THE
ORPHANAGE
OF GODS

Also by Helena Coggan

The Catalyst
The Reaction

THE
ORPHANAGE
OF GODS

Helena Coggan

HODDER &
STOUGHTON

First published in Great Britain in 2019 by Hodder & Stoughton
An Hachette UK company

1

Copyright © Helena Coggan 2019

A CIP catalogue record for this title is
available from the British Library

Hardback ISBN 978 1 444 79474 8
eBook ISBN 978 1 444 79475 5

Typeset in Sabon MT by Palimpsest Book Production Ltd, Falkirk, Stirlingshire

Printed and bound in Great Britain by Clays Ltd, Elcograf S.p.A.

Hodder & Stoughton policy is to use papers that are natural, renewable
and recyclable products and made from wood grown in sustainable forests.
The logging and manufacturing processes are expected to conform to the
environmental regulations of the country of origin.

Hodder & Stoughton Ltd
Carmelite House
50 Victoria Embankment
London EC4Y 0DZ

www.hodder.co.uk

To my mother,
for your wisdom and endless kindness
I remember everything you taught me

PART ONE

Hero

CHAPTER I

Lightning

It's raining. We're sitting in an empty tavern by the side of the road. The windows are dark, the torches snuffed out. Joshua looks very tense. He's tapping the wooden table, *duh-dum, duh-dum* over the thrum of the rain on the corrugated roof. He's staring out of the window, his eyes glazed.

'Calm down,' I tell him.

He nods jerkily. His hands are clenched into fists, knuckles pale against the polished wood. They keep tapping, like they're not a part of him. *Duh-dum, duh-dum.*

He saw this coming an hour ago. I don't know what else he saw with it. He never talks much about the premonitions. We were walking beside the road, silent in the thinning dark, and suddenly he stopped dead, the colour draining from his face as his eyes glazed over. I stood and watched him in the rain until it was done.

He swallowed and looked up at me. He tried to hide the terror on his face, but I could see it.

'Patrol car,' was all he said, just that, though I knew by his face he must have seen more.

So we came in here and sat down and waited.

I don't want to ask him for details, but still I burn with anxiety, sitting in the darkened tavern. Was it only a patrol car he saw? A flash of sirens and tyres, a sense of dangerous proximity? Or was it something else, something darker? Us standing handcuffed against a car window in the darkened rain, pistols pressed to our heads, the Guard yelling into our faces? Silver blood dripping into the mud? Would he tell me if he'd seen that? Would I want him to?

I close my eyes and lean back in the hard wooden chair. I can feel myself tensing up again and I try to make myself relax. If I can't do it, he won't be able to either.

We've never been found by a patrol car before, but I know it only takes once. It's Joshua who's the problem. He just *looks* more like a god than I do. It's not just his blood – we can hide that easily enough. It's his height, his beauty, his nervousness. His general aura of awkwardness, of always being in the wrong place. The way lights seem to brighten ever so slightly when he walks into a room. Any one of those things might not be enough to give him away. All of them together, that starts to set off alarms.

It used to be Kestrel's job to shut them off. To hide him, to keep him safe. But now she's gone, and I'm not as good at it as she was. She'd never have let—

Joshua stops tapping suddenly and stares out of the darkened window. Then I hear it. Over the drilling of the wind and rain. Tyres.

He turns and looks at me.

'Now,' I tell him, and he nods. The last dregs of light in the room gather on his fingertips, bright as candlelight, and I have a last vision of his face in the chalky glow, drawn and frightened. I ache to go to him, comfort him, but I can't, we're not children anymore. He has to do what must be done, and he can't with my voice in his ear, telling him it's all going to be all right. It won't be. He has to understand that.

The light goes out, and then there's only darkness, thick and black and breathless. I can't even see his hands on the table.

He whispers, 'What now?'

'We wait.'

'If I need to, I can—'

'I know what you can do.' My mind is thrumming, strung taut like violin wire, the cold metal press of a knife against my throat. 'Don't. Not yet.'

He doesn't say anything. I just hear his hoarse breathing through the blackness.

The tyres come closer. Screeching through the dark towards us. The road is deserted; it's the middle of the night. I can feel Joshua beside me, itching to take the glow from their headlights and send them careening into the brush. But then more of them will come, and they can drive here faster than we can get away on foot. We have to stay.

We wait. The tyres slow down and then stop. Right outside the tavern, by the sound of it. They know, they *know* there's someone in here. I hear Joshua realise it a second after I do, his breath hitching in his throat.

We stay very still, listening, like rabbits crouched in the dark. Outside the wind pushes the hammering rain harder against the windows. We hear the slams of car doors. Voices, harsh and unintelligible.

Then someone shouts, clearly over the rain, 'Come out with your hands up!'

We are completely motionless. I can't breathe.

'Come out! Come out with your hands—'

Joshua makes a sudden movement like he's about to get up.

'*Don't.*' The sharpness in my voice surprises me, the sudden authority.

I hear him stop. Very still in the blackness. I wonder what he's seeing through the dark. Can he see my face?

'Hero—'

'We have a plan.'

'It's a stupid plan.'

'No it isn't. Calm down.'

'Come out with your hands up!' shouts the voice. A man's, deep and rough. The rain is driving harder now. There's a bang on the door. 'Come out or I'll *break* this thing down!'

'I have to go out there.'

It's Joshua who says it, not me. I get to my feet, steadying myself against the table. Everything is dark. I can't see him.

'Don't. We planned for this.'

'If I go—'

'Then you die.'

There's a note of petulance in his voice, beneath the hard ferocity. 'I don't care. I'll kill them too.'

'*Joshua*—'

Another bang on the door. 'Come *out!*' He howls it over the wind. 'Come out or I'll drag you out!'

Joshua makes a sudden movement again, and I say, 'She'd kill you for doing something this stupid.'

I hear him turn towards me, on the other side of the table. Feel his eyes on me. He knows I mean Kestrel.

Silence.

I take a step forward, and he doesn't move to stop me. I have hit the right nerve. I don't let my relief show in my jagged breathing.

I walk towards the outline of faint light that marks the tavern door, trying not to trip over chair legs or loose floorboards in the dark. I will do this with dignity.

Another bang on the door. '*Come out!*'

I take a deep breath.

'I'm coming, I'm coming!'

The banging stops. They're waiting for me. I can feel a light behind me, soft and white and low, and I turn to see Joshua's face, cowled by the darkness, ghostly in the light from his fingertips. He writes in the air with his finger, leaving a scorched glow that lasts only for a moment before fading, long enough for me to read it.

It says, *If they hurt you, I'll kill them.*

I hold his eyes and nod. What I'm thinking is: if they hurt me, they will kill me. The Guard don't do things by halves. And after that it doesn't matter what happens, really, because once I'm dead so is Joshua. He can't survive for long without me there. Sooner or later he'll snap and do something stupid and then he'll get caught and he'll die.

I turn away from him, back to the door. Behind me, the light goes out. I hear him sink to the floor, under the table. I take another breath, gathering all my courage in a closed fist. I open the door.

For a moment I don't recognise them. Six figures standing in the mud, their grey shirts black with rain. Their battered metal car, smoke still rising from the exhaust. The gas lamps in their hands. The letters engraved on the side in fading paint. I can't make out what it says, but I don't need to, I already know. *Guardsmen.*

I thought we'd escaped them when we escaped the orphanage. But no, of course, here they are again. How could I have been so naive? You can never escape the Guard. Panic rises in my throat.

The one who was knocking on the door is pointing a rifle into my face. He lowers it when he sees me. The road behind them is deserted and beyond that the cloudy sky stretches over the black hills to nothing.

'Who are you?' says the one with the rifle, the one who shouted.

We prepared this. I feel their eyes on me like the burn of cigarettes on my skin. I know they have more guns than I can see.

'Jessica,' I say. 'Jessica Markham.'

'What are you doing out here in the middle of the night, Jessica Markham?'

I can feel my heart struggling against my ribs. I try to make my voice break, to sound as scared as I feel. 'I'm running away.'

I feel their gazes sharpen.

'From what?'

'My parents.'

'Oh yes? And what have they done to you?'

'I want out.' My voice trembles. 'I'm sick of their crap, I'm an *adult*, I'm leaving—'

'Who are your parents, Jessica?'

A dark-eyed man near the back says it. He watches me, his face impassive. I know he's trying to read me, and I show him only angst and fear and resentment. But as I open my mouth to speak, the names Joshua and I prepared all those weeks ago vanish from my mind. *Who are your parents, Jessica? Who are—*

Panic beats in me again, under my heart. A too-long silence. I can feel them watching me.

'Let's get on with it,' says the older Guardsman near the front, roughly. 'Hold out your arm, girl.'

I hesitate. This time he puts his hand on his gun quite deliberately, making sure I see.

'Hold out your arm, I said.'

I let the silence stretch for just a moment, and then hold out my arm. The Guardsman takes a knife from his pocket and advances towards me, his eyes glinting.

And suddenly I feel my heart jolt, the dregs of my panic swirling sickeningly in my stomach. The plan Joshua and I devised only worked if we were captured in the dark. If it were daylight, if I were standing in the headlights, if they had starlight, we'd be in trouble. But it's two o'clock in the morning, pitch black, there's no reason our plan shouldn't work. My heart is too fast.

The Guardsman pushes my sleeve up to my elbow and tightens his grip on his knife. I wonder if he can hear my thundering pulse, feel it under his palm. I expect to see some glint of sadistic pleasure, a shine of bared teeth, but there's nothing.

He does it quite matter-of-factly. He turns my arm over and makes a single sharp cut across the skin of the back of my wrist. The cut is shallow and stings, but the pain seems far away in my head, across a flat moonlit lake.

I feel the others move closer, watching my blood. I'm watching it too. I can't breathe again. I feel the Guardsman's grip on my wrist tighten, squeezing, and then blood fills the cut like water, and gathers, and then a bead of it overflows and hangs, trembling, on my skin, until at last it drips towards the mud.

The Guardsman catches it. I see him raise his fingers to his face, staring at the bead of blood. I keep hoping the rain will wash it away, second to second, but it doesn't.

'Anything?' one of the others calls.

The Guardsman doesn't say anything. He's still examining my blood, watching for the glint of silver. With every moment that passes in silence, I grow more certain his next move will be to pull out handcuffs to clamp across my blood-stained wrists, or to wrench his rifle from his belt and shoot me. I can see it happening very clearly, inside my head, with dizzying clarity. He's going to kill me, right here.

Then he does something I've never seen before. He raises his hand to his mouth and licks my blood off his fingers, staring at me.

I feel sick. He's still gripping my wrist with his other hand. I want to run, to get away from here, away from him.

There's a long moment where his eyes don't leave my face.

'Doesn't taste like it,' he says, quietly.

Behind him, a shard of lightning appears in the sky. There's a rumble of thunder, deep and dark.

'You don't think she's one of them?' says another Guardsman.

The Guardsman who tasted my blood shakes his head slowly, still staring at me.

And then suddenly there's a clap of thunder so deep I feel my bones tremble. I see them start to turn, slow, dreamlike. I know what's going to happen, but I can't move.

The bolt of lightning strikes the field ten yards behind them.

The world goes suddenly white. I close my eyes against the blinding heat. The Guardsman slackens his grip on my wrist and I pull free instinctively, clutching my bleeding arm.

The grass in the lightning-struck field is smouldering, blackened. I can smell smoke in the rain.

'Let's go,' says one of them, at the back. He looks the most nervous. 'She's not one of them, there's no point—'

The Guardsman nods, and the men behind him all start filing into the patrol car. But he doesn't move. He doesn't take his eyes off me. The rain is soaking into his hair. I stand perfectly still, not wanting to provoke him into anything. Then, finally, he says softly, 'Be careful, girl.'

I just look at him, not moving. Then after more seconds than I dare to count he turns and walks back to the car. I watch the door close. The rain pounds on the car's metal roof. It doesn't move for a moment and I know they're all watching me from inside. I stay still.

Then I hear the engine rev, and the car moves slowly away. A hundred yards from the tavern it speeds up, so that I can hear the hiss of the tyres against the flooded road. I watch until it's out of sight and then for another few minutes, the rain soaking into my skin, until I'm as sure as I can be that they're not going to double back.

The lightning doesn't strike again. I pass my hand over the cut on my wrist and when I look down at it the skin is smooth and pale, healed. I sway slightly where I stand. I hear the door of the tavern open behind me.

'Hero! *Hero!*'

Joshua behind me, running towards me. He looks pale and terrified.

'It's okay,' I say, and as I say it I realise how soft my voice is, how drained. 'I'm okay.'

'Oh, Hero . . .'

He gathers me in his arms. I let myself collapse into him. He is warm and soft, even against the soaking cold of the rain. I am very tired.

'I'm sorry, I should have gone with you—'

'You called the lightning, didn't you? To scare them away.'

He doesn't say anything for a moment, just holds me, swaying slightly. Then he says, 'I'm sorry.'

'We had a plan.'

'I know. I'm sorry. I panicked.'

'You can't, Joshua. Not anymore. They could have got suspicious, they could have looked closer—'

'I know. I'm sorry.'

'It's okay.'

'I won't do it again.'

'Okay.' And I believe him.

Raindrops thick and cold in my hair. A mutter of thunder.

Later that night, we find a grove of oak trees and try to fall asleep beneath them, sheltered from the rain. In my head I'm in the orphanage again.

Some part of me is always there, I think. It comes over me when I think I'm alone in my head, a swelling chorus in the back of my mind. A glimpse of torchlight on granite, the smell of kerosene and soap. It scares me. I thought once I escaped I would be free of it. I guess that was stupid.

There were a thousand kids there, packed three or four to a room, so it was never truly quiet. It's taken me weeks to get used to the silence out here in the woods. Even at night there, some new foundling kid was crying three floors below us, and the river whispered softly at the bottom of the hill. And always, if we listened, we could hear the Guard walking the corridors, their slow, thudding patrol, listening for any disturbance. Sometimes I think I still hear them. I wake gasping, a sawing violin note of fear in my chest. The fear, at least, hasn't left me.

I close my eyes and curl up in the grass beneath the oak trees, and I vanish. In my head I'm standing in the doorway of the bedroom the three of us shared. This was my favourite place in the orphanage; I feel calm here, and silent. I stand and imagine the room around me, its comforting walls, and I breathe.

It's daylight, and the windows are open, sunlight settled in the corners like dust. The corridor was always full of restless teenage chatter, fights and gossip, but in my head it's quiet.

I walk to the window and run my fingers over the bars. When I was eight, a seventeen-year-old boy threw himself out of one of these windows. He was two weeks away from his last finding-day here, and he knew there was no way to stop the Guard finding out what he was. He preferred death to that. I admire his bravery.

I didn't know then that I was like him. After I found out, the story gave me hope, in a way. It meant someone like him had lasted seventeen years in this place, under the Guard's constant, unblinking eye. Most kids like him – like *us* – had disappeared from their beds by the age of ten, but somehow he had been clever enough to make it, had hidden his blood and his gifts, and counted on the Guard's overconfidence.

But there was always one last check. A blood test on every orphanage child's eighteenth finding-day, to make absolutely sure they were human, before they were released into the world. There was no escaping that, no keeping your head

down, no more quiet evasion. The boy must have known his
time had run out.

After he died they barred the windows and watched us all
more closely. I resented the dead boy for that.

The few orphanage books that talked about gods and half-
gods were full of torn pages, words blurred out with old ink.
If they could have, I'm sure the Guard would've tried to pretend
there were never any gods at all, that they never lived and
were never slaughtered. But they couldn't pull that off, of
course. Even if they locked every door in the place and assigned
each of us our own watchful Guardsman, they couldn't stop
us knowing the world. Kids talk.

So they destroyed some books and mutilated those that
were left, to make sure those few god-kids who managed to
evade them would know as little as possible about what we
were. The less we knew about our gifts, the harder they were
to control, and the easier we were to discover.

But even that didn't work, at least not entirely. We still
found things out.

Here's what I know for certain: Joshua's premonitions aren't
usually like this. Usually they taunt him, make him think he
knows the future when he doesn't. We learned a long time
ago how vague and fleeting they were. Most of the time, when
we were kids, they came to him in dreams, and they told him
stupid, childish things, the answers to questions in class, who
had kissed who in empty classrooms. Only once before this
have they told him anything useful. I saw it happen. I saw
him dream it.

That was how we met. The three of us had been put, by
chance, in the same dormitory. In those days we slept three
to a small room, ten feet wide and ten feet across. They put
boys and girls together, because what did the Guard care what
teenagers did in darkened rooms, so long as they stayed there?

It's not like there would have been children born from it; the Guard had ways to deal with things like that, if it came to it. Girls with swelling bellies were taken away in the night, returned with hollow eyes and flat stomachs. But we didn't know about that, then: we were twelve, too young to dream of that kind of horror.

The room smelled of granite and varnished wood, and the light seeping in faintly from under the doorway was gas-lamp yellow. Lights out at nine o'clock, the darkness imposed.

We lay in silence, not daring to speak. We knew what happened to those the Guard overheard making trouble.

Then, an hour into that silence, as the moonlight through the window vanished behind a cloud, Joshua began to moan.

I remember him, as he was then. A small, nervous child. Frizzy black hair, big teeth, darting eyes. Terror clung to him like a shadow, the gnawing fear of being discovered. I had that fear too. I felt sorry for him. If he was a god then he would be discovered sooner or later, and it would do no good to try to help. That was what I thought, in my youth and my cowardice.

He lay in his bed, his eyelids a stark, bruised blue, staring into his own head. The moan seemed to be pulled slowly out of him, like a cord of blood. He looked anguished, even in sleep.

I saw Kestrel's eyes glint in the darkness. Then, after a minute, she got up, and went to the rotting bookshelf that hung from the wall. She folded her arms and stood in silence, watching him.

When I was certain she wasn't going to do anything, I raised myself up on to one elbow. My mouth was dry. I hesitated.

'Joshua.' His name was all I knew about him; we'd met maybe three days beforehand, and had barely spoken. 'Joshua, wake up.'

I was too quiet. He didn't move. He moaned again. It made me shudder and I glanced up at Kestrel. She was motionless, staring at him. Reluctantly, I sat up and slid out of bed.

'Joshua.'

He shuddered under the weight of the dream.

'Joshua—'

And then at last his eyes flew open, and he screamed.

I'd never heard a scream like that. It wasn't a child's scream, it was worse than that, long and high-pitched and filled with terror. I couldn't move.

Kestrel darted forward, pulled a pillow from her own bed, held it down over his face. The shrieks became muffled and he started kicking, crying out. His flailing feet thumped against the bed.

'Kestrel, no! You'll kill him—'

She pressed the pillow down harder. Her teeth were gritted and her eyes cold.

'Stop! You're going t—'

She lifted the pillow. Joshua gasped, his eyes focused at last. He lunged for her but she put a hand over his mouth. 'Scream again,' she said quietly, 'and this time I *will* kill you. Understand?'

That was Kestrel at twelve.

Joshua was staring up at her, too scared to move. We all knew that we were in danger already; if the Guardsmen who patrolled the corridors at night had heard him, they would be on their way towards us even now. But nothing happened, and after a few moments Kestrel let Joshua go. He lay quite still on the bed, barely breathing. He looked haunted, hunted and grey-faced in the starlight through the window.

'What happened?' I said, at last, as quietly as I could. 'A nightmare?'

His eyes focused on me. Reading my face. Wondering, I think, if he could trust me.

'Yes,' he said at last, and swallowed. 'Yes. Nicholas. He's gone.'

We stood still, just looking at him. The words didn't make sense in my head. 'What?'

'Nicholas. I saw his face. You know—' He waved a hand, wildly. 'Room three sixty-seven. With Kelly and Chase. He's gone.'

Corridor Three was where the six to eight-year-olds lived. Kestrel and I glanced at each other.

'How do you know?' said Kestrel at last.

'I *saw* him.'

Kestrel sat down on the end of his bed, watching him intently with her bright amber owl eyes. She spoke with slow and deliberate calm. 'What do you mean, you saw him? You saw him being taken away, out of here?'

'No! I saw him and I just—'

'Just what?'

He swallowed, trying to slow his breathing. I saw the terror of the dream leaching back into his eyes.

'I saw. . . his face. He looked scared. And I felt. . . like, I'd been standing on a floor and it had just vanished. Like something was gone, like I was falling. And I knew. . . I just knew. . . he was. . . gone.'

'You mean he's dead?' said Kestrel evenly.

Joshua flinched. I tried very hard not to. I wanted to be calm and brave, like her. Neither of them looked at me.

'I don't know. Maybe. He's not here. He's just . . .' He swallowed again, convulsively. 'He's *gone*.'

Kestrel got to her feet, but I kept my eyes on Joshua. I wanted to explain this away. 'Did anyone tell you that? Did you see what might have hurt him? Was there anything you saw today that you might have dreamed about?'

Joshua shook his head mutely.

'It must have been just a nightmare, then,' I said. I knew

if I said it aloud, it would help me believe it was true. 'Just a dream. If we go back to sleep now, we can check in the morning if he—'

Kestrel reappeared beside me. She was holding something in her hand, gleaming and silver. Joshua realised before I did; he didn't cry out again but his eyes widened and he scrambled backwards on the bed, away from her. Kestrel was faster, but only because Joshua was so disoriented. She lunged for him and grabbed his wrist, and then she did something terribly familiar, something I had never seen but had heard about all my life – the test carried out in small rooms and tight corridors, away from nervous eyes, on everyone's eighteenth finding-day, the day they left the orphanage.

She flipped his wrist over and drew the knife across the taut skin and squeezed. Joshua's lips were pressed together to stop himself from crying out. He stared at her, terrified.

'Watch,' was all she said.

It was hard to see in the thin light from the window, but clear enough. A bead of blood formed in the cut and hung there, trembling. I knew at once it wasn't normal blood. Normal blood glistens, it doesn't glow. But Joshua's did. He shifted in Kestrel's grip, shaking violently, and the moonlight caught the bead of blood and I saw it properly.

It was silver. Not just the strange greyish metallic gleam of my own blood, but pure, brilliant as molten steel. The blood of a god.

Kestrel looked up at him. There was a moment of silence.

I knew what Kestrel should have done. She should have screamed for help, for the Guard to come, to be saved. Once they came running she could show them the silver blood on her fingers; that was more than enough evidence. I saw him have a *dream*, she could have said, disgust and fear in her voice. He's one of *them*.

Kestrel is human, not like us. She would have been safe,

rewarded. The Guard would have taken Joshua away and no one would ever have spoken of him again.

There was a long silence, and the whole of our lives hung in it.

Then Kestrel let go of Joshua's wrist, stepped back, and grinned.

'All right,' she said. 'Can you do anything cool?'

Joshua just stared at her, trembling.

'Go on,' she said. 'You can trust me.'

Neither of them glanced at me; the moment was theirs. The look between them was living, writhing, shining. Slowly, the fear left Joshua's face.

He lifted his fingers and a light, pure gold and steady, appeared at their tips. He stretched it out slowly towards her, hesitant, like a cat with a vole it had hunted and was presenting now as a gift. I stared at it in wonder.

Kestrel just laughed, joyful and melodious, and from then on, we were all bound together as surely as by blood.

I should have known it from that first shining look, the way she was going to love him. I want to go back, now, to that moment, and sit us all down, the three of us. I want to say: you don't know what you're getting into. Back out now. This doesn't end well. I want to say to Kestrel: sweetheart, leave us, you don't know what you're doing. You're human, this isn't your fate. Go and have your life. You don't have to do this.

The next morning, Nicholas's bed in room three sixty-seven was found empty. Kelly and Chase, his seven-year-old roommates, swore they hadn't heard anything. No one ever saw him again.

CHAPTER 2

Seaborne

The rain has stopped by morning. The sky is clear, blue and cloudless. The ground is soaked with mud. Joshua picks his way through it to the road.

'Look at this,' he says.

I follow him, look down. Black tyre tracks, encrusted in the dried mud. Joshua follows them with his eyes to the open rain-soaked hills ahead, and grins. 'They must have been in a hurry to leave, huh?'

I shoot him a dark look.

'What?'

'Don't.'

'Don't what?'

'Act like it was a good thing. Scaring them away with the lightning. It was dangerous, Joshua.'

'Yeah, I know, I know.'

We start walking beside the empty roads. In the three weeks since we escaped from the orphanage I've got used to the weight of the leather pack on my shoulders, but it still hurts. I shrug, trying to shift it around, shivering in the deepening autumn cold, hugging myself. I don't know what we'll do when winter comes. There's nothing here big enough to skin for a cloak, even if I knew how to skin anything.

The fields on either side of us are dark and swimming with mud. In the far distance, we can hear the clipped rhythm of hooves. There's no one here. That's good, very good. We haven't talked to anyone since we left Fitzgerald House. It would be far too dangerous. We know there must be warrants out for our recapture, posters with our faces on them. No one's supposed to leave the orphanage until they turn eighteen, and to the best of our knowledge, no one ever has. We were the first. I am fiercely proud of that.

Before the patrol car last night, we hadn't realised the Guard even came this far north. There didn't seem anything to patrol. There's just farmland up here, a few towns where people keep their heads down and don't look at us. This was one of the last counties to fall during the rebellion, and it still bears the marks. Whole fields razed bare, even after twenty years. Moss-covered rubble where our map says some towns should be. They tried to defend their gods, protect them, wouldn't give them up to be murdered. In the orphanage it was rumoured there were still gods up here, hidden in quiet, straw-thatched villages, or camps in fields, thinking themselves fighters for some long-dead resistance movement. We didn't believe it, but obviously the Guard must, or they wouldn't be here.

The map was quite clear about this place, though. Fields, roads, small towns and cattle. No city anywhere close; no shelter but forest.

And then, a hundred miles away now, Elida.

When we stop to eat I try to talk to Joshua about it.

'You know, she might not be there.'

He looks up from his bowl of syrup and oats. His face is closed. He reads my expression slowly, playing for time.

'What do you mean?' he asks at last.

'I mean, if Kestrel—' It's difficult to say it. 'I mean, they might not have taken her to Elida.'

'Why not? They think she's a god. There's no reason they wouldn't take her there.'

'Yeah, but if she couldn't fake it . . .'

He takes a bite of his oats, chews slowly, swallows. Stares levelly at me. Then he says, 'She could.'

'Yes, but only if they didn't check. They could have done it any time. It's been three weeks. They'd only have to look at her blood again—'

Joshua shakes his head. 'They wouldn't have.'

'Why wouldn't they?'

Joshua takes another bite of the oatmeal. It takes him a long time to reply, and when he does his voice is full of unexpected heat.

'Do you *want* her to be dead, Hero?'

'No!' And suddenly I'm angry, when I promised myself I'd stay calm. 'Of course I don't! I . . . Joshua, I love her just as much as you do, but even you have to at least allow the possibility—'

'What do you mean *even me?*' Joshua leaps to his feet. I see his skin gleaming, the air around him starting to shimmer with heat. The anger in him sudden, strong and wild. I step back. 'You think I just want her to be alive because it's my fault they took her?'

'Joshua.'

'You think I don't lie awake at night wishing I could—'

'Joshua. Calm down.'

'You think I don't hate myself for it *every second*—'

'*Joshua!*'

The sleeve on my jacket has caught fire. The gleam from the glass of my watch is so bright it hurts to look at, and I clench my teeth to stop myself crying out. The light sears into my skin, white hot, brightening with his fury.

At his sudden intake of breath, it goes out, and the world seems dimmer.

I kneel and shove my arm into the puddle by the side of the road. There's a hiss and a cloud of steam. I wince. I hear Joshua moving around, but I don't look at him.

One. Two. Three. Calm down, breathe. *Eight. Nine. Ten.* Okay.

After a moment I lift my hand out of the puddle, dripping with filthy water. I take off my watch with one hand, awkwardly, wincing, and look at the damage. Part of my sleeve has been burned away, and the skin beneath it is reddish, shiny and painful. The metal of my watch is red-hot. The marks of the chain links have seared into my wrist. The skin there is almost black. I concentrate, taking deep breaths, and slowly the pain drops away, like water off the edge of a cliff. I am half-god, and my gift is healing; pain is where I live and work.

This isn't a problem, not really. My problem is Joshua.

I look up at him at last. He's staring at my wrist. All the unearthly shimmer has vanished from him. His rage has disappeared as quickly as the sun going in. He looks horror-struck, and my anger almost vanishes when I see his face, the hurt there. My heart nearly breaks for him. Nearly.

'Oh, Hero,' he says, with quiet anguish. 'Hero, I'm so sorry—'

'Don't worry about it.'

'Hero—'

'Calm down.'

I can smell searing meat. My stomach flips. The fury is low in my chest, overlaid by shock.

'Give me a knife.'

He hesitates, then reaches into his pack and takes out a thin, sharp blade. He doesn't take his eyes off my face. He throws the knife over to me and I catch it by the handle. I put it to my elbow and hack away the burned sleeve clumsily with my left hand, leaving my wrist bare. I close my eyes.

'Hero, I'm so sorry.'

I pass my hand over the charring black skin at my wrist, not quite touching it, and feel the skin stir and cool. Then I slide it up my arm until I find the burn. It's deep, whitish, shiny and hot. I put my hand over it. I wait thirty seconds, counting them off in my head, keeping my eyes closed.

Here's what I'm scared of: three weeks ago, when we escaped the orphanage and she did not, I think something broke in him. I know he wakes in the night, breathless, haunted by her terrified face. I've seen it in his eyes.

I don't know what to say to him. I know something's happening to him but I don't have the words for it and I don't know how to heal it.

That twelve-year-old boy who woke screaming in his bed from a nightmare of a child vanishing, was terrified of his own power. He would never have called lightning near either of us. He would never have threatened, to kill anyone, not until the very last moment. And he would never have lost control like this. He would never have hurt me.

I take a deep breath in and out, and stay very calm, and try to think. My right hand is wrapped around my healed arm.

When I look up, Joshua is sitting in front of me again, his head in his hands.

'Joshua,' I say, softly. I am very aware of the silence surrounding us, thin and sharp as a knife blade. He acts like he can't hear me. 'Joshua, look at me.'

He looks at my arm first, sees the skin healed, smooth and pale and unblemished, and some of the colour returns to his face.

'Joshua, listen to me.'

His eyes flicker unwillingly up to my face. My voice is very calm.

'The next time you do something like that, I'm going to leave you here and let the Guard have you.'

His head jerks up and stares at me. There's sudden, blank shock in his face.

'You don't mean that,' he says softly.

I don't mean that, of course I don't mean that, I'd never leave him, but I'm scared now and that means I have to scare *him*.

'I do.'

'You wouldn't—'

My voice rises in spite of myself. If I'm doing this I have to do it properly. 'I would, Joshua. If you're going to get us killed, what the hell is the point of me even being here?'

He just looks at me for a long time. When he speaks, his voice is constricted.

'I didn't mean to hurt – you know how it is, I can't control—'

'I don't mean my *arm*, Joshua.' I do. It hurt. 'I mean, what was *that?*'

'What was—'

'You don't talk to me like that.' The frustration and fear of the last few days are high in my throat. I'm buzzing with it, I want to scream at him, but I take deep breaths and stay calm. 'You don't *ever* talk like that to me. You don't get angry like that, not with me. Has it occurred to you, even *once*, that I'm on your side?'

He looks down at his feet. I can see blotches of colour starting to come into his face. I speak curtly, acidly.

'I'm your sister, Joshua. I love you. I'm not the Guard. Try to remember that.'

There's a silence. Joshua takes a deep breath in and then out again, and for a terrible moment I think I've gone too far. He gets to his feet and walks restlessly to the side of the road, his hands in his pockets.

'I'm sorry,' he says at last. 'Really, I am.'

'Okay.'

He turns to me. 'I mean it. I'm sorry.'

I am so tired. 'Sure. I know.'

'I just—' His face is contorted, full of anguish and guilt. 'I don't want her to be dead. I can't *imagine* her dead. I don't know what I'd do if she weren't here. I just . . . I can't bear it.'

It feels, as it sometimes does, like she's standing between

us: smiling at me, in her tattered leather jacket, her eyes glinting in the sun. The sight of her face, even in my head, is a swooning sickness, a knife in my throat.

'Yeah,' I say dully. 'Me too.'

The orphanage had rules, and it took years to learn them all. The most important one was not to ask questions. Terrible things lay beneath the surface of the questions that went unasked in that place. About all the children who had disappeared, for one thing. Where our parents were, for another.

I was pretty good at surviving there, all things considered. My gift was healing; quiet, unflashy, not the kind of thing that could burst out of me when I was angry and bring the Guard down on me. My blood didn't turn grey until I was sixteen, and by then I had long since learned the art of hiding, of lying, of looking normal and unafraid. The Guard never had reason to look at me twice, to suspect me of being anything more than human, and the older I got, the less worried they were about me. Most gods and half-breeds were discovered young, as their gifts came in, six or seven maybe, too young to understand or control themselves. To hide for seventeen years in the orphanage, under the Guard's constant eye, was almost unheard of. But I did it.

Joshua had it worse. He was blazing, even as a kid, a burning god, full of irrepressible power. His blood turned the brilliant silver of full gods when he was only twelve and from that moment on he was in danger. If he slipped and cut himself, he would reveal himself and be taken. If he lost control for only a second and called lightning down on someone, conjured light in glowing handfuls from a clenched fist, if he struck a wall in frustration and cracked the stone, that would have been it, time up. He would have been taken from his bed in the middle of the night and vanished dreamlike into the annals of the disappeared. We would have fought the Guard when they came for him, Kestrel and I, but what use would we really have been? Two young girls against the Guard with their guns, their numbers and strength and their dead eyes. We had no chance.

And then we would have vanished, too. That was the punishment for those who fought back. The Guard were clever. They knew how to turn us against each other. They knew how to make us cowards.

But most of the kids there have nothing to fear. Nearly everyone in the orphanage now is human, twenty years after the rebellion killed all the gods; there are so few of us left that the Guard believe themselves safe. Most of the kids we grew up with were found as infants in alleys and stairwells, their origins shrouded in darkness, their parents taken by illness or storm or famine.

Joshua and I weren't like that. We know exactly how our parents died. The Guard murdered them.

I know how to count. The rebellion was twenty years ago, and as far as I know I'm seventeen, so my mother spent three years in hiding, waiting for the Guard to find her, to drag her away and kill her, like they'd murdered so many other thousands of gods. Three years in some cavern, shivering and waiting. I can't imagine it.

How did she do it? Where was she on that first terrible, sunlit day, when the protests began outside the Palace of Peace and the first Guardsmen – nameless then, with no uniform, just a mob with hearts full of hatred – marched through Amareth pulling gods and half-breeds from their homes, screaming, and slaughtered them, there in the streets where they'd lived openly and without fear? How did she survive those weeks of slaughter, of rotten fury and blood? Where did she hide? Who died for her, to keep her safe? You don't survive that long without sacrifice, without love. Someone must have loved her.

I ask myself, what would I have done if I were her, in a terrible new world with the Guard in power, my family dead, no future but running, a newborn daughter in my arms?

And the answer is obvious. I would leave that baby behind, abandon it and run. If my mother had been found, the Guard would have cut her wrists and seen what she was and murdered her. And if I'd been found with her, it would have been obvious that I was one of her kind. They'd have killed me just as quickly, snuffed me out and moved on.

But without her? My blood was still red then, like all newborns. It wouldn't turn grey until I was sixteen. Abandoned in the streets of Amareth, with thousands of other motherless children, I would look human. I would look human for *years*. I could hide in an orphanage, growing in silence, learning to control myself, to hide.

And my mother . . .

My mother is dead. I can't lie to myself, I'm not a child anymore. Seventeen years is a long time. They found her long ago.

We knew in the orphanage that we could escape the notice of the Guard for only so long. No matter how well we hid, after eighteen years, on the day we were released, the Guard would cut our wrists and test our blood. That was the final test, to root out those few lucky gods and half-breeds who hadn't yet been discovered under the Guard's dead-eyed, lidless gaze. By eighteen everyone's blood had turned silver, if they were divine. The moment the Guard's knives cut through our skin, under the harsh argon lamplight of the orphanage, they would see and they would know. And then we would disappear. Like Nicholas, like Clarissa, like the hundreds of others before them. All my mother's courage for nothing, in the end.

So that was how long we had, Joshua and me. Eighteen

years from the day we were found, abandoned in the streets of Amareth. A clock in the back of our heads, endless and cold. *Tick. Tick. Tick.*

'I don't think they kill gods anymore,' said Kestrel, as we sat in our dormitory, talking quietly by the golden light that drifted above Joshua's hand. She had taken off her leather jacket and dropped it on the floor, and sat curled on the bed. 'They just take them away. That's where you go when you disappear. Elida, it's called. Junie told me.'

'Where is it?' said Joshua. He said it casually, like it was of only trivial importance to him, but I could read him by then.

'North.'

'Yeah, but *where?*'

Kestrel shrugged. 'I don't know. Keep walking north and I guess you'll get there.'

'Kestrel—'

'Hey, do I look like a map to you?'

She made jokes about it. It takes my breath away, remembering that. She made *jokes*.

I remember a boy called Janus disappearing from his bed one night when I was younger, long before I met Joshua and Kestrel. We were all curious about where he'd gone, but not scared, not yet, we were too small for that. No one but me was stupid enough to ask. The nurse who taught us arithmetic was young, and had a kind, open face. I asked her in the middle of the lesson, as she stood beside the blackboard. The room was cold, stone grey.

'Where's Janus?'

I must have been about four. She looked at me with flat and empty eyes, so terrible a look I was scared to meet her gaze. Then she just said, with nothing at all in her voice, 'Who's Janus?' She was standing right next to his empty wooden desk.

*   *   *

The next town on our list is called Seaborne. Joshua looks at it apprehensively on the skyline of the greyish hilltop ahead.

'Are you sure about this?' he asks.

'Yeah.'

'We could get food later. We don't have to eat at all if we don't want to.'

This is true. As a full-blooded god, he could last months without eating; I could maybe make it a couple of weeks. But that's not the point.

'We need food if we're trying to walk twenty miles a day. We'll be skin and bones in a week.'

He glares at me.

'Joshua—'

'Fine.'

We keep walking.

We're by the coast. Seaborne is a fishing village, the walls of the houses rough with salt and lichen-encrusted rope. It's autumn, so the streets are thick with leaves. No street lights, no electricity at all I'd guess, just torches in brackets on the brick walls. The people are all very quiet. Gods are usually tall, so in the past few years it's become fashionable to walk stooped. Everybody keeps their eyes down. That's good; there might be posters of our faces up here. We stare resolutely at the gravel-grass streets, and nobody speaks to us.

We go into a shop, its chimney bare. I shiver at the sight of it, stark red slate on the thatched roof. I know the stories. Two hundred years ago, when the first generation of gods were born, inexplicably, to human parents, gangs of silver-blooded teenagers would tear through human villages, killing the people and setting the houses on fire so that columns of smoke rose into the sky to mark where they'd been. We were told by the Guard that they'd rip through swathes of the countryside, never going back to the same place twice, systematic in their brutality.

Centuries later, during the rebellion, when the gods were murdered, the humans burned the bodies in piles in the centre of the villages, as a warning and a mark of victory. Gods live longer than humans; perhaps some of those same teenagers had survived to be murdered in the rebellion, old men and women by then, weak and terrified. They died and were burned and the sky filled with ash. Now everyone fears the smell of smoke.

Joshua has to duck to get through the doorway. The shop is dimly lit, and smells of leather and salted meat. Skins of water are lined against the wall, balls of dried fruit tied with string. I hate the walls, the closed room, the dimness.

We have a plan. I take the left side of the shop, he does the right. Food, in tins and in salt and bound with string. I take anything that will last. The shop is empty but for the two of us and I feel the shopkeeper's eyes on the back of my head, the single flickering gas lamp hanging from the ceiling.

Joshua puts our supplies on top of the shopkeeper's desk, including a sheepskin jacket for me to replace the one he ruined yesterday. I take our money out of my leather bag. We stole it the day we escaped the orphanage. Joshua was uneasy about it but I told him we didn't have a choice and I was right.

The shopkeeper eyes me. I keep going over the signs in my head, feverishly. There are seven signs that mark a god out from a human: speed-and-strength, premonition, beauty, endurance, the ability to heal oneself, the silver of the blood, and the god's particular gift, their demesne. I only have the last four because I'm only half-god, and three of those are invisible, so he shouldn't notice anything strange. Please let him not notice anything strange.

His eyes are grey. 'Hello, lovely,' he says.

I feel myself tense up, and he laughs.

'You're all right. What are you on the road for?'

Who are your parents, Jessica? 'Holiday.'

'Nice.'

He's making a small note of everything we buy, writing down the prices on a sheet. 'That your boyfriend, then?' He indicates Joshua behind me.

I feel, rather than see, Joshua's sudden stillness.

'My brother.'

'Ah.' There's something careful about his laugh. 'Sorry.'

'How much will it be?'

He pauses again to write on the sheet. 'Sixteen silvers.'

'Thanks.'

I count them out in my hand. He watches me. Joshua, standing in the shadows behind me, stirs.

'Where are you from, then?'

I hesitate, then curse myself for not being faster. I keep my eyes away from the shopkeeper. I smell smoke and know he's tending to a fire. The heat is uncomfortable, prickly. 'Amareth.' That's the truth.

'Ah. You're city kids, then.'

'Yeah. Here's your money.'

I place it on the counter and he straightens up from the fire behind the desk. 'Thank you, lovely.'

I nod curtly. Joshua has packed the food into the bag. We glance at each other as we walk, not too fast, towards the door. The heat beneath my skin shifts slickly. I feel sick.

I reach for the doorknob and feel Joshua stop dead beside me.

I look at the door, my mind slowing. It's been barred shut behind us.

We turn. Joshua is staring at the shopkeeper, who is standing in front of the desk, pointing a pistol into his face.

'Joshua and Hero Fitzgerald,' he says. 'Right?'

Joshua shakes his head mutely. My voice is shaking and so am I. 'No, we're . . . I mean I don't know what you're—'

The shopkeeper lowers his pistol and shoots Joshua in the arm.

There's a *crack* and a spatter of silver blood. Joshua cries out, and so do I, flinching as though the wound was mine, but before I can move I see the pain switch off in Joshua's eyes. The skin smooths over, sealing the bullet inside. Joshua's arm is covered in silvery blood but he's stopped bleeding.

He straightens, panting, staring at the shopkeeper with deep, palpable hatred.

'So,' the shopkeeper says. 'You're one of them.'

Joshua doesn't say anything. The shopkeeper turns his gun on me.

'What are you, then?'

I don't say anything. I've gone dead, like we practised, my eyes are blank. *Don't feel, just think.* If I let myself feel, I'll be afraid.

'Smoke,' I say. 'You sent up smoke.' I think of the flat fields around us, the bodies of gods burning in the centre of town all those years ago. It's not yet cold enough to justify a fire at high noon, and if I turn my head I see the wood in the grate is sycamore, dark-smoked, not the kind you'd use for fuel or heat. It's a signal. 'The Guard will see it. From the road. They'll know there are gods here.'

He turns to me, hands steady. 'You want me to shoot you too, bitch?' He snarls it with real hate, a fury I've rarely heard before. I raise my hands above my head, cold fear lightning-sudden in my throat.

'No. No. Don't shoot me.'

I hate the way the words sound, the cowardice in my voice.

He smiles. 'What are you, girl?'

I don't know what I should say. I can tell him I'm human, but he won't believe me, and then he'll shoot me, which will tell him anyway. I don't have the advantage of darkness now to hide the grey steel gleam in my blood. 'I'm a half-breed,' I say.

'Oh yeah? What are your *gifts,* then? What're you going to

do to me?' He enjoys this, the gun to my head. I wonder which of his loved ones was killed by a god, how many gods he killed himself in the rebellion. 'Tell me what you can do, bitch.'

I say nothing. Joshua's looking at me and I know he, like me, is working through our options in his head. Staying here long enough to be captured by the Guard is not an option. We *have* to get to Kestrel.

The shopkeeper points his gun at Joshua's head again, and I try not to flinch. 'Answer me. He won't heal so prettily if I blow his brains out, will he?'

I swallow, feel my breath catch in my throat. 'I'm a healer.'

'That's not a demesne. Don't lie to me, girl.'

'Healing others – other people, I mean – if you're sick, I can help, I can—' *Please don't shoot him*, I want to say again, but I stop myself. Pleading won't save us. 'I can help you. I can heal you.'

He ignores this. 'And what's his?' He jerks the pistol towards Joshua and I say nothing. There's urgency in his eyes now, the slight bones of fear. He wants to know who he's provoked.

I look at Joshua. His eyes are wide, pale gold in the gas lamplight.

I think, *trust me.*

And I say, 'Now.'

The room goes suddenly dark, pitch-black, dizzying, all the light sucked from it. I hear a gunshot. Glass breaking. I duck, I can't breathe, I feel the sharp pain of wood cracking against my legs. I try to keep my breath quiet, I'm thinking *Joshua, please*, and then—

Light. Sudden, overwhelming light.

I keep my eyes closed, swaying, my clenched hands pressed into the wooden floor. I don't want to open my eyes. I'm terrified I'm going to see Joshua dead.

But even if he is, I have to survive to rescue Kestrel from

Elida (*if she's even still alive*, says the malicious little voice in my head) and so I have to get out of here.

I look up.

Joshua is standing with his arm around the shopkeeper's neck. The pistol is lying on the floor. The light from the lamp above their heads, swinging dead from the ceiling, is dancing on Joshua's fingertips. I can see the shimmer of heat, the fluid white-hot glow. The shopkeeper is turning blue.

'Call off the Guard,' says Joshua to him, quietly and calmly.

'Joshua, he can't.'

'Then he'll pay for calling them here.'

'There's no point.'

I see that golden gleam in his eyes. 'Yes there is,' he says, and I see something wild is in him, the shards of the thing that broke when Kestrel was taken. He presses his glowing hand into the shopkeeper's throat.

The shopkeeper howls, his eyes blanching with agony. Joshua's eyes are blank, his face is steady. I can smell again that stench of burning flesh.

Shock stops me only for a second. '*Joshua!*'

He doesn't move. The shopkeeper's screams are choking away into nothing; I can see reddish blood beneath the crackling black skin of his neck. I want to be sick. I think, should I hit him? But he's stronger than me, and I flinch at what he might do to me in return.

So I try to hurt him. I say the first thing I know will cut him open at the heart. I hiss it at him.

'She would hate you for this.'

His eyes meet mine and they're dead, hopeless. My heart is pulsing faster. The spectre of her rises between us again, and I can see her in my mind's eye, standing next to me, she's saying, *Go on, you're right, I'm with you.*

'Drop him,' I say, 'drop him *right now*, if you ever loved her. On her soul, Joshua. Do it.'

For a terrible second I think it hasn't worked. His eyes are full of nothing. Then, abruptly, he releases the shopkeeper, who falls to the floor, not moving.

I don't look at Joshua. I drop to my knees beside the shopkeeper. The skin of his face is white and bloodless, his eyes milky and still. I know he's alive; I can feel it. I press my hand against his red-hot neck. I feel my hand sticky with his blood, the ash of his skin. I close my eyes. Behind me, the door rattles. The shopkeeper's skin stirs beneath my hand, and I feel it start to knit together.

Joshua says at last, above me, 'How could you say that, Hero?' His voice is empty and cold. I don't look up at him.

Someone slams against the door again, shouting. 'Ignatius!'

That must be the shopkeeper. He doesn't stir. The blood beneath my hands is drying. I can feel his pulse. His skin is still red with the heat of the burn, but the skin of his neck is smoothing. I look up at Joshua, fight down the guilt and fury burning my throat. If I don't stay calm, neither will he. 'Bar the door.'

He says nothing.

'Bar the door if you want to live.' My voice is shaking and I steady it. I'm not afraid of him. 'If you want to save her, *do what I say.*'

There's a silence. I think of him standing beside the road after he burned through my arm, the anger in his eyes, and for the first time a jolt of fear rises in my throat. I can't breathe, I can't look at him, I don't dare.

Then slowly I hear him walk over to the door, pick up a chair, and drive it with vicious shattering force under the doorknob.

I let out a shuddering breath.

There's another slam against it. '*Ignatius!*'

The shopkeeper gives a moan. I take my hand away from his neck. It's sticky with blood and blackened ash but the skin beneath it is smooth and cold, healed. I get to my feet. The shopkeeper's milky white eyes flicker. He'll be blind for the rest of his life. Healing that would take me hours, and we don't have hours; we don't have minutes.

I close my eyes.

Joshua will be no use now. He'll be too angry with me to think straight, to help me think. And Kestrel is in Elida. So now it's just me.

What are we going to do?

Option one, stay where we are; that way we'll get captured by the Guard, everything over. I can't let that happen.

Option two, fight our way out. Okay, think about that. Fight out of what? Through whom?

The shop is surrounded, let's say by a dozen people – I can't imagine Seaborne could muster much more than that, even with a smoke signal to summon them. How do we get through them? We'd have to kill them all, and that's not really an option either. If we slaughtered a village, we'd be upgraded from a couple of runaway orphanage kids to confirmed gods and mass-murderers. The whole country would be on the lookout for us. We wouldn't make it ten miles. And how would we fight? We have the shopkeeper's gun, but they will have more, pistols and hunting rifles and weapons I can't even name. What do we have that they don't?

We have Joshua.

Option three.

I stand up and look at him. Our eyes meet over Ignatius's body. He's still shaking with anger. 'Good news for you,' I say, keeping my voice flat and calm. I cannot show doubt. 'You might still get to kill him. Pick him up.'

A long stretch of silence, flat and dead as the fields around us. His eyes are narrowed with a hate I never thought I'd see in him. I didn't know he even had this rage. Where was this part of him that I've never seen it before?

His voice is soft, a whisper, rough with fury. 'How *dare* you use her like – like *that*, like—'

'To stop you becoming a murderer? You think she wouldn't have done the same thing?' I have to look contemptuous, ruthless. I will not show fear. 'Pick him up. If you want to shout at me, save it for when we get out of here alive.'

Another moment of silence, unspoken rage pressing down on us like fear.

Then at last he walks forward, bends down and pulls the shopkeeper to his feet effortlessly. The shopkeeper, Ignatius, lets out a long, agonised groan. His fish-blind eyes flicker. Joshua places a hand over Ignatius's heart. I can see the bones in his hand.

I close my eyes again. The light creaks above my head, swinging dead from the ceiling. Nothing else moves. Don't think.

The door slams yet again. 'IGNATIUS!'

'If I say your name,' I say to Joshua, over the shouting, 'I need you to injure him. Injure him, but not kill him, you understand?'

Joshua nods slowly, his eyes on the door. He's breathing quickly now. I think fear has finally cracked open his fury. *Good*. Let him hate them, not me.

'And if I tell you to kill him . . . I mean, look at you and say the words, *kill him* –'

'IGNATIUS!'

'– then you do it.'

Joshua looks at me. For the first time in years, I can't read his eyes.

'Do you understand me?'

The door rattles. 'IGNATIUS!'

'Sure,' he says. The hate is still there, under the adrenaline. I can hear it. 'If you want me to.'

I am not used to giving orders. I was never the one leading

us before all this happened, that was always Kestrel. But since she was taken everything's different. *He's* different.

'IGNATIUS!'

I bend and pick up the gun. It's smooth and still hot in my trembling hands. I aim, as carefully as I can, at the door, and fire at the lock.

There's an explosion of dust, a crash of metal. Then the door slams apart; the light opens on to our faces as though through a window in a temple. I raise my pistol. A man stumbles into the shop, looking desperate. He sees the shop-keeper in Joshua's arms. 'Ignatius!'

The woman behind him has a revolver. Behind her, there are others. They stay still, watching and waiting.

'If I tell him to, he'll kill Ignatius,' I say to the woman. Breathe in, breathe out. 'Do you believe me?'

Our guns are pointed into each other's faces.

She nods slowly, her eyes on Joshua.

My head hurts. I have to think. Be reasonable, don't make her angry.

'If you let us walk out of here, unhurt, we'll leave your Ignatius by the treeline, and we won't hurt him. Come after him when we're gone. If you choose to fight us, I can't guarantee we'll survive. But we'll fight to kill as many of you as possible – and the first person we kill will be him.'

She looks at me. Her hands are trembling but her eyes are clear. The man looks aghast. 'You can't kill him,' he says. 'You wouldn't. You're kids, I swear to . . . we can just—'

I close my eyes for only an instant. Then I say, 'Joshua, do it. But very gently.'

I don't look at him. I only see their eyes widen. The man starts forward, crying out, 'Ignatius, no—'

My voice catches. I have to fight not to let it break. 'Joshua, stop.'

Behind me there's only silence. The man and woman fall still. The woman is looking very levelly at me. Her face is grey, the muscles in it taut.

'Do you believe me now?' I say. I'm looking at the man. He nods so furiously it looks like a spasm. He's shaking. The woman isn't.

I say, 'Will you let us pass?'

The woman nods, very slowly.

'Then clear a path for us.'

She doesn't move. 'Where will you leave him?'

'We'll go into the woods and leave him by the side of the road. Give us half an hour and then come and get him. Any sooner and we'll know.' That's a blatant lie, but with luck she won't realise that. 'You'll be able to see him the whole time.'

The woman hesitates, and then nods again. I try to stop myself asking the question.

'Are you his wife?'

She nods again.

I don't want to say it, but the words come unbidden. 'I'm sorry this happened. We didn't want to hurt anyone.' Stupid, stupid, why does she care what you wanted? 'But we can't be captured. Do you understand?'

She doesn't say anything. I'm not even sure she's heard me. Her eyes are fixed unblinkingly on her husband's face. I don't think she's noticed yet that his eyes are boiled white beneath the closed lids.

At last, she moves aside. The man, now trembling furiously, follows her.

'Joshua,' I say, without taking my eyes off them, 'walk with me. Bring him.'

I move forward, then wait until I hear the shuffle of Joshua's footsteps behind me. I take two steps, then three, and then I'm six feet away from the woman, who's nearest.

We stare at each other. I'm not going to move until she steps out of the way of the door and she doesn't want to leave me alone with her beloved Ignatius but neither of us has a choice.

The woman looks at me. Then, very slowly, she steps back. We walk past her.

The sun has come out while we've been inside. The shop is surrounded. There are more people than I thought. I can feel Joshua's breath behind me, hear our footsteps on the hard cobblestones. I know he's frightened, at last, but I'm not. I've gone numb and cold inside my head, my mind a flat black lake.

They're all staring at us. Guns pointed into my face.

The woman's voice behind us. 'Let them pass.'

They look past us, at her, bemused.

'Julia?' one of them says, quietly, to Ignatius's wife.

'Let them pass. They're gods, Lauren.'

A collective, frightened intake of breath. Hands tighten on weapons. My mind is racing. I'm trying to work out what my next move should be but my mind has shut down. *Who are your parents, Jessica?* I can feel the Guardsmen's hand on my wrist, outside the tavern in the rain, their soft voices, their questions. *Who are your parents, Jessica?* No, don't think about that. Concentrate.

Another step. Joshua moves with me. The salt-crusted houses in front of me have their doors and windows bolted shut. Our presence here has put the whole of Seaborne on lockdown.

No one says a word. I walk faster. I feel their hatred, their fear, their stirring breaths, eyes on my face. *Who are—*

Then, suddenly, a voice behind me. 'What's happened to his *eyes?*'

I whirl. Joshua is staring at a man who is looking into Ignatius's stirring, blind-white eyes, pointing his gun straight

into Joshua's face, which has gone suddenly blank. The woman
– Ignatius's wife, Julia – runs towards her husband.

'What is it? What's happened to him?'

'His eyes—'

Julia's too close to Joshua. She grabs Ignatius's arm, tries
to pull him from Joshua's grip, but Joshua's much stronger
than her, and he stays where he is, his grip on the shopkeeper's arm too tight. He's looking at me for help, fear beneath
his anger.

'Hero—?'

He means, What do I do? *Where are your parents, Jessica?*
I can't focus, can't think. I'm panicking and my mind has
jammed like a gun and as I watch, stupid and helpless, Julia
steps back and raises her gun very calmly and points it between
Joshua's eyes and clicks off the safety.

'Don't shoot him,' I say. My voice carries across the square,
over the smell of smoke, and it does not tremble.

'Why shouldn't I?'

'It won't bring back his sight.'

'His sight,' Julia says, and for the first time her voice is
shaking. 'His *sight*. You think that's what this is about?'

'If you kill my brother,' I say, 'I will raze your village to
the ground.'

I say it with as much authority as I can, because I don't
have that power or anything like it and there's a good chance
they know that by now. The woman, Julia, looks at me and
her eyes are huge and hard and her hands are shaking.

And then the man next to her raises his gun and fires.

Everything snaps. Joshua throws himself out of the way as
the man's hands are moving and drops Ignatius into the mud
and rolls. The shot is clear and bright and I feel a sharp, cold
pain in my hand and shut that off immediately.

There's uproar. Julia is still standing exactly where she was,
pointing her revolver into the space where Joshua's head was

seconds before. The crowd is swirling and coalescing around Ignatius. Joshua is crouched in the mud, frozen in panic.

'*Run!*'

He scrambles to his feet. Someone fires a shot behind us but they go wide and we're already running. The road and the treeline, the road and the treeline. My breath is salt-steel in my throat.

'DON'T MOVE, SCUM!'

We keep running. There are tears flying from Joshua's eyes, he's much faster than me and pulling ahead; that thought trickles slowly through my mind like a raindrop down a window. Mud sucks at my feet. The road is so close, the sunset bright. There's greyish blood streaming into the air from my hand but I don't look at it. Another shot and I wait to see Joshua fall or for me to hurt but nothing happens and we keep running running running over the road and now we're on the other side—

'COME BACK, YOU SCUM!'

Treeline, treeline feet away, I realise I'm still wearing the leather bag slung across my back, everything hurts, and then we're into the trees and darkness overwhelms us and we're still running. Another shot far away, and then the silence of the woods breaks over our heads like the surface of an ocean. The quiet broken only by our quicksilver breaths. The trees whip past us and time is sliding blackly through my mind and then there's just breathing, footsteps, pain in my lungs, blood in my mouth. I need to slow down, I can't—

'Joshua—'

He keeps running, ahead of me. I stop, doubled over, wheezing, trying to speak, voice hoarse.

'Joshua – stop. We're . . . we're safe.'

He doesn't, for a moment, but then slowly he falters and stops. He doesn't bend over and clutch his knees like I do, he doesn't need to, his god-blood is stronger than mine and keeps him standing. We're under a canopy of pine trees, shielded from the dying sun. I throw my bag to the floor and sink to my knees. My hand is still bleeding.

'Joshua, please, give me the knife.'

He doesn't move. His eyes are dead. The hate is gone but there's nothing else there either. It frightens me.

'Joshua, please.'

He doesn't do anything. I look down at my hand. It's pouring blood, and I know the agony would be paralytic if I allowed myself to feel it. I can see glistening bone beneath the gristle and blood, the bullet gleaming softly at its centre, a pearl in a bloody oyster. This will be difficult to heal.

'*Joshua!*'

He pulls his bag from his shoulders at last, slowly and mechanically. I'm still holding the shopkeeper's pistol. He gives me the knife and his hands aren't shaking. The knife is still smooth, sharp and shiny. I pull up my sleeve, close my eyes, fight off the pain, and start prising the bullet out of my hand, between muscle and sinew. A normal bullet would have gone straight through me. The realisation trickles like cold water up from the recesses of my brain. This is a god-killer bullet, the type they used to slaughter our kind during the rebellion. It's meant to stay inside a god, make it hard to heal around the bullet. How long had Julia kept that gun, waiting for another god to wander across her path, so she could kill them with it? Twenty years? How old was she then, ten, fifteen?

I'm still holding Ignatius's gun in my other hand, I realise. It trembles in my shaking hand and then slips from my grip and hits the grass. I take slow deep breaths, staring at it. The world swims gently around me.

'How could you?' he says at last, above me. His voice is soft and low, but it cuts through the quiet, makes me flinch. 'How . . . I don't . . . how dare you say that to me? Use *her*—'

'Because I had to, Joshua.' Can't he understand that? I want to sound angry, but the words come out gentle, weak. I'm so exhausted. 'I can't let you kill.'

He drops his hands suddenly and the look on his face is so violently murderous that it scares me. He growls at me. 'She's not *yours*, Hero, she's not . . . how dare you use her like she was *here* . . . and say . . . how dare you say she wouldn't love—'

I see the exposed nerve I have touched, the deep guilt, and I think of his nightmares, and his fear of letting her die.

But I don't care how he feels anymore. I am so sick of trying to heal him. I want my brother back, I want advice and calm and comfort, I don't want this angry broken boy I have to shout at and control. Doesn't he think I wake in the night? Doesn't he know she haunts me, too, the last sight I had of her terrified face? However much he hates me for leaving her, it cannot be more than I hate myself. Doesn't he get that?

But the truth, obviously, is that no, he doesn't. He hasn't given one moment's thought to the inside of my head since we left the orphanage. He lives in his own grief, and I hate him for that so much right now I can't breathe.

'Don't talk to me like that,' I say, at last. My voice is trembling. *Stay calm.* 'I told you not to talk to me like—'

'*I can speak to you how I want!*' he roars, so violently I see birds lift from the trees around us and flap away, cawing. 'You had *no right* to say that, to try to use her to make—'

'I had every right in the world. You were going to kill him, Joshua—'

'*Yes I was!* Yes, I was, I should have, I had the—'

'You are insane,' I tell him. That shuts him up. The last birds fly away, crying out in low pained caws. 'You are high on your own power. Being a god doesn't mean you get the right to take a life just because you're angry. If you think that, you're no better than the Guard. You're *worse* than them. She'd never love you if she saw you like this.'

I have never seen him this furious. His eyes are wide and gold and full of rage. He looks inhuman.

I can't move. I just stand there, breathless.

He lunges towards me, and the ground vanishes under his feet, with his god's speed, and he raises his clenched hand.

I don't move. I can't. I just stare at him. The seconds slow. And then I realise they've stopped.

He's standing over me, his fist raised and trembling. I'm gazing at him in blank shock. I know – I *know*, despite the evidence in front of me – that Joshua, my brother in all but blood, would never raise a hand to me, so what I am seeing does not make any sense. I wait, patiently, for the world to adjust to what I know to be true.

The seconds stretch on. The woods around us are perfect and still. And then he crumples. 'Oh, crap,' he whispers through his hands. 'Oh, Hero. . . '

Nothing stirs for a second. Then there's a movement in the air, like a brush of wind, and he's gone. Vanished into the woods, with his god's lightning speed. I stand staring after him for minutes afterwards, immobile. The only sound is the steady drip of blood from my hand into the earth.

In the first years of the orphanage, in the chaos and the silence and the fear, children used to slash at each other with knives, make each other bleed. Trying to find the gods amongst them, to root them out, pre-empt the Guard. Eventually, a couple of kids bled to death, and after that you were hard-pressed to find anything sharp in Fitzgerald House.

That wasn't to protect gods, of course, but the human kids. It'd been a problem for years, out there in the world, though we orphanage kids had no way of knowing that. It was too easy to mistake human blood for a half-breed's, to think you saw a gleam of silver in the dim, dark-wine red. Thousands of humans died in the rebellion for that, killed for a trick of the light. And kids, too, murdered by bloodthirsty god-hunters, convinced they were half-breeds or gods too young for their blood to have turned. Maybe some of them were, I don't know.

After a few years, once the frenzy had died down, laws were passed. To stop kids being tested too young, and to make sure that when tests were carried out, the Guard could be sure of who they were killing. Blood was taken in brightly lit rooms, with witnesses, on the day that marked eighteen years since an orphanage child had been found abandoned, and not one day before. They were meticulous, the Guard, in protecting humans from the slaughter they meted out to us.

As we grew up, the disappearances slowed to a trickle, and then became sparse enough that barely anyone could remember the last one: maybe six months ago, or a year. Almost all the foundlings of Amareth are human, now; nearly all the gods are dead, or if they were alive, they were up north with the resistance, hiding like cowards, while we rotted under the undying gaze of the Guard. There was no way any children of the resistance would end up being abandoned in Amareth.

But the Guard didn't care. It was worth a thousand human children being confined needlessly to an orphanage, worth the care and the expense, if it meant even one stray god-child could be rooted out and disappeared to Elida. They hated us so much. I could feel the weight of their hatred pressing on my chest every morning when I woke, feel it in their eyes. It burned inside me, how much the humans hated us.

But Kestrel didn't hate me.

Inexplicably, gloriously, Kestrel with her safe human blood had decided not to hate us. Kestrel thought it was all nonsense, had accepted Joshua's abilities without question, had thrown herself eagerly into our plans to escape, to protect him. She let us trust her, and for that, we loved her forever.

Trust was what let us escape from Fitzgerald House. Trust between the three of us – god, human and half-breed – which should have been impossible in that evil place. That was what saved us.

I can't leave Joshua now. I don't care what he does, who he becomes. I swore vows, to Kestrel and to him. If the Guard break us apart like this, without having to say a word to us, then they win, don't they?

I went into this prepared to die for him, didn't I?

And what the hell do I do if I change my mind? Where do I run to? *How* do I run? He'd chase me down, call me a traitor, do . . . I don't know what he'd do. I flinch at the thought, the cold sick fear in my stomach.

He was *angry*. He wanted to kill that man and I stopped him. He was scared. I'm being . . . I don't know . . .

It was just a moment, a bad moment. He'd never hurt me, not deliberately. He's not *evil*. He stopped himself and he ran away. He wouldn't do that if he wanted to hurt me.

He's my brother. He's my *brother*. What the hell am I thinking? Kestrel would kill me if she knew I'd even thought about leaving him. Or no, she wouldn't kill me. She'd just look at me, shocked and hurt and betrayed, like she didn't know who I was anymore.

I love him. I don't care how he feels about me. He's my brother and I love him and I'll never abandon him. He must know that. I'd never, never leave him.

So I'll wait here.

He's there when I wake, lying beside me in the thin, dawn-grey dark. He doesn't say anything. He just waits to hear the change in my breathing, and after a moment, he kisses me on the forehead. Neither of us moves or speaks. I don't think I could take it, anything he said. I'd break at last.

I lie there in the silence, listening to his breathing get slower and slower.

After a while he falls asleep, and I sit up and watch him, curled in the dimness, still and quiet.

CHAPTER 3

Cairn

Now we move faster, waking before dawn and walking long after sunset, guided through the darkness by the light in Joshua's hands. The Guard will be truly hunting us now, after our escape from Seaborne – now that they know what we can do, that we can kill. They know where we are now, to within fifty miles. We have to get to Elida as quickly as possible, before they can find us.

I suppose speed was always our priority, but I never thought of it as being for *our* sake. Joshua always thought we had a chance of getting to Elida before the Guard could hurt Kestrel, but I knew that was delusion. If they wanted to kill her they'd kill her, and there would be nothing we could do, not from here. It was more important to keep ourselves hidden. Kestrel would want me to keep him safe.

Joshua wakes every night muttering, but it's never a premonition. I can't sleep, so I sit guard. When I close my eyes, I try to trace heartbeats on the edge of my vision, blinks like radar against the darkness of my eyelids. Part of my demesne, I think. I can sense faults in the heartbeats, irregularities that I've come to understand as cuts or breakages or bruises in the people around me. I could find my way to an injured person blind and deaf. But there's never anyone here but me and Joshua. Not that that makes me feel any safer.

Sometimes he wakes in the night with light glimmering on his hands, the white-hot fear of a nightmare, and he looks at me and I swear there's a few seconds when the dream's thick in his mind and he can't remember who I am.

I don't know what he'd do if he believed I was a danger to him. He could kill me with a thought, a flash of white-hot light. I am at his mercy, always.

The days sink into a blur of grey cloud and paranoia, the scent of the sea. The last forest fire before winter burns gold and grey to the south, and whenever the smoke blows towards us I can't breathe through the fear. I see Guardsmen in every shadow. I keep Ignatius's gun at the bottom of the bag, where neither of us can reach it. On the map Elida lurks just out of sight.

Kestrel and Joshua found out I was a half-breed when we were thirteen. It wasn't even me who told them.

I'd known I was godly for years, but I didn't know what my demesne was for a long time. My blood wouldn't turn grey till I was sixteen, but I could make my bruises smooth to pallor if I wanted them to, make cuts heal over, find the switch in my head that released me from pain. I heard heartbeats, sometimes, though I didn't know what they were – a thrumming of pulses at the base of my skull. But I didn't realise I could heal other people until Kestrel broke her leg.

It happened when Clarissa came for Joshua. She was a god too, or so it was rumoured, though she'd been too clever to let anyone see proof of it. That only made us more worried. Gods and half-breeds, especially the paranoid ones, the ones with powerful demesnes like Joshua's, which were bound to spill over and be discovered – they were the ones you had to watch out for. They'd try and find other gods they could rat out to the Guard, in the hope of saving their own necks. It rarely worked, of course, but that didn't stop them trying.

It went like this: Clarissa came into our room one evening and asked to speak to Joshua alone.

There was a silence. I remember the silence very clearly, thick as cloud, a humidity. The window was half-open and our black curtains stirred uneasily in the breeze.

Then Kestrel said, 'No.'

Clarissa folded her arms, raised her eyebrows. 'I'm sorry?'

'No,' Kestrel repeated. She, Joshua and Clarissa both looked round at me and I realised I'd said it too. Clarissa flashed me a contemptuous look and turned back to Kestrel.

'Joshua can speak to whoever he wants. I'm sure he wouldn't mind—'

'Yeah,' he said. 'I would, actually.'

The temperature in the room seemed to drop. Clarissa stared at Joshua, and then at Kestrel. Her eyes hardened. She took a step forward, slowly, as though hoping we wouldn't notice.

'Excuse *me*,' she said softly, 'but I think—'

Kestrel lunged towards her, pushing Joshua behind her. *Strike first*, that was her motto. I don't know what her plan was, honestly. What was she going to do, hold Clarissa down and beat her up? It was insane. Panic made her do it, more than anything else.

And it was never going to work. Clarissa was a god, after all. She stepped forward, calm as anything, and stamped on Kestrel's leg, with a god's vicious strength. I heard the clear white *snap*. Kestrel crumpled, screaming.

Clarissa looked between us. I could see the sudden terror in her eyes, like waking from a dream. She knew, I think, that she was doomed; she had revealed herself. There were people in the corridor watching us, who were running towards the sound of the scream. The rumours now would be too thick ever to escape.

She turned and ran, and we never saw her again.

Joshua lunged after her, stopping at the doorway, screaming at her, all caution forgotten. 'Come back! You *coward!* Come back and *fight!*'

Kestrel was on the floor, sobbing with pain. I was standing in the corner, staring down at her, half-paralysed. Some deep sense in my brain had come alive at the sight of it, a spark lighting up in my throat, white-hot. I'd *felt* Kestrel's leg being broken, like a jolt in my chest, more than shock, the ghost of that clean *snap*.

I stood very still. I couldn't stop looking at the way her leg bent. I could hear, more clearly than ever before, the heartbeats around me, a thrumming drumbeat at the base of my skull. Kestrel's was in front of me, and there was something in it, jagged, like a blockage . . .

Outside me, Kestrel screamed again.

There was an obstacle in the thumping of Kestrel's blood. It felt wrong. I wanted to fix it, set it right, like scratching an itch. The impulse was all-controlling. I moved without thinking, wanting to obey it.

I don't remember anything after that. Sight and sound had suddenly become irrelevant; I had new senses now, and they spoke to me surely, telling me deeper truths. This is how you fix her bone, see, the fraying of the flesh, *here* and *here*. This is the play of muscles and sinew under blood, listen, isn't it beautiful? And if you look *here* . . .

When I came out of myself I was kneeling beside her on the cold floor, hands on the break in her leg, feeling the bone and gristle knit together beneath my hands. Sound came back only slowly. Joshua had fallen quiet and Kestrel had stopped crying. She was staring at me, at her healed leg. I looked up at her and she wiped her face impatiently.

There was a long silence. I was numb with shock, too astonished even to realise that I should have been afraid.

'What the *hell*—'

'I didn't know,' I said. I couldn't think what else to say. I looked down at my hands, and saw with a dull throb of shock that they were covered in blood. 'I didn't . . . know I could do that.'

Kestrel looked at me, at my hands. I could feel her considering.

'Joshua,' she said at last. 'Close the door.'

He did. I felt the darkness thicken. The room was musty, and our beds set against the wall cast long shadows in the sunset. Joshua turned with his hand on the doorknob to look at me.

'You're a god?'

I turned and looked up at him. There was a shine of hope in his face. I understood for a moment how lonely he must be, and ached to be able to fix it, heal it like bone.

'No.'

He was intent. 'Are you sure?'

'Yeah. I don't have premonitions . . . I'm not strong or fast, or . . .'

I shook my head, trying to avoid his eyes. I sounded too defensive, but I didn't know what else to be.

There was a silence.

'But you've got a demesne,' said Kestrel. She took my hand and helped herself to her feet, testing out her healed leg in mild astonishment. She was looking at me like she'd never seen me before, but it was with appreciation and respect, not disgust. Something in me started to lift, weightless, the beginnings of joy. 'Can you heal yourself too?'

'Yeah.'

Kestrel walked to her bookshelf, still testing the weight on her leg, and drew out the knife she had threatened Joshua with a year before from between the pages of *A Comparison of Human and Divine Biology*. She hesitated, and then handed it to me. I slid it gingerly across my wrist. The pain throbbed once and then vanished under the shock.

The blood that welled up was red, still. It was three years

then until my blood would turn. Joshua turned away, but Kestrel stared. I felt that same urge to heal, and obeyed, and felt something in my mind fall away. The pain stopped. The skin sealed, and the cut vanished.

There was another silence. Kestrel raised her eyebrows. 'Not bad,' she said.

Not bad. Sometimes I forget how much I love her.

It's just before dawn, the light greyish. I sit up, breathing hard. Something's woken me and I don't know what it is. Joshua is lying beside me in his sleeping bag. I can't hear anything. We're far away from the road, in a shadowed clearing. I can smell the clouds, heavy with rain.

I can't imagine what would have woken me, what could have stirred in my mind to warn me, what I could have—

Yes, I do. *Idiot.* Heartbeats.

I close my eyes and touch that sense in the corner of my mind and suddenly everything's clear. I think for a moment that there's nothing, because I can't sense any one beat in the darkness around us. Then I realise the whole wood beyond the clearing is pulsing, throbbing. My breath catches.

We are entirely surrounded.

I open my eyes quite slowly, winded with shock, my own pulse hammering. For a moment the vision – if that's what it is – of the heartbeats dies away in a thundering echo, and the trees are silent again. Joshua is lying beside me, his face blank in sleep, and the heartbeats could almost have been a nightmare.

I need to think, I need to calm down, I—

Something moves behind me. A pulse extricating itself from the whole.

I keep very still.

'Get up,' says a voice from behind us, very softly.

Joshua jerks awake, whirling in his sleeping bag, a drop of

light appearing from thin air on his fingertips. He scrambles to his feet. I act on instinct, dive for the bag, pull out the pistol, click off the safety and roll up with it pointing into the face of the woman in front of us.

Then we both stop.

She's not a Guardsman. Or at least, she's not wearing a Guardsman's uniform. She looks to be alone, though I know from the heartbeats she's not, and she's very calm, standing there in a worn leather jacket and breeches, looking steadily at us. She looks about forty. Short, blondish hair, very pale eyes.

'Go on,' she says. 'Have a go.'

Joshua hesitates, even though he could burn a hole through her face in an instant if he wanted to. I don't. I level the gun at her throat and fire.

Even before I feel the jolt of the recoil I know there's something wrong. She's too calm, too quiet. The bullet hits her with a strange popping noise, like a stone dropping into water. She rocks back on her heels slightly.

'Exactly,' she says. 'So maybe you can put down that gun.'

Joshua is staring at her. 'You're a god.'

The woman looks levelly at me. 'Well?'

I gesture roughly with the pistol to the trees. 'Get rid of them.'

Her expression barely flickers, though I can tell she's taken aback. She looks at me, then says, with a decent attempt at cool incomprehension, 'What do you mean?'

'You've got a whole battalion back there. Order them a hundred feet away and then maybe we can talk.'

A hundred feet away is out of my range, but it also means we'll be out of theirs. The woman gives me another hard look. I'm still pointing my gun into her face, but she seems entirely unperturbed. Then she says, 'All right.'

I can tell Joshua is itching to turn and look at me, to speak to me, but he doesn't dare look away from the woman. The light is still hovering, diamond-bright, in his hand. She looks into the trees, and calls, 'Retreat. A hundred and fifty feet. Mark, Eliza, stay with me.'

We wait, silent. Joshua takes two steps backwards, closer to me. I get slowly to my feet, never taking my eyes or my gun off the woman's face. There's rustling in the trees. Then two people, a boy and a dark-haired girl a few years older than us, slip out of the trees to stand beside the pale-eyed woman. They position themselves automatically on either side of her, watching us.

'Who are these?' I say. I wave the gun to point at them, and neither flinches.

'This is Eliza,' says the woman. 'And this—'

'That's not what I meant.'

The boy and girl glance at each other. I see the woman's eyes harden. Finally she says, 'Mark is human.'

'And *Eliza*?' I'm not sure why I lace the name with hostility.

'Eliza is . . .'

'I'm a god,' says the girl quietly. Her hair is cropped to her scalp like the boy's, and she stands straight and tall as the boy, her eyes bright. 'Are you?'

There's a strange pull to her voice, like the drag of a tide on your ankles. I can feel the word form in my throat, smooth, easy, *yes*. I want to say it, want to answer her.

I choke the instinct back, say nothing, tighten my grip on the gun. The girl doesn't take her eyes off me. Joshua's hand twitches slightly to the left, as though he's not sure whether to aim it at the woman or the girl. But I'm more worried about Mark.

'Why is he here?' I jerk the pistol towards the boy, who doesn't flinch. 'If he's human?'

No one says anything. The boy glances at the woman.

'I'm not here to hurt anyone,' he says. His voice is gently

reassuring; I recognise it, from the nurses in the orphanage, as that of someone who has spent a lot of time around children.

Where could he have done that? Where are there children, out here in the hills?

Very slowly, I lower my gun.

Joshua is aghast. 'Hero—'

'It's all right,' I say. I'm still staring at the pale-eyed woman. 'They're not here to hurt us.'

'Hero—'

I meet the eyes of the woman and say it aloud. 'They're resistance, Joshua.'

It's the only thing that makes sense. If they'd wanted to kill us, we'd be dead by now. And to willingly admit they're gods, shamelessly and without fear . . .

They must think themselves far out of reach of the Guard.

My heart is thumping. The resistance hate the Guard, and the government, and everyone who helped to kill my mother. *They will not hand us over.*

Joshua stares at me, and at last I see the light flicker and die in his hand.

Mark, Eliza and the pale-eyed god are all watching me as well. I have to look tough. I stare at the woman. 'What do you want with us?'

'I want to ask you questions.'

'Do you?' I glance at the girl. 'Or do you want *her* to ask us questions?'

To my surprise, the girl, Eliza, shifts uncomfortably. I speak to her, pressing my advantage. 'What's your demesne?'

She doesn't meet my eyes. 'Truth.'

'What do you—'

'I can tell if you're lying,' she says, very softly. Her eyes are on Joshua now. 'I can make it . . . uncomfortable if you are.'

Joshua advances on her, a light glowing in his hand again, and this time I can see the shimmer of heat around it. Mark and the pale-eyed woman immediately move to block his path to the girl, and to my relief he stops.

'Is that a threat?' he says roughly.

'No.'

The pale-eyed woman glances at her. Mark's eyes are still on Joshua, on the light in his hand. I think he knows he wouldn't stand a chance against Joshua, if it came to it. One bolt of white-hot light into his face and everything over. Kestrel believed firmly that Joshua didn't have it in him to kill, and maybe she was right, then, but this isn't that Joshua anymore. His power comes easily to him now, effortless, fire on his skin, his eyes cold. Maybe even the woman's demesne wouldn't protect her, if Joshua wanted her dead.

The same thing seems to have crossed her mind, because she turns to me now fully, her eyes hard and determined, like she knows what she says now is vital.

'My name is Cairn,' she says. 'I think you know who I am. We heard about you, and we wanted to know why you had come here, what you wanted, and if we could help. We have absolutely no intention of hurting you.'

I smile without feeling. 'Unless we hurt you first.'

Her eyes harden. She pauses before nodding slowly, like she's trying to read me but can't. Good. 'Unless you hurt us first. But I don't think you will, Hero.'

I flinch slightly at the sound of my name in this woman's mouth.

'Help us?' says Joshua. He says the words like they sound strange in his mouth. I understand the feeling. Nearly a month of complete isolation, of unrelenting mortal peril, has made the idea of help almost unthinkably alien. 'Why would you want to help us?'

'Why would we *not* want to help you?'

'That's not good enough.'

Cairn looks at me evenly. 'All right,' she says at last. 'We'd like to know how you escaped the Guard. So far as we know, you're the first kids ever to make it out of an orphanage alive.'

'The first kids who weren't human.'

She jerks her head slightly, almost irritably, as if she thinks I'm being pedantic. Maybe I am. 'Yes.'

Joshua and I look at each other for a long moment. His face and its expressions are so familiar, it's a relief to be able to read it after minutes of staring into their impenetrable eyes.

'You don't have to tell us anything if you don't want to,' says Cairn. 'All we want is to protect you from the Guard. Every life is precious.'

Every life? Easy for them to say that now. What about Nicholas, what about Clarissa? They could have used this woman's help, trapped in Fitzgerald House. What have the resistance been doing all these years, to help the disappeared children? What makes our lives more valuable than theirs, trapped in Elida?

But of course there's an answer to that, an obvious answer. *Think, you idiot.*

Why appear to us now? They've heard about us. They've heard about Seaborne. They think us warriors, murderers. They've heard how Ignatius was blinded. They know what we are . . .

Every life is precious.

'Especially *his* life,' I say, slowly. I think I understand now. 'You want him on your side, don't you?'

'We're already on your side,' says Eliza gently.

But I'm not listening to her. They want Joshua. Obviously. They want people with powerful demesnes, gifts that can kill.

And Joshua could kill fifty people at a stroke, if he wanted to, just by burning through them. A flick of his hand.

No. My revulsion is immediate. I won't give him to them.

They don't deserve it. If they could really protect us, they wouldn't be here only now, after we'd already escaped the Guard three times. If they were worth anything, if they had any strength, they would have swarmed Amareth and rescued us all from the orphanage when I was still a kid. If they were worth anything at all, they would have saved my mother. Either they're too weak to do anything against the Guard, or they were powerful enough to help us and chose not to.

'No, thanks,' I hear myself saying, in a flat voice. 'We can't accept your help.'

There's a strange, strained silence. Then Cairn says, in a voice that has lost its smoothness, 'What do you mean *can't*? If you're going to Elida—'

Panic flares in me. 'How do you know that?' It's a stupid thing to say.

'You're at least fifty miles north of any major city,' says Eliza quietly, 'and still going. There's only one place you could be heading for. And our reports said a girl you associated with was taken to Elida on the day you escaped.'

I say it again, stiffly. 'We don't want your help. Thank you for the offer.'

There's a pause before Cairn speaks. Her tone is not angry, but low and persuasive. 'You must understand the insanity of this plan. You want to get this girl out of Elida, on your own, with no help—'

'No,' says Joshua, his voice rising, 'we're not—'

'When you know your path must have been clear to the Guard for days,' says Cairn, as if she cannot hear him, 'as surely as it was to us, when they are prepared for your arrival – you do realise that if that girl is even still alive, it's only because they're keeping her as bait, to lure you there? And even if—'

'No,' says Joshua, more angrily, 'that's not what we're—'

'And *even if* you do,' says Cairn, her voice even quieter but somehow more audible over Joshua's, 'do you expect to be able to live your lives in peace and comfort, having stolen a prisoner from the Guard from *Elida*, of all places – from their *lair*? You won't be orphanage escapees anymore, I promise you. They will never let you sleep. They will never rest until they have found you and they have ended you.'

There's a silence. I don't look at Joshua.

'I'm sorry,' I say, yet again, and my voice has hardened, cooled, like glass. 'We don't want your help. Thank you for the offer.'

Cairn is staring at me very intently. Something in her breathing has roughened. Eliza's watching me in silence. Mark's eyes still haven't left Joshua's face. Then Cairn says, with what seems like considerable effort, 'All right. All right. Well, if you change your mind . . .'

She trails off, and after a moment she just shakes her head, turns and walks out of the clearing. The shadows swallow her at once. Mark takes one last look at Joshua, then follows her.

Only Eliza remains, watching me. There's a long pause.

'Elida's in the sea,' she says quietly. 'It's on an island. We weren't sure whether or not to tell you. And—' She pauses. Her eyes linger on Joshua for a moment. Then she says, in a different, flatter voice, 'Well, good luck.'

And then she's gone, and we're alone again in the clearing. The silence around us is thick and pure and clear. Joshua turns to me, his face still colourless. I can't breathe.

CHAPTER 4

The Ocean in Sunlight

Joshua's eighteenth finding-day dawned bright and searingly hot. Those were the last days of summer, and the sky was bleeding out the last of its heat.

Finding-days were strange in Fitzgerald House. For one thing, of course, it was an orphanage, so no one's ages were real. As far as the Guard and the nurses were concerned, we hadn't been born at all, but *found*, in alleyways and on doorsteps. Everyone knew they were weeks, months, maybe even years older than Fitzgerald House's records suggested. But who you'd been before didn't matter. Now you were just one of a thousand, named from a list, raised in a dormitory. You had no birth, no parentage. You were nothing until your blood changed, and then you were prey, a hunted thing.

This was only a few weeks ago, so unlike many of my memories from the orphanage, this one has the absolute clarity of glass. I remember, for instance, that I woke hours before that glittering dawn and lay unmoving in bed, watching the sunlight creep across the varnished wooden floor. Joshua's skin shimmered gently with the silver of his blood as the light touched him, his features smooth with sleep. I waited for the dawn to reach Kestrel's bed, to slide over her face. Her amber eyes were open and staring without focus at the ceiling.

We watched the light dance on his face, as if he were lying underwater, until it was too bright for him to hide any longer. His eyes opened as suddenly as if we had shouted at him. I was close enough to see his pupils dilate slightly as he realised where he was, *when* he was, what was coming. I saw the fear calcify in his face.

Kestrel was the first to speak into the brittle silence. 'Congratulations.'

'For what?' Joshua's voice was very hoarse.

'It's your finding-day, you dolt. You're an adult.'

We got up silently, dressed without speaking. Nothing needed to be said. We had a plan. It wasn't going to work, of course, but it was worth a try.

I tried to avoid looking at Kestrel. We had worried about whether Joshua would have the nerve to go through with it. In the days before, he had seemed brittle and exhausted under the weight of his fear, barely eating or sleeping. But that morning it seemed we should have had more faith. His face was the soft grey of my blood, but his jaw was set and he seemed determined.

None of us spoke until the bell rang for breakfast. Kestrel grimaced at me apologetically. I understood, and walked towards the door, trying to seem casual. I know Joshua always hated this kind of awkwardness, and I had no intention of causing him more discomfort than necessary, not on his last day here.

And that was when I realised for the first time that whatever happened today, this was Joshua's last day in Fitzgerald House. He would never come back here. I would never wake again to see him lying there, in that bed, peaceful and calm . . .

Out of the corner of my eye I saw Kestrel take a tentative step towards Joshua, who was staring fixedly at the floor. The mirror in the back of the door as I swung it open showed her placing a hand gently on his chest, turning his face to look at her.

There was a burning look in his eyes. His voice was gruff and quiet. I heard him say as I left, 'You've got to understand, whatever happens now . . .' and then fall silent when she kissed him.

Breakfast in Fitzgerald was held in the main dining hall, a cavernous, glittering room with a curved metal and glass roof, which in summer turned the place into a furnace. It never bothered Joshua, of course – light likes him – but the rest of us were sweating. I saw Kestrel wipe her forehead as she lifted a forkful of eggs to her mouth, slowly. She wasn't eating much. Her unblinking eyes were fixed on Joshua's face.

Someone walked behind me. 'Hey, Kestrel. Joshua.' No one ever noticed me. For a while I'd thought that might be my actual demesne, until Clarissa broke Kestrel's leg.

They both said 'hey' back, automatically, without taking their eyes off each other. The passerby, whoever it was, whistled mockingly. They both looked up.

'Look at you two . . .'

'Shut up,' said Kestrel, flatly. Usually she took things like this in good humour, but not today.

They did shut up. No one ignored threats from Kestrel.

Joshua was still staring down at his plate. He had barely eaten either. I leaned forward.

'Joshua,' I said, very quietly. 'Look at me.'

Very unwillingly, he raised his eyes.

'Don't worry. We'll get you through this. You trust us, right?'

He didn't speak for a second, still staring at the table. Then he said suddenly, 'If it does go wrong—'

'It *won't*.'

'Yes, but if it *does*, what happens then?'

'They'll take you to Elida,' I said. 'It *won't* go wrong, Joshua, but if it does, then we'll follow you. North.' After nearly five years, that was still all we knew about it. 'As far as it goes, and as long as it takes, we'll follow you, and we'll rescue you.'

Later, I would remind myself that it was me who said that; it was me who promised it first. Joshua had begun to tremble.

'It won't go wrong,' said Kestrel, gently. 'Hero and I will make sure of that. Trust us.'

I nodded. Joshua said nothing.

There was a silence, broken by the clinking of cutlery and plates around us. Kestrel and I looked at each other again. I could see her wondering whether to broach the subject, but I knew she didn't want to smash whatever resolve Joshua had mustered. Then, finally, I said, 'Joshua, you haven't had any. . . any premonitions, about this, have you?'

He shook his head. And I believed him. I can't imagine he would have kept it secret if he'd known what was going to happen.

We got up to put our plates away in silence. Behind us, people were talking, laughing. We took one last look at each other and walked out.

It takes us the better part of two days to walk to the coast. We get there near midnight. There are no towns here, nothing to farm. There's a fishing town about ten miles west of us, but something tells me Elida won't be near there. The Guard would have wanted to build it as far out of sight as possible.

We sit down on the cliff top together. We can't light a fire without giving away our position to anyone within twenty miles, so we sit in darkness. I'm rubbing my shoulders to try and numb the lingering sensation of the bag straps cutting into my skin. Beneath us, the sea whispers against the cliffs, a gurgling sigh. The darkness around us is complete. I can hear the water but can't see it.

I hear shifting from my right. Joshua's lain down on the grass.

'What are you thinking about?' he asks.

'Amareth.'

His voice goes flat. 'What about it?'

'It's just . . .' I'm thinking about how far south it is now. Hundreds of miles, certainly, after a month of walking. And I'm thinking about how warm it was there, the grass, the rolling fields, the whispering river, the glass city.

'Nothing.'

'You think it's out there? Elida?'

'Must be. If she said so.' I mean the resistance girl, Eliza, but I'm too tired to say it.

'You trust them, then? The resistance?"

'No.' I'm sure of that. In the orphanage they told us the resistance were brutal in their revenge for all the murdered gods, that they killed and ate human children, tortured their captives, that they were artists of violence. That was the Guard talking, of course, and I don't believe a word of it, but none-theless I don't trust their sudden helpfulness.

We sit there in silence for a while, the only sound the roar of the waves and our hair fluttering in the salt wind. Then I say, 'We can't be more than a few hours away now.'

'Yeah? So what?'

'What do you mean *so what*?'

'Well, we've still got to get her out, haven't we?' He sounds grim, and very tired.

'Yeah,' I say, 'but think about it – we're not going to be able to stay in there more than a few hours, are we? So what-ever happens' – I say it very quickly, so neither of us can dwell for long on the myriad horrors contained within that *whatever* – 'this ends by tomorrow night. Tomorrow, we could be back here, with her.'

'Yeah.' I can hear his smile. 'Yeah.'

We're quiet for a moment.

'She'll be okay,' says Joshua softly. 'I know she will.'

I don't say anything. I'm thinking of the last time I saw her, the fear in her eyes. I'm imagining her dead in a black cell, sprawled and limp. I can't make myself say *yes*. Love wells up in my throat, too strong to breathe, and a guilt I can't let myself feel yet. She might still be alive.

'What are we going to do afterwards?' he says. I can hear he's sat up, restless. 'We can't just stay here. Where will we go?'

I swallow, try to get my voice back. 'I don't know.'

'We can go somewhere she'd like,' he says. I can see him in my head, I just know he's staring over the cliff top, at the black tower shrouded in darkness. Trying to see her. 'The coast. Not this hellhole, somewhere nice. The south. Where the Guard won't get to us.'

The Guard are everywhere.

'There's a harbour town in the southeast, Nurse Rachel said. Joelle. They eat salt fish and lie on beaches and watch the ships come in—'

'We could get on a ship,' Joshua says. I can hear his excitement, it thrums in his voice. 'Go somewhere else. Somewhere different, another country. The whole world can't really be like here.'

I don't know, can it? 'Karkaran,' I say. 'That's to the south. A hundred miles across the sea. The Guard won't find us there.'

'Yeah,' says Joshua. 'Yeah. There must be loads of places we could be safe. The nurses at Fitzgerald just didn't want us to know about them.' He shifts in the dark. 'And how much of the world have we really seen, anyway?'

'We've seen Amareth.'

'Only from the windows. And then the woods, and the roads up to here, and Seaborne' – he flinches away from the word, I can hear, but he makes himself say it – 'and now this place. There must be loads of things we haven't seen out there, things Kestrel would like. Mountains, rivers . . .'

'Silver oceans,' I say. I can feel part of his excitement glowing in my stomach, despite myself. 'To the south, they're so clear and bright, at dawn they shimmer like metal, Nurse Carter said.'

I feel him turn towards me in the dark. 'You like the south, don't you?' He's smiling, I can hear it.

'Why not? Salt fish and white beaches, and the ocean in sunlight. That was what it said in Kestrel's books, anyway. What's wrong with that?'

'Nothing,' he says. He turns back, stares at the tower through the dark, the traces of his smile are still in his voice. 'Yeah. I could get used to that. That's where we'll go.'

I nod.

'Hero?'

'Yeah?'

'Don't think . . .' It sounds like it hurts him to speak, his throat constricted. 'Don't think I don't know how much you've done. To get us here. I really . . . I mean . . .'

Thank you, I think he's trying to say. 'I know,' I say. 'It's okay.' And then I tell him, just to make sure he knows: 'I love you.'

'I love you too,' he says.

And then there's silence.

We knew they'd come for him, but we didn't know when. It turned out to be the middle of our mathematics lesson, the second of the morning. That was a relief. We'd said our good-byes now; all we wanted was for this to be over.

The Guard never knock. Just past eleven o'clock in the morning, Joshua's Guardsman simply walked in, and stood in the corner with his arms folded, looking around at us. The nurse who was teaching us put her pen down and looked up at him.

'Joshua,' said the Guardsman. There was no upwards inflection in his voice; it was not a request.

Everyone in the room turned to stare at Joshua. Joshua's skin, normally warm brown, had gone greyish. His eyes were hard. He rose to his feet, and I was relieved to see he wasn't shaking.

The Guardsman said, 'Come with me.'

Joshua nodded. He didn't look at anyone else, not even us. He picked up his bag from under his desk, swung it over his shoulder, and walked to the front of the classroom, his eyes on the Guardsman, who opened the door for him and let him walk through. I saw Joshua go still, just for a moment, in the doorway. Nobody else noticed.

The Guardsman closed the door behind him, and the room was silent.

The nurse was still staring at the doorway where they'd vanished. Then she seemed to collect herself. 'Right,' she said to the class, though all of us were still motionless, transfixed by the doorway where Joshua had vanished. 'So, when you differentiate implicitly with respect to x, you get a quadratic in terms of y . . .'

We had agreed on a forty-five second gap, but it felt like much longer than that before Kestrel raised her hand and said, 'Excuse me, Nurse Jacobson . . .?'

'Yes, Kestrel?'

'Could I please use the bathroom?'

The nurse said yes and I saw Kestrel rise, perfectly steady this time, and follow Joshua's path to the door. She didn't look at me, either – that would have been too suspicious, given what I was about to do.

She opened the door and walked out, closing it behind her smoothly, and I was alone in the class.

Everything in my ears was hazy, a low deep buzzing. My blood felt thick and cold in my veins. I was overcome by nerves. I didn't know what I was doing, only that I was terrified, that I didn't want to move. I needed Kestrel and Joshua back, someone to tell me to do what I was meant to, to hold me to account, to provide some recourse other than my own faltering courage.

The breath caught in my throat and the world reasserted itself.

'Hero?'

I was sitting at my desk. One hand grasping the wood, white-knuckled. The other up in the air. The voice calling my name was Nurse Jacobson's.

'Yes, Hero?'

'I . . . I don't feel well.' I imagine I sounded convincing. I felt cold and pale, sick to my stomach, and my voice was trembling.

The nurse eyed me. I was lucky, thinking back on it now; she wasn't one of the cruel ones. I think she might have known in passing how inseparable Kestrel and I had become from Joshua, how much he meant to us. If all three of us had been human, I would have been facing a six-month separation from him until my own eighteenth finding-day, nothing more terrifying than that, but I suppose it could still have explained my distress.

If all three of us had been human. What a thought.

'All right,' she said, quite gently. 'Go on, go to the doctor.'

I got to my feet shakily, my fingers slipping with sweat on my bag as I picked it up. I don't remember walking down through the desks, or through the door. I don't remember whether I looked back at my classmates, whether I was fully aware, at that point, that I would never see them again. I suspect I wasn't.

My memories resume quite suddenly in the corridor, by the biology classrooms, when I was leaning against the cold stone wall, holding my bag in violently shaking hands, breathing too fast.

I pressed my head against the cold wall, held myself there

in silence until the breath stopped rasping like iron in my throat and my blood felt thinner than water. I did what Kestrel had taught me to years ago – pushed away my doubts and unwanted thoughts, closed them down, ruthlessly, brutally, unreasonably.

I was going to die. *No.* I'd stayed here too long, ruined the plan. *No.* The plan was stupid, it wouldn't save Joshua, it would only make things worse for him. *No.*

I fought them off, fought doubt with faith. Failure was not a possibility. I knew where I had to go.

I pulled myself away from the wall, wiped the sweat from my face and looked around. I knew what I was looking for. If I couldn't see it now, step one of the plan would already have failed. We didn't know where the Guard would take Joshua to test him, and it was imperative that we find him.

But I saw it, after maybe ten seconds. Along the side of the wall. Faint, black scorch marks. He'd burned them into there with the tips of his fingers. I reached out, brushed one. I could still feel the residue of his white-hot touch.

Then I hauled my bag over my shoulder and started walking.

The marks led all the way down the corridor to the stair-case and then deeper, down, into the chemistry corridor on the ground floor and then out into the courtyard. There, they stopped. The day was still dazzlingly bright, and I felt a wave of terror-borne heat pass over me as I faltered, staring out at the buildings in front of me. The courtyard was empty.

Where would they have taken him?

They never told us where they did the blood tests; it would have been too easy for frightened god-children to find and sabotage it. They changed the room every test to make it untraceable, to stop exactly this kind of thing from happening. Of *course* they were three steps ahead of us, how could I have imagined we had any chance—

Stop. Calm down. Think.

It was lesson time. They couldn't pick a classroom, or anywhere near one. They wouldn't use a dormitory, either – that was our home, our territory. They'd want to have all the power. Somewhere big, somewhere impressive—

And then I knew. The entrance hall.

It came to me with crushing certainty. I was so lucky. Kestrel always said I was clever. I'd never believed her before then.

But I worked it out, and I walked, dreamlike, across the courtyard towards the lone wooden building, the straps of my bag cutting into my shoulder.

The entrance hall was dark and empty. I saw Kestrel crouched beside one of the anterooms.

'Finally,' she whispered. 'I thought you weren't coming.'

'I got nervous.'

She glanced up at me. 'Are you okay?'

'Yeah. I'm here.'

It was all I could say.

'Good.' She touched my hand and turned back to the doorway. As she did I caught a flash of her face in the dim slatted light, the tension in it. All the years I'd known her, she'd been almost preternaturally calm. She kept us together. I'd never seen her break before, not even close. It sobered me. I felt suddenly much older than seventeen.

She reached out and gripped my hand, gave me a quick, encouraging smile. Didn't lose my eyes. 'Ready?'

I couldn't speak. I nodded.

We both bent to stare through the crack in the wood at the room within. It was dim, and the windows were shuttered. Joshua was sitting at a desk in the back. Two grey-uniformed Guardsmen were sitting opposite him.

Where were the others? I'd thought there would be more of them, I thought they all gathered together for a blood test. Unease slid long tentacles down my throat. I couldn't breathe.

One had her head bent, writing – taking down his details, I think. The other was staring at Joshua, hard-eyed. Joshua was sweating. His foot was tapping against the ground, next to his bag, and he was staring dead ahead of him, as if the patch of wall behind the Guardsmen's heads was his lifeline. I knew what he was waiting for, why he was so anxious. *Us.* He was waiting for us.

My hand was still in Kestrel's. She gripped it tighter. There was a moment of acute silence. I closed my eyes and heard her take a deep breath.

Then she screamed.

It was right next to my ear, bloodcurdling and high. I opened my eyes to see the Guardsmen leap to their feet, turning towards the door.

Joshua had frozen. I knew a moment of absolute terror, thinking that he would be too paralysed by his fear to do what the plan relied on. But he wasn't. He raised his hand while the Guard were staring at the door, and all the light vanished from the room. The blackness was complete, unyielding. I couldn't see my own hands in the dark. All I had was touch, the floor against my right hand and Kestrel's fingers in my left, and then even that was gone, as she vanished from my side.

Here was the plan: Kestrel was to go for the Guardsman on the right, me for the one on the left, provided we had memorised their positions before the lights went out, which I had. They wouldn't be expecting two people to be flying at them from the darkness, so we'd have the advantage of surprise. Then we'd grab their weapons, shoot them if we had to, run out of the room, Joshua would bash down the doors with his godly strength, and we would run to freedom.

If we'd known what he could do, of course, I could have told him to kill them. Kestrel wouldn't have wanted him to become a murderer, not if he didn't have to, but he wouldn't have cared, if that was the only way to save her. I would have taken him aside and said: blind them, first thing you do, and then kill them. They'll be easier to kill once their eyes have melted away. I'll help you. Do it before she gets here. Don't risk her getting hurt.

But we had no idea how easily Joshua could kill. He didn't yet know how powerful he was, he'd never had a chance to try out anything more than conjuring his firefly lights in the darkness of our room, behind the closed door. Once we had escaped, and were safely into the woods, he could burn down trees if he wanted, call lightning, push himself. But in here anything like that was much too risky, and so most of his power lay deep and unexplored within him, a well of deep water.

So this was the plan. Disarm them, then escape.

We weren't naive, of course. We already knew there were a hundred things that could go wrong. And those were only the problems we had foreseen. Another problem had arisen already, one we had not prepared for and which I don't think Kestrel and Joshua had noticed yet, which was this: in the half-second before the lights had gone out, while Kestrel was screaming and the room was starting to dim, the hard-eyed Guardsman had begun to turn, not towards the door, but back towards Joshua, her hand moving to the gun at her waist.

I knew then that it was over, that we'd lost, but Joshua and Kestrel were still in that room and fighting, and that meant I had to be as well. I scrambled to my feet, nearly whacking my head on the doorway in the dark, and stumbled into the room with my hand still on the doorknob.

Then I stopped, my breathing fast and shallow, panic budding in my chest. I couldn't see anything, let alone the Guardsman I was meant to be tackling, and I knew with a terrible sinking dread that they'd already have their guns and I wouldn't stand a chance even if I *could* find them—

I felt a hand grab my wrist in the darkness. Kestrel. I twisted around blindly to face her, and suddenly there was a line of pain across my palm. A knife. I felt the slick warmth of blood well in the cut, her hand crushing mine. Then she was gone.

I stood there stupidly in the dark, bewildered, trying to find her. I closed my eyes to the darkness and pulled heartbeats from the base of my skull, but the world around me was a staccato mess and I couldn't tell one from another—

I realised she was still screaming.

'No, *no*, get off me, *get off me*—'

The lights snapped back on at once. Later I asked Joshua why he allowed them to, and he said it was the anguish in Kestrel's voice that did it; her screams had terrified him. Of course, Kestrel must have known he'd do that. It played perfectly into her hands. I hate her for that, that brilliance. I love her for it.

I just stood there, blinking stupidly in the sudden light. It took me a while to absorb what was happening, to adjust to the stillness.

Joshua was pinned to the wall by the hard-eyed Guardsman, whose arm was over his throat. She could have broken his neck in an instant if she'd decided to. The other Guardsman was standing about four paces away from us, by the desk.

Both of them were staring at Kestrel, who had shoved herself suddenly away from me as though pulling herself from my grip and had now crumpled against the wall, sobbing. Her hands were covered with greyish blood. My blood.

'No!' she shrieked, her face pressed against the wall, her feet kicking uselessly against the ground as though she hoped she could push herself through the wall. 'No, *no*, Hero, tell them I'm not one of them, Hero, please—'

I didn't understand what she was doing for almost three full seconds. Then Joshua shouted, 'Kestrel, no!'

'*Joshua!*' she shrieked, eyes wide, as though she had just

realised he was there. 'Oh, Joshua, please, tell them I'm not, tell them I don't, I'm not one of *them*, I'm not—'

The Guardsman closest to us began to advance upon her. Kestrel screamed again and threw up her grey-blood-covered hands. 'No! No, please, don't—'

'You did that,' said the Guardsman holding Joshua, and it was flat-voiced, the way she said it, more a statement than a question. 'You made it go dark.'

I saw a flash of something like triumph in Kestrel's eyes.

'No!' shouted Joshua. 'No, she didn't, it was—'

But Kestrel had turned her tear-stained face up towards the Guardsmen, and the look of terror and despair in her face was so pitiful I remain convinced it was genuine.

'Yes,' she whispered. 'I did it. Please don't hurt me, please . . .'

That seemed to settle it for them. A confession like this was too tempting to ignore. The Guardsman holding Joshua released him and advanced upon Kestrel, drawing her gun as she went.

I was still paralysed, speechless, aghast; Kestrel's eyes met mine for a single moment, orbs of cat's-eye amber, wild, the terror in them suddenly real, before they closed in on her.

'*RUN!*' she shouted.

She should have said, *kill them*. I want to go back there to her, trapped against the wall and screaming. I want to go back to the boy Joshua who died in that moment, the one who wasn't yet a killer. I want to say, with the preternatural calm I discovered at Seaborne: let us go and he won't kill you. I want to look those Guardsmen in their eyes and break their necks with my bare hands.

I wake in the night in this moment, trapped, fingers dug into the grass, Kestrel's terrified eyes burning into mine in the darkness. Joshua burns ants alive, power effortless in his skin now, and I know every one is that Guardsman, in his head.

He would kill a hundred people, a thousand, if it would allow him to go back and kill those two.

I don't think Joshua would have run, if it hadn't been for me. I knew there would be no saving Kestrel from the Guard now, not while they were closer to her than we were and still had their guns. If they thought she was a half-breed, they would kill her sooner than let her escape. Our choice, as Kestrel must have known it would be, was now between letting her be captured and getting her killed. But there was still hope for us. I am amazed, still, at the utter dispassion I displayed in thinking this.

Joshua was still staring, horrified, at Kestrel. I grabbed his arm.

'We have to run.'

He didn't move. My voice broke.

'Joshua, if you want her to live, *run*.'

He seemed to react to that, at least. He turned and hit the stone wall with all his strength, and the bricks cracked under his hand, his shuddering power. The Guard started to turn at the noise. Kestrel screamed '*Go!*', and Joshua struck again, wild and desperate, and the wall of the room collapsed with a rumble and a cloud of dust, and sunlight broke on our faces through the sudden air.

But still he turned back to look at her in anguish, even as the Guard twisted to stare at us.

I turned with him, though I couldn't bear to look at Kestrel now. The Guard had her pinned to the wall and they'd cuffed her hands, still stained with my blood. One had her gun pressed to Kestrel's head and I saw she had the safety switched off.

My terror had been numbed. Some part of me knew this had been Kestrel's plan all along, and that it would do no good to rail against it – though later, in the woods, I would cry myself to sleep, cursing her for making us abandon her.

She must have planned this for weeks, months. She must have lied to us a hundred times.

I met her eyes. She was shaking violently in the Guardsmen's grip, terrified, but her gaze was hard. She was determined.

Joshua opened his mouth, but nothing came out. The other Guardsman swung his pistol up to point into his face. For the first time, I felt a thrill of panic: no one, god or half-breed or human, can survive a shot to the head or the heart, and if Joshua died now, everything Kestrel had done would be for nothing.

But Kestrel saw it too, and screamed 'GO, JOSHUA!', and finally, with such swiftness it alarmed me, he picked me up as though I was an infant. There was a rush of wind, cold on my face, and then he was running, out into the empty, sunlit grounds and towards the dark, labyrinthine woods where they would not find us, his speed a wind on my tear-stained cheeks in the warm summer air.

CHAPTER 5

Murderer

I wake before he does, and sit there in the cold mist of dawn. The sea is soft and black and whispering in the salty air. Joshua is curled in front of me, asleep. I don't know why they say people seem peaceful in their sleep. None of us were ever like that. Even Kestrel had nightmares.

Joshua is never still. He twitches, his fists clench. He must bite his nails or they'd be long enough now to draw blood from his palms. I look at him and try to be dispassionate.

If it had been me who'd been taken, and Kestrel had escaped with him, would he be here right now?

No. He wouldn't, of course not. He wouldn't have let Kestrel put her life in danger for me, the way I risked myself for her. He loves her as he never loved me. I'm his sister, in all but blood; but she was his partner and soulmate. She was everything to him.

But that was a long time ago, before the power flooded into his skin, his eyes and hands. Before he tried to kill the shopkeeper. Before I felt his eyes burning into the back of my head, full of suspicion and resentment. He isn't the boy Kestrel fell in love with anymore. Would she have stayed with him, the way I have?

That's easily answered. She would never have had any reason to leave. He wouldn't have scared her, the way he scares me. He would never have hurt her, not ever.

Oh, sweetheart, we're so close to you now. A few more

hours and this will all be over. I can see the black tower in the fog, in the dark water, a shard of obsidian, a knife against the cold sky. You must be somewhere in there. Can you see me, from inside?

No. The Guard wouldn't have put windows in their prison, they wouldn't allow you sunlight. They would have wanted to crush all hope. Oh, please tell me it didn't work on you. Look, we're here. We came all this way. I believe that you're alive, I believe it fiercely, a bright flame in my heart. Please be alive. I don't know what he'll do if you're dead.

I don't know what he'll do to me, if you're dead.

He twitches in his sleep, as if he can hear my thoughts, and I flinch. I get to my feet and look down at him. He's gone suddenly taut, all the muscles in his face stretched tight. He convulses once, violently, and starts shuddering. His face is greyish-brown and greased in sweat. He moans through his teeth.

I feel helpless, panic rises in my chest, and in my head a twelve-year-old boy is twisting in his sleep in a dormitory far away, his face wreathed in moonlight, through the fog of six years and imperfect memory.

Then suddenly the tightness of his jaw cracks and he says, aloud, anguished, '*Hero* . . .'

I just look at him. I don't know what to do.

He gives a shuddering gasp and his eyes fly open. This time he doesn't struggle, just stares up at me. There's no recognition in his eyes, not for long seconds, and the song of the ocean is cold on my skin.

'Joshua.' My voice sounds strange in my ears. 'Joshua, what did you see?'

He was dreaming and the dream turned into this. A field, the grass freshly cut, as if for grazing. Bubbling with mud. A dark woodland edging it. The sky grey with cloud, soaked in darkness. Was it night-time? He thinks so, but he isn't sure.

He was watching from slightly above, so he knows he wasn't seeing through his own eyes; he had, he says, no sense of a body, a consciousness. He wasn't there. But I was.

I stood in the field, bloodied, panting. My hair shorn, shorter than it is now, dark with rain. I looked no older. Were there people around me? What was I wearing? He doesn't know, or remember.

But he remembers what happened to me.

I was holding something, a gun he thinks, in my right hand. I checked it, then threw it away in disgust. Then something moved at my feet. A Guardsman was lying in the mud. Is he sure it was a Guardsman? Yes; it was the same uniform, mud stained, he knows it perfectly from their night patrols at Fitzgerald House, and the same kind of gun.

The Guardsman rolled over and pointed the gun straight up into my face. There was a moment of silence, of stillness. The Guardsman and I were both staring at each other. I had frozen, he says.

Then the Guardsman fired. There was an explosion of grey blood and I was blasted backwards. I fell to the ground and didn't move again.

The Guardsman let his arm drop and lay in the mud, panting, staring up at the sky.

His words were *you looked no older* – I'm quite sure of that. In the cabin of the ferry I sit and stare at the wall, thinking. I paid the captain extra to take us within a mile of the black tower, but that's not going to be enough, I know that; it's a sightseeing ferry, it won't want to go three miles out of its route into the dark sea to pass by a prison full of trapped children. Most likely the captain will renege on his promise and we'll be back at the coast in an hour. I paid in stolen money and kept my head down, but that's not going to be enough either. Sooner or later some part of the plan will crack open and give way, and I will stand in a field in the mud and die at the hands of a Guardsman.

I looked no older. He said he saw the scar on my right hand, the one I got at Seaborne, shiny and purplish and gleaming. I look down at it, running my fingers over the baby-soft skin. I'm better at healing other people's wounds than my own. The wound was too deep for me to vanish the scar entirely. In a year or so, it will fade to white, and then to nothing.

I have less than a year, then.

It's nearly dusk; it took us a long time to find the village. The ferry is on a scenic tour of the coast, but it is so cold and grey today that there are very few passengers. An elderly man and woman are in the back of the boat, watching the coast with a bright wonder, the skin of their old faces nearly translucent in the dim light.

If I look over the side, fifty yards away from the boat, faint and almost hidden by spray, I can just make out Joshua's sleek back rising and falling through the water. He keeps up with the boat effortlessly, with his god's strength. I can't swim like that, and even if I could, we have a bag full of supplies – food, clothes, Ignatius's gun – that needs to reach the island dry. The boat is our only option, although deeply risky. Even up here, there might be posters with my face on them.

Joshua thinks I might survive being shot in the face. I call that optimistic. I forswore wishful thinking on the day Kestrel was taken. All I have to do is not think about it, I suppose. It will happen, of course; there's no point trying to run from it. The pieces will all come together in their own time and, in my experience, trying to evade them will only make them assemble faster, from spite. Fate dislikes cowards.

I lean back and close my eyes. My heart beats very slowly. I am so tired.

Minutes pass. At last, from the front of the ship, I hear the captain say wearily, 'Now we're at our easternmost point. You can see the cliffs over there if you like, we're going to start circling back now . . .'

And that's my cue. But I don't move.

Why aren't I feeling anything? Why am I so calm? I'm going to *die*, and violently, I know that for certain now. I should be angry. I should be afraid. But I'm not. I feel nothing just weary resignation. I'm so tired.

Is this shock? No, I know shock. Shock was those first days in the woods, waking in tears, feeling Kestrel's absence like a cavity scraped in my chest, the hard weight of guilt across my shoulders. This isn't shock. This is . . .

. . . acceptance?

Yes, I think it is. Reluctant acceptance. I accept that I'm going to die.

Doom is nothing new to me. Haven't I kept us from being captured by the Guard all these weeks, even when the whole country is looking for us? Aren't we alive, haven't we almost made it to Elida, when that should have been impossible?

I have fought certainty before and won. I will do it again.

'And here,' says the captain, 'these are the Black Cliffs of Aliphia, you can see the crevices where the seagulls—'

I get to my feet so suddenly the bag nearly falls off my lap on to the floor. I grab it hastily. If we've turned around already we're in trouble, but I can feel the boat under my feet and we haven't, not yet. I look out of the greasy window again and catch a flash of Joshua's back in the water. I try to look reassuring, in case somehow he can see me.

I start walking purposefully towards the bridge. I dodge sliding chairs, old, tired-looking couples staring listlessly out of the window. This whole boat smells of age and boredom.

Back in Amareth they had trains, lamplight, cars, electricity, spices, great trade ships that slid along the horizon from the port, carrying salt and money to far-off lands. Here, up north, the closest things they have to modernity are guns. Everyone travels by horse or boat, except the Guard with their patrol cars. Everyone looks tired.

I think I make it to the door to the bridge without anyone seeing my face. Then, as quietly as I can, I knock.

A voice from within. 'What?'

I try to make my voice nervous and shaky. 'Uh, I was looking for the toilets? I feel sick.'

There is no toilet on this boat. I try to emphasise my southern, Amareth accent as much as possible so it seems plausible I might not know this. I doubt there are any flushing toilets for a hundred miles.

'Look, lady, you're not allowed in here, it's not—'

I knock again. I see faces turn towards me out of the corner of my eye and pull the hood of my cloak up tighter. I speak as though I haven't heard him.

'Excuse me? I was wondering where—'

A man on the other side of the boat gets suddenly to his feet, staring at me. He taps the shoulder of the woman beside him. I pull my hood up even higher. He's muttering to her, but his narrowed eyes are fixed on me. My heart jolts and speeds up. She looks up just as the captain's door opens.

He's standing inside, one hand on the wheel, looking exasperated. 'Listen, there isn't a—'

I slam my weight into the door and push past him. He whirls, stumbling and staring at me, and I pull Ignatius's gun from my bag and point it at his head. There are three bullets left in it, I checked after I shot at Cairn in the clearing. Three bullets. And how many people on this boat? No, don't think about that. *Concentrate.*

'Close the door.'

'What the—'

'Close it. Now.'

There's just a moment's hesitation as he looks me up and down and decides that yes, I am capable of killing him, and he closes the door. No sooner has it clicked shut than someone hits it behind him, as hard as they can, ramming it with all their weight. A roar.

'*That's her, that's the girl the Guard are looking for! That's the Fitzgerald girl!*'

The captain's eyes widen and I see him swallow, but he doesn't let the door open. The boat is dead, bobbing gently in the water. Can they see it from Elida? What must Joshua be thinking? Oh, crap, if he panics he'll have to kill everyone on this boat if they see him, and if they have *guns*—

I tighten my grip on Ignatius's pistol. I want to close my eyes and take a deep breath, but I can't show weakness.

'I'm not doing anything you say, girl,' says the captain roughly, before I can speak. 'If you think I'm going to—'

And against his anger I find my voice again. 'Turn the boat around. We're going to Elida.'

He makes a sudden movement towards his belt, but I'm ready. I do what has to be done.

I raise the gun and shoot him in the hand.

The recoil is a snapping blow, a crackling bolt of pain. There's an explosion of blood, the shot echoes in my ears. He howls in agony.

'I'll heal you if you stay still,' I say, over his screams and the hammering on the other side of the door. I feel sick, but I have to sound cold.

'*Murderer!*' he howls. '*Bitch – murderer –*' He's panting, clutching his ruined hand. He looks at me with white-cold hate. I do not flinch. I raise the gun again to point into his face.

'Keep screaming and I will be.'

His breathing slows at last, ragged with agony; his screams quieten to whimpers. His hand is dripping blood on to the floor. I doubt he'll ever be able to use it again if he doesn't let me heal it. Still, it's better than being dead. I tell myself that over and over again inside my head. I have to stay calm.

'I'm not a murderer,' I say, when I have control over myself again. 'I don't want to kill anyone. But if you attack me again—'

'You killed,' he says, struggling for breath, 'don't lie to me, you killed . . .' But he can't get the words out, and then he looks up at me with blood soaking into his shirt and the hate in his eyes is blinding, corrosive. 'You killed, at that village . . . all those people . . . don't try to . . . to lie, you bitch . . . I *know* . . .'

Anger rises in me, despite myself, and part of me is thinking of Joshua. If this boat doesn't start to move towards Elida soon he's going to panic. He might have heard the gunshot and think it's me who's been hurt, and what will he do then, will he come to save me? But another part says, out loud, 'What the hell are you talking about?'

I think I already know.

'You . . . slaughtered . . . that whole village,' says the captain hoarsely, gritting his teeth. I think he's trying to stop himself from crying out again. 'In the south. *Seaborne.* You bitch. I'll kill you, I'll—'

I move the gun downwards to point at his heart. My mind is completely blank. Power surges into my hands, white-hot fury. As he looks down, fear seeping into his face, I snap the barrel up and slam it into his chin so hard I hear bone crack.

I hope it hurts. I hope it's agony.

He collapses in silence. I stare down at his body, crumpled on the floor. I am breathing very quickly. That was a mistake. I can't turn the boat around now without him, I don't know how. Someone is still hammering on the door, but my blood is singing with fury, drowning his voice.

Did the Guard just spread the story, or did they kill everyone in Seaborne themselves, to give it weight? Would they do that, just to make us look evil?

What am I talking about, this is the Guard. Of course they killed them. They killed everyone.

Ignatius. Julia.

A slow weight settles in my stomach, like cold milk. They're dead. Everything I did not to kill them, and they're dead.

I think of the smoke that drifted across the village square when Ignatius lit his chimney. Did the Guard burn those bodies in a pile, too, like the villagers did when they slaughtered their gods?

Were there children?

I did not kill them. I have to remember that.

But the knowledge that the Guard are telling everyone I did burns in my stomach, sour, it brings tears to my throat. It matters to me, it shouldn't but it does. I am helpless. They have all the tools to shape the truth and I have none.

Except this.

The certainty hardens inside me as I kneel there, the boat bobbing gently beneath me, the shouting from outside the door pressing into my ears and the captain's rough breathing beside me. His blood is spreading over my hands, pooling on the floor.

I will not give them this. I won't give any truth to the Guard's claim that I have killed innocent people. I won't hand them that victory.

I kneel beside the captain's body, and wait, and gather myself together, around the pain in my head. I breathe in and out.

One. Two. Three.

Kestrel would say to me: sweetheart, what are you doing?

This is stupid – they'd kill *you* in a moment, what kind of mercy do you think they deserve?

Four. Five—

The door finally splinters. I turn, hand on my gun, but too late. There's a blast that wipes out the hearing in my left ear but doesn't hit me, and I look up as the man who has been shouting my name with such fervour aims at me again with the pistol, his face white and twisted with fury. He is shooting at my head, I realise, shooting to kill.

I point Ignatius's gun at his stomach through the splintered wood of the door and fire as he fumbles with the catch. There's a blast I don't quite register. Then a ringing beat of silence.

The man is still standing but something has vanished from his eyes. He sways and then collapses, gracelessly, folding flesh and bone, a seam of spreading blood across his leather jacket.

I get to my feet and find I am shaking. I open the door and the wood pushes against the man's ankle.

There are four people on the boat apart from me. One, the woman, is screaming. The elderly couple are frozen where they sit, terrified. I kneel down beside the man who tried to kill me and put my hand against his stomach. He draws in a rough, agonised breath as I do so, trying to flinch away from me. Out of some flash of spite I look deep into his eyes. I see his pupils dilate at the sight of me. He thinks I'm going to kill him.

I sink my fingers into his open stomach, blood bubbling under my fingers, and feel the flesh begin to knit. The man makes another rasping noise of agony. It takes him a very long time to realise that he is not dying.

After long minutes, I stand up, holding the bluish bullet in one hand and Ignatius's gun in the other. My hands are covered in blood. I look around at them. The elderly man raises his trembling hands to cover his eyes. His wife looks terrified.

The other woman is still screaming.

'When you tell the Guard about this,' I say, not sure they can hear or understand, 'make sure you tell them I saved his life.'

The old man's wife gets to her feet. Her husband tries to pull her down, terrified, but she stares at me with hatred and defiance in her face. She pulls out a knife, edged with copper, and spits. 'Die,' she says. 'Die with the rest of your kind. You killed my daughter. She was *three*.'

'I didn't kill anyone,' I say, but she's already thrown the knife at me. I duck. There's no fear left to feel. The blade catches me across the back of the hand and clatters on to the deck. I look down at it, the welling grey blood. Silence.

Then we look up at each other. I see a vicious hope in her face and I remember: the old myth, passed down through ten generations and whispered in the orphanage, that a copper blade will kill a half-breed. I wonder how long she's been carrying that knife around, waiting to be able to use it.

I crouch there, wondering for a moment if she's right, if I am going to die now, but there's nothing, the cut on my hand seals and is gone.

There's a high, murmuring silence, the only sound the soft splashing of water against the side of the boat.

It takes all the strength I have to get to my feet. My brain is numb. I heave my bag over my shoulder, closing the gun inside it, and turn around.

I jump off the side of the boat, because I have no choice. The salty white air slakes my face and I feel a rush of dark speed in my stomach before the water swallows me.

The darkness underwater is entirely complete. I breathe in the cushioned airlessness, feeling my ribs tighten, my lungs close, my god-blood hardening my body against the lack of oxygen. It will not work for long.

I hang there like a corpse, feeling my hair float around my

head, my waterlogged clothes pulling me downwards, the cold caress of the sea on my face. I could stay here forever and rest.

Then I feel a hand close around me and the water pulls apart. Joshua's grip on my wrist. His speed drags us forwards and we are away.

There's a boy called Idris who lives on Corridor Six, in a bedroom on his own. He's a month older than me, so he'll be up for his blood test in another six weeks or so. I know he'll fail. He's a god as surely as Joshua is, but he's quiet about it.

How do I know? He's beautiful. Tall and strong. But more important is the awkwardness in him, the way he stoops when he walks, like he's trying to hide himself. He's survived this far without the Guard getting enough proof to disappear him, so who knows, maybe he'll find a way to make it, like we almost did.

He's clever, so clever. I used to watch him in class, the ease of his mind, the carelessness of it. I used to guess at the darkness in his head. I am an absolute sucker for the dark ones. Kestrel used to laugh at me for it.

I never made a move, though. I didn't have the courage. I had a brother and a sister, I told myself, I was fortunate already in the love I had managed to build in this hellish, detached place; there was no point pushing my luck.

But I watched him. And in my head I played out futures delicate as butterflies. Most solid of them, in my head, was the one that took place on the night before my blood test. I'd go to his room in the middle of the night and talk to him. Reveal my . . . not *love*, this wasn't love, but tell him he was . . . whatever he was to me.

And he'd accept me, tell me he felt the same way . . .

In the end, it didn't work out quite like that. I woke up

quite suddenly in the middle of my last night in the orphanage, the night before Joshua's eighteenth birthday, while he and Kestrel were both asleep. I had never been brave before that. I don't know what happened to me.

I got to my feet as quietly as I could and stood there in the bleak silence, the darkness. I expected Kestrel, at least, to wake up, but her breathing didn't change. I went to the door and pressed my head against it. No movements outside, no Guard.

So I opened the door slowly and crossed the corridor to stand outside Idris's room.

It's hard to explain why I did it. I can't remember making the decision. In my head were cold facts: I would die for Joshua; the Guard might try to kill Joshua tomorrow; therefore there was a good chance I had under a day to live, and I wasn't going to let that happen without at least trying this.

I did not knock. It would have risked the Guard coming. I just opened the door – the ones to our dormitories didn't lock – and stepped inside Idris's room.

The candle beside his bed was lit. He was reading, some old crumbling book from the library downstairs. He looked up in alarm as I came in.

'Hero—'

But I put a finger to my lips.

I know he thought, for a good few seconds, that I had come to sell him out, to attack him, even. I closed the door. He just stared at me.

I remember how the light glowed across his beautiful, angular face. I had no idea what his demesne was, and I didn't care. I opened my mouth to speak and was surprised when the words that came out were, 'I'm a half-breed.'

Idris just kept staring at me.

My hands were shaking. I sat on his bed and stared back at him. I'd never been this close to him before, never been alone with him. An inkling of the truth was dawning in his eyes.

I reached one shaking hand up to the buttons on my shirt, thinking, *am I really doing this?* But I wanted him to realise. If he was going to reject me, I wanted to know now. His eyes widened.

My voice was low, hoarse. 'Idris, just tell me if—'

There was a pause. When he moved his hands were steady, unhesitating. He reached out to the candle and pinched it out. We sat in darkness. I was trembling.

There was a rustling and I felt his hand on mine, the shocking velvet coldness of it, his flesh, the nervous terror of his touch. Then his lips on my hand, on my face. The salt silk of them, the warmth under his clothes. He was so gentle.

I'm glad I did it just so I have something for the water to remind me of. I can imagine the caress of the sea as his hands, and its grip can be his. I can survive the hatred of the people on that boat, the disgust in their faces, so long as I can descend into the memories of him, his eyes on my skin, his touch. Someone wanted me, someone wanted me to exist.

CHAPTER 6

The Black Tower

Joshua drags me out on to the beach. I cough up salt water.
He just stares.

'What the hell went wrong?'

'He wouldn't do it. The captain.' I have neither the time
nor the will to explain why. I can see the shadowy obsidian
tower behind Joshua. We need to move now. 'Does the gun
still work?'

He reaches for the bag, peering down into it, then grimaces.
'Everything in here is soaking wet.'

I swear viciously. Wipe my wet hair out of my eyes. 'Then
you're our only weapon. Leave the bag.'

'Where?'

'Behind a bush, if you can find one. But it doesn't matter.
They'll know we're here soon enough.'

Joshua stares at me. 'Hero, what's going on?'

'We don't have time,' I say, and then I fall to my knees. I
am coughing up seawater again, retching it. Joshua rushes
forwards and holds me until I am still.

'Hero,' he says quietly, 'what happened on that boat?'

I'm shaking too badly to reply. Then I say, in a narrow,
constricted voice, 'I shot someone in the stomach.'

I feel Joshua go very still. 'Did you heal them?'

'Yeah.'

'Why did you—'

'The Guard murdered everyone in Seaborne,' I say, and hear
the break in my own voice. I didn't know I knew it for certain

until I said it aloud. 'And now they'll kill everyone on that boat. Just to say we've done it.' My voice trembles and dies, and then I realise I'm going to cry.

'It's not our fault,' whispers Joshua, but there's a crack in his voice. 'I . . . it's not our fault, Hero, it's . . .' But words fail him too.

I can't control myself and fear wells up in me like blood in a wound, and I'm heaving with sobs, the world at the corner of my eyes is going dark. I need to calm down, I need to calm down *now*.

Joshua hugs me. He doesn't say anything else. He doesn't need to, just doing that is enough to quiet the voices in my brain, the ones that say that Kestrel is dead and he doesn't love me anymore. I am alive, and I'm with him, and I'm okay. I can feel blood and water trickling down my arms. I breathe in and out, regaining control, steadying my voice. I close my eyes.

Don't think about it now. Any of it. Think about Kestrel, not Seaborne.

'We've got to move,' I say at last, and am relieved to hear I sound calm. 'Don't bother with stealth. We've got to get in and out as quickly as possible, okay?'

He doesn't let me go.

'Joshua.'

He pulls back and looks at me. 'Are you okay?'

I swallow and nod. We both get to our feet and look around. There are no doors in the black tower, only smooth stone. Joshua looks at it.

'You reckon I can bash this in?'

'Pull it off,' I say. 'There are seams, look . . .'

He nods; he's found them. For a second I wonder how he could ever get a finger hold in there, but he pushes and there's a scream of stone as the obsidian gives way, soft as clay in Joshua's hands. Sometimes I forget how strong he is.

He throws a great slab of it to the ground with a crash. Inside there's only darkness. He looks back at me. And I think dully: that was too easy. If a god can tear apart that stone with their bare hands, how do the Guard keep anyone trapped in here? What do they do to them? What will they do to us, when they find us?

I shut down the thought. 'Use your light,' I say.

He nods and a spark of sunlight coalesces in his palm into a bulb the size of a pebble. He flicks his wrist and the light soars ahead, illuminating a stone corridor, stairs leading upwards into flickering darkness. He peers ahead.

'Can you hear anything?'

He doesn't mean with my ears. I close my eyes and tilt my head upwards, and with all the strength I have, detach myself from my sight and sound and touch, let everything fade to blackness except for the pulse at the base of my skull. The silence of my head. And then suddenly, heartbeats.

Hundreds of them. Like the orphanage, a rushing clamour that makes it impossible to tell one from another, a constellation. I can feel Joshua beside me, strong and steady, his heart out of time with my own, and everything beyond that is a tumble into discord. A deafening offbeat orchestra. I can't breathe with it—

I open my eyes, gasping. The world comes back in a rush, and I stumble. Joshua grabs my arm so hard it hurts.

'Did you hear her?'

'No,' I say, trying to catch my breath. 'No. I can't . . . too many of them, I can't—'

He lets me go and turns away, disappointed. I put a hand against the wall to steady myself. The silence around me is a dizzying chasm, suddenly dead of the heartbeats I know it contains. I look up at the blackness above me. How many people are in here?

Please let her be one of them.

I never imagined I'd pray for that.

There is no way forward except up the spiral stairs. Joshua is trying to be as quiet as he can and I'm on edge, I can't breathe, I'm waiting for the first Guardsman to appear, from a shadow. We'll have to kill him as quietly as possible, before he can scream.

And then how will we know where Kestrel is?

Panic rises like blood in a wound, a bubbling terror. I dig my nails into my palm. I have to suppress it. If I panic, so will he, and then we'll both be dead.

We start climbing. I wince at every footstep, the echo of it in the darkness. At the top of the first flight of spiral stairs, Joshua puts a hand out to stop me.

'What the hell is that?' he whispers.

I stop so quickly I nearly fall backwards down the stairs, my mind suddenly high-pitched with terror. The silence around us is thick but for the sea.

'What?'

Then I hear it, melodic and lilting. A child's singing voice, lilting and gentle, from our left.

Joshua turns, ignoring my urgent whisper to be careful, and sends the ball of light in his hand drifting along the corridor, golden and steady, like a firefly. I'm motionless, frightened beyond wit or reason, trying not to breathe.

Glossy black doors shine in the walls, but I can't see any Guardsmen yet. That's wrong, there's definitely something wrong with that, but what's more wrong is the child, singing. *Singing.*

Joshua moves along the corridor, looking around. The light falls away from him like a pebble into a well, into the darkness of the corridor, the endless black doors.

'Where is it?' he whispers. 'The kid?'

'Joshua—'

But he's stopped dead. His face is suddenly sick and grey,

the colour of melting snow. He's staring at the door in front of him. I step forward towards him, and when I do something changes, something deep in my head, and I realise the child is not singing at all.

'Joshua—'

He lunges for the door, slamming his weight against it, his lips pressed together with the effort of not calling back, as the child cries out in agony, and it's the very *sound* of hopelessness, of the knowledge that no one is coming to help, a scream made just because the pain is too great to do anything else.

The door is made of something stronger than the walls, and does not even rattle in its frame when Joshua hits it. The noise echoes down the corridor.

'Joshua.' I'm not sure he hears me. The child keeps screaming, and I don't want to hear it, I want to cover my ears, and I hate myself for the impulse. 'Joshua. You can't, you can't do anything for her . . . we're here for Kestrel . . . for *Kestrel*—'

My voice breaks and he stops at last, panting, sobs in his throat. He kicks the door desperately, three beats staccato, and then collapses against it.

'How many?' he whispers at last, under the terrible sobbing screams, and I close my eyes and open my mind again to the thrum of heartbeats in the rooms around us. It's deafening, overwhelming, and I feel my heart break, cracking under the pressure of so much pain.

'All of them,' I say, at last. 'All the doors.'

He turns to me, and as he does, something behind the door *thumps*.

He leaps away from it, but it keeps thumping. Three beats. *Boom boom boom.* A mirror of his own desperate kicking, call and response. Sardonic. Mocking.

Something is in there with the child.

Neither of us moves.

'Run,' I whisper at last, staring at the door, and Joshua nods, his face taut. As we hurry away down the corridor, the child's screams jag, crumble, descend into sobs. They follow us up the stairs and into the echoing dark.

We can't speak after that, not for a while. We climb the stairs in silence. The doors aren't airtight, is all I can think, if we can hear the child. Maybe it was Clarissa. Maybe it was someone I knew. One of the children from the orphanage, on Corridor One with the infants. Oh, no, no—

Kestrel. I close my mind to everything but her, her face. Kestrel is what matters, nothing else. Not the sickness in my stomach, not the child's screams, nothing.

'How will we know where she is?' says Joshua at last, as we climb the stairs. His face is still drawn and pale, the light still glittering on his hand. 'What if . . .'

If she was there, I know he's going to say, but I can't allow myself to think like that, and anyway she's not a child, Kestrel couldn't scream like that, she couldn't . . .

'She'll be at the top,' I say.

'Why?'

'Do you remember what Cairn said?'

He looks at me blankly. 'If she's still alive,' he says at last, he's never said *if* before, 'it'll be bait to catch us. That's what she said.'

'The top is where they'll expect us to go.'

He doesn't argue with me, just gets up and climbs the stairs, the silent corridors, the light clutched in his hand.

We keep climbing. At the third corridor, we stop. I peer over Joshua's shoulder. The floor is covered in blood and broken glass. All I can think, in my numbness, is: no screaming. Good. The heartbeats of the prisoners beat slowly inside my head, as if I had a hundred pulses. The blood is all silver. It spatters the doors, the walls. The broken glass looks crystalline.

Something else is scattered on the floor, small and black in Joshua's light. He bends and picks one up.

'Cork,' he says.

'A vial,' I say quietly, looking down at all the broken glass. 'Crystal vials.' I want to be sick. 'There were vials of blood here. They smashed.'

Joshua turns back to me, and his face is full of misery, of horror, of questions that should not be asked, and I am about to tell him something, I don't know what—

And that's when we hear footsteps at last.

Before I can say anything, the light in Joshua's hand goes out. I move beside him, clutch his hand, and we press ourselves against the smooth black walls. The heartbeats are clamouring inside my head, panicked and irregular. We stand in complete darkness. I am tense, listening as hard as I can, waiting.

Footsteps. One person, coming slowly towards us. Ambling, a lazy rhythm. Someone's patrolling the corridors on the third floor. They don't know we're here, I'm certain of it, or they'd be walking faster. I can feel the muscles in Joshua's shoulder hardening against my hand. He wants to run, to attack, but I hold him back. It hasn't come to that yet.

Maybe the Guardsman will walk away. Everything would be perfect then. I won't breathe, I am invisible.

Walk away, walk away . . . come on . . .

For a moment it seems like he won't. I'm holding my breath crushed in my stomach, and so is Joshua. The footsteps are maybe six feet away from us. A terrible silence. I want to scream with frustration. *Walk away*—

And then there's another *tap*, boot on the obsidian floor, this time on the other side of us. The footsteps begin fading away into the opposite direction, into silence and dark.

I feel Joshua give a deep shuddering breath beside me. The darkness is thick and slimy in my throat. For a moment I don't dare to speak.

'Can you see?'

'Yes,' he whispers.

'I'll hold your hand.'

I feel his grip tighten on mine and we move tentatively up a single step, my feet following clumsily in the wake of his.

Suddenly, something moves behind me. More footsteps, closer. I hear Joshua's gasp, try to turn, and then—

The blade slides slickly into my back.

I stop dead, swaying. My breath is suddenly solid. All feeling vanishes but for the hard black ice of the metal between my ribs, my lungs. It's like having something stuck in my throat. I can't breathe. I put a hand to my chest and feel something sharp and wet. It's slid right through me and broken the skin of my chest.

I feel the ground slam into my knees before I realise I've fallen, and hear Joshua's terrible cry. There are bright spots swimming in front of my eyes. The world rushes away and then back, the sea against a cliff. My breath is coming in short cold gasps that congeal in my throat before they reach my lungs.

Then the pain hits.

I can't draw breath. Every nerve in my chest is screaming, consumed with a terrible black fire. I'm being peeled off my bones like meat, this blade is laced with poison, I can't—

I force my hand down with effort on the lever in my head and the pain vanishes.

I'm kneeling with a long knife through my chest. I can't move, can't breathe. I know I don't have the strength to stand. This will kill me, I know, even if I can't feel the agony of it anymore, but I can't remember why. It can't have touched my heart or I'd be dead already, but people don't survive being stabbed through the chest.

How will it kill me?

My lungs. It's punctured my lung, yes, that must be it. I

can't heal that while the sword is still in there. Joshua needs to pull it out before my lungs fill with blood, why isn't he doing it?

That's when I realise the corridor is filled with light again.

The Guardsman who stabbed me is standing over me, watching me gasp for a breath that isn't coming, blood dribbling from the corner of my mouth. Joshua is facing him. The light he's conjured is drifting in his hand. The black corridor gleams.

The Guardsman seems to be taking a long time to look up from me to him and I know I'm seeing things strangely, as if through water, slow. Maybe I'm passing out. But I can't do that. I know that if I go to sleep now I'll never wake again; I have to be awake to heal. My god's blood is trying to harden me against the lack of air, but something, shock, is preventing it.

There's a cold, dispassionate look on Joshua's face, power made flesh. He flicks his wrist and the light hovering above his hand shoots from his palm straight into the Guardsman's eyes.

There's a high scream that isn't mine. The Guardsman stumbles back, clutching at his face. The light has shattered into a thousand white-hot strands, spreading over his skin like a spider's web, his flesh blistering, crisping, drooping, liquid and bright. He tries to wrench it off but the skin of his hands tears under the heat. He flails, screaming, slams into the wall. The words in his cries become torn and gargled. He slides down the wall, leaving a smear of dark, burned blood, and lies quite still. The light in his face glows red and then fades.

Joshua is staring down at him, a hard look on his face. I try to say his name but all that comes out is a gargle of blood. This is a nightmare; I am asleep. Joshua stares down at me.

'Hero. What can I . . . what should I do?'

'Take,' I whisper, but it's lost in the hard buzzing in my head. I can feel the hot, washed heaviness in my lungs, the taste of blood in my throat. I try to lift a hand to my chest, my back, but I don't have the strength. I think, *Take it out*, with all my effort, but no sound comes out. I feel a sleepy trickle of panic. If he doesn't do it . . .

Would it be so awful to go to sleep, though?

'I'm sorry,' he whispers, his anguished voice in my ear, and I feel a terrible sliding rush in my chest, the scream of ice, and realise he's drawing the sword out of me.

I collapse on to the floor, trembling, blood seeping from my chest. I lie there with my face to the cold hard stone, and with an exhausted shudder I summon all the strength I have and will myself to heal.

But it's too late, I'm too far gone, and death has taken me, or delirium . . .

Count. *Stay with me, Hero*. His hand under my head, am I dreaming it? Count your way back to me. *One. Two. Three.*

I'm fifteen and sick, sicker than I've ever been, lying in a sweat-drenched bed in darkness. I'm maybe the hundredth kid to fall – we've started calling it the *plague*, and maybe it is. Some foundling kid had it when she was brought to the orphanage, and she was dead in three days, the nurses who cared for her gone within a week, and now everyone else is being struck down with it, too. A god could heal themselves of it, but I'm not a full god and I'm weak. Nearly all the gods are gone from the orphanage now, vanished to Elida, there are none of us left anymore, and so the plague scythes through us like barley corn, human kid to human kid until it reaches me.

My lungs are full of slime and all the blood in my head has congealed and oh it hurts, it hurts so much. My bones ache, all the nerves and muscles wrapped around them have tautened and now it hurts too much to move. The world comes and goes. I don't really mind when it's not there, I swim in the darkness of my head. My skin is covered in sweat, a slick greasy oil. The pillow is hard against my throbbing head.

I think: well, okay, am I dying? I'm not angry if I am. I just want to know.

Somehow, sometime, the world coalesces slowly around me, and I can see the stone ceiling above my head, hear my rattling breaths. I'm in *my* bed, in our room. I didn't know that. The thought calms me slightly.

Voices around me.

'She needs essence of rue.' Nurse Madeline.

Joshua. 'Give us a moment.'

'Within the next hour.'

Joshua, calm and insistent. 'I'll give it to her.'

A hesitation, but there are too many sick kids around to care much about me. I hear the nurse walk out. The movement of the door out of the corner of my eye. Joshua, locking it.

Then, at last, a grip on my sweating hand. Warm and sure. For days he has refused to let anyone else in the room. Even Kestrel can't go near me now, when I'm this sick. But he is unafraid.

His voice is in my ear. 'Heal yourself,' he says, softly. 'You can do it. Come on. Stay with me, Hero.'

I try to speak, but it hurts too much. He shushes me, and strokes my head.

'You're gonna be okay,' he says. 'You hear me? You're gonna be fine. You're gonna live, Hero. We love you too much.' The ferocity in his voice. 'Heal yourself. Come back to me. Come *on*.'

After a long time, the bleeding stops.

The black tower around me congeals into solidity. The heat in my lungs, the wetness, starts to drain, and I feel a cold stab in my chest as the lung tissue mends. My breath comes slowly and raggedly. I can feel scar tissue congealing on my back, heavy. I am more scar than flesh by now.

I lie there in a pool of my own blood, trembling violently, too tired to move. My breath is coming in bright, warm gasps.

I am alive.

Joshua is kneeling beside me. 'Hero? Can you hear me?'

I summon the strength to nod with difficulty, and hear him breathe out in relief. He presses his blood-stained hand into mine.

I try to roll over, speak. 'The . . . Guardsman—'

'What?'

'The Guardsman, he has to . . . bring him here . . . I can . . . I can heal him—'

'Oh. Him.' There's a strange, blank look on Joshua's face. 'He's dead, Hero. Can you stand?'

He grabs my hand and tries to lift me, but I stay on the ground. I roll over slightly, feeling a washing heat of exhaustion and light-headedness, to see the Guardsman. He's not bleeding anymore, which I guess is as sure a sign as any. His face is a melted, burned mess. Yes. He's dead.

I close my eyes. Our clothes are filthy after a month in the woods and now I can feel grey blood soaking into my dirt-crusted shirt. He's dead, because Joshua has killed him.

'Are you . . . okay?'

I don't open my eyes but I feel him shift.

'I'm fine,' he says, lightly.

A silence. Then he speaks again, restless.

'He tried to kill you. He would have killed me, too, if I'd stayed still long enough. I couldn't see any other way.'

I don't say anything. I just keep breathing slowly.

His voice tightens. 'Could you see one?'

I shake my head. He tries to pull me to my feet, and I shake it again, more vigorously.

'Hero,' he says, sharply. 'Come on, we have to move. They'll have heard the screaming—'

'Give me . . . ten seconds. I can't . . .'

It's too tiring even to speak.

'Okay,' he says, at last. He sits down beside me. I know he's staring at the Guardsman's body. When I close my eyes, I can see his face as he stood facing the Guardsman, the light glowing in his hand. That look of cold power. I try to push it away, but find only the heartbeats beneath it. They're worse than the screaming: quieter, accusatory. The pain of ignoring them sits deep in my chest.

'Okay?' says Joshua, after a minute. His voice is drained and dead.

I nod without looking up and grasp his hand.

When I'm on my feet, I say hoarsely, 'Don't turn the light back on.'

And we climb again, each breath tearing a cold seam in my chest, an empty well of exhaustion.

I thought it was bad going up these stairs in the faint gold of Joshua's light, but this is a hundred times worse. No matter how grim the corridors look, how bare and terrifying and black, it's worse not to know what resides in them.

I am so tired. My head is still throbbing with the shock of what has just happened. Every step drags at my lungs. I can still feel the blood wet on my chest, the staring melted eyes of the Guardsman, the hard ice of the blade inside me. I want out. I want this never to have happened.

Joshua stops again. I grip his wrist more tightly.

'What?' I keep my voice as quiet as I can.

'No more stairs.'

It's like being thrown off a cliff and into the wide vanishing air. My stomach disappears. I lift the quiet from my voice with effort. 'Then,' I say, as loudly and calmly as I can, my voice echoing off the unseen walls, 'we're here.'

There's a buzzing above our heads. Then a bulb of white argon light appears, solid and glass, the kind I've only ever seen in Amareth.

I blink, taking everything in. The exhaustion has taken my terror and beneath it there's only numb, white cold.

We're in a gleaming, circular black room at the top of the tower. No windows, no doors. No way out but the staircase behind us. Around us, covering every inch of the walls, are at least forty Guardsmen, grey-uniformed and impassive, pointing their guns at our heads.

And at the centre of the room, straight in front of us—

Joshua gives a terrible, strangled cry. I realise a few seconds later that I've stopped breathing completely. My brain is full of light. Nothing else around me is real.

At last, at last . . . strapped to a chair, looking right at me—

Kestrel.

CHAPTER 7

The Fall

At first all I see is her face, and the bright, hungry light in
it.

She's looking at us like we're her whole world, some golden
angels descended from heaven into the darkness of this place.
Oh, my darling . . .

And then I *see* her.

Her dark eyes sunken, her bones stark in her thin, bare
arms. Her black hair lank and damp. There's a slight tremor
in her right hand, under the ropes binding her to the chair,
and there's something not right, too, about the darting quick-
ness of her eyes. They swell, wide and bright, and I know
she's seeing the fresh, grey blood on my shirt, the exhaustion
in my face and in Joshua's.

I try to stare at her, to catch her gaze in mine and tell her
wordlessly that she will be all right, that I'm so sorry we
abandoned her, that I'm so sorry for all of it, but she's looking
at Joshua, her breath slow and taut, like she's keeping calm
with deliberate effort. I try to send the words to her, inside
her head. *I love you. I love you.*

'Let her go,' says Joshua in a low voice. I see her breathe
in quite suddenly at the sound of his voice. 'Now.'

None of the Guardsmen does anything. Their eyes are all
on me. I remember suddenly, over the roar of joy at my sister's
return, that they all have guns. I need to think of something
to get us out of this, but my mind is suddenly blank.

Then the Guardsman nearest to Kestrel speaks.

'Jessica Markham.'

The name rings a faint bell in my head. So does his face. Then I realise who he is, and a sweep of revulsion and fear grips my stomach. His voice in the mud-streaked rain, by a deserted tavern. Joshua's presence in the lurking dark behind me.

This is the Guardsman who led the patrol that caught us, days ago. The one who tasted my blood and thought me human.

I feel suddenly sick again, but swallow it down. I feel the ghost of the knife sore in my chest, and my heart thundering. I keep my face impassive.

He stares at me. His eyes are hard and bright. Kestrel and Joshua's gazes are locked with such intensity that the air between them is trembling, on the verge of catching alight. I do not expect Joshua to be able to handle this situation, or to come up with a plan; all I need him to do is control his powers, and use them when I need him to. We are not going to be able to walk out of this by just talking. We're going to need Joshua's light.

My heart slows, certainty steadying me.

I need to force a fight as quickly as possible. They don't know what Joshua can do. The last thing I want is to give them time to work it out.

I look at Kestrel.

'Stay calm,' I say quietly. She does not look away from Joshua, but I see her twitch; I know my voice, too, will give her strength, prove to her that I am not an illusion. 'Keep still. We're getting you out of here.'

'Oh, you are, are you?'

A Guardsman to my right speaks, his voice low and trembling. His gun is pointing straight into my face. In the fight, we will need to take away their guns. But there must be over a dozen of them. How are we going to do that?

'Alec Cragg,' he says, in a querulous voice. He doesn't look much older than us. Why on earth would a boy that age want to join the Guard? 'He was stationed downstairs. Where is he?'

I must seem calm: they will be hungry for any sign of weakness. 'He's dead,' I say, flatly.

I revel in the way he flinches. He raises his gun.

'You murdering—'

'Close your eyes,' I say, over him.

The Guard don't move. The one to my right still has his gun pointed into my face. In fact, no one moves but Kestrel, who squeezes her eyes shut and presses her face into her shoulder, her hands still tied to the chair. I can see her chest rising and falling rapidly.

Joshua glances at me and I nod once. His face hardens.

A little of the colour has returned to the Guardsman's face, the one who threatened me. He glances to the Guardsmen next to him, and I see fingers tightening on guns. They're frightened at last, I realise.

The Guardsman with his gun pointed into my face puts his finger on the trigger.

'Give me one reason not to kill you, bitch,' he says softly.

I know I can't.

'Joshua, *NOW!*'

I step backwards and throw my arms over my face, shielding my eyes. There's uproar amongst the Guard, shouting, a spatter of gunshots – one, two, three, four – deafening in the closed room. I wait for the pain but none comes. Then, an explosion of light.

The inside of my head turns white. The heat is rippling, shimmering; I can feel the skin of my arms burning, and it takes all my effort to heal them. The moisture in my mouth evaporates. Even through my closed eyelids, I can see the shadow of the bones in my arms through the red glow of my flesh.

Then it's over.

I can hear screaming over the buzz in my head. I keep my eyes closed for a few seconds. There are no more gunshots.

Slowly, I lower my arms and open my eyes. All I see for a moment is the white, blinding dots shimmering over my retinas. Then my vision clears.

The Guardsmen have dropped their guns. They are stumbling around, into each other and the walls, the skin of their faces red and shiny or blackened with burns. Their eyes are webbed with stringy white flesh, boiled and set in their faces. They're all screaming, a terrible, bloodless sound that echoes around the walls in a strangled mess. They are blind.

I don't have time for horror. I dart past one of them with his hands outstretched and flailing towards Joshua, who is kneeling beside Kestrel, pulling with shaking hands at her restraints. She's staring down at him, her eyes blank with horror. Her chest is still rising and falling rapidly.

I crouch beside her chair and look up at her.

'Kestrel. Can you hear me?'

She doesn't move. Her eyes are still fixed sightlessly on Joshua's face. For a terrible moment I think he blinded her, too, but her eyes are still bright jewelled amber. Just unfocused, nothing worse.

'Kestrel.' I put my hand on her arm, her living flesh. What a miracle she is, in front of me, alive. 'Come on. We need you awake.'

One of the blind Guardsmen beside us gives an incoherent, agonised roar at the sound of my voice and lunges towards me. I punch him hard in the chin, feeling the crisped heat of his skin, and he stumbles away. Kestrel's wide eyes blink unseeingly.

I take a deep breath, and slap her across the face.

Joshua's head snaps up. He looks for a wild, terrifying moment like he's about to hit me, too. Kestrel's moved with the blow; her long, lank, dark hair is hanging over her face, moving gently as if in a breeze, the echoing screams against her ears. The Guardsmen around us are still blundering around.

For a moment all three of us are quite still.

Then Kestrel murmurs, 'Yes. I'm here.'

Another Guardsman lunges towards me out of the melee. I hit him again. Out of the corner of my eye I see another fumbling blindly for his gun on the floor.

'Joshua,' I say, 'take them out.'

The Guardsman has picked up his gun and is rotating it, his milky, unseeing eyes staring at the wall behind us. His hands are moving like spiders, swiftly, instinctively, along the barrel towards the trigger.

Joshua gets to his feet and turns to him, just as the Guardsman raises the gun blindly and fires.

I cry out and try to throw myself in front of Kestrel, but it's too late. There's a *crack* and her blood, bright scarlet, splatters on to the floor. Her gasp of pain is tiny, pitiful.

Joshua gives a roar of rage and lunges towards the Guardsman. At the first crushing blow the blind man crumples, but now other Guardsmen are turning towards the noise. Joshua smashes through them, blood spattering his knuckles, his face taut with fury, his god's strength bright in his eyes.

I kneel beside Kestrel, my heart beating too fast. 'Kestrel. Talk to me. Are you all right?'

Kestrel's face is pale and grey, sticky with sweat, her eyes on my face. The muscles in her wrists are taut against the restraints binding her to the chair, her teeth gritted. 'My back,' she says.

A low hum of panic starts up in my head. I put my hand to her back, behind the chair. I can feel the deep black well in her skin, the gunshot wound, the slick seeping of blood.

She hisses. I close my eyes, feel through the place where my fingertips meet her skin to find the switch in my head that will turn off her pain, and hear her breathing slow and ease. Beneath my fingers the skin melds and smooths over.

But I know the damage goes much deeper than that.

I open my eyes. Around us the screams of the Guardsmen have changed in pitch. Kestrel is staring at me, her eyes bright. She says quietly, 'I'd forgotten you could do that.'

I give a very faint smile. She is so much thinner, gaunter, but the light in her eyes is the same. A month in the dark, in Elida, at the hands of the Guard . . . I cannot imagine being brave enough to survive that.

'I was waiting for you. All this time. I knew you would come.'

'Of course we did.'

'No, but I thought—' She hisses once more, and hastily I touch her bloodied back again, ease her pain. I start untying her restraints. 'I thought . . . I thought you might have been captured, but then I realised . . . why else would they not have killed me . . . unless you were alive . . . and they wanted you to come here?'

I think my heart breaks when she says that. 'I'm sorry.'

'For what?' she whispers. She touches my hand. 'I'm alive, Hero.'

We look around. The screams have stopped. Joshua stands alone, panting, his hands bloodied. The blind Guardsmen lie on the floor, collapsed on top of each other, unconscious or dead. I can feel heartbeats thrumming at the corner of my mind, far below us. He looks at us both. There's still that miracle-struck, hungry look in his eyes as they rove over Kestrel's face.

She isn't looking at him but down at the mangled face of the nearest Guardsman. She says quietly, 'Joshua—'

'Don't speak,' he says. 'Relax. We're getting you out of here.' He rounds on me. 'Hero, what's wrong with her?'

I am staring at the wall, but not seeing it. Under my stirring hands I can feel the edges of the injury. A sudden dread
settles in my stomach.

'Kestrel,' I say gently, to her, 'raise your foot off the ground
for me.'

There's a silence. In the darkness around us a Guardsman
groans and stirs. From outside the tower there's a faint thundering, like the pattering of rain. The heartbeats below us
seem stronger, denser.

Joshua says, 'Kestrel, did you hear—'

'Yeah.' Her face has paled slightly, the muscles in it taut.
She holds Joshua's gaze but her breathing becomes shallower.
'I . . . I can't.'

I touch the skin of her leg through her torn and filthy jeans.
'Can you feel that?' She shakes her head. I pinch it. 'Anything?'

Joshua stares between Kestrel and me. 'What's happened
to her?'

'The bullet went through her spine,' I say, holding Kestrel's
eyes. 'What's the lowest you can feel?'

She takes a shaking hand and moves it down her torso. At
her hip she stops. 'Here.' Her breath is shortening and I know
she's panicking despite herself. 'Hero—'

'Heal it,' says Joshua, his eyes bright with terror. 'Hero,
can you heal it?'

I shake my head, then see Kestrel go pale.

'No—' I'm so tired, I can't think straight. 'I can heal it, I
just . . . it won't be a clean break, the bone will be shattered,
there'll be nerve damage and . . . it will take a long time.
Hours. Maybe days.'

'We have time,' says Joshua at once. 'You can start now.'

There's something about the dismissiveness in his voice,
the insistence, that pulls at the ghost of the sword through
my chest, the memory of the hate-filled eyes of the ferry
captain, and brings exhaustion clamouring into my head like

fever. Some terrible, selfish instinct makes me want to say *no*. I am not a limitless resource. I want to sleep, I am so tired. I want this to end.

He stares at me. The shade of that dark suspicion stirs in his eyes again. I see his fists twitch. I don't know what to say.

Then behind us, a blinded Guardsman in the corner stirs and struggles to his feet.

Joshua turns away from me and lunges for him. Kestrel shouts, '*Joshua*—' but it's already over. He moves with brutal surety. There's a *crack* of bone, and the Guardsman drops with a thud.

Below us, at her cry, the thunder of rain shifts and grows louder.

Something stirs in my head. Why is the rain under us?

'Is he dead?' says Kestrel, quietly. Joshua turns to her, defiant. I don't know who he's angry with now. There's a shadow of that cold power in his eyes again.

But before he can speak, I say sharply, 'Quiet. Listen.'

It's not rain at all, of course.

It's *heartbeats*.

They surface from the recesses of my brain, slowly, hundreds of them, a pattering drumbeat inside my head, below our feet. Not in my ears but deeper, in the base of my skull. Close together, dense, a thundering cloud.

Guardsmen. Coming closer, rising through the tower.

'There are more of them,' I say, feeling my stomach drop. 'More Guardsmen. There's . . . of course there was—'

'What?'

But Kestrel says it for me, her face taut with horror.

'There was another trap.'

A beat of dead silence. The footsteps are audible now, getting louder, thundering up the tower stairs.

Joshua steps over the unconscious Guardsmen, towards the door. 'I'll hold them off.'

'No. Stay here.' My hands are pressed over my face. Let him be quiet, just let me think, if I can think I can find a way out of this, there *is* a way out of this—

'I can carry Kestrel down.'

I shake my head, *stupid*, trying to think past his voice. 'No, you can't. We won't make it even halfway if we try that.'

'You don't think I can fight them off?'

I raise my head, momentarily stunned. 'What the hell do you mean? Of course I don't think you can. What do you think you are, Joshua?'

He flinches, and I see Kestrel's eyes dart from him to me. I point at the door.

'That's a narrow stairway. All they have to do is stand their ground long enough to get a shot at your head. They don't even have to be able to *see* to do that, Joshua, all they have to do is point and keep firing—'

'Then I'll kill them.' His face is determined, angry. Beneath my irritation, I realise that he thinks he's being brave.

'A *hundred* of them?'

'Of course,' he says, curtly. 'You got a problem with that?'

I am speechless at his idiocy, his stupid bloody-minded heroism. He turns back, towards the door.

And suddenly I know this is it, the last moment I have to turn him back, to break whatever suspicions of me he's built up in his head. If I just acquiesce, if I let him do this, he'll trust me again. All he wants is for me to stop fighting him. If I let him do what he wants, he'll stop resenting me. If I just *shut up*.

Everything seems very clear, suddenly.

'Joshua,' I say quietly, to his turned back, 'don't you dare.'

He whirls. That strange light is in his eyes again. We stand there, feet apart in the dark tower room, and I can feel the half-healed wound in my chest aching, the newly formed scars, the burns on my arms. Inside my head we're standing again in that clearing outside Seaborne with his fist raised, hate in his golden eyes.

I think: go on, you bastard. Do it if you're going to do it.

'Don't give me orders, Hero,' he says. His voice is full of soft menace. I think he expects me to recoil.

Kestrel is staring at him. I can feel my pulse in my hands.

'I don't have time for this, Joshua.' I keep my voice very low and calm. 'Don't go out there.'

He walks slowly forward, his face contorted in fury. I stand my ground. He's so huge, suddenly, the shimmer of heat on his skin. I am terribly aware, again, of how easily he could hurt me. When did I start fearing him?

'You're not my master, Hero.'

'I'm the reason you're alive!'

Sudden silence. All the things I never said are rising in my throat, months of hurt and anger and resentment. I can't stop myself talking.

'You owe me *everything*. I've saved us from you more times than I can count. Seaborne, the orphanage, that patrol car – we would have died ten times over this last month alone, if I'd listened to you! And you . . . you dare to . . . you *threaten*—'

He's looking at me like he doesn't know who I am.

'You've *never* given a shit about me!' I am bitter, furious, a child. 'This whole time, I've had to save you, over and over. I'm so tired, Joshua, can you just *once*, please, forget your bloody pride and *do what I say*, and then if you want to hurt me, you can hurt me, okay.' Kestrel's eyes are so wide. I can feel myself on the edge of tears. Joshua's face is still very blank. 'I'm just trying to save you. This whole time I've been trying to save you. Just, just *once*, do what I tell you, okay? And then it'll all be over.'

There's a very long silence. My throat feels hoarse. I'm about to cry, I swear, I am actually about to break down in this dark room full of blind men and corpses and curl up and weep. I'm so, so tired.

Joshua's face is completely expressionless. I wonder if he's deciding whether or not to hurt me.

The footsteps of the Guardsmen below are loud enough now to distinguish one from another.

Joshua says softly, at last, 'What are you talking about, Hero?'

I try to speak, but I can't.

Beneath us, behind one of the blood-spattered doors, someone is screaming. It drifts up towards us like a breeze. Slowly, my mind returns to me.

The world in my head condenses. We are in the tower. We cannot be in the tower. If we stay here, we will die. We must get out of this room, whatever it takes.

'Joshua,' I say at last, into the silence. He raises his head slowly to look at me, the rest of him still. 'Please. Make a hole in that wall.'

For a second I think he isn't going to do anything. Our gazes meet, and I try to plead with him. His eyes are flat and empty. Kestrel's chest rises and falls very quickly.

'Please. We need to get her out of here.'

That gets to him like nothing else. Slowly, he turns around and walks towards the wall. I see the way he glances at me before he turns. Everything I said is still ringing in my head. I can't believe I said it, hate myself for saying it, but it's worth it if he obeys me. I'm sure of that.

I bend down beside Kestrel's chair. She meets my eyes with a brave attempt at nonchalance. Her voice is faint.

'What was that?'

I want to say, *you don't know what it's been like without you*, but she's beaten and bloody and I can't bring myself to hurt her more. She studies me.

'Are we . . . doing . . . what I think we're doing?'

'I'm sorry.'

'Don't apologise. We don't . . . have a choice.' Her breath is shorter again.

'We won't have any way to break our fall.'

'I know.'

'I can stop your pain, and I'll heal you as soon as we hit the ground, but that's only going to work if we all stay alive. Can you do that for me?'

'I'll try.'

'I love you.'

'I know.' Her face is grey with sweat but her eyes are steady. 'I stayed . . . alive . . . for you before.'

I pick her up with difficulty. The footsteps from just below us are thunderous now. I stand up.

And then at last grey hair appears above the rim of the staircase, dark eyes. I turn, in slow motion, to look at him, holding Kestrel in my arms, and our eyes meet.

What is he doing? He doesn't raise his gun. He's just holding up his hands, as if in surrender, a slight smile playing around his lips.

And there's a shimmer around his hands like gathering light. Maybe it's just in my own head, from exhaustion and fear. I'm staring at him, and I need to move—

Joshua turns and sends a pulse of light straight into the man's face, and he falls back, screaming. There are cries from below, the shattering thuds of his body as he falls down the stairs. There's a hole in the wall now big enough to squeeze through.

Joshua turns to me, hard-faced. 'Let me carry her.'

I hand Kestrel over. Clamouring, jumbled voices rise from below. I turn to Joshua, holding Kestrel in his arms. My heart is beating fast. I want to tell him to climb down. The words are there on my lips. But we don't have time. They'll just lean over the edge of the tower and shoot us as we cling to the walls.

I see it there reflected in his eyes. The bright, cold wind is sharp on my face.

Say it. *Jump.*

But will he do it? Will he take the risk of hurting her? And if he doesn't, and she dies . . .

A grey-uniformed head appears over the threshold, snarling. '*They're here!*'

I turn and shove Joshua in the back.

He stumbles, and then something in his legs gives and he pitches over the edge. I live in the terrible moment of his scream, the whirl of her hair as they vanish into the darkness.

Then it breaks and I'm alone in the tower, as if they never existed, in silence. I breathe in and out.

I turn and look at the Guardsman, who has those same shimmering hands, a glow building up around them like Joshua's, a gathering heat, I'm going mad—

He raises his gun. Points it straight between my eyes. We stare at each other. *Come on, you coward, fire—*

Then I lean back into the open air, and the wind swallows me.

There's a gutter of gunfire and suddenly the black tower is gone and I'm falling, the air glistening in my eyes, my throat bulging with fear. I kick uselessly in the air, away from the tower.

Gravity envelops me like water. My hair is in my face. There's a terrible vanishing in my stomach. Thought is gone. I can feel, but not hear, my breath shortening in my chest. I curl up in mid-air, there's the taste of salt, my own rough cry of fear, and the icy wind screaming, sharp as a knife, as I tear through it.

I manage to shut off my pain just as the water slams into me, bright as starlight and as hard, and I feel myself break, the cracks racing through my bone like wildfire.

The world vanishes for a brief, terrifying moment and then

returns. I'm underwater, the night black, in a silver storm of bubbles. I'm paralysed in a breath that won't come. Fear boils in my brain.

A voice, more Kestrel's than mine, speaks inside my head. *Heal, come on, heal—*

And something moves within me, a shuddering heat. A last surge of power. My body convulses as my bones fuse and mend, a shivering rush of cold. I feel a broken bone withdraw itself from my punctured stomach. I flex my hand in the darkness, feel a crack in my skull smooth over, and realise my mouth is filling with water.

I kick upwards and the surface breaks against my head. I gasp, trying to breathe and see in the dark.

The gleaming tower of Elida shines ahead of us in the night. I cough and feel salt water brim in my mouth like blood. My lungs clear themselves and fill with air. I'm treading water. I see a head bobbing in the distance. Short, wet-slicked hair. Joshua, not Kestrel.

'*Kestrel!*' he screams.

I take a deep breath and duck beneath the water again. There is no starlight here, but the water is shallow. I can't see anything. I surface again, gasping.

'*Joshua!*'

I see him turn towards me wildly in the darkness ahead, start swimming towards me.

'*Joshua! I need to see—*'

He nods and I duck beneath the water again. I wait, my heart racing, and then suddenly there's a flash of light from behind me and the water is transparent, as clear as daylight, and I see Kestrel, lying ghostly white, her arms and legs broken, on the sand just beneath me in the water. Her black hair is drifting in the currents around her. Her mouth is slightly open. I can see the whites of her eyes.

I feel myself scream, see the cold rush of bubbles, but the

water is soundless. I push through the viscous water towards Kestrel's body, grab her broken arm, not caring about pain, and drag her to the surface. I can feel the fabric of her sodden clothes trying to pull her downwards in my rough grip.

I am holding anything I can, her skin, her hair. I kick out towards the island, the ground, and my feet gain traction in the sand. Kestrel's face is wraith white in the starlight, bobbing in the water. Through my grip on her wrist I do not feel a pulse.

'Hero!' Joshua's faint voice from the water. 'Hero, where is she?'

I can't answer him. I drag her on to the sand, her sprawled limbs heavy with seawater. Her head lolls on the sand, grains clinging to her hair like crystal, her breeches dark and crusted. Her head.

I stare at it and understanding pushes gently through my senses. Her neck is broken.

I put my hand on the skin there and feel soft slime beneath my palm, seaweed. The bones fuse together beneath my touch. Kestrel is silent and still. Slowly, my brain is laying out the facts before me, like dishes on a table. If breaking her neck didn't kill her, she drowned.

I pull up her filthy shirt and press my hand to her slimy, pale stomach. My mind contracts and a spasm, like electricity, convulses her body. Water fountains from her mouth.

I do it again. I want her to cough but she doesn't. I reach for the switch inside my head that will turn off her pain but there's nothing, no pain inside her, no feeling.

Shadowy figures appear in the doorway of the tower, but I don't look up. I am focused completely on Kestrel's starlit, empty, sand-crusted face, her sprawled limbs, her slack mouth, as I kneel beside her on the beach.

Come on. I am a healer. This is an injured person. This is the point of me, why the hell am I even *alive* if she's—

Dead, whispers a voice in my head.

No, no, not dead. Not if I can help it.

I run my hands over her arms and legs as gently as I can and feel the cracks in her bones seal along my touch, as easily as smearing paint. I am focusing as hard as I can on the wet body lying on the sand beneath me but there is no heartbeat there, only empty space, my mind feels nothing. Veins close and punctured organs seal and mend, bruises fade to pallor on her skin, but it's a corpse's skin, an unliving thing. She doesn't move.

I stare down at her face in the moonlight, out of options, my hands pressed into the warm sand at her side. The two of us alone. I can hear my own panting breaths, too loud in the silence.

In my head I hear her living voice. *I stayed alive for you.* Kestrel, don't be dead. Please don't let me have killed you. I had to get you out. Kestrel, *please*, neither of us can live if you die . . .

A scream from the doorway. Gunfire again. A splashing from beside me. Joshua is dragging himself from the water. 'Hero! Where's— Oh, Kestrel, oh thank—'

I don't say anything. I can feel my pulse in my wrists again, a screaming rage gathering in my brain. Exhaustion and terror like a rushing wind.

Guardsmen are gathering in the doorway of the tower. Out of the corner of my eyes I can see them shimmering, blurred. There's that strange light around them again. Like Joshua's light, but weaker.

When I open my mouth to speak, it's to say, 'She's gone', but instead what I hear myself say is, 'Stand back.'

'Hero,' he says. He hasn't looked at her properly yet, he can't see she's dead. 'Come on, we have to get out of here—'

'Stand back, Joshua.'

Beat. Her heart, dead in her chest. *Beat.* That's all I need it to do. If her heart beats, she lives. All the wounds I've healed, the blood I've made blossom, the bones I've fused. My demesne has never failed me before. All I need is one heartbeat. One convulsion of flesh. That's all she is, flesh. I stare into the whites of her eyes for a gleam.

Out of the corner of my eye I see Joshua slide away over the sand, salt water dripping from his hair. I look into Kestrel's empty face. *Beat.* Come on. That bright power is hard in my chest again. I feel my hands buzzing.

I press my hand to the cold skin of Kestrel's chest and breathe out.

I feel a concentration of power so intense that the air between us heats up; there's a kind of glow, like a mirage. I feel it leave me, I'm lightheaded, drained, I don't know what I have left, but I don't stop to think, just press my fingertips to Kestrel's wrist, desperation hard in my chest, a living thing. You will not die now, Kestrel. You *will not die* . . .

Something stirs beneath my fingers, in my head. A pulse.

Everything in me vanishes into a rough exaltation. I grab Kestrel's shoulders, shake her. 'Kestrel!'

Her head lolls, the muscles in her neck pulled taut as a marionette. She doesn't move. I put my hand over her mouth and feel a stir of air, a breeze. She's definitely alive, she's got a pulse—

'Kestrel!' Not my voice but Joshua's. He scrambles over to kneel beside her face. 'Kestrel.'

He looks up at me, all his rage at me forgotten, fear bright as a child's. 'Why isn't she moving?'

'I don't know—'

And now I'm looking over his shoulder at the Guardsmen who have gathered warily to stare at us, these horrific other-worldly beings who jumped fifty feet from a tower into unforgiving waters and have survived. I know they're preparing to attack, perhaps debating whether bullets can hurt us or will merely rile us. We don't have long.

'Joshua . . .'

I don't know what else to say. This is it, the end of my thoughts. I haven't been past this moment in my head. We can't swim away; Kestrel will drown. We don't have a boat. We are stuck here.

And now I can see the Guard stepping forward, spreading out. They mean to surround us. I'm so tired. I search my head for a way out but find nothing. My brain is dead in my skull. I have nothing left to feel.

Joshua's staring at me. 'Hero?'

'I'm sorry,' I say, and hear my own voice sluggish with exhaustion.

There's panic in his eyes, sharp as a blade, the realisation that we have no way out. His mouth falls open slightly. I put a hand on his shoulder, feel apologies and excuses bubbling at my lips, too tired to speak. Kestrel's pulse stirs under my hand, steadying me.

The Guardsmen have surrounded us entirely, their faces shrouded in impassive darkness, their guns aimed into our eyes, and still they shimmer, a ghostly light around their hands. Why can't I see properly? What does it mean?

Wake up, Kestrel, please . . .

That sense of powerful calm has settled over me again. There is nothing to be done now. We will die no matter what I do. It is such a wonderful release, and as I look into Joshua's terrified eyes I want to tell him that, to say, I'm sorry, I'm sorry we have to die like this, what wouldn't I give . . .

And that jolts the truth into me like lightning, and I remember. The clearing, and a pale-eyed woman . . .

What wouldn't I give? I would give *us*. I would give anything, for them, for her – myself, soul and body and life . . .

'Joshua,' I whisper.

My voice makes some of the Guardsmen start, flinch backwards. One of them says, 'On three.'

'A light. We need a light – something that can be seen –'

The words are disintegrating in my mouth even as I say
them. I see the look he gives me, terror fighting deep mistrust,
and I think: well, this is on you now, then. If he trusts me,
fine. If not, we die. I am suddenly at peace.

I close my eyes and put my hand over Kestrel's face, shielding
her. I wait.

Then, by a clammy fever-soft heat on my face, I start to
feel the moisture in the air grow tight and heavy. Thunder
growls in the distance. I hold my breath.

Then the world turns white, a blaze of red behind my
eyelids. I squint as it fades to the cries of Guardsmen, and I
see the sand melted into a swell of glass behind the black
tower, and I know Joshua's lightning has struck too far away
to hurt either us or them. But hurting them wasn't the point.

The Guardsmen have fallen back in shock, crying out to
each other. Joshua is panting, his face glistening with sweat,
his eyes bright in the darkness.

I don't know what I expect to happen. Kestrel's breaths are
slow, and she doesn't stir on the sand, and the Guardsmen
are gathering again, bringing their guns up, shielding their
eyes from the residue of the light, and Joshua turns to me—

And then.

The sand is suddenly crawling, and people are standing
within the circle of Guardsmen. They cry out again in fear
and shock and raise their guns. In the darkness I see Cairn's
pale face, and Eliza, who grabs mine and Joshua's hands, and
two figures I don't recognise, one who's holding Eliza's
shoulder and another who throws up his hands and sends
three Guardsmen flying through the air, screaming.

'Hero!' Eliza is shouting at me, her grip tight on my hand.
'Grab her!'

I seize Kestrel's wrist with my other hand. Someone screams: '*It's her!*' There's a sputter of gunfire and I see bullets ricochet off Cairn's skin like pebbles.

Someone yells, '*Have you got them?*' I hear Eliza shout back through the darkness and then suddenly—

The air is filled with firelight, yellow and gold and grey. Joshua's stunned face is lit with it, his wide gold eyes gleaming.

We're kneeling on grass.

I feel Eliza release my hand. There's a rush of heartbeats like the return of sound from underwater. We've moved. The island is gone and I don't know how—

Kestrel suddenly gives a great rattling gasp and coughs. I kneel beside her. 'Kestrel, please . . .'

Someone beside us says, 'She's dead,' and then another, above me, 'No, she's breathing.'

I slap Kestrel across the face again, but her neck rolls and she doesn't wake. Joshua growls at me, a low animal noise I've never heard.

'Make her wake up!'

'I can't—'

Someone grabs Kestrel's shoulders, another her legs. They start carrying her away, over the grass, and Joshua gives a howl of rage and lunges after them. I move weakly to follow him but Eliza kneels down in front of me. I stare blindly into her green eyes.

'Hero,' she says gently, 'it's all right. You're safe.'

'But Kestrel—'

'We'll look after her. You did the right thing, calling us there. You're okay now.'

The world is glittering with stars and torchlight. I kneel in the grass, soaking wet, covered in sand. The pale-eyed woman Cairn is with them, watching me, hands in her pockets. Eliza grasps my chin and pulls it upwards.

'Hero. Look at me.'

The world swirls, shadows blurring my eyes. I feel Joshua's name congeal in my throat, Kestrel's, an undying throb of panic in my heaving chest, my speeding breath . . .

'You can stop now,' she says quietly. 'Your friends are safe. You did well.'

Her face shimmers like the air over a fire. I feel the world sway, the earth swelling under my back.

Cairn turns away, her eyes glinting in the moonlight, and I lie down in the soft grass. I watch the stars in the sky go out, one by one, like bubbles in seawater.

PART TWO

Raven

CHAPTER 8

Lessons

When the lightning strike comes, we're sitting on the cliff top, waiting. The thunder comes first. Then the sky goes suddenly white, a crackling electric *snap* that makes everyone jump.

Cairn scrambles to her feet. 'That's them. Come on.'

The twins are closest. Caleb grabs Luca's hand. Eliza, who's been gazing into the fire, moves too, quick as the sparking of flame, grabbing the frayed edge of Luca's sleeve. Caleb reaches over to grasp Cairn's shoulder.

I'm quicker than any of them, around the fire in an instant, hand on Luca's belt.

She tries to shake me off. 'Raven, no!'

'No . . . I'll come, I'll fight—'

Caleb pushes me off, and he's not unkind about it, either, which makes it worse. His hand is on my cheek, stroking, gentle, and then suddenly there's that *pulse* of force and I'm thrown backwards over the fire.

In mid air I twist and I'm a falcon. I dive for them in a scream of wings, but Luca closes her eyes and then they're gone, vanished, swallowed by the air. There's silence but for the crackle of the flames.

I shriek an angry *caw* of frustration and then land in the grass, and become a girl again. They *never* let me fight.

Mark comes running out of the darkness, looking wild. 'Where are they? Where did they go?'

'To the island.' *Without me.*

He blanches. 'To the *island?*'

I don't want to say it again so I turn into a lizard and crawl into the warm lick of the flames, crouched among the logs flaking white in the blue heat. Mark just stands there, a lost look on his stupid face. I curl up into a ball, lizard head resting on my scaly talons.

I *could* fight. They should let me do it, I'm their sister, I'm meant to help them. It doesn't matter how old I am, I don't care what Caleb says, I could have done it when I was nine and now that I'm ten I can do it even better. I could be a wolf for them, a bear, a shark, a dog with slobbering fangs, I could fight and hurt the Guardsmen and keep all of them safe. But instead they went alone. Stupid, *stupid.*

'The island?' Mark says again, softly. I expect him to hurt or throw something, like I would, but of course this is Mark, he doesn't do stupid things like that. Instead he takes his knife from the sheath at his hip and sits on the grass and stares over the cliffs at the great black sea, turning the blade over and over in his hands.

Across the cliffs the black tower rises like a knife blade. The tower of the Guard. No one's told me what's in there, but if the Guardsmen live there it can't be anything good.

But the boy and girl from the city went into it alone, and Cairn says we need to protect them. We have to believe Cairn when she says things because if we can't trust Cairn we can't trust anyone, that's what Caleb says when Luca's angry. *If we can't trust her, we're all dead,* is what he says, but I try not to think about that last part.

I growl inside my head. Ugh, I want *to help.* I crawl out of the fire over the crumbling logs on my scaly lizard arms and the cold washes over me like water, so I curl into the crackling mud and bury my head in it, warm. I want them to come back—

'*Kestrel!*'

The scream comes from behind us. Mark leaps to his feet and I turn into a girl again in an instant and run towards them.

They're all there, appeared out of the air. Cairn, Luca, Eliza, Caleb and three other people, a boy and a girl and another girl who's lying unconscious on the grass. They're all soaking wet and covered in blood. The boy is yelling '*Kestrel! Kestrel!*', and Cairn is standing over them, and Eliza and Luca are kneeling by the unconscious girl. She's pale as death, her wet hair dark and spread over the grass like the feathers of a drowned bird. *Kestrel.*

'Kestrel, please,' says the other girl. She's shaking, and her face is drawn with pain. 'Kestrel, *please—*'

Mark kneels down beside Kestrel and puts his hand over her mouth.

'She's dead,' Luca says flatly. I can see she's shivering, hugging herself in the cold.

'No, she's breathing . . .'

Kestrel isn't coughing anymore, just lying still, shivering and taking long rattling breaths. The boy is still screaming '*Kestrel! Kestrel!*'. Then the other girl, Hero, hits Kestrel across the face, but Kestrel's head just rolls to the other side, her cheek slowly reddening with the mark.

The boy, Joshua, stops screaming and makes a growl like my voice when I'm a wolf. '*Make her wake up!*'

It takes me a moment to realise he's talking to Hero. She just stares back at him. She looks empty, lost, her eyes blank, like she left something on the island of the black tower when Luca vanished her here.

She says softly, 'I can't . . .' and her voice is so hollow it makes me shiver.

'Get her to the fire,' Eliza says sharply. 'She'll freeze to death.'

Mark and Luca move like people shaken awake and grab Kestrel's legs. Joshua howls again and lunges after them, grabbing at her arms, her face, but then with a sound in his throat like a sob he collapses into the grass, his arms pressed over his head, making awful muffled noises into the dirt.

Eliza has Hero by the chin, speaking softly to her. Eventually Hero's eyes go blank and flutter closed, and Eliza lays her down gently on the grass. Joshua isn't moving anymore, collapsed in the dirt.

Everyone else is just standing very still. I'm waiting for someone to talk, to explain what happened.

Then Caleb says my name, very quietly.

Everyone looks at him. He's almost as pale as Kestrel, and his eyes, on me, seem blacker, empty in the firelight. He sways and then falls to his knees.

I scream.

Luca doesn't. She vanishes and then appears out of the air by his side in a moment, a long moment where Caleb takes a breath and we see the blood that trickles from his mouth, over his hands as he presses them to his chest. Thick and black and glistening in the darkness.

'Raven,' he says again, and the word is slick and bubbly. Then he falls forward, on to his face.

This is our second day on the cliff top, waiting for the boy and girl from the city – *Joshua* and *Hero*, I have to remember their names – to signal for our help. My sister Luca asked why on the first evening, as we all sat around the fire, eating a rabbit that Mark had caught in the woods.

'They've already refused our help once,' she said. 'Why are we wasting our time on them?'

Eliza is cleverer than Luca, cleverer than any of us, except maybe me when I get older. Everyone says I'll be cleverer than all of them one day, that's why it's so important to keep me safe. I think that's a stupid reason. She said, 'They'll change their minds.'

'How do you know?'

'Desperation.'

Cairn was pacing the cliff top. She doesn't eat when she's anxious. That's how we know she *is* anxious. It never shows in her face but I can tell sometimes, I'm good at reading people. We're here on her orders, she wants to save Joshua and Hero, and we always do what Cairn says, even if we don't understand why. Cairn knows what she's doing, that's Rule Number One.

'If they come out of there at all,' Mark said, pulling a strip of rabbit off the roasted leg he was holding and throwing it to Caleb. Caleb's eyes narrowed, and the rabbit meat slowed and hovered in the air. I made sure he was still watching it, and then I grabbed it and stuffed it in my mouth.

Mark roared with laughter, and Caleb made an outraged face and started tickling me.

'I think they will,' said Eliza. 'The girl, Hero, she's clever.'

Cairn turned to look at her from where she stood on the cliff top. 'You think so?'

Eliza was quiet for a moment. Cairn almost never asks for our opinions on things and I think Eliza thought this might be a trick. She said, 'Yes. She has to be, to keep herself and the boy out of the Guard's hands for this long.'

'That could just be luck,' said Mark, and threw a strip of beef jerky to me. Caleb tried to grab it out of my hands but I was too fast. 'They've made enough stupid decisions.'

Eliza said, 'Have they, though?'

'What do you mean?'

'If I walked into Amareth right now, unarmed, yelling *here I am, come and get me* at every Guardsman I saw until one of them shot me, would you just leave me to it?'

'Of course not. I'd go after you.'

Eliza smiled. 'And does that make you stupid?'

'It makes *you* the biggest idiot alive.'

'Exactly.'

'Exactly what?' A little grin was playing across Mark's face, like he was waiting for someone to tell him the joke. He looked at me. 'Raven, do you understand what she's on about?'

I thought I did. 'An army is only as strong as its weakest division.' It's what Cairn says sometimes in strategy lessons, when she's telling me not to send an infantry battalion over a hill in the centre of a cavalry line. The Guardsmen would go straight for the people on their feet and then there'd be a big hole in the middle of your offence.

Mark was openly grinning now. 'What are you talking about?'

'It doesn't mean they're *both* stupid,' said Cairn. 'It only means *one* of them is. The girl might still have brains. She just keeps running into danger to save the boy.' She turned away from the cliff top, towards us. 'When it comes to it, she'll ask for our help. She'll know she won't have any other choice.'

'And how will we know when she does?'

Cairn shrugged and sat down beside the fire. She took a strip of beef jerky from Mark. 'I think we'll know.'

Dawn comes over the distant sea, the black tower against the yellow-grey sky. I don't think I'll ever sleep again.

Caleb's still alive. Eliza says that's a very good sign. She's not a doctor but her mother was, in Amareth before the rebellion, and she knows some things. Like how to bind a bullet wound, and how to pack it with herbs and salt water so it doesn't get infected. She tends to him and we stay out of her way. Nobody speaks.

I'm a bird in the trees, watching the camp, a hawk, my

eyes sharp and my body warm under my feathers. Beside the fire, Joshua and Hero and Kestrel lie asleep. Cairn is standing over them, waiting for them to wake. I don't think she wants to look at Caleb, and I hate her for that a tiny bit. He went to the island on *her* orders, she's the reason he got shot. I know she cares so much about these strangers, Joshua and Hero and Kestrel, but I don't care, I don't care at all. I care about Caleb, my brother. I want them to be dead so he would wake up.

But no, that's a stupid thought. I wish I were older, grown-up, like them. I wish I could help.

I'm going to watch for the Guard and make sure they can't come here to hurt Caleb ever again. I want him to wake up and say he's all right, but he's sleeping now, shivering and pale, and Eliza says we can't wake him because sleep helps you heal. She hasn't slept herself in a day and a night, not since before they went to the island to rescue the boy and the girls. Her hands are crusted with Caleb's blood and she's kneeling beside him, watching as he sleeps, with a dead, exhausted look on her face that makes me think she's not seeing him at all.

Joshua is shivering violently in his sleep. Kestrel isn't shivering, she's just lying there still, breathing in and out like she has ever since she got here, like if a dead person could breathe. Hero sleeps beside her, one hand on hers, like she's scared Kestrel will be stolen away from her in the night. I get that. I want to go cling on to Caleb's hand like that. I used to do that when I was a little kid, after our parents died.

Luca and Mark are sitting beside the fire. Luca hasn't slept either. She's holding a cup of tea that Mark made her, not drinking it, just letting the steam wash over her face, staring bleakly at Caleb. I know she blames herself for letting him get shot. Cairn and Eliza both say it wasn't her fault, but she doesn't listen. She hasn't said a word since they came back.

It's my fault too, because I wasn't there, but no one has told *me* it's going to be okay.

I know it's stupid, but that frightens me more than anything. The whole of the rest of my life, it's all been about me. Where I am, if I'm safe, if I'm learning, if I'm growing right. They always talk about me being *ready* one day. Ready for what, though, I don't know. I should have been ready for this. I should have fought with them when they went to the island.

The night lasts forever. Caleb hasn't stopped bleeding yet. He's so pale. I can see the sweat shining on his face whenever a cloud passes and the moon comes out. I wish I'd been shot instead. I can heal myself when I get hurt or sick but Caleb can't, not even a stupid cold like the ones Mark gets sometimes. I *hate* the Guard, more than anything, I wish one of them was here so I could turn into a wolf and hurt him.

I asked Cairn once why they hate us. She said people are stupid and evil when they want to be, but that wasn't a real answer.

Cairn is getting restless, pacing on the cliff edge. It wasn't in the plan for her to be here this long. I know she wants to go back to the camp.

I told Luca I can take care of him for a while if she wants to sleep, but she just ignored me. It was like I wasn't there at all. I'm trying not to get mad at her because I know she's scared too, even though she doesn't say.

Except there's nothing to be scared of, because—

I say it loudly to myself, in my head, so I believe it.

He's. Not. Dying.

After we eat, Mark stands up and says loudly that it's time for my lessons.

No one says anything. I curl up and stare at Caleb over Luca's shoulder, but Mark nudges me with his foot and says, 'School time, tiny one.'

'I'm *not* tiny.'

He just grins at me, but beneath it he looks tired and worried. He loves Caleb too, I know. He's been with us since the beginning, since I was only four, when the twins and I went to Cairn for help after the Guard murdered our parents. Cairn sent Eliza and Mark to live with us, on the run, because we can't live in the camp like everyone else. It's a huge camp, they say, full of tents, thousands of people of godly blood, all living in secret, hiding from the Guard. Cairn is in charge of them all, which is why it's such an honour for her to come and visit us as often as she does.

Before, when I was very young, there were other children who travelled with us, others of the blood with different demesnes. But by the time I was six, Cairn had sent them all back to the camp. I miss them sometimes, but Cairn says they weren't good enough to stay with us. When I ask what that means, she just shakes her head and smiles.

Cairn knows what she's doing. That's Rule Number One, I have to remember that. Even if we get angry with her, we have to do what she says and not ask questions.

It's Mark's job to teach me to fight. Mark is very good at fighting. *Cleverness will win you more battles than strength*, he says. Sometimes he calls Caleb *little brother* and me *little sister*. He's offered to take over cleaning Caleb's wounds as well but Luca ignored him too, and since then he's left her alone.

'Come on,' he says, nudging me with his foot again. 'You've got to. If you stop learning your brain will melt and drip out of your ears, like syrup . . .'

'Stop it,' I say, but I go with him anyway, because lessons will make things seem more normal and make it easier not to worry about Caleb.

First lesson is words, from the big leather book Luca took from our father's library when we escaped the Guardsmen.

All the words in the world are in there, she says. Normally it's she who tests me, but today Mark does it because we don't want to bother her.

'*Cannibal.*'

'A person who eats another person.' I make a face.

'*Sage.*'

'Wise.' I poke him. 'You're making it too easy.'

'Oh, fine then. *Hypocrisy.*'

'You, when you tell me not to eat any more sausages from the pack and then I see you eat two more.'

He widens his eyes like he's outraged and grabs my feet to tickle them. I almost giggle but then over his shoulder I see Luca kneeling beside Caleb, pale and shivering, and suddenly all my laughter is gone.

Second lesson is fighting, just with fists and elbows today, no knives. I ask why we have to train without weapons, because surely in a real fight I'll have weapons with me, and he says, 'You never know, you might get caught off-guard one day.' I say I'll *never* get caught off-guard, not ever, thinking of Caleb, and Mark laughs and says, 'Even you have to sleep sometimes, tiny one.'

'I'm *not tiny!*'

I kick him but he dances away. His eyes gleam. 'A tiny person wouldn't be able to beat me.'

So then I fight fierce and hard with all the muscles I have until everything hurts, changing my shape over and over to try and confuse him, but even then I still can't quite beat him. Mark is older than me, older than the twins even. He's human, not of the blood, so he's not fast and strong like Caleb and Luca and Cairn, but I'm not fast and strong either so that makes it fair. I have five blood-gifts of seven, healing and beauty and my demesne and the premonitions, and when I get older my blood will turn grey like the twins'.

But I don't have the *useful* things, like speed and strength.

Luca says not to complain, five signs out of seven is more than people usually have when they're half-human like us; she and Caleb only have four each. But it still makes me angry. What use is stupid *beauty*? I'd much rather be able to crush rock in my hand, like them.

I kick at Mark's knees and drive him back a step and dart away, turning into a wolf again to bite at his heels, but then he dives at me quick with his hands open to catch me by the scruff. I become a bird and flutter through his grip but suddenly his hands are on me, not crushing but hugging, and the fight is over.

He lets me go and I turn back into a girl. I make an angry growling noise, but he grins. 'Good work.'

'I *lost*.'

'Yeah, but you lost well.' His head is tilted to one side, and I can see the exhaustion of the last days worn into his face, like wind into rock. He rubs his eyes. 'Kid, you don't get it, do you? Losing is pretty good, from where you're standing. Do you know how many people have ever beaten me in a fight like that, without weapons?'

I think about it. 'None.'

He smiles. 'Two.'

'*What?*' No one *ever* beats Mark at fighting, he's the best. He grins.

'The first time, I was about your age. This eighteen-year-old kid came up behind me and grabbed me and took everything I was carrying. I started going around with a knife after that.'

I try to imagine Mark that young, but I can't. 'Who was the other one?'

He grimaces. 'Cairn. That fight hurt.'

'Why did she fight you?'

'She was testing me. To see if I was what she was looking for.'

Cairn and her stupid tests. Before, it was the other kids she was testing, the ones who travelled with us, and before even that it was Mark, and now it's me, and I don't even know what she *wants*. All the frustration and fear wells up in me and rises in my voice.

'What *is* she looking for? I don't understand, what was she—'

'*Keep your voice down,*' whispers Luca from beside us, sudden and hoarse. I clap a hand over my mouth and look out over the sea, to where the black tower stands against the pale silent sky, full of listening Guardsmen.

Mark takes my hand away from my face, gently. 'It's okay. They can't hear you from here.'

I look up at him. 'What *is* Cairn looking for?'

'She was looking for you, kid.' He smiles down at me, a little sadly, his hair all ruffled in the wind. 'She didn't know it yet, but it was you she was looking for. All right. One more time.'

Then we fight again and I *still* don't beat him, but this time I last a little longer before he catches me.

The third lesson is tactics, and after that it's truth-telling with Eliza. Telling truth from lies is her demesne; nobody can lie to her without her knowing. You can't teach demesnes, of course, but if you read people's faces really closely you can sometimes see the lie there. That's what she says, anyway. I've never been very good at it.

This time, she calls Mark over to make him try to lie to me. He glances at Hero as he sits down, careful not to wake her.

'Oh, man,' he says, 'I can't think of anything.'

'Yes, you can. Tell her about the camp.'

'What about the camp?'

'Anything.'

'Okay.' He thinks while Eliza goes back to staring into the fire. 'When I lived there, my tent was . . . green.'

I look at him. There's the slightest twitch at the edge of his lips, but then this is Mark, he grins at everything. I consider for a moment. 'Lie.'

He holds out a fist and I bump it. He does his impressed face at me, the one where his mouth goes all round like an o, but I see the look he gives Eliza, too. They always give each other that look when I get things right. I hate it.

'How did you know?'

'Your favourite colour is blue.'

'Aw, that's cheating. Okay, another one.' He thinks for a moment. 'When I came to live with you, I was fourteen. Truth or lie?'

I think about it, trying to do the maths in my head. Cairn sent him to live with us when I was four, so six years ago, so that would make him twenty now. I don't know exactly how old Mark is, I've never really thought about it. I try and remember what he looked like when I was little, how young he seemed. 'Lie,' I say slowly.

'Nah, that's true.'

I stare at him. 'Really? You're *twenty*?'

'Yep. And Eliza's twenty-one.'

I turn around and stare at her. 'True,' she says, without looking up from the fire. 'Although that was going to be *my* next question, Mark.'

He grins. 'Sorry.'

I gape at them both. 'You can't be that old!'

'Sure we can.'

Twenty-one, wow. I've never met anyone that old, except Cairn. It's a strange idea, really, Mark and Eliza growing up. They don't ever change, they never have, they're just *here*, always, our protectors and our friends, teaching me lessons or fight training with Caleb and Luca or helping us make camp. I never really thought about their ages, the fact they must have been kids and grown older.

Then I have another thought. 'Where are your parents? Do you *have* parents?'

'Sure I did,' says Mark. 'They're dead.'

I look at him. His face has gone suddenly very clear and closed, expressionless, like Cairn when she's thinking.

'I'm sorry.'

'It was a while ago. I was eight.' There's a kind of tightness in the way he says it. 'Well, that was when my mother died, anyway. I never knew my dad. He never showed up, so I guess he might as well be dead, for all the good he did me.'

The bitterness in his voice is strong as salt. I stare at him. 'That's not . . . I mean . . .' I swallow. 'Maybe he tried, and—'

'Did he?' Mark is staring at his fingernails, turning his hand over but not seeing it. 'After my mother died I took to stealing, to get food. I got so good at it, people started paying me to steal stuff for them. I got famous, in my own kind of way. The Boy Thief, they called me.' He takes out his knife and starts turning it over and over in his hands again, just looking at it. 'The people I worked for kept a list of everyone who came looking for me. The Guard were after me most of the time, because they knew I used to steal stuff for people of the blood who were in hiding in the city, food and clothes. I used to find empty houses and steal the keys.'

He takes the slate slowly from his belt, but he doesn't start sharpening his knife, just stares at that, too.

'Then there were people who wanted to hire me to steal things, people I'd stolen *from*, who wanted revenge . . . all sorts. But I was always on the lookout for him. My father.' He twists the knife sharpener between his fingers. 'I was always watching for a man with my face, my name. But he never came to look for me.'

Eliza's looking at him over the fire. Her skin is warm and

gold in the sunlight. He glances at her and puts the knife sharpener back in his belt.

'Anyway,' he says abruptly, but he doesn't say anything else.

'What *is* your name?'

'What?'

'Your last name. The one your father would have.'

He shakes his head. 'You're meant to leave your last name behind when you come to live in the camp. It was one of Cairn's rules.'

'Did she invite you?' You can't live in the camp except by Cairn's invitation or if you're born there, that's why we can't go and we have to live like this, moving from place to place in case the Guard catch us. We can't go there until I'm *ready*. Whatever that means.

I think it's because of Anthony. I don't know who he is, but I overheard Eliza telling Luca one evening that Cairn was worried about how Anthony would react if we ever went there. *He'll be furious*, she said. *He always thought it was going to be him.* I hate not knowing what it all means. What is *ready*? What am I meant to do? What *am* I to them, except just me?

He nods. 'When I was ten. Cairn came to find me when I was still working as a thief. I guess she thought my skills would be useful.'

He says it with a kind of hardness in his voice, like Luca does sometimes when she talks about Cairn.

'Why did you go? You could have made loads of money as a thief, if you'd stayed—'

He laughs. 'Nah. It's easy to steal when you're a kid, you're smaller and no one notices you. And I wasn't going to be a kid forever.'

'Yeah. I guess so.' I look down at my hands and try to imagine myself older. I can't. I wonder how long my hair will be when I'm Mark's age.

'I think I'd be a good thief,' I say, after a while. I could be a mouse, and climb through windows.

Mark smiles, and ruffles my hair.

Then we just sit there, together, looking at Caleb as he sweats and murmurs in his sleep.

CHAPTER 9

Twenty-Three

I wake curled beside Caleb in the middle of the night. The salt air is cold in my hair. Everything is quiet. I can hear their breathing around me, soft and smooth and warm. The sea murmurs against the rock.

Something is wrong. I've turned into a wolf in my sleep. I can feel the teeth in my mouth, newly sharp. Claws dug into the grass. I want to attack something, but I don't know why.

Everything around me is still dark. Caleb's breathing beneath my paws has become slower and more hoarse, I can hear the rattling in it. There's a raw white pain of panic in my chest, and I don't know why, I don't even know why I've woken up, except—

There's a woman behind me, crouching in the dark.

I know it, vividly, with the surety of the premonitions I get sometimes. Maybe it *is* a premonition. I turn around—

And yes, there she is.

She is silent. The sky is flushed grey with the rot of dawn over the cliff tops but the sea is still ink-black, and I realise that the woman is crouched over our pack. She's opened it but she's not looking through it. She's staring over the cliffs, at the sharp knife blade the black tower makes against the sky, against the salt-grey clouds. She can sense me, too, I can tell, and when I wonder how, I realise I'm growling, low and soft.

Slowly, very slowly, she pushes herself to her feet and turns to face me, and that's when I notice one of the sleeping figures by the fire is gone.

This is her. The short-haired girl. Hero.

She looks very tired. Her face shifts grey to blue in the light, bruises and the shadowed hulls beneath her eyes, and with my wolfish senses I know she smells of lavender somehow, and sweat and salt water and blood and more weariness than I've ever seen on anyone, even Cairn. Her hair isn't really that short at all, it goes halfway down her neck, ragged and matted and nearly as dark as *my* hair, *raven black*, the hair our father named me for.

I wonder how this girl was named. Luca says that in the orphanages in Amareth they name all the babies off two lists, one for boys and one for girls, and they reuse a name whenever someone grows up and leaves the orphanage. Maybe there's a baby Hero now, squalling in a crib, surrounded by Guardsmen, a thousand miles away.

'I'm sorry,' she says, and her voice is smooth, melodic. That word came up in dictionary lessons three weeks ago, it means *songlike*. 'I was just hungry. Have you got food?'

She's talking to *me*. Me, in my wolf-body, as clearly as if she knew I was a person, warily but with respect. I growl again. She doesn't step back. Her eyes have a strange kind of clarity to them and glitter darkly.

Suddenly I know that her hesitation is not because of fear, not at all. She seems *clean* of fear somehow, like all of it has been used up. 'I think . . . I think you saved us,' she says. 'Thank you.'

It's a statement, laid flat on the air between us like clothes on a line.

'My name's Hero,' she says. She's keeping her voice quiet so as not to wake the others. Her eyes keep flickering back to the boy and the girl sleeping by the embers of the fire. 'What *are* you?'

I don't do anything. She's staring at me in fascination.

'I don't think you're really a wolf,' she whispers. 'I can see that in your eyes.'

And suddenly the breeze is colder on my skin and without even deciding to do it I know I've turned back into a girl.

Hero doesn't even flinch. Her eyes move over my face, my tangled hair. I hate this body, but however hard I try, I can never change its shape, to be older or bigger or stronger. If I'm human I'm always me, the same face in Eliza's cracked mirror, still only ten and weak and a *child*, still just—

'Raven.' Again, I don't decide to say it.

Hero looks at me, calm and wary. She still hasn't screamed, most people scream when they see me change shape for the first time. Mark did, I remember. 'I'm sorry?'

She means *I don't understand*, not a real apology. I try to read her, like in lessons. 'Raven. It's my name.'

'Oh.'

She glances again towards the fire where Kestrel and the boy sleep. 'Have they . . .' She seems nervous, biting her tongue, scared. 'Have they woken up yet?'

'No. You're the first.'

She flinches back a bit, her face paler, and closes her eyes. It's a while before she speaks again, and even then it seems like the words hurt. 'Who . . . who are the others? Where's Cairn?'

'I don't know. She went for a walk.'

'A *walk*?' Hero's voice is hoarse. 'What do you mean? Where did she go?'

I don't say anything. Hero puts her face in her hands and crouches down again by the fire. There's a moment of uncertain silence, and then a strange, croaking, muffled sound starts coming through her fingers.

I stare at her.

'What is it?'

'I'm alive,' she says, muffled, and I realise she's laughing, but a kind of hollow laughter, mirthless. Not the way Mark laughs, all humour and joy and release. 'I'm alive. I'm *alive.*' She looks up at me. She sits down then, wraps her arms around her knees, and stares out over the fire, pushing her hair out of her eyes. 'Who is everyone?' She stares over at the twins, sleeping away from the fire. 'Are those your parents?'

I nearly choke. 'No!'

She looks at me, again with that open look. Unoffended and unafraid. 'Who, then?'

'I'm their sister.'

'Oh.' She looks back at Kestrel and the boy again but this time she doesn't flinch when she sees them asleep, she just swallows. 'And these are . . . Mark. And Eliza. Yes, I remember.' There's an odd look of lightness about her that came with the laughter and hasn't left yet, like everything around her is beautiful just for existing. I guess she really thought she was going to die on that island.

'How long have you been here?'

'Three days. We were waiting for you.'

She looks back at me, slowly. 'Waiting for us . . . to what? To call for help?'

'Cairn and Eliza said you would.'

Hero gives a low, bitter laugh. 'Of course they did.'

I'm excited. 'Were you really *inside* the black tower? Did you fight the Guard?'

'Yes, we—'

She goes still, suddenly. Her knuckles go white, clasped around her knees. She's looking past me. I turn, trying to see what she's looking at, and when I look back she's in a crouch, hunted, her face pale with shock, and in the dying firelight she looks almost *feral.*

And then I realise it's Caleb she's staring at, *Caleb* across the fire—

I'm on my feet. 'What's wrong?'

'His heart,' she says. 'I felt it. His . . . his heart just stopped beating.'

The world around me vanishes, and all there is is fear. I run towards him, leaping over the fire. No, of course he can't be dead, the girl is lying, of course she's lying—

But when I look at him with Luca curled on his shoulder, there's no movement in his chest, no dawn-mist rising from his face, and his eyes are closed, eyelids blue in the dusk but no fluttering, his mouth half open.

No, no, *no*—

And then I scream.

Everything moves suddenly, a terrified scramble, shouting. Hero's kneeling beside Caleb, her fingertips on his wrist.

Luca jerks awake blearily, and sees Hero crouched beside Caleb and lunges for her, but there's movement out of the darkness and Mark's there, pulling her back, away from Hero and Caleb.

I'm just standing here, silent, voiceless, *useless*—

Then Mark says, hisses, '*Look at him, Luca!*'

And at last she does.

I see her eyes go wide suddenly, blank. The sound she makes is the worst thing in the world, like her soul is being ripped out through her mouth, a mess of sinew and blood.

'He's not dead,' says Hero quietly, over Luca's moaning. As if she's talking to an animal, soothing and calm. '*Listen* to me. He's not dead yet, he's got two minutes – no, *listen* to me – just because his heart has stopped doesn't mean he's dead, but he *will* be if you don't let me heal him.'

Luca looks up at her as Mark lets go of her arms, her agony etched upon her face, and seems to truly *see* her for the first time. That bitter acid-hatred is in her eyes again, and I know what she's going to do before she does it.

She vanishes and then she's behind Hero, appeared out of

the air, but Hero's quick. She turns and swings a punch and it catches Luca in the stomach and she stumbles back.

Suddenly my voice is back in my throat, I can't bear them fighting. I scream at her. '*Caleb!*'

Hero has Luca's fists caught between her hands, her glinting dark eyes burning into Luca's face. Luca should be stronger, but her eyes are on Caleb. Her strength is broken. Hero whispers, half-pleading.

'Let me *help*, please, we don't have time—'

Mark's crying, kneeling down, staring at Caleb, wiping tears from his eyes. 'Help him, please . . . heal him, please, heal him . . .'

He looks helplessly over my shoulder and I realise Eliza's there.

'She's telling the truth,' says Eliza. Her eyes are full of tears too, and when she looks at Caleb, she speaks faintly, like she can't hear what she's saying. 'Please, heal him. Please.'

I don't think Hero hears her at all, she's still just staring down at him, and she said *two minutes* and it's been forty seconds easily and I find my voice again and scream.

'*Please!*'

Hero's head turns. Then she drops to her knees and presses two fingers to Caleb's wrist. She takes a long, shuddering breath.

I see Luca take it with her, a rattling gasp, the agony, the absence in her face and the terror and grief behind it.

And Hero closes her eyes.

One two three four five six seven eight nine ten eleven twelve thirteen fourteen fifteen—

Caleb, please—

The world blurs inside my head, all the voices and the sobbing and the darkness swims and fades, and I sit in the window of a house, and I'm smaller, and watching a woman running barefoot across the lavender field—

– no, stay here, don't—

– and I fight to stay here but I can't, I'm sinking inside the memory of the worst day, the day I try not to remember *ever—*

Run, Luca! Take them and run—

The day was beautiful, sunny and blue. I was sitting at the windowsill, playing with a wooden horse Caleb had carved for me.

We'd stayed hidden our whole lives before that morning, but no one stays hidden forever, that's what Cairn says and she should know. I was four and the twins were twelve, and I was sitting in the window when my mother came running home from the village, screaming our names.

Go! Luca, take them and run—

The Guardsmen were running behind her, dead-eyed. Even with her speed and strength there was no hope, Luca says, not when the Guardsmen had guns.

Our mother had Luca's pale brown hair, I could see it streaming behind her as she came running towards us, and heard the faint strains of her voice. She was barefoot. Her eyes were green like mine and Caleb's, and wide with terror.

As she got closer I could hear more clearly what she was screaming. *Go, Luca! Go, take the others and GO!*

We were alone in the house. Our father had gone to teach at the school that day. The Guardsmen had probably killed him already by then. He was human, not a god like our mother, but the Guard hate god-lovers just as much as they hate us, Cairn says.

The twins were upstairs. Everything was silent, but for the creak of wood and the rising terror of our mother's voice from outside, a thin note, like the call of a bird in the woods, easily ignored. I don't remember being afraid.

There were two Guardsmen running behind her. We called

them *grey-faced men* afterwards, before we found out who and what they were, because they looked so pale, wan and cold, and expressionless, like they were sick. Their uniforms were grey as well and they ran exactly together. *Mechanical.* That's another dictionary word.

They both had guns, and after a moment one raised it, aimed, still running, and fired two shots.

One grazed our mother's ear. When I saw the spurt of blood, the thick silver rivulets running down her neck, I was finally scared. Terror was in my skin, a cold white heat.

She kept running, screaming for us, and stumbled once, the blood dripping down her shirt.

Luca! Go! Take Caleb! Take Raven and—

The second shot took off the top of her head. She dropped at once, but a faint mist of blood lingered where she'd stood, like perfume.

And suddenly the silence in our house was pure as clear water.

The Guardsmen kept running towards the house. One of them saw me sitting in the window. He looked at me across the garden, still running, and raised his gun. I could see the concentration in his dead eyes.

Then Luca's hands were around my waist, lifting me from my seat. There was a high-pitched ringing in my ears that might have been a scream. And then – with the breathtaking suddenness of Luca's vanishing – we were on a hilltop in the wind, with a thousand coloured tents spread out below us, gleaming in the sun.

We stood there trembling. The rasp of Luca's breathing was hoarse and rapid and numb as gunfire. The taste of Caleb's silence was worse than anything else. I didn't understand, not yet.

I remember our mother's face as she screamed. I see it sometimes when I sleep. I don't remember our father's face at all.

They died, and we lived. We *lived*, like they would have wanted.

Caleb's so old now, our mother wouldn't know him anymore. He was only twelve when she died. Look at him lying on this cliff top, breathless and cold. If he dies . . .

I'm going to kill every single Guardsman on this earth, I'm going to kill them all, and then he'll wake.

– sixteen seventeen eighteen nineteen twenty twenty-one twenty-two twenty-three –

At last, he opens his eyes and takes a rattling bloodshot breath and coughs, and his eyes haven't changed, they're hazel. I was so scared they'd be milky-white, the colour of dead things.

I can't hear I can't feel I can't breathe–

Luca is screaming something, and Eliza behind me has collapsed on her knees with her head in her hands, and Mark is crying harder than ever. Only Hero doesn't look into Caleb's face. Her eyes are set and cold and trembling, and there's no joy in them. I remember the way the sleeping girl looked when they brought her here, how hard she screamed for Kestrel to wake.

She doesn't look up, doesn't say anything. She just pulls Caleb's shirt up and keeps her hand on his wound, and eventually the bullet comes worming its way out of his skin into her bloody hands. She throws it on to the grass and presses down on the wound, with its pus and blood, and closes her eyes. When she takes them away the skin is smooth and unmarked and clean and whole.

I'm on my knees too. When did I fall? I don't remember.

Luca crawls over to Caleb's side, cradles his face, and now she's crying too. I can't take my eyes off him. In a voice that doesn't feel like mine, I hear myself say, 'Thank you.'

Hero looks at me and doesn't smile. Everything about her seems tired. Only Eliza is looking at her.

After a while she brings her a blanket and some food and says thank you too. Hero takes it slowly and sits in the corner, eating it alone.

Luca and I sit beside Caleb, wiping the blood from his face. The sun is almost fully up. I can feel his skin, fever-warm, in the cold sea air.

Luca meets Cairn at the edge of the woods when she finally returns. There's a snap in her voice. I tense when I hear it, against Caleb's shoulder. We do not snap at Cairn, not ever.

'Where have you *been*?'

Cairn doesn't answer her, just looks around at everyone, at Hero blood-stained and exhausted, eating her beef strips on the edge of the cliff in the dawn, and Caleb, ragged and pale but *awake*, sitting up and talking and laughing with Mark.

After a moment she just says softly, 'Ah.'

Luca looks so angry she might hit Cairn, but after a moment she just takes a single deep, shuddering breath and walks back towards us. Cairn watches her go, an eyebrow half-raised. Luca sits down beside us, and Caleb puts an arm around her shoulder.

Out of the corner of my eye I see Eliza walk up to Cairn almost casually, her expression strained. I turn into a bird where I'm sitting on the grass beside Caleb, a hawk with sharp ears. I want to hear what she says.

She lowers her head and speaks softly and intently, and Cairn listens, her hands in her pockets.

'Cairn – with respect – I think it's time.'

Cairn looks at her for a moment, then speaks quietly. 'You do?'

Eliza looks relieved. 'Yes. Caleb will make as good a recovery at the camp as here. And I think Raven's ready for it. She was very calm when the Fitzgerald girl woke, she didn't panic until

Caleb's heart stopped. And even if she weren't, it's not safe to stay here. Cairn . . .'

She falters at Cairn's expression.

'The Fitzgerald girl?' says Cairn at last, looking over Eliza's shoulder towards the fire. 'She's awake? She's talking?'

'Yes, but . . . Cairn, please, listen to me—'

'I am listening to you, Eliza,' says Cairn. Her voice is suddenly dangerously quiet, and I see Eliza's face go blank. 'My answer has not changed. There is still Anthony to deal with. And Raven is too young.'

'She'll be young for years still, and we don't have years. Things are changing. The Fitzgeralds – what happened at Seaborne . . .' Eliza's expression is strained, and I can't believe she's being so brave, to talk to Cairn so boldly. I'm scared for her. She swallows. 'Cairn, when we were on the island, I think . . . I mean, I saw—'

'Eliza, we can talk about this later, but right now I have to—'

Something shifts beside the fire, a drop in cold water, a silence that ripples outwards in a shivering rush. I turn. I don't see anything at first, don't understand why everyone's gone suddenly still.

And then, beside the fire, Joshua stirs at last.

CHAPTER 10

The Traitor

The air is gone, and everyone is breathless. Cairn and Eliza turn, very slowly it seems to me. Everything is quiet.

Joshua murmurs a name, vague and slurred. Then he says, 'Kestrel?', and opens his eyes, gold in the sunlight. Hero is on her feet and running towards him.

Then he starts awake, properly, sits up and cries out, '*Kestrel!*'

Everyone stares. His eyes are wide and bloodshot, and he's trembling.

Hero kneels beside him, her face full of wonder and grief, and wraps her arms around him. She's nearly crying. 'Shush, it's okay, Joshua. I'm here . . . Kestrel's here . . .'

He flinches slightly, and there's a shivering moment where his eyes are blank and I can tell he doesn't know her. Then something breaks, and he opens his arms.

She hugs him. Everyone watches them. Her eyes are closed, there's such fierce love in her face, and she stares over Joshua's shoulder at the black tower with a kind of sharp hardness, like how I felt when I slept beside Caleb, the kind that says *no one will ever hurt you again.*

But there's a terrible sadness in the way she looks between him and Kestrel, too, and I know suddenly something's terribly wrong.

'Where are we?' he says, blearily.

He catches sight of us over Hero's shoulder, Caleb with his arm around me, protective, and Mark and Eliza standing, and Luca's sharp gaze, and then he sees Cairn.

He scrambles to his feet, stumbling. '*You!*'

And suddenly everything changes.

Mark is on his feet and beside Cairn in an instant, hand on the knife on his belt, wary. Eliza is crouched behind the fire, pushing me behind her. Luca vanishes and appears on Cairn's other side. She reaches for her longsword but it's not there, it's still lying beside the fire. I see her glance back at it but she doesn't move.

Caleb is on his feet in front of Eliza. He forces me behind them, his other hand outstretched, but he's still so pale, the blanket wrapped around his shoulders. Will he still be able to move things with his mind, when he's this weak?

And now I know what I'm meant to do. Their silences and their movements mean they think we're in danger, and if we're in danger I'm meant to be a bird and fly away and *save myself* . . .

But no, never again, I don't care what Cairn says. I'm never leaving them.

I growl and I'm a wolf, crouched by Caleb's side. He pushes me back, murmuring, 'No, Raven,' because I'm not meant to show strangers what I can do. But Joshua isn't looking at me, just at Cairn.

There's a terrible anger in his face. It says, *don't provoke me*, it says, *don't make me hurt you, I can hurt you, I can make you wish you weren't born*, and it speaks of power. You can't tell by looking, but I know Cairn's turned on the switch in her mind that makes her invulnerable, makes her skin and bones hard as diamond. It exhausts her to do that for more than a few minutes, she's told us. When she came back from meeting Joshua and Hero in the clearing, she slept for hours and hours. Eliza sat beside her all night, even though she didn't need protecting, we were far away from anyone who could attack us. And now—

Now we're weak.

I realise it suddenly. There are six of us and only one of him, but still he is stronger than us. This boy could kill us all, if he wanted to.

'How?' he whispers, staring at Cairn. 'Hero . . . how did they find us?'

'They followed the lightning,' says Hero, quietly. 'Joshua, listen to me. Luca's a vanisher, she can move from place to place, she brought them to the island. They *saved* us, Joshua, they saved us from the Guard.'

He turns to her slowly. Their eyes meet and the moment shines between them in the sunlight.

'You asked me to call the lightning,' he says, at last.

She nods.

'Did you *know* they would come?'

Slowly, she nods again.

He makes a strange breathless noise, like he's been punched. Out of the corner of my eye I see Mark's hand twitch towards his knife.

Joshua steps backwards, away from Hero. 'You *called* them to us?'

'Joshua, it was the only way!' Hero is anguished. 'The Guard would have killed us, there wasn't a way out, you know that—'

'But you said . . .' The confusion in his face is still stronger than the anger, that's good. 'You said they'd use us. We agreed to say no, they'd hold us hostage, make her kill for them. Hero, we agreed, don't you remember?'

I expect Cairn or Eliza to say something then, something like, *of course not, we'd never make you kill anyone*, because they *wouldn't*, I know they wouldn't . . .

But both of them are silent. Eliza's fists are clenched by her side. Cairn's face is blank and calm.

'Have you . . . have you talked to them?' Suddenly, he sounds scared. 'What have you told them? Have you promised her to them?'

'No!' Hero moves like she wants to take a step towards him but holds herself still. The pain in her voice is hard to listen to, I want to cover my ears but my hands are only paws. 'No, Joshua, I'd never . . . come on, they *saved* us!'

'Never?' he says. '*Never*? What is it you think they want from us, Hero? Don't you remember what they *are*?'

The little-girl part of me wants to hide behind Caleb and close my eyes, but the wolf part stays strong, and growls.

'I don't care,' says Hero, quietly. 'Whatever they want, I'll do it. As long as it keeps you two safe.'

'They want *me*, Hero.' He turns to Cairn. 'Am I wrong?'

She just looks back at him, hard-eyed and patient, and in my head her voice is swirling. The reason we came here and risked our lives to save them from the Guard, the hunger in Cairn's eyes when she looked at them—

'You owe us,' says Cairn quietly, and her voice is harder than I've heard it. 'We saved your life.'

He stares at her for a moment, then turns bleakly back towards Hero. When he speaks it's very flat.

'You said we would go to the south. Somewhere peaceful. Together. All three of us. Salt fish and white beaches.'

'Joshua.' Her voice is soft and sad. 'We were never going to be able to have that. You know that.'

'And instead you sold us to *them*? Don't you remember what they do?'

'They don't, Joshua. That was the Guard, the Guard told us all that . . . that rubbish, they saved our *lives*, Joshua, come on . . . please, just listen to me—'

But I see the mistrust that flashes across his face, the dark, deep terror.

'You told me you didn't trust them. You promised me you'd keep us free. You *lied* to me.'

'To save us,' she says. 'To save *her*.' She gestures behind him, to Kestrel curled beside the fire.

His face is suddenly twisted, his voice full of contempt. 'To save yourself.'

She flinches, and for a moment all the guilt is wiped from her face. There's only shock and hurt, and then, slowly, the beginnings of anger. *Yes.* I want her to be angry. She saved my brother, and I do not like this boy.

Joshua turns away, towards Kestrel sleeping by the fire. He kneels beside her, places his fingers against her neck. I remember that from medicine lessons, he's checking her pulse. There's a tenderness to the way he does it, slight and gentle, and I remember the way he screamed for her two nights ago. The way Hero looks at *him* is like Luca looks at Caleb, sister to brother, but this girl Kestrel isn't a sister to him, not at all.

'Kestrel?' He shakes her, I can tell he's putting a lot of effort into ignoring us. 'Kestrel?'

'She hasn't woken,' says Cairn. 'Not yet.'

He ignores her and turns back to Hero. 'Have you healed her?'

She presses her hands to her lips and shakes her head. 'Not yet.'

Joshua's on his feet in a moment. Everyone goes very tense. Mark's hand tightens on the hilt of his knife.

'Why? You've been awake all this time—'

'I was healing *him*,' says Hero. She nods towards Caleb. Her voice is tight and her eyes move too quickly, flickering between him and Kestrel and us.

'Him?' Joshua takes a step towards Hero, and this time all four of the others twitch in unison. Cairn stays very still. '*Him?* And she's just been lying here, alone—'

'He was dying. I saved his life.'

There's no defensiveness in the way she says it, no emotion at all. My claws are digging into the grass and I can feel a growl building in my throat.

'You saved,' says Joshua, very quietly, '*his* life?'

Another step towards her. I can see every muscle in Mark's clenched hand.

'You saved *him* instead of her? What the *hell* happened to you? Have they—'

'They haven't done anything to me,' says Hero. 'He was dying, so I saved him. Joshua . . . her spine is broken, the bullet is still in there, I didn't have the energy, the—'

It's the wrong thing to say. Another flash of rage passes across his face. 'You're lying. You're lying to me. That's not why.'

Everyone glances towards Eliza, she gives the tiniest of nods, her eyes still on Hero. It means *yes*. She's lying.

Hero looked at Eliza too. I see her face tighten. 'Joshua . . .'

But nothing else comes out.

'Tell me what you did,' he says, quietly.

'Joshua . . . I . . .' A terrible flush of pain and guilt is creeping up her face like a blush. 'Joshua . . .'

Everyone is very still.

'Joshua . . . she died.' Her voice breaks. 'I don't think healing her is going to. . . She fell in the water and her neck broke and . . . and she died.'

There's a terrible silence. Joshua's face is pale as sand, sick, and there is no expression on it. Maybe he didn't hear, I think, maybe he doesn't understand.

And then—

He moves suddenly, quick as lightning, and so does everyone else. Luca vanishes from Cairn's side to appear at Hero's, grabs her elbow, and vanishes away again to appear behind Mark. His hand is on his belt. Hero bends over with the shock of it and retches, hands pressed into the dirt to hold herself up.

Mark steps in front of her where she kneels, gasping for breath, between her and Joshua, and takes out his knife.

Caleb and Eliza are pushing me further behind them, away

from Joshua, towards the trees, forming a wall I can barely see past, forcing me away. Eliza always said I was the most important thing, that any of them would kill and die for me. I struggle against them. No, *enough*, I'm sick of being protected, I want to help. I couldn't help the night they went to the island, and look what happened then.

'Give her back,' Joshua says, softly.

'We're not going to let you hurt her,' says Mark. His grip on his knife is steady, his voice is calm, he's ready to fight, I know it.

'She's lying,' says Joshua. 'She's a lying bitch. Kestrel isn't dead, she *isn't dead*—'

'Her neck broke,' says Hero, so softly that for a moment none of us realise she's said anything. 'When we hit the water . . . and I . . .' Again that flush of guilt. 'I tried, Joshua, I *tried.*'

'*But she's breathing!*' Joshua's face is wild and hard with fury, his voice a whiplash of white rage. 'She's got a heartbeat, I can *see* it—'

'Joshua . . . I started her heart, I healed her neck, I made her breathe, but none of that means she's *alive*, she was gone . . . I mean, the . . . the *her* bit of her, her soul, might have gone the moment we hit the water, and . . . and making her breathe again, I don't think it's going to bring her back. I'm sorry, I'm so sorry.'

There are tears in her eyes, on her cheeks.

'But we . . .' The pain and confusion in Joshua's eyes, his hands dangling useless by his side. 'I don't understand . . .'

And then something changes in his face, something deep inside him like it's snapped. There's a silence. Hatred has welled up in his eyes, sudden and strong, like blood in a wound.

'You,' he says, so quietly.

Hero just looks at him with that terrible sadness. Her

hands are pressed into the dirt, pushing herself slowly to her knees.

'You pushed me,' he says, and his voice is dead. 'You pushed us from the tower. That was why you wanted me to . . . to make that hole in the wall. You did it. It was all you.'

A silence. Caleb's grip on my shoulder is rock, he's still trying to push me towards the trees but I won't go. Eliza's eyes move slowly between Hero and Joshua.

'You did it,' he says. 'You were trying to kill her. You were always trying to kill her. You never wanted her to get out of Elida. Even on that road, you were always trying to tell me she was dead. You told me to run, to leave her in the orphanage. You lying bitch. *You* did it.'

Hero's just staring at him, her face entirely wiped blank, like she doesn't understand him at all, like his words are too terrible to make sense.

He raises his clenched hands, and for a second I think he's going to hit her. Something is gathering around them, like all the light of the fire is congealing on his skin, a shimmering, pulsing—

Eliza shouts '*No!*', and Caleb lets go of my shoulder and clenches his fists. Joshua is thrown suddenly backwards, off the cliff, suspended in mid air, kicking. That look of cold rage doesn't leave his face.

The pulse of light that shoots from Joshua's hands soars over her head and past Mark's shoulder. Mark throws himself aside and it hits one of the trees behind us. The tree goes up in flames at once and there's the smell of wood smoke, in my throat and my eyes.

Suddenly I'm a bird again, an eagle with crushing talons. I leap into the air at Joshua even as Caleb screams '*No!*' and reaches for me. But I'm faster, I'm soaring past him over the cliff. My talons scrape through Joshua's hair and leave streaks of silver blood. I flap around his head, screaming my bird-rage. It's not *fair*, you don't just attack people like that. He nearly hit Mark, he *meant* to hit Hero, and it doesn't matter what she did, you don't kill people ever—

'Raven, no! Raven, come back!'

But the fury in Joshua's face is so bright, like madness—

And his next pulse of light brushes my wing, and I feel the searing heat.

Then *pain*, shining unimaginable pain, and I cry out and the wound is smoking. I'm kneeling on the grass and I'm a girl again, a girl, and my hand, my hand, my—

It's got a hole through it, my hand has a hole through it. I smell charring meat, but no blood, *cauterised*, yes, that word was in the dictionary.

I'm going mad, can pain drive you mad?

But I don't need to feel the pain. There's a switch in my head, Mark told me, I've done it before, I can press it and *self-anaesthetise*, that was also in our father's dictionary but my head is a haze of agony and I can't think I can't think I can't—

'*Come back!*'

Hero's voice, rippling like flame, the fire in my hand.

The pain washes over me, a drowning wave of blood, water with metal spikes. I moan.

Please . . .

'Raven.' Luca's kneeling beside me, holding my good hand. 'Raven, come on, can you hear me?' I can hear tears in her voice. 'We need you to focus. We need you to *heal*. Heal yourself, come on, please, I know you can.' I think she's crying.

'*Come back!*'

Out of the corner of my eye, I can see that it's dark. Hero's kneeling at the edge of the woods, sobbing.

'What . . .?'

The word is soggy in my mouth.

Someone strokes my hair, says 'Shush', soothing, it's Caleb, my head is lying in his lap. He strokes my face, his hand is cool. 'Ignore her. Come on, Raven, it's okay, just heal yourself, all right? It's okay, we're here.'

But my hand and my hand and the pain and my hand and Hero's crying and the *pain*—

When I wake again it's nearly dawn, my hand is wrapped in bandages. Luca is curled round me, asleep, my head is on her chest.

The pain is gone, or part gone; it's a dull throbbing ache. Gently, so I don't wake Luca, I unwrap one of the bandages and prod the skin of my hand. There *is* skin there, there isn't a hole anymore. The skin is red-raw and painful to touch but it's there, *regrown*. How did that happen? People can't heal in their sleep, Cairn taught us that in medicine lessons when I was younger.

Caleb and Mark are asleep on either side of me and Luca. I turn into a bear, fur against the cold, hopefully that will warm Luca as well. There are tear tracks through the grime on her face. I'd become a lemur and curl round her neck like a scarf but I don't want to wake her.

'It started after we left the orphanage.' Hero's voice is quieter, she wipes tears from her face. Cairn and Eliza are watching her in silence. 'He didn't trust me anymore. Or at least . . . maybe he thought he did, but . . .'

She closes her eyes. There's a silence.

'I shouted at him,' she whispers. 'I couldn't control him. I said . . . terrible things. I threatened to leave. But I never thought . . . I never thought he'd leave. I swore, on my life, I promised her I'd protect him . . .'

Eliza puts a hand on her arm. No one says anything.

'This thing that's come over him,' says Hero at last, constricted, 'I thought it would go, when she came back. I

thought if he had her back . . . but if she doesn't wake up
. . .' There's so much pain in her face. 'He'll come back,' she
says at last. 'If we wait, he will. He wouldn't leave her, I know
that.'

Neither of the others speak. Hero turns to Eliza.

'What do you think? Am I crazy?'

Eliza hesitates. 'I don't know him.'

'You do know. You know about people. You're a truth-teller.'

I see Cairn and Eliza exchange a look.

Eliza says, slowly, 'I don't think you want him to come
back. I think if he comes back it'll be to finish you off. I don't
think that was a mistake, in his head. I think he's serious.'

Hero puts her face in her hands. She looks very small in
the firelight.

After a moment, Cairn gets up and starts pacing again.

'They killed a whole *village?*' she says at last.

Hero looks up again, wiping her face with the heel of her
hand. 'I think so.'

'If it got out,' says Eliza to Cairn, 'if we put it out, if we
told everyone that it was the Guard who did it—'

Cairn shakes her head. 'No one would believe us.'

'Some would. It would cast confusion over it, and that's
worth the effort in itself.'

Cairn gets up, strides restlessly to the cliff top. Hero watches
her, her face bleak and grimy.

I think Joshua's gone, I can't see him anywhere. He ran
into the forest.

My hand throbs dully in the cold. I wonder if I'll have a
scar.

'There are two ways we could defeat the Guard,' says Cairn
eventually. She's still staring at the black tower, over the cliff
top. 'One would be to overwhelm them. We've never had much
of a chance of that. But the Guard get their power from the
people. If the people turned against them, they'd be lost.

That's how we do it.' Her fist is clenched in front of her. 'We make them look worse than us. We show them that we're better than them. That we're not the monsters they've made us out to be.'

'You have no chance,' says Hero at once. 'None at all.'

Cairn turns back to her, eyebrows raised. 'You think so?'

'I grew up with them,' says Hero. 'In Amareth, with the humans. If you've been out here for the last twenty years, if you haven't talked to them . . . you can't *begin* to understand how much they hate you.'

'*Us*, I think you mean,' says Cairn softly. 'You're one of us.'

Hero shrugs. It looks like it takes her all the effort in the world, and her eyes keep darting back to the forest.

'It doesn't matter. I mean, if I were you, I'd want to think that people had been deluded, too. I'd want to think there was some better instinct in there. That they'd be compassionate if they were given the chance. But they won't, I promise.'

There's some anger in her voice now, it's higher and clearer. I can see some of the fury that sparked and then died in her eyes when she fought Joshua. She stands up and looks Cairn in the eye. Cairn regards her coolly.

'They saw what happened in the rebellion. They *helped*. They like feeling safe from us. They don't care what the Guard do, they don't want to know. And you can't make them want to.'

A silence. My hand throbs gently in the cold.

'We have a plan,' says Eliza, after a moment.

'Eliza,' says Cairn warningly.

There's a silence. Then at last, Eliza starts talking again, low and intent and restless.

'We have *goodness*. We have strength and courage and love. We have all of that, in one person.' Eliza points towards me over the fire without looking, and I close my eyes very quickly, my heart racing, pretending to be asleep.

'With her at our head, how could they fight us? How can you say she's is a monster? How could you hate her? You only need to meet her once and you'd kill and die for her. She's *everything*. Nothing the Guard say can stand against her. She's half-human, she's as much one of them as she is of us. Her father was Amir Herath, did you know that? The Guard captain who fell in love with a god?'

She is still talking, but she's much further away now, and I am falling.

'They can try to make the people hate us,' says Eliza, 'but when we show *her* to them, their hatred won't stand. It can't. If she is our face, they *can't* hate us.'

There's a silence. The words hammer into my head, meaningless, a clamour of nothing. The fire crackles red behind the dark of my eyes. I don't understand. Our father—

'That's your plan?' I hear Hero say at last. She's half-laughing despite herself, wiping her tear-grimed face. 'Raven? She's a *child*.'

'She won't be a child forever. And by then we'll be stronger. We'll have more fighters, more supplies.'

'And then what? You declare war? What do you think *this* is, if not war?'

But Eliza doesn't say anything else. Cairn is walking slowly around the fire. I hear her footsteps, soft in the grass.

'You idiots,' says Hero, quietly. 'You think you're going to win this by being *right*? By being *better*? You think if you've got the moral high ground, that's enough? How *old* are you?'

'No one thinks that,' says Cairn. Her eyes glitter as she looks at Hero, measuring her. None of us would dare to talk to Cairn like this, not even Eliza. 'There will be bloodshed, on the way to victory. There will be justice and execution and revenge. But *she* won't do it. Her hands will always be clean.'

Kestrel's still curled and sleeping by the fire. Or at least Kestrel's body is. If Hero was telling the truth before, her soul is somewhere else. Maybe in heaven with our parents. This is just meat, a dead thing breathing. I watch it out of the corner of my eyes, but it doesn't move.

My breathing is much too fast. I want to get up, to stop them talking, stop them saying these words about me. I don't *understand*. What am I to them? What am I meant to do?

'He *will* come back,' says Hero suddenly. She wipes her eyes again, I'm watching her now that they've stopped looking at me. 'I know it.'

'Hero,' says Eliza, and her voice isn't gentle now. 'He tried to kill you.'

She shakes her head, presses her face into her palms.

'He injured Raven,' says Cairn, her voice is flat and hard like flintstone. 'And then he ran into the woods. Do you know how many years we have spent protecting that child? Do you know what it's cost? And *he* came here, in our debt, and nearly ruined all of it—'

Hero flinches. 'I know. I'm sorry.'

'If I'd known what he was, I'd never have—'

'You wouldn't have saved us?'

She says it flatly, bleakly, and Eliza looks away.

There's a pause. Then Cairn gets up and walks to the cliff top, staring out over the ocean. She has that pale absent look on her face that means she isn't seeing.

'Please don't kill him,' says Hero quietly. 'I couldn't live.'

'We wouldn't kill him,' says Eliza.

'Really?' Hero isn't looking at her, but at Cairn on the cliff top. 'I know you'd sleep easier knowing he was dead.'

Cairn doesn't say anything, but I can read her stillness like we're doing the lying games, I know she's listening.

'Capture him,' says Hero, her voice raw, 'punish him, do whatever you want, but please don't kill him. I'll do anything.'

Cairn turns to her, her gaze slow and hard in the dark.

'Anything?' she says, quietly.

Hero looks up at her. She pushes her hair out of her eyes. I can see Eliza watching her, unblinking.

'What do you want?'

'I think you know.'

'You can have me if you want,' she says, and her voice is flat, numb. 'I'm yours. The resistance's. I'll do whatever you want.'

Cairn pauses for a moment, but I can see from her face she's decided. 'Okay,' she says. She steps forward and holds out her hand, but Hero's already turned away, pressing her face into her knees. After a moment, she picks up a sharp rock from beside her and starts shearing away at her hair, absently, staring into space, her movements slow and dreamlike.

I see Cairn and Eliza look at each other. Cairn beckons her and they walk together away from Hero, towards me. I narrow my eyes, trying to look more asleep.

At last, Cairn says softly, 'I think you're right.'

'About what?'

'I think she's ready.'

I see Eliza look up, her face still half in shadow.

'Anthony still won't like it,' says Cairn, looking out over the cliffs. 'He'll be angry. He might try to hurt her. *He* wanted this.'

'You can deal with him,' says Eliza. She's watching Cairn intently. 'They love *you*, not him. And if you tell them to, they'll love Raven as well. You have more power than you think, Cairn.'

'I have exactly as much power as I think,' says Cairn. 'No one is invincible, Eliza. You need to learn that quickly. Before the lesson finds you on its own.'

She turns and strides into the woods, the heels of her hands pressed to her forehead like she does when she's thinking.

Eliza stares after her. It's dark, and the clouds in the wind make the starlight flicker in and out, but even in the gloom of night I can see the stricken look on her face.

The Taste of Blood

It's still dark when I wake. I'm lying between Luca and Caleb but I can't sleep. My head is full of things that don't make sense, that I don't want to make sense. I'm scared of what they mean. I don't want to know.

Our father . . .

But that absolutely can't be true, put it away, put it in a box in your head, like Mark says. Cairn made a dumb mistake, people do that sometimes, don't think about it.

Think about something else. Be as clever as they think you are.

I think she's ready, Cairn said.

What am I ready for? What's going to happen? Who's going to die? I want to be Luca, able to go wherever I decide to, to vanish from place to place without even breathing and never have to *think* if I don't want to.

But Luca can be trapped too, I guess. If you strap her down skin to skin with something big, she can't vanish without taking it with her so she has to stay where she is. She never walks barefoot, or she'd try to take bits of the cliff with her whenever she tried to go anywhere. She's the last vanisher the resistance has.

There was another called Joanna, Eliza told me once, but the Guard captured her and trapped her in Elida, chained her to the walls so she couldn't vanish away. *That's if she's alive*, Mark said when he heard Eliza telling me, but Eliza gave him a *shut-up* look, so I'm pretty sure she's dead.

They're asleep, all of them. I can feel their breathing. I

imagine being like Hero, sensing their heartbeats. I'd be able to count them, *one two three four, Luca Caleb Eliza Mark,* and know they're there even when my eyes were closed. An instinct clear as my own heartbeat, a steel wall in my head, unmoving. *I'm never leaving them.*

I close my eyes and try to be four years old again, sitting at the window and watching our mother run towards us through the field outside our house, blood-stained, barefoot, the smell of lavender. Screaming our names. And the men behind her with their dead faces—

Bang.

I open my eyes, heart racing. For a second I think it wasn't real and then reality breaks over my head like water, the smell of the sea, the grass beneath my feet and the darkness and the *echo*, sharp in my ears and clear—

Bang.

Hero wakes suddenly, her eyes wide. I see her mouth open, the embers of the fire gleaming in her face.

I turn, a silhouette in the darkness. Mark is standing facing the woods, his throwing knives in his hands. They're the real ones now, I see the glint of blood-stained steel. I'm so still, I'm not breathing.

Eliza's pushing herself up on to one elbow, bleary. 'Whassgoingon?'

'Guardsmen,' says Mark tensely. 'In the woods. Get up.'

Bang. Bang bang.

'*Caleb,*' says Mark, his voice a low growl, but Caleb's already on his feet. Mark kicks the leather pack towards him. Caleb pulls up his sleeves and the other knives, rusted and blood-stained, soar out of the pack towards him. They hover around his head like fish around a shark, shifting slightly in the air as he breathes, gleaming white teeth.

I run to his side, a wolf. Caleb pushes me back, away from him.

'Raven, don't you dare.'

No. If he thinks I'm going to hide while they fight, he doesn't know me. I'm so scared I'm shaking, but they can't see that. This is it, I'm going to fight.

Mark says, his eyes on the woods, 'Luca, take Raven and go. Get her to the camp and then come back.'

No. I growl again, low in my throat.

'I can take all of you,' says Luca. She's staring at the woods as well; her longsword is in her hands. Eliza's eyeing the trees warily, her hands are empty, she fights close-combat like Mark but she's not nearly as good. She's crouched slightly, her eyes fixed.

'I have to stay,' says Mark, he's not shaking but I can feel the strain in his voice. 'Cairn went into the woods, I can't leave without—'

Something shifts in the darkness of the woods. Everyone's silent. In the trees I see a glint of eyes, glazed sharply white in the firelight, and then they're gone.

Hero's crouched beside Kestrel's body staring at the woods, her eyes steady and dark. 'Give me a weapon.' Her voice is low and strange.

Mark glances back at her. 'Give her the spear. Eliza, get behind me. Caleb, do what you have to do. Anything they throw at us, you send it right back.'

Caleb nods. He flicks his hand and the spear glides back towards Hero and hovers in the air in front of her. She grasps it, weighs it in her hands. It's five feet long and has sharp knives tied to each end. Mark taught me how to use it in training. *Throw from the shoulder.*

There's shifting from within the trees. I see a hand move in the dark.

'Luca,' says Mark. 'Go. *Now.*' His knuckles are pale on his knife-hilt. She looks at him, I can't read her face in the darkness. I know she doesn't want to leave him here.

Then something rolls out of the forest towards us.

All the knives around Caleb's head jerk forward in the air, and then stop dead. The thing has stopped rolling. It's bulky and long, like a log, kicked and floppy, it's in the shadow of the trees and so dark I can't—

Mark takes a hoarse, rattling breath, like he's been shot. One of the knives drops from his hand. I see it catch the light.

Cairn. The thing is Cairn.

Her clothes are dirty and soaked in blood, *red* blood, Guardsman-blood, but the blood matting her hair is silver. The back of her head is flat. Part of her skull is gone and she's covered in blood and her eyes are open and empty and staring, full of stars.

She's dead.

The air in my chest is ice and my veins are on fire and my head is light, spinning, and Cairn is dead.

Luca makes a terrible high-pitched noise like a strangled scream. Eliza is silent, staring at Cairn open-eyed in the grass. Caleb is shaking uncontrollably like he's going to fall. Cairn's eyes are blank and do not recognise me.

'Cairn Abernathy.' A young man's voice comes from the trees. 'That was her name, correct?'

Cairn stares at me with her dead, empty eyes in her crushed head.

'She was invulnerable,' says the voice, lightly, from within the trees, curious. 'Unbreakable skin and bones. That was what we were told. And yet . . .' He kicks Cairn's body with his toe. I hear Mark make that horrible half-scream in his throat again. Cairn rolls over so that her face is pressed into the earth, and the wound stares up from the back of her head like a monster's eye.

'She didn't give you up,' says the voice, and I look up and it's a man in a grey uniform, standing above Cairn in the shadow of the trees. His machine gun pointed straight into

Caleb's face. 'We asked her where you were, over and over again, but she wouldn't say a word. We asked her who she was protecting. After a long time, she told us it was *the child*. The child . . . I'm willing to bet that's her right there.'

He gestures towards me with the gun and the violin-screech of terror in my head gets high enough to block out everything. I can't think. Caleb pushes me further behind him, his hands shaking.

'Why would the chief bitch of the scum of the earth be out here protecting a *child*?'

'Caleb,' says Mark, his voice is strained like knives in his throat, 'Caleb, *now*—'

'Don't!'

Everyone goes still. I turn my head the slightest tiny bit to see out of the corner of my eye. Hero's on her feet over Kestrel's body, pointing the spear at the Guardsman.

'Don't do it,' she says breathlessly. She shakes her hair out of her eyes but her hands are steady. 'There are more of them. In the trees. I can feel them.'

The Guardsman looks at her and smiles.

'Very good,' he says.

'We've met,' says Hero, and her face is cold and so are her eyes. The hatred in her is thick as blood, it scares me.

The Guardsman licks his lips.

'I tasted you,' he says, softly. 'Yes. I remember your blood.'

The way he says *blood* is sickening, it grows claws, sinks into the earth and stays there, in the salt air.

'You were in the patrol car,' says Hero. 'By the tavern, days ago. You didn't know what I was. I fooled your whole patrol.' Spite in her voice and snarl.

He smiles again, and the way he does it, his teeth look almost silver.

'You tasted of salt,' he says. 'Human blood is salt, but gods' blood is *sweet*, so sweet. I couldn't taste it in yours, but it was there. I know that now. Soft on my tongue, and *deep* . . .'

Hero flinches. 'Stop.'

' – deep, deep and *sweet*, I could taste everything of you there, the beat of your heart, the raw *meat* of you—'

'You were in the tower,' says Hero. The knuckles in her right hand, the one gripping the spear, have gone pale, bloodless, like Mark's. 'The black tower. You were *blind*, I *saw* you. Joshua melted your *face*, I saw the blood—'

'And the pain,' he says. 'Oh, you should have felt it, the pain was exquisite. It was beautiful. The whole world was white agony, and I was alight within it, a mote of dust, burning . . .'

He raises his hands, pale and wide and clean, and lets the machine gun drop to his side on his hip, and I stare at his hands. They're shimmering, pale as moonlight, *pearlescent*, that was in our father's dictionary too, and I'm going mad again—

'*LUCA!*' roars Mark, turning, and suddenly the world is on fire.

Luca vanishes. The roar of the sea is drowned under gunfire and I'm frozen to the ground, waiting for the punch of a bullet in my stomach, but there's nothing. Out of the corner of my eye I see knives buried in the earth, hilt-deep. Caleb's knives.

Caleb.

He's staring fixedly into the trees, his hands raised. As I watch I see the glimmer of the air, the silvery rain, except it isn't *rain*, but bullets. They hurtle out of the trees towards us and when they get within ten yards of us they fall. Caleb is swatting them aside with his mind, but there are too many for him to stop them all. I see one pass straight over Mark's head as he runs towards the Guardsman, one passes so close by my ear I hear the *pop*.

And Mark is screaming and lunging with his knife whilst the Guardsman just watches him and smiles, and Caleb's eyes are bloodshot with the strain, and I—

What the hell am I doing?

I'm just standing here behind them, useless, *protected*—

I run, hearing Caleb shout my name. Hesitantly at first and then quick, over the death-rattle of bullets. I have to get to Mark, because I do not like the way the Guardsman is smiling, not at all. Mark is still running towards him, that terrible fury-grief in his face, and Cairn is lying facedown in the grass.

Everything is so slow. They are human-slow but I am wolf-quick.

Luca appears behind me as I run. I hear her scream, pain or rage I don't know. I don't even turn. If I turn I'll die, I know that for sure. I'm running towards Mark and the Guardsman, they're the only two things in the world.

The Guardsman looks towards me as I come closer, he's still smiling. He raises his gun.

Just as his finger touches the trigger I transform, quick as lightning, rear up in his face and rake at him with my claws. I don't even know what I've turned into, I can feel teeth in my head, long and sharp, scales on my legs.

He reels backwards, his face is covered in blood, gristle beneath my claws, his gun fires into the earth and I hear Mark shout my name.

Caleb cries out and I turn, terrified.

But no, it's not him, it's Eliza kneeling on the ground with her chest covered in blood. Her eyes are wide and black. She looks at me. My mouth is open and I realise there's blood dripping from my fangs.

Luca vanishes with Hero struggling in her arms, her spear in one hand and Kestrel's limp ankle grasped tight in the other, and then they're gone, and for a moment everything's silent. The whisper of the sea emerges again from under a sheen of terror, slow and singing and sweet.

And then Mark screams.

I've never heard him scream like that before, and the way his eyes meet Eliza's feels like there's a line in the air connecting them, thin and silvery, a rope of pain.

At last it cuts off. The world breaks again and emerges to the rattle of gunfire, the Guard are still firing at us, and this time more and more bullets are getting through Caleb's wall of air, his eyes are wide and black in the light with the strain. Luca appears behind Mark and grabs him by the neck, she vanishes again with him.

Eliza's lips are moving, silent in the air. *Raven*, she's trying to say, she was the one who taught me to read lips. *Get Raven.*

The Guardsman beneath me is panting, his breath thick with pain, and reaching for his gun. Maybe he wants to shoot me. The thought doesn't seem to mean much. I lean down and bite at his hand, he screams, I taste blood and gristle, I want to be sick.

Eliza. Eliza is what matters. I lope towards her and realise dully I'm a crocodile. Bullets scream over my head, maybe some hit me, I'm shaking so badly I can't feel them.

'Raven,' she whispers when I get near. Her hand is on her chest, covered in greyish blood. I just stare at her.

I take a breath, the word in my head is *Kestrel*. I try to think of what it means but before I can Luca's standing above us holding Caleb and she grabs my head and he takes Eliza's hand and we're gone.

CHAPTER 12

Inheritance

I'm sitting in a tall chair, my feet just reach the ground. The light is blue. The light.

'*Raven . . .*'

It feels like I'm waking up but I can't be, because I haven't been asleep. The hours have vanished and now they're back, time has started again, and I'm here. Sitting in a chair, in blue light. The *light*.

'Raven.'

'No, she's not talking to me. You try.'

I can still taste blood in my mouth, but my hands are clean, like Cairn said they'd be. Someone has washed me. Someone's gentle hands, soapy, I remember the touch.

The light is blue because the canvas is blue.

I'm in a tent.

'*Raven . . .*'

I wish they would stop talking. So long as everything's quiet I can keep my mind clear and I won't have to think about anything.

I swing my feet below the edge of the chair, my toes are bare, they touch the grass. Pain is everywhere, dull and pulsing. The skin of my hand is red raw from a wound a strange boy made a thousand years ago and the back of my right leg is throbbing bluntly, a hammer against my nerves. The soreness, the ache. I feel like I've been punched all over.

And *Cairn*.

Count to fifty, one hundred, two hundred, waves on a beach. Waves on a beach. My thoughts are calm and mean nothing.

The voices have stopped now.

I'm in a tent.

We were on a hill, at night. Luca had dropped me when we appeared, fresh from the cliff top, and had run to Eliza's side. Eliza's chest was covered in blood and she was taking long shuddering breaths, her eyes wide and black, blood everywhere.

Luca was screaming at Hero. '*Heal her! Please, heal her—*'

Below us the valley glittered with tents and little fires. I could hear the murmur of voices. Thousands of people. The camp, the camp of the resistance.

We're in the camp.

I slide off the chair and on to the grass. The tent is silent. Outside I can hear voices, but they're meaningless, they talk but don't speak. Here I am safe, they can't touch me.

Touch.

Blood in my mouth, and gristle—

It's only a memory. Memories can't hurt you, that's what Caleb always says, and Eliza . . . but no, Eliza's chest, and the *blood* . . .

Time vanishes again and when it comes back I'm kneeling on the ground, my mouth tastes sour, I'm staring at vomit beneath me, it's on my hands.

I wipe my hands on the grass, then I sit down and stare at the canvas, it rustles in the breeze. Daylight. The whole night came and went and now we're here. In the camp.

Just like Cairn wanted.

I don't want to think it but I do, it's a joke, a stupid sick joke, I want to throw up again, and no I can't think of Cairn I can't or I'll remember—

'Luca,' I whisper, through my hands. Sound comes back in a crashing wave, the way it did on the cliff top, and suddenly I can hear birdsong in the distance and the voices outside and within the tent there's breathing.

Someone slides off a bed next to me. I turn so suddenly my neck cricks.

She stands there awkwardly. Her hair is matted and her face is grimy, streaked with tears. She looks more tired than anyone I've ever seen. Hero.

'It's okay,' she says. 'They're coming back.'

Something catches in her throat and she covers her face with her sleeve. I look away and after a moment I hear the bed creak as she sits down on it. I turn, and there's Kestrel lying on the grass, the breathing-meat girl, blood-stained, water splashed over her mouth where Hero's tried to make her drink it.

'They left him there,' she says, after a moment. It sounds like it hurts for her to speak, it's like the pain in Mark's voice when he saw Eliza shot but somehow worse. 'They won't let me go back for him.'

I don't say anything. I remember the darkness of the woods, the way the Guardsmen with guns emerged like shadows from between the trees. Joshua went into those woods, where Guardsmen were hiding. He must be dead, too.

'Eliza.' Her name slips from my mind on to my tongue and flits out into the air and it's gone. 'She . . .'

My mind feels slick with blood. I remember her chest, the wounds, the black gleam of her pupils, and I press my hands to my face.

When I open them Hero's standing there with her hands outstretched towards me. They're covered in blood.

I look up at her.

'She's alive,' says Hero. 'I'm no use in a fight, you saw that back there, but never say I can't *heal*.'

My heart is hammering, relief pours over me like a water-fall, Hero's lips move again, maybe a smile maybe not. She looks at me and then looks away. Her eyes are black. I never noticed that before.

After that we sit in silence.

'He's ready for you now.'

'Took him long enough.'

'Luca—'

'Fine.' She coughs, and when she speaks again her voice is smooth, louder, carefully polite. 'We'd be honoured to see him.'

Footsteps, shuffling flap of canvas. Someone leaves the tent.

Caleb's voice, urgent. '*Luca*, you can't—'

'I know. I'll be respectful.' She sounds resentful.

I open my eyes blearily as someone comes into the tent. Mark, sitting cross-legged by the flap, gets to his feet hastily, stretching out his hand to the man who enters.

'Anthony. Thank you for seeing us. We know you must be busy, it's a difficult time . . .'

Anthony? I remember the name, it flutters up from under-neath everything, from a thousand years ago. Cairn was worried about him, she was worried about what he would do if he saw me. Eliza said Cairn would be able to deal with him. But she can't now.

Anthony regards Mark coolly. He's tall, grey-haired, ageless in the way that Cairn was too. 'You'll understand,' he says at last, 'if I can't touch you.'

Mark lowers his hand. His eyes are deeply shadowed, his face drawn in lack of sleep, or grief.

'Of course,' says Mark finally.

The man called Anthony turns to Eliza. He has a wide smile that does not reach his eyes. He moves with a smooth, precise grace, a practised charm. 'Eliza Ehler. A pleasure.'

Eliza. I try to sit up but someone on my other side pushes me back down. I twist uncomfortably in the grass to see Hero's hand on my shoulder, her eyes on Anthony, Kestrel lying silent at her feet.

I turn my head the other way and see Eliza. Joy and relief pulse through me at the sight of her, *alive*, a miracle. She's on her feet, but she looks weak, her face is bloodless, feverish. She's pressed one hand to her chest, to where she was shot, and she's holding herself oddly, wincing slightly at the movement.

Anthony says to her, 'I knew your father.'

'I know you did, *elioka*.' I've never heard the word before, she says it respectfully, but none of that is mirrored in her eyes.

Anthony studies her curiously, as if watching for hesitation or weakness. His voice has changed, become curt. 'Where was he born, can you tell me?'

Eliza looks back at him. 'A town on the east coast. Iolanthe. His father was a fisherman.'

'I met you once when you were a child, just after your parents died. After Cairn took you under her wing.'

'I remember, *elioka*.'

'Do you remember what I said to you, then? When I walked into the tent?'

Eliza straightens, and looks him steadily in the eye. 'You said, *you're luckier than you'll ever understand. Little one,* you called me.' I don't think he knows her well enough to hear the contempt in her voice.

Anthony studies her for a moment, then says, 'All right, it's her.'

Only then do I realise that two men have walked into the tent behind him. They're holding knives. Caleb's eyes are fixed on them both, one hand pushing Luca slightly behind him, towards my bed.

'I thought Cairn was with you,' says Anthony lightly.

'She was. She decided to stay behind. She said there were things she needed to do.'

I see Caleb and Luca exchange a look, but no one says anything. Hero's grip on my shoulder is iron. I don't breathe.

'And those things were?' Anthony asks, quietly.

Eliza smiles slightly. It shocks me how much I believe that smile.

'I don't ask questions, *elioka*.'

'I'm sure you don't.' He turns away. 'Mark . . . Lorcan, was it? I used to have a better memory for these things.'

Mark doesn't stretch out his hand again. 'Mark Leran, *elioka*.'

Anthony turns to the twins. Caleb takes his eyes off the men with knives at last.

'Caleb Herath,' he says, at Anthony's look of polite expectation. 'And these are my sisters.'

He doesn't turn toward me, doesn't introduce me, tries as hard as he can to get Anthony not to look at me. Anthony does anyway, examining me appraisingly. I look up at him, into his cold grey eyes. I don't say anything. I know it's not safe. *He might try to hurt her*, Eliza said. Why would he hurt me?

'Ah yes,' he says softly. 'Lorelei's daughter.'

Luca twitches. Caleb says, 'You knew our mother?'

Anthony smiles thinly. 'I knew her very well. A fine woman. A terrible loss.'

Silence in the tent. Caleb's face has gone carefully blank. Luca has stopped dead. Anthony glances at her, then turns at last towards Hero beside me.

'The Fitzgerald girl,' he says. 'You're sure it was wise to bring her here?'

Over his shoulder, Mark and Eliza exchange glances.

'Cairn told us where to find the camp,' says Eliza.

'She told you to bring *her* to the camp?' Anthony sweeps around to look at Eliza, his eyes suddenly cold, piercing. 'You're sure? She gave you explicit permission?'

Hero's eyes burn, moving between Eliza and Anthony, her fists clenched by her side.

'Yes,' says Eliza, calmly.

'Because obviously,' says Anthony, 'you would never have brought a stranger here *without* explicit permission. That would be terribly dangerous. *Treasonous.*' His tongue traces the word, giving it a slight hiss. I see Mark's hand move almost casually towards the knife at his belt.

'Of course,' says Eliza.

They stare at each other for a very long time.

At last, Anthony says, 'I thought there was a boy.'

Eliza shook her head.

'A shame.'

'Indeed.'

Anthony tilts his head. 'You have no idea of when Cairn will come back?'

'None, I'm afraid. She'll return when she's ready.'

'I'm sure she will,' says Anthony, and smiles again. He claps his hands together and looks around at us all. He doesn't seem to have noticed Kestrel at all. 'Well, I think it's best if you all stay up here for now. People aren't used to seeing unfamiliar faces in the camp. I don't want them to worry we've been found. That might cause a panic, and we wouldn't want that, would we?'

'We would not,' says Eliza, gravely.

He gives her another slow smile, then turns and sweeps from the tent. His henchmen go with him, eyes fixed on the back of his head. Mark moves to speak, but Eliza raises a hand to stop him. We listen to their footsteps until they are too faint to hear.

When at last they're gone, Mark says, 'Damn him. He knows.'

'Yes,' says Eliza. She sits down slowly on the grass again, then suddenly gasps and stops dead, trembling. Her hand goes to her chest, her breath coming in quick agonised rasps.

Mark bends beside her. 'Hero, please, could you . . .?'

'Of course,' says Hero. She moves towards Eliza, one hand outstretched, wiping her face.

'What do you mean he *knows?*' I ask quietly.

'He knows Cairn's dead,' says Mark, watching Eliza as Hero closes her eyes in concentration. 'He's her brother. Maybe he knew the moment she died. He used to have very accurate premonitions.'

'He's her *brother?*' says Caleb.

'Yeah,' says Mark. 'Younger by ten years. Not that age carries a lot of weight with your kind, I've heard.'

He tries to smile, but fails.

'If he's her brother . . .' Caleb presses his hands to his face. 'I mean, surely we *have* to tell him, if he—'

'We can't tell him,' says Eliza hoarsely, pushing her hair out of her eyes. Hero's hand is still pressed to her chest. 'It's what she'd want. Caleb, look at me. It's what we have to do.'

There's a silence. Hero opens her eyes and sits up, taking her hands from Eliza's arm, looking suddenly drained. Mark throws her a flask of water and strips of beef jerky from the pack.

'Anthony was head doctor here for years,' says Eliza, 'that's what it means, *elioka*, healer, but it's . . . an honorific. A Karkaran word. It means, *most learned healer*, something like that. It's what he liked to be called.'

'And why—'

'He disagrees with Cairn,' says Eliza tersely. 'About the Guard.'

Caleb looks blankly back at her. Luca sits down on the grass and puts her arm around me. I lean into her. Behind me, Kestrel still breathes in and out, in and out.

'Cairn always thought the Guard could be defeated,' says Eliza, sitting up – I see everyone in the room flinch at the past tense – 'if we could show the people that we were better than them. Or that they were worse than us, whatever. She used to . . . plant gods and half-breeds in human villages, make them reveal themselves, so that the Guard would descend and the humans could see what they were really like. Oh, she'd get everyone out in time,' she adds quickly, at Luca's horrified expression, 'but you see the strategy. The Guard are only powerful so long as they have human support.'

'And I told you before,' says Hero, her voice almost as hoarse as Eliza's, 'there's no point. There's nothing you could do to make humans stop hating us. They'll turn a blind eye to whatever the Guard do, so long as it keeps them safe from us.'

Caleb says, 'And Anthony thinks . . .?'

'That we can only defeat them the way they defeated us, twenty years ago. Fire and blood. Revenge for our slaughtered parents.'

There's a pause. Then Luca speaks at last, very quietly. 'I agree.'

Eliza looks at her for a long moment.

'If they knew she was dead,' she says at last, 'there'd be panic here, riots, who the hell knows, but *he'd* be in charge by the end of it, I can promise you that. Even if the whole camp was ashes and dust. Believe me. I knew him. And Cairn certainly knew him.'

There's a silence.

Caleb says in a low voice, 'I can't understand how they killed her.'

'It wore her out,' says Eliza. 'Being invulnerable, it cost her effort, it drained her. She was just going for a walk in the woods, you know how restless she was. If they captured her . . . held her for an hour . . . she wouldn't have lasted that long.'

Mark winces.

'I'll kill him,' says Luca suddenly. 'If it takes me my whole life, I'll kill him. The one who kicked her.'

There's another pause. Hero looks up and opens her mouth to speak, but before she can, Mark says, 'Don't say it.'

'What?'

'You're going to ask to go back and get that stupid kid. Don't say it. He's *dead*, Hero.'

A silence.

'He's not,' says Hero quietly.

'What, have you had a premonition, or—?'

'No. I don't get premonitions. I'd just . . . I'd know. If he were dead.' She takes a deep breath, closes her eyes. 'I couldn't *not* know it. And he's not.'

'We can't go back for him,' says Eliza. 'You know that, Hero. If he was in those woods, the Guard captured him. We can't risk it.'

No one speaks for a long time. Hero presses her hands to her face, but says nothing more.

And now I know I have to speak, because I have to know the truth, but I can't say anything.

Ask it. Ask the question. Cairn is inside my head, looking at me, a map spread out in front of her, like in our strategy lessons, drawing with a stick in the dirt. *Courage, Raven,* she says. *Courage is the key to any battle. Cowards win by accident, or luck, or the sacrifice of braver men.*

I blurt it into the silence, the thing I need to say. My palms are sweaty, I'm so scared and I don't even know why yet, not really.

'Cairn didn't want Anthony to take over from her.'

Eliza raises her head slowly to look at me. The silence in the tent has changed suddenly, become harder, colder. Mark is looking at me, but I keep my eyes on Eliza. I have to look brave.

At last, she shakes her head.

'Who *did* she want?' I ask, trying to sound casual. My heart is beating very fast.

A long, long quiet. Caleb gets slowly to his feet, but I can't look at him. I see him exchange a look with Luca over my shoulder. *Courage*, whispers Cairn to me, inside my head, *courage, girl, that's all that matters in the end.*

I hold Eliza's gaze.

'You know, sweetheart,' says Eliza quietly. Everyone is watching us. 'Surely you know that by now.'

The silence in the tent is deep and dizzying. No one is surprised, or angry. No one is shouting *What?* or asking Eliza what she's talking about. Luca is stroking my head very slowly.

Use your brain, says Cairn. *They know. Look at them.*

They know. They always knew, my whole life. They were just waiting for me to figure it out.

My heart is cold inside my chest. I can't breathe.

'I don't understand,' I say, and my voice is so small and not-mine. 'I don't get it.'

'Raven,' says Caleb. 'Raven . . .'

'Any of you would be better. *Anyone.*' My voice is rising despite myself. 'You're cleverer than me – Mark's better at fighting—'

'I'm cleverer than you *now*,' says Eliza calmly. I hate the look in her eyes, the measuring shrewdness in them. I look away. 'In ten years you'll be way beyond me. I've watched you grow up. I've taught you, I've seen you learn. Your mind works faster than you could know, growing up around us. Cairn picked us because we were the best she had. She chose us to take care of you.'

'But I'm not . . .' I can't breathe, I can't think. I'm sick of being watched, I wish they'd all look away from me, I wish they were all gone. 'I'm *nothing*, why would she want me?

What did I do? I'm not . . . I'm not special, I'm not ready, I'm—'

'Don't say that,' says Luca quietly, beside me, her hand still on my head. 'You're *everything*, Raven. Haven't we always told you that?'

I twist round to look at her, my stomach full of a sick hurt I can't name. 'You said yes to this?'

Luca looks at Caleb over my shoulder, then says, 'We both did.'

'*Why?*'

'Because there are more important things than what we want,' says Luca. She's stopped stroking my head now and is looking straight into my eyes, unflinching. 'Of course we didn't want this for you. We hoped Cairn would pick someone else, anyone else . . . but then you got older, and we saw—'

She cuts off, glancing at Caleb again. Her jaw is set, her face pale.

'They saw she was right,' says Mark softly. I turn back to him, not wanting to look at Luca. 'Cairn was right about you. I wasn't sure, either, not at the beginning, but you are . . . you can't know it yet, Raven, but you are *prodigious*.'

He sinks down to his knees and looks me in the eye, level with me, like he did when I was younger. I stare back at him. He speaks calmly, and it makes my heart beat a little slower.

'Cairn sent those other children away so you wouldn't grow up around anyone your own age. She didn't want you to know how incredible you were. Kids like that grow up arrogant and stupid. And you *still* could have grown spoiled, and selfish, and cowardly with all you've been through – but you didn't.' He smiles at me, so tired and sad. 'The number of people who could survive what you've survived – being hunted by the Guard, seeing your mother get killed – and come out with your sense of right and wrong, your courage . . . There's not a lot of real goodness in this world, but *you*, Raven, you've got it. I believe that.'

There's a deep silence. They're waiting for me to speak but I don't have anything to say.

'You're only ten,' says Eliza at last, glancing at Mark, 'and you're cleverer than half the people in this camp already, and braver than even more. You can nearly beat Mark in every fight you have, you can tell truth from lies almost as well as I can and more than that – no, *look* at me, Raven—'

'I don't want to,' I whisper. 'I don't want to lead anyone. *You* should do it. I don't want—' My head is full of Cairn still, her crushed skull, her staring eyes, and I can feel tears in my eyes again, I hate myself. 'I don't want to—'

'Look at me, Raven,' says Eliza, from above me.

I raise my head, take a slow deep breath and meet her eyes.

'I love you,' she says, and tries to smile at last, through her exhaustion and her pallor and her pain. 'Everyone who has ever met you loves you. You can't understand what that means, you're too young, but there it is.' She shrugs, then winces. Mark's hand goes to her shoulder, steadying her, with his eyes still on mine, and she grasps his hand and keeps talking. 'You're powerful, but that's not what really matters. Cleverness and skill and sheer power aren't what matter. If they were, you'd be right, one of us would have been Cairn's heir. But they're not. What matters is *love*.'

Love. I can't believe this. I stare at her. I'm not stupid, I want to say, you've got to do better than that. You all loved Cairn and she's dead. But I can't speak.

'You make people *want* to follow you, to do what you say, to do anything for you. None of us can do that.' She gestures to the twins, watching me and waiting, to Mark with his calm gaze. 'You had all of us captivated by you by the time you were five years old. *Cairn* loved you. Do you know how many people in the world Cairn loved?'

'You,' I whisper, before I think better of it. My eyes are full of tears, I can't stop them. 'She loved *you*.'

Eliza looks stricken. I see a flash of her face in the firelight from last night, the loss there when Cairn spoke to her too sharply, a shard of memory lodged inside my head.

I turn to Hero, desperate. 'You didn't want this. Last night, when Eliza told you, you said it was a terrible idea. *Tell them*.'

'I didn't say it was a terrible idea,' says Hero quietly, looking at Eliza. 'I said you were too young.'

'Yeah! Yeah, I am!' I feel stupid, a spoilt child stamping my foot and wanting the truth to go away, so frightened. I can feel the weight hovering over my head to crush me, a terrible hawk-like shadow. 'I'm *ten*—'

'No one's asking you to start leading armies, Raven,' says Mark, still crouching, looking at me. I stare at him. *Armies*. 'But the resistance people need to know there's a different choice. When Anthony starts trying to build up power, and he will soon, they'll follow him if they think there's no one else. But *you* were the one Cairn wanted.' He looks so tired and he rubs his face. 'She thought she had years, *decades . . .* I thought she'd live forever. We all did. But if she's gone' – his face creases with pain as he says it, but his voice doesn't break – 'I'd follow you over Anthony any day, Raven, and I don't care how old you are. I trust you.'

'You shouldn't,' I say, and my voice trembles. '*I* don't trust me.'

A silence, shivering. The weight of years-old secrets, spilt at last on to the floor of Mark's old blue tent. I feel so drained, tired, alone. I've never felt lonely before, not in my whole life – not with them, my family, who kept me safe, who never lied to me—

Everything breaks and I start crying at last, dry sobs into the silence of the tent. I can feel them all watching me. I *hate* them.

At last, Caleb comes and hugs me. I hug him back, and I can feel what he's trying to say, what none of the others have said – *I'm sorry* – and I'm still crying. Luca strokes my head and I feel like a stupid kid in their arms. I'm so scared, more scared than I've ever been. I feel smaller than ever, a stupid fragile human girl, because I know what they don't know yet: that Cairn was wrong. I'm not the right person at all, how could she think I was? There's no *goodness* in me, I'm nothing, I'm not even clever, I'm just scared and stupid and weak and cowardly. They wanted someone to believe in because they're desperate and frightened, but it's not me, of course it's not me, don't they *know* me?

But if they want me to do it—

If they *need* me to do it, to be this magic other Raven they all think I am—

Then what can I do but try, for them? I love them.

Cairn knew that. She knew I'd do it, for them.

Outside, the wind on the hilltop is harsh and cold, and inside my head Cairn stares at me with glassy dead eyes, unforgiving. Her voice reverberates in my head, like music. *Her hands will always be clean,* she says. *She won't be a child forever. There will be bloodshed . . . there will be blood . . .*

CHAPTER 13

Mala Kralovna

The camp is the most beautiful thing I've ever seen.

I sit staring down at it for almost an hour. I try to count the tents and fail. A thousand, two thousand, maybe five thousand, who knows. Little fires burn in clearings between the rows of tents, like village squares, and kids play around them; kids older and younger than me, boys and girls. I wonder if any of them are the kids who travelled with us when I was younger, the ones Cairn sent back when she decided she wanted me as her heir.

I take a slow breath, let the thought move into my head and out and away.

Good, says Cairn, inside my head.

The tents are all kinds of colours, dreamcatchers and ribbons and flags hang from them to mark them out, signs with names on. It's in a valley, like the bottom of a well, surrounded by four green hills. A river runs through it, gleaming in the low autumn sun. It must have rained yesterday. Mud flows down the hill in slow, thick rivulets.

I turn to Caleb, sitting beside me. 'I want to go down there.'

'We can't, sweetheart. Anthony told us not to, remember?'

Anthony. His name makes me think of Cairn again, and what Eliza said in the tent, and then all the frightened voices in my head rise and rise until I can't hear anything.

I take long deep breaths until they go away. Calm is the first thing I have to be if I'm going to be a leader they want.

I can't be a stupid frightened kid anymore. That's the new Rule Number One, the place in my head where Cairn used to be.

There's only one tent up here and that's ours, the blue one that used to be Mark's. There are six people gathered around a fire that burns silver-white. They're here as watchers, looking down from the hill to make sure there are no Guardsmen coming near. If there are, we have to pack up and leave and move the whole camp somewhere else. There are three other fires, more watchers, on the other hills.

'It's clever,' says Caleb to me in a low voice, as we sit down, 'because the camp is hidden behind the hills, you see? So the Guard wouldn't be able to see it.'

One of the watchers is on the other side of the hilltop, a grey-haired woman with sharp brown eyes, talking quietly to Eliza. Their eyes keep flickering towards me.

I ask even though I think I already know. 'What is Eliza telling her?'

Caleb doesn't meet my eyes. 'We have to start spreading the word.'

'About me?'

He makes himself look at me, smiles without eyes. 'Yes. It's all okay. It's to keep you safe, in case Anthony tries anything. We're all here. No one's going to ask you to do anything.'

I don't believe him anymore. I raise my head and try to breathe slowly. My palms are all slick again. Calm, I have to be calm.

After a while the grey-haired woman comes over to our fire. Caleb gets to his feet, but her eyes are on me, looking me up and down. Then she smiles. 'Well, *mala kralovna,*' she says. 'It's an honour.'

The words are Karkaran, from the cold southern lands across the sea. Eliza taught me as much of the language as she knew when I was little, which wasn't much, but it's enough

for this. *Little queen*, this woman called me. I straighten my
back and try to look proud instead of scared.

Caleb shakes her hand. 'Caleb.'

'Anna,' she says, and I remember there are no surnames in
the camp, that's what Mark said. 'So, she's the one Cairn
wants?'

Caleb tries to smile again. It doesn't work. I can see the
blue-black shadows under his eyes.

Anna is examining me, her head tilted slightly. I raise my
chin. 'I think I can see it,' she says. 'Perhaps. You're a
shapeshifter?'

'Yes.'

'You can fight?'

I nod.

'You can read?'

I almost laugh. 'Of course I can read!'

Caleb shoots me a warning look, but Anna doesn't seem
offended. She smiles. 'I like her,' she says. 'Oh yes, I like her.
She has fire. As much as Cairn, and more than that Eliza, I
have to say. Does she scare you, *mala kralovna*?'

'Eliza?' I think about it, the coldness in her eyes when the
Guardsmen came through the woods with Cairn's body, the
way all feeling left her face. 'I think . . . she could be scary
if she wanted to be. But she doesn't.'

Anna smiles. 'I meant Cairn, *maladra*.' *Little one*. I try to
look taller and older. I am not little.

'No,' I say. 'Not anymore.'

Anna laughs, and we sit down, and then I think the test is
over.

I try to sit a little way away from Caleb and not to lean
against him. I want to look like a grown-up.

'How do they not see the fire?' I ask Caleb, as Anna and
some of the others pass lumps of charred fish around to us.

'Who?'

'The Guardsmen. If they came near here trying to attack. The camp is hidden by the hills, but they'd see the fire from here.'

'Good question,' says Anna, smiling, 'but no, they couldn't, not from this side of the boundary. Show her, Declan.'

Declan is another of the watchers. He reaches across the fire to shake my hand. 'You scared us before, let me tell you. Coming out of nowhere like that, right inside the boundary. We worried you might be Guard until we got close to you.'

I don't know what to say to that. 'What boundary?'

He gets up, leads me by the hand a few feet away from the fire. I can see Caleb watching him out of the corner of my eye. 'Close your eyes,' he says.

I look at him suspiciously. 'Why?'

He grins. 'I'm not going to hurt you, *mala kralovna*. Don't want to piss you off, do I?'

I didn't see Eliza talking to him. Someone else must have told him. Word spreads fast here.

'Step forward,' he says, and I do. I wait for him to say something else but everything's quiet. *One, two three,* I stand there with my eyes closed.

Silence. I open my eyes and turn around.

He's gone. The *camp* is gone.

All of it, the thousands of beautiful tents, the children playing and the fires, vanished. The valley is bare and empty, just grass and the lonely silver river, everyone's gone. Our blue tent is gone too, and the strange pale fire, and Caleb, the hilltop is empty and silent, I'm alone—

No, no, no—

My blood is cold and shivery, but I walk forward slowly, the silence deep, my heart beating too fast. This is some kind of trick, it has to be. *Stay calm,* that's Rule Number One. Whole camps don't just vanish like Luca. Caleb would never let me be taken away.

I close my eyes, I have to stay calm, *stay calm*, I can do this. I step forward again—

– and there's a rushing noise like emerging from underwater and suddenly they're back, appeared out of nowhere, and the camp behind him has un-vanished from the air, just as it was. They're all watching me in silence, gathered around the fire. I stare back at them. Caleb is on his feet, looking very strained.

'Gotta hand it to Cairn,' says Anna, getting to her feet, 'she knows what she's doing. I've seen grown men scared out of their wits by that trick.' She shakes my hand. 'All right, *mala kralovna*?'

I try to smile, wonder if she can feel how fast my heart's beating through the skin of my wrist.

'How do you *do* that?'

'It's a pretty big camp. There are, what' – she looks around – 'twenty people here who can make things invisible, with their demesne. On their own they can only make themselves invisible, maybe a couple of other people, but if they all work together, concentrate very hard, they kind of . . . *compound* each other. They can disguise the whole camp.'

'So the Guard can't see us at all?'

'Not unless they get really close. And if they do, we can see *them*.'

She pulls out a long knife, stained with dried blood, from her belt and shows it to me, grinning. Caleb steers me away from her after that.

I walk along the boundary for a long time, trying not to talk to any of them in case they ask me more questions. I become an owl, a beautiful snowy white one, and fly above the camp, looking down at it, at the kids and the grown-ups talking and laughing in the setting sun. I fly over the boundary again and again, watching the camp vanish and reappear, the silence lifting and falling. It's amazing.

For a while I can pretend no one knows who I am, but

when I look down, Caleb and the watchers are there, looking at me, silent and awed. I don't like it.

There aren't many shapeshifters in the world, Eliza said. Is that why I'm special? Maybe if I had Luca or Caleb's demesne, she wouldn't have chosen me. I wish so much that I could ask her.

When I land at last, Anthony's back, with a group of about twenty people all sitting around him. He's talking very intently to a little girl, who nods and shakes her head as he talks, too scared to speak herself. Luca is sitting across the fire from us, watching them darkly.

'Where are Eliza and Mark?' I ask Caleb.

'Gone for a walk. You know how Mark gets. And we agreed we wouldn't be alone, any of us.' Caleb looks at me sternly. 'Which *you* need to start remembering, *mala kralovna*.'

I stare at him, alarmed.

'*Don't* call me that, stupid!'

He grins and I punch him a little in the arm, relieved. He laughs and tickles me, and I collapse giggling.

'I can still pick you up and throw you thirty feet whenever I want,' he says. 'Just remember that, if you think all of this means you can steal my dinner. *And* I've got a better aim than you.'

I try to tickle him back, but I'm no good at it and he gets me under the arms again.

Then suddenly he's serious, looking at me.

'I think you were awake last night,' he says, quietly so the others can't hear. 'Before the Guardsmen came. I saw your eyes open. You were listening to Eliza and Cairn.'

I look at my feet. I think for a second he's going to be angry with me, but he doesn't sound angry. I can feel his warmth, next to me.

'Raven,' he says, softly, 'do you want to ask me a question?'

I look up at him. The question worms its way slowly out

of the box I put it in, inside my head, from beneath the taste of blood and Cairn's crushed head and Eliza's blood-soaked shirt. Eliza and Cairn, talking while Hero lay curled beside Kestrel's sleeping body. Firelight and whispering. A long, long time ago.

'Our father,' I say, at last.

'Yeah.'

The words come out slowly, painfully. 'He was . . . a Guardsman?'

Caleb hesitates.

'Yeah. Before we were born.'

'What happened?'

'Our mother.'

He's watching me very intently.

'Was he . . . was he trying to kill her? When he met her?'

'I don't know,' he says. 'I don't know the whole story. Not even Cairn did. Our mother was a resistance fighter, and Cairn knew her, and then she left, and the next thing Cairn heard she'd had me and Luca. I don't know what happened, to make her fall in love with him.'

He puts his arm around my shoulder, and I lean into him.

'People make mistakes,' he says, softly. 'I know he loved her. He loved us, too, he didn't care what we were. We were his kids. And when you were born . . .'

He squeezes my shoulder. His voice has roughened.

'Luca and I were waiting outside the house, it was twilight, we could hear our mama screaming, we were so scared, and then we heard you crying, and ten minutes later he came out holding you. And the smile on his face, Raven, honestly. He said, *look at her hair*. You had a full head of hair already.'

He hugs me more tightly. I don't know what to say.

'He loved you,' he says. 'With his whole heart.'

'I know,' I say, but I don't, I don't even remember him.

For a while we just sit there in silence, by the crackling

white-flame camp fire. All I can think is: Cairn didn't want
us to be here.

'Why did they pick her?' I ask. 'In the beginning?'

'Who, Cairn?'

'Yeah.'

Caleb sits there for a moment. I know the look on his face,
I can tell he's running through the story in his head, stripping
out the parts he thinks I'm too young to hear.

'There was someone else,' he says at last. 'Before her. Irina,
her name was. Cairn was her lieutenant. Her deputy,' he adds,
at my confused look. 'Irina was like Anthony. She wanted to
fight back against the Guard, to stop the rebellion. It was
very bloody. There were too many humans, and too few of
us. Irina wanted to make everyone in the camp into a soldier.
But some of them were too old, or too sick, or too young.
People started resenting her.'

'But why did they want Cairn? If Cairn had worked for her?'

'Good question. Cairn was in charge of the rescue missions.'

'What rescue missions?'

He rubs his eyes. 'During the rebellion, I mean. Once the
resistance realised the Guard were coming north, she organ-
ised raids to get all the gods and half-breeds she could out
of the towns, before they could be killed. She brought them
all back here, to the camp. Half the people here are only alive
because of her.'

It's starting to come together in my head. 'So when Irina
died—'

'What makes you think she died?' says Caleb sharply.

I just look at him.

He rubs the back of his neck. 'Irina . . . started to get
paranoid. She thought everyone was against her. People who
complained about her started to disappear. Eliza's mother,
for one. Eliza still doesn't know where she's buried.'

I didn't know that. I examine it in my head, the horror of it, and Eliza's grave face.

'And then,' I say, finally, 'Irina tried to kill Cairn?'

Caleb nods again. 'There was open revolt. Nobody knows exactly what happened. Irina was dead by the end of it, and Cairn was in charge.'

There's quiet.

'It should have been Eliza,' I say. It's not a compliment, it's not even a wish, it's just the truth. I'll never be even a tenth as clever as her. 'Cairn should have chosen *her.*'

'You think so?'

'Yeah.'

'I did too, for a while,' he says. 'But Cairn was adamant. It had to be you. And if she says it's you, then I believe her, sweetheart.'

He kisses my head, and then we sit in silence for a while, eating lumps of charred fish.

I nod at Anthony. 'What's he doing?'

'Holding court,' says Luca darkly, from right behind me. I jump. I didn't know she'd vanished there. She ruffles my hair and sits down beside me. 'Sorry.'

I lean into Caleb's chest, and he strokes my head. He says to Luca, 'What do you mean *holding court?*'

'Everyone talking to him had a premonition in the last few hours. They have to tell him, it's camp law or something. So if someone sees something important, we all know about it.'

'Like what?' I ask, but I think I know. That sick feeling is back in my stomach again.

They exchange looks. 'Like an attack,' says Luca at last. 'Or like the river running out of fish, things like that. So they know to move the camp.'

My head is full of Cairn again, the monster's eye in the back of her head, and I have to take deep breaths. *Premonitions,* Mark said once, *will tell you what you're going to have for*

breakfast tomorrow, but not whether it's going to be poisoned.
Premonitions are evil, sneaky things. They leave out the important stuff. Caleb and Luca and I all get premonitions sometimes
and still none of us saw that Cairn was going to die. The
weight of the secret is heavy in my chest.

More people introduce themselves to me as darkness falls,
shaking my hand, looking me over curiously, asking me and
the twins questions, grinning, or testing me like Anna did.
People here don't trust easily, Eliza told me before we left the
tent. *Show them who you are, be open, and they'll respect
you for it.*

So I hold my head high and answer their questions,
wondering what Eliza's told them about me, what she's promised. Some of them call me *mala kralovna* too, sometimes
jokingly and sometimes not. That makes me feel sick and
nervous again so I stop thinking about it.

How many people have Eliza and Mark told about me? I
look down at the glittering lights of the camp below us, the
low roar of a thousand voices. It can't be many yet, I think,
not compared to the people in this camp. That makes me feel
slightly better.

A young man called Damien comes up and starts talking
to Luca. He's the reason the fire burns white, it's his demesne.
They use it because it doesn't make smoke, which could drift
over the boundary and reveal us by accident. Damien is talking
to Luca very enthusiastically about the different kinds of
wood you can use to make a fire when an older woman
detaches herself from Anthony's party and comes to say hello
to us.

Caleb gets up to receive her, throwing a look to Luca, who
sees it and moves towards us at once. I get to my feet.

'I'm Beth,' the older woman says to Caleb. She smiles. 'My
husband told me all about you.'

By her look back towards Anthony, I understand she means

him. This is Anthony's wife. I study her carefully. She looks kind and gentle. I wonder what she sees in him.

Luca shakes Beth's hand. 'It's an honour to meet you,' she says, with stiff, careful politeness. 'I'm Luca. Lorelei's daughter.'

'I know, child. You have your mother's face.' Beth studies the three of us with a scholar's interest. 'She was a gifted, brave woman. And your father was a good man. A very good man.'

Caleb's face is very empty. He, too, extends his hand to shake hers. 'Thank you.'

'Do you have everything you need? Anthony told me—'

But she stops. Someone's shouting at us, a rough voice from across the fire. I turn.

'Look, look! That's her! The wife!'

One of the men around the fire has just got to his feet. He sways slightly in the cold, his face pale, his cheeks reddened. He's wrapped in a big coat. He's been watching us for a while, I know from the way he looks at Caleb.

At once, Luca pushes me slightly behind her. On my other side, Anna and two of the other watchers have got to their feet. They step between me and the drunken man, their knives out, pushing me backwards away from the fight. *Mala kral-ovna*, I think, suddenly dizzy. I wanted to stop being protected, and now everyone in this whole *camp* wants me safe.

Beth turns slowly to look at the shouting man, her face set. 'Yes?'

The man grins drunkenly. Everyone around the campfire has fallen silent. He raises a finger to point at Beth, wobbly. 'Beth, right?'

'Yes,' says Beth, more coldly now. I can see her edging backwards, looking around. A couple more people have got to their feet, watching the man. 'What's it to you?'

The man in the big coat shakes his head, still grinning. He

picks his way through the watchers. Everyone stares at him but he doesn't seem to notice. Eventually he's very close to us, maybe five yards. Beth stands her ground, but Luca and Anna push me further behind them. Caleb's hand is on his knife.

'You're Beth?' the man says again. 'Anthony Abernathy's wife?'

And suddenly he's very steady, his hands on the buttons of his coat perfectly still.

I don't think he's drunk at all.

Beth nods slowly. She starts to take a step back, too late.

The man in the big coat turns quickly and looks at me. There's an odd look in his face, furtive, but then the shutters come down behind his eyes and it's gone. He turns back to Beth. She looks up at him, but his right hand is already in his coat. He takes a small pistol from his pocket. Their eyes meet. Then he raises his hand and shoots her in the head.

There's a shot but I don't hear it. All I see is her, dying.

It's so quick, like her head was made to burst. There's an explosion of silver, like rain hitting earth. It splatters his coat, splatters the grass.

Luca's behind me, her arms tighten around my chest like a snake, I can't breathe with fear.

The man turns around and looks at me again, and his eyes are such a bright blue. I've seen them before, I remember, staring out from the darkness of the trees in the woods on the cliff top—

A Guardsman.

A *crack* of bone, and time speeds up again. The world is moving quick-as-heartbeats, shining with colour. Behind me Luca lets me go and twists and vanishes and I see her appear on the Guardsman's other side. Beth's body hits the ground in a mess of silver blood. Luca grabs for the Guardsman's wrist, the one with the gun in it. Beneath us in the valley, distantly, I hear sudden screams, the rattle of gunfire, sobs. There are other Guardsmen hidden in the camp. The gunshot that killed Beth was their cue to start firing, to start *killing*, I—

Some part of me thinks *Mark Eliza Hero Kestrel* but the rest of me is bright and calm, clear water in sunlight.

I am on my feet.

Beth is lying on the ground, dead, her head is gone. Luca's grabbed the Guardsman's wrist and my whole body is a scream of terror, my nerves are electric wires, but my mind is clear and I feel myself changing, in the air, leaping towards the Guardsman, feet changing to claws, skin rough, teeth sharpening—

Someone screams. Blood in my mouth.

Blood in my mouth and—

The world returns. I'm a lion, crouching over the Guardsman. My teeth are in his throat. His blood is red and salty.

I retch and I'm a girl again. I crawl away from him. He stares at me. He clutches at his throat, the gushing blood black in the firelight. It pours over his hands, his neck, his coat.

His gun is lying on the ground. Luca picks it up and says, 'Look away, Raven.' Her voice is odd.

I look away and there's a bang. Blood splatters my arm.

Caleb is on the ground, he gets up on his knees. Everyone around the fire is frozen silent, there's only the fire left making noise, crackling white static. People are still screaming in the darkness around us, crying. I look down into the valley and see smoke. The tents are on fire. On the edge of the camp, at the foot of the hill, a woman crawls out of her tent blearily. Then there's a *crack* and her head explodes like Beth's. She falls. The twins don't see it, but I have no voice to tell them.

'Luca,' says Caleb hoarsely, 'Luca, they're here, they're in the whole camp. How the hell did they find us?'

She looks at him, shaking, and says nothing. Her hands hang slack and bloody by her side, trembling.

'Luca, there are *kids* here. You have to—'

'I know,' she says. She turns and looks at me, still holding the gun. She holds my gaze for a moment. I open my mouth, I want to say *please don't go* but there's blood on my lips, my teeth.

Another gunshot in the distance, a child crying. Luca's eyes are dark like mine in the firelight.

Then she vanishes.

Caleb crawls over to me, wraps me in his arms. He's shaking too. 'Raven.' Beth and the Guardsman's bodies are lying behind us, earth stained black and silver. 'Oh, Raven.'

More gunshots. People are screaming all around us. At the bottom of the hill, the woman's body is still lying on the ground. I tremble in his arms. I think I bit my tongue, I can taste sweet blood beneath the salt. My arms are leaden and cold.

He pulls back and looks me in the face. Behind me, I can feel people stumbling around, panting, crying.

'If the Guard are here . . . in the camp . . . they have guns . . .' He licks his lips. He opens and closes his right hand to stop it trembling. Something changes in his eyes. 'I have to go fight. I have to help Luca get everyone out. I have to find Eliza and Mark . . . and Hero . . . wherever they went . . . oh, Raven—'

His voice breaks and he looks up from me, over my head at the dark and the screaming people around us. I see the firelight gleam terror in his eyes. Then he looks down again, at me.

'Raven – do you understand?'

I just look at him.

'Raven . . .' He's shaking so hard I can feel it. 'You have to get out. Promise me. *Promise me.*' He shakes me, staring at me, fear-glazed eyes gleaming like cut glass. 'Run. As far as you can. We'll find you later. Promise me. *Raven.*'

'I promise.' My voice is a whisper.

'On everything.'

'On everything.'

He wraps me in his arms again, presses a kiss to my head, tender and fierce. His arms are shaking as he holds me. I can feel the trembling against my chest.

Then he gets to his feet and, with what looks like all the effort he has, he turns and runs down the hill into the blackness.

I watch him until he's gone. Wait. Around me people are screaming. I can't breathe.

'*Mala kralovna.* Raven.'

A voice behind me, someone's hand on my shoulder, blood-stained and trembling. I turn and there's Anna. Her face spattered with silver blood, all the colour gone from her. 'Come with me. We have to get you away from here.'

Eliza Hero Mark. A heartbeat in my chest. I press myself to it, clinging to it. *Eliza Hero Mark.* They're alive in this camp somewhere and in danger and I—

'Raven, come on.'

Promises mean nothing, not even promises to Caleb, not compared to their lives. I have a choice and I will not choose wrong.

'*Raven!*'

'I'm not going,' I say aloud. I expect my voice to tremble but it doesn't. Around the fire, people turn to me, the gasping and sobbing and stumbling falling still and silent. Everyone's looking at me. I can see the shock in their glazed eyes. My heart isn't racing any more, it's not beating at all.

Anna pulls my shoulder. 'Come on, you have to come with me—'

'I'm not leaving,' I say, louder. Cairn's ghost is standing behind me, I can feel her. Her hand on my other shoulder, listening and nodding.

And suddenly I understand, through my singing blood, what I'm meant to do, clear as vision.

I will not run away.

'I'm going to fight,' I say to them. Sound is rising and falling in my ears, there and then gone, buzzing. 'You can come with me or you can not.'

No, says Cairn's ghost in my ear, *no, that's not how it works. They're frightened, more frightened than they've ever been, more than you. Tell them what to do.*

'Come with me,' I say, into the screaming from down below, and their terrified stillness. My voice doesn't sound like mine. 'Come and fight. There are people down there. It's what we have to do. It's right.' And when I say it I believe it.

Anna has let go of my shoulder. Everyone is looking at me. No one says anything at all.

I close my eyes. Breathe in and out. Fear is shining on the edges of my mind, but if I keep it there it can't hurt me. If Caleb Luca Mark Eliza, if they die, it doesn't matter what happens to me, so what do I have to lose? Dying is quick as shattering, painless if you do it right. Gunshot, snap, splatter of grey blood on grass. And then I'm over. Death is just sleep but longer. I am not afraid of dying.

I am not afraid.

My soul is steel, threaded through my bones. I open my eyes, the terror washes over me, the depth of the bloodied night. Then I get to my feet shaking, change shape and I have wings. The air in my feathers is cold.

Behind me, Anna has got to her feet too, her hand on her knife, her trembling gone at last. Declan is standing beside her. Everyone around the fire is looking at me. I can see the life coming back to their eyes, the fear brightening there. What they do is their decision. It takes all my strength, but I turn away.

I flap, strong against the wind, take off from beside the crackling fire where Beth and the Guardsman lie silent. The night around me is full of screaming, and my blood is thunder in my ears. *Eliza Hero Mark* . . .

And beneath me, I can feel footsteps, thrumming like the beat of my eagle-heart.

I look down.

The watchers by the fire are walking beneath the path of my flight, holding each other, silent, trembling. I see some of them pointing at me, crying out; the cry takes, like wildfire, spreading through the crowd and the darkness, their shining eyes upturned. A held breath.

As I watch them they start to run with me, towards the gunfire and the screams and the blood, a thundering rush, cries rising from their throats.

Yes, whispers Cairn's ghost flying beside me, *that's right, good girl, yes, you're doing so well.*

My mind is clear and bright. All my courage is balled into iron and trembling in my stomach. I fly down the hill, leading the running people below me, my ears full of their cries of *mala kralovna*, and we go together into the screaming, cavernous dark.

PART THREE

Kestrel

CHAPTER 14

Waking

Water is the first thing I think. Flesh of my throat like razors, cool air a torture. *Water*. I try to say it, force it out of my mouth, bloody and raw, but I have no voice.

'Oh, look—'

'She's *awake*! Eliza, she's awake.'

Someone presses something into my hand and all of me vanishes into *touch*. Cool metal, cold and smooth. My hands dry as kindling. I can't lift it to my mouth; someone's hands are on my wrist, gentle. 'Open your mouth,' she says, and I do.

Water clear and cold and pure in my mouth down my throat in my chest and oh, *oh*.

A moment, and then hunger. The throb of acid in my stomach, a low pulse of agony, my body eating itself. I try to say that too with my new lips tongue teeth, but someone is already opening my mouth, hands gentle on my chin. 'Can you chew?' she says, and it turns out I can.

Soft bread, salt fish, hard cheese, berries, until someone says, 'Stop, you'll kill her.'

I flinch away, thin muscles in my thin arms wrapping over myself, protective. No good if they want to hit me, no good if they want to kill me. The woman says, 'No—'

Later I wake again.

It's silent. Someone's crying outside. Grass beneath me.

Grass. The meaning of that filters through to me at last. I'm not in my cell.

I look for it, the smooth stone, the black walls of the black tower. Maybe it's hiding somewhere in my head. *Maybe you've gone mad*, says a tiny voice. That's fine, I can live with this madness. It's giving me a tent. Canvas flapping gently in the breeze.

It's autumn, I can smell it on the air.

I lie there for a while, just feeling it.

Eventually a nub of memory grows at the edge of my mind and starts pushing gently against it. There are things that have happened and I don't remember them and I don't *want* to . . .

I'm in a tent. That's all I have to think about now.

I'm in a tent, I'm lying on grass, smell of the earth.

Calm down.

I drift in and out of sleep. The tent is always full of daylight. Someone comes in.

'Eliza!'

'*Luca*. Oh, thank—'

Sound of an embrace. Ruffled clothing. A soft intake of breath.

'Oh, crap, you're hurt—'

'I'm fine, I'm fine.'

'But your arm—'

'I'm *fine*.' Firmly. 'You're okay? What happened to you?'

'Yeah . . .' Pause, swallowing, a breath. 'Caleb . . . in the fighting, last night . . . he told me to get the kids out first . . . vanish them out, I mean . . .'

Soft voice. 'I know.'

'People kept shoving their children at me . . . they were screaming. This woman, she put her baby right into my arms—' Luca's voice breaks. 'I know it isn't safe here. I shouldn't have come. It was just the first place I could think of.'

The woman called Eliza gives a terrible raw laugh. 'I don't even know where we are, Luca.'

'It's the lake. The lake we were camped at before we went to the cliff top. Raven used to swim at dawn . . .'

'Yeah. I remember.'

'I should have gone somewhere else, somewhere we hadn't been in years . . . but I was so scared, I couldn't think, and the *kids*—'

'Luca. *Luca*.' Eliza's voice is soothing. 'You're okay. You got us all out. They're alive.'

'Not enough of them.' Luca's voice breaks and she stops, then takes a long shuddering breath. 'There was this six-year-old, I saw after, back in the camp . . . the Guard got to her first . . . her eyes were still open . . . oh, Eliza . . .'

She breaks down, sobbing. My mind pulses gently in the sunlight. Don't think. I don't want to know.

I open my eyes. The dark-haired woman, the one called Eliza, is holding Luca in her arms, stroking her head. They're both covered in blood, red and silver and grey. Eliza's eyes are open, and she stares at the walls of the tent.

I close my eyes again quickly. I don't want them to see me awake.

'Is Caleb all right?'

'Yeah.' I hear Luca swallow, the change in her voice. Shifting. She wipes her eyes. 'Yeah, he's with Raven.'

A silence.

'Raven.' Eliza is hesitant. 'Is she . . .'

'We found her. After the fighting.' Luca stops herself, a shake in her voice again. Flap of canvas in the wind. 'I didn't know where she was, I was going out of my mind. I went back to find her – just before dawn. The camp was empty, everyone was either gone or dead, or I'd brought them with me here. And all the tents had been ripped out of the ground . . . and the Guard had left . . . and I was just wandering around, in the mud, calling for her, I was so scared . . .'

Another shuddering breath.

'I came back here, and someone found me, caught my arm, I don't even know who it was, they said I'd taken Raven here with me hours ago, they'd seen her with me. I hadn't even realised. I must not have known her, in the dark.'

Her voice is tight again, thick, tears in her throat.

'There were so many people. And the kids – I had whole chains of them, they were grabbing on to the ones that had hold of me. I could barely move, there were so many – and she must have been one of them – but I didn't *know* her, Eliza.'

The other woman's voice is gentle. 'It was dark. You were scared.'

'Caleb told her to get out, to run, to get in the woods, out of danger, but she . . . she didn't. She stayed. In the camp. In the fighting.'

Silence. The rustle of clothing. Eliza doesn't speak.

'She – Raven – she saw things. And she was there when that Guardsman . . . and Hero's . . . I mean, what happened to Hero, when that Guardsman . . .'

A pause, a slow deep breath. In and out. *Hero*. The name nudges the edge of my mind, it means something very important, but I push it away. I don't *want* to remember, please, not now, it's so peaceful just lying here in the grass not thinking about anything.

Luca speaks again, more slowly, hesitant and shaking.

'I mean . . . Raven wasn't *hurt*, not injured . . . but Caleb's with her now.'

Another silence.

'How is she?'

I know they mean me, I can feel their eyes on me. I try not to tense, to keep my hands from clenching into fists.

'She's alive,' says Eliza shortly.

'Wasn't she always?'

'Not really. Not *living*. She breathed, but that was it.'

There's a pause.

'Can she speak?'

'I don't know. She hasn't yet. She's screamed, if that counts.' A false lightness in Eliza's voice.

'Did you manage to get food into her?'

'Yeah.'

'So she's going to make it.'

'Looks like it.'

'Good.'

Silence.

'Yeah.' I hear Luca swallow again, clear her throat. 'How's Mark? Did he get hurt? I saw him fighting.'

'I don't know, I haven't seen him yet.'

'What do you mean? Where is he?'

Silence, suspended in the air.

Eliza's voice is suddenly terrible. 'Luca – wasn't he with you? Didn't he—'

'You haven't seen him?'

'No, I haven't seen him, I thought – I saw him in the fighting, in the camp, he had his knives out . . . and you were there . . . don't you *remember*? I thought you'd brought him here!'

'No, I thought he'd stayed with you!' Luca's voice is high-pitched, panicky. 'When did you see him?'

'Just after the Guard attacked. It was hours ago. In the camp.'

Silence, long and black and suddenly airless.

'Oh,' one of them says, her voice is dark and terrified. 'Oh, no, *no*—'

Silence again and then the rustle of canvas. Someone's run out of the tent. The other one stays. I can hear her breathing, deep and quick and rasping and a rip in it beneath, like a collapsed lung, a gunshot wound.

* * *

Silence. I'm awake again. I can hear breathing. My mouth is dry.

'Water. *Please*.'

For a moment I don't recognise my own voice. Someone presses cold metal into my hand, I lift it to my mouth but it slips in my hand and splashes over my face. I flinch and splutter at the cold.

Someone says, 'Sit up.' An arm under my shoulder. I move slowly with it, aching. The world swoons around me.

I blink. The light is fading, the tent walls are dusk-grey. A woman is sitting in front of me, holding out the metal canister full of water. 'Can you take this?'

I try, gripping it with shaking fingers. The woman nods and lets go.

'Drink. You need it.'

I drink from the canister. The water is gloriously cold.

I look around. There's a girl no more than ten or eleven sitting by the tent entrance, watching me, with matted shoulder-length black hair. Her solemn dark eyes are familiar. I stare at her.

The woman glances over her shoulder. 'Go to Caleb, Raven.'

The girl called Raven doesn't move. She watches me.

'Raven. *Go*.'

'Do you know where Mark is?' The girl speaks straight to me. I flinch. 'They won't tell me.'

'Raven.' The woman's voice is cold, fierce. 'I told you to go.'

Raven looks at the woman, terribly sad. 'You said you wouldn't lie to me.'

The woman gets to her feet, turns slowly to look at Raven. 'I'm not lying,' she says.

'Would you tell me if he was dead?'

'Yes.'

Raven tilts her head slightly. 'I don't believe you.'

'Raven, *please.*'

Raven glances at me one more time, then gets up and leaves the tent. The woman looks back at me, exhaustion carved deep into her face.

'Can you get up?'

It's a question, not a demand, but at once I want to answer. The pull of her voice drags the words with it, up through my throat and over my lips. 'I don't know.'

The woman gives me a fleeting, humourless smile. 'Well, let's see.'

She gives me her hand and I grasp it. Slowly, gently, I pull myself to my feet. I feel the blood pumping very fast through my heart, a dizzy rush. The woman is watching me.

'You all right?'

I nod, then stumble slightly into her. My legs are trembling violently. Everything hurts. Take slow, deep breaths. I'm alive, at least I'm alive, I'm not in my cell.

'Can you walk?'

'I think so.'

She nods and lets go of my hand. I lean against the tent flap, breathing slowly and carefully.

'You washed the blood off.'

She looks up at me, as if woken from a reverie. 'What?'

'Your face. There was blood on your face. Before.'

The dark-haired woman stares at me. *Eliza*, that's her name, I remember now. 'When *before*?'

'You didn't know I was awake. You were talking to Luca.'

She lets go of the tent flap and walks suddenly towards me. I flinch and she stops, three feet away. The canvas murmurs in the wind.

'How do you know her name?'

'You used it.'

Eliza looks at me intently for a second. When she speaks there's that pull to her voice again, like the inrush of a wave on a beach. I *want* to tell her the truth, I can feel the tug of it in my throat.

'Do you remember any of us?'

'From when?'

'From *before*. The camp. The cliff top. Any of it.'

I stare at her. 'I don't know what you're talking about.'

She looks at me, presses her tongue to her lower lip. Then she says, 'Okay.' She opens the tent flap again, watching me. 'You want to take a walk?'

'I don't know.'

Another fleeting smile. 'No one's going to hurt you.'

'Who hurt *you*?'

'How do you know anyone hurt me?'

'The blood. On your shirt.'

'Oh, yes.' She shakes her head slightly. I can see the flicker of pain in her eyes. Then she says, 'They're gone now.'

I look at her. My breath is tight in my chest, hard and cold.

'It was the Guard,' I say.

'Yes.'

'The Guard came here. They found me.' Panic rising, burning white hot in my throat. 'They'll find me again—'

'No. The Guard can't come here. I promise you.'

There's a sudden strength to the way she says it, a searing intensity, and almost against my will, I believe her. The pull of her voice draws me to the truth of her words, inescapable, like staring into the sun.

'The woman who was in this tent before. Luca.' She runs a hand over her face, eyes closed. 'She's a vanisher. She brought us all here when the Guard attacked the camp. We're safe now. They can't find us here.'

'How did they find the last camp?'

Eliza opens her eyes and stares at me for a second.

Then, finally, she says, 'I don't know.'

'So how do you know they can't come here?'

She tilts her head slightly. 'I don't know. I *hope*. Does that worry you?'

'Yeah.'

Eliza opens the tent flap again, slowly. Beyond it I can feel the dark winter wind. I shiver.

'Take a walk with me.'

Slowly, I step forward. The grass is soft and cold against the skin of my feet. And then I'm out of the tent and into the cavernous blue night. I just stand there, staring, for a long, long time.

It's the sky that gets me. I haven't seen it in weeks (*don't think about why*) and I forgot how huge it was, how deep, frayed with mountains at the edges and studded with stars, silk and diamond. The air is musky, cool and bright. I turn slowly and at the bottom of the hill, beyond the rows of blood-stained tents and campfire smoke, I see a pine forest, thick and soft and green-dark, furred like velvet, and beyond it the metal gleam of a lake, silver in the moonlight.

I speak quietly, remembering what Luca said before.

'Raven . . . the little girl . . . she swam in *that*?'

I feel Eliza stop behind me. There's a silence. I turn to see her with her hands in her pockets, staring down the hill at the lake.

'Yes,' she says. 'As an otter. Or a dog. She likes being furry things. They keep her warm. She's a shapeshifter, it's her demesne.' She looks harder at me. 'You're human.'

I glance down at my wrists, the deep blue veins. My hands are clenched into fists. I try to open them. 'Yeah.'

'There are other humans here. There were humans in the camp.'

Eliza's voice catches, she pauses and when she speaks again it's steady, slow.

'When the Guard attacked, last night . . . well, there are

stories . . . that they were blood-testing people. They'd cut wrists, and if you bled human – you know, red – they'd let you go if you didn't fight. They weren't interested in killing humans. Only us.'

Us. I look at her, comprehension swimming at the edges of my mind. 'You're a god?'

'Yeah.'

What's your demesne? I want to say, but I don't. Eliza's expression is oddly pitying. I look away.

'I know what you're doing,' she says.

I shake my head.

Her voice is gentle. 'I understand. I do. I promise. But you've got to stop.'

I turn to face her. Anger pulses in my chest underneath the weight of panic, hot as stone. 'Who *are* you?'

Eliza shakes her head slowly.

'That's the fourth question you should be asking.'

'What?'

'I said, that's the fourth question you should be asking me.' She catches my eyes. Her gaze is burning. 'The third question is how long you were unconscious, the second is where you are, and the first—'

'No.' I hold up my hands, step back, as if that could stop me hearing her. 'No, please.'

Eliza steps forward, away from the tent, eyes deep and intense, voice low and soft and terribly kind. 'You can't forget it forever.'

'There's . . . there's nothing . . . *please* . . .'

'There is,' says Eliza quietly. Her voice is inside the nub of memory, pressing it into my head, echoing, red-hot steel. I press my hands to my face. 'I'm sorry.'

'No. *No* . . .' My throat is hard, my breathing is too fast, and my heartbeat underneath it is thundering. 'Please. I can't. Not now.'

'Yes, you can.' She takes another step towards me, but this time I don't step back. 'Look at me.'

Slowly, slowly, I raise my head. My temples are pulsing, there's a knife through my brain, I don't want to remember. I don't *want* to, please—

'All I'm going to ask is one question,' says Eliza, softly. Her eyes burn in the dark, I can't look away from them. 'One question, that's all, and then you'll answer it, and I'll leave you alone. Can you do that for me?'

I stare at her. My breathing is too shallow, too quick. *Calm down.* I am dizzy, lightheaded. I nod before I realise what I'm doing.

She touches my chin and raises it slightly. I'm shaking. 'What's your name?'

I stare up at her. My head splits open, and suddenly I hear another girl's voice, younger, asking me the same thing. *What's your name?* It was years ago, we were standing in our dormitory—

I push the memory away. No, *please*, I don't want to, I *can't* . . . let me have peace, let me forget . . .

'Come on,' says Eliza softly. Her eyes are burning into my head.

I stumble back, trying to push her away, and she follows me. She grabs my wrist to stop me falling.

I hear my own voice, faint. 'I don't know.'

'That's a lie. Come on. It's not hard. Tell me your name.'

There's no mercy in her voice any more, and the memories are searing the inside of my skull. I hear the young girl again in my head, asking me *What's your name?* I push it away again, harder, fighting it desperately, closing my eyes, but then I see her, clear and bright inside my head. We were standing in our dormitory. It was the first time I met her, we were twelve years old—

No—

She was holding out her hand to shake mine, polite, looking up at me, dark-haired and dark-eyed—

No, please—

And she asked me my name—

It slams into me with the force of a wave, a screaming howl of memory. The orphanage, and the black tower, Hero, Joshua, all of it, my capture, my name, my whole *life*. A month of darkness trapped in my cell in Elida, a month, and then at last the Guard came to take me to the tower room where they waited with their guns, and suddenly, like blinding light—

They were there.

Hero and Joshua, both of them, exhausted and blood-stained and filthy but *there*, in the tower room in Elida, come to save me, and then there was a gunshot—

Joshua conjured a light more powerful than I'd ever seen, sudden and blinding, and the Guardsmen were melted and screaming, and Hero was talking to me calmly, untying the ropes that held me to the chair, her solemn dark eyes keeping me sane, keeping the screams trapped inside my throat, and then—

What happened then?

I fell.

We fell together from the tower and Hero was near me, falling too, and my heart was full of terror and love, and then—

Nothing.

Blackness in my head, my memory. I hit the water and the world ended.

What's your name? Hero asked me, the first time we met, standing in our new dormitory. And I told her, *Kestrel.*

I raise my head to stare at Eliza. All of me feels new, new hands, new skin, and when I speak my voice is hoarse but my own. My heart is still pounding.

'Where are they?'

Eliza looks at me for a moment. I realise she's let me go. I clench my fists, aware that I am weak, aware that I am thin and swaying in the wind, but my head pulses with their names, *Hero Joshua Hero Joshua*. Where have I been, what have I been doing trying not to remember them, while they—

'*Where are they?*' My voice is high. Fear sings in my blood. I can see their faces clear in the darkness, like I used to in my cell in Elida. 'Where *are* they? Please! Are they dead?' I say it before I truly think it, and then a moment later the terrible reality of it touches me, the grip of cold rotting fingers around my heart. I almost crumple. If they are dead, I will die too. 'Are they dead?'

Eliza just looks at me. Panic is choking me. I can see Hero's face in the dark.

'No,' she says. 'No.' Then she walks to me, wraps her arms around me gently. She strokes my head while I keep the sobs tight, hard, closed in my neck, my chest. *Please don't hurt me.*

She raises my head.

'Be strong,' she says gently, 'for five minutes. And after this, I promise you, nothing will ever be able to hurt you again.' She's kind, I understand, this strange woman. It takes all my strength, but I nod.

Hero isn't dead, not yet.

Eliza takes me to her tent, walking behind me like a gentle shadow. People in other tents glance at me, but I don't feel their eyes. I hear the moans of the wounded in the distance across the hill.

A boy and a girl are sitting in Hero's tent. The girl has laid a blood-stained longsword across her lap. When she looks up, I recognise her as the one who broke down crying in our tent. Luca. She stares at me.

Eliza says quietly, 'Let her through. We'll talk later.'

Luca and the boy stand up at once. The boy moves with her grace, so alike he could be her twin. He has Luca's eyes, and he looks at me with the same terrible kindness. I look back for a moment, my fists closed by my sides, for a moment, not seeing him.

Then at last, slowly, I turn to look at Hero, wrapped in blood-stained sheets in the straw bed, and my heart tears apart in my chest.

Oh, my love. What have they done to you?

The blood is everywhere, and half her face is gone. The bullet smashed through her cheekbone and up into her skull. Her left eye is gone, jelly and blood smeared across the raw red canyon of the wound, and I can see threads of muscle frayed beneath, raw meat. Grey blood oozes from her ruined eye, dripping on to the grass beneath her bed. She's perfectly still but for the slow, steady rise and fall of her chest. Her face is grey, and her fingers are blue at the tips.

I know just by looking at her that she isn't going to live.

I sway in the tent doorway. They're all looking at me, Eliza and the twins and the little girl. I open my mouth, soundless. The screams in my chest are gone, there's only an appalling quiet. I can't take my eyes off her.

Faintly, I hear myself speak.

'When?'

'Last night,' says the boy. I can't look at him. 'During the fighting in the camp. A Guardsman did it.' He glances over my shoulder, and I can feel the look he exchanges with Eliza behind me. 'She was protecting you, Kestrel.'

Hearing my name aloud is like a knife in my chest. It jolts my heart, a searing pulse of adrenaline.

'I know,' I say. Hero is clever and quick and brave. She would never have been hurt if she hadn't been weakened. *I* weakened her.

My voice is quite calm, outside me. 'Is there anyone here who can heal her?'

They don't answer. Of course there isn't. Hero's demesne is a miracle, an aberration. Most gifts are good only for killing. If it had been anyone else, she could have healed *them*, that's the exquisite horror of it. But so long as she's unconscious like this, she can't heal herself any more than I can.

I walk to her bed, sit down beside her. Her hand is cold. I stroke her face and my fingers come away sticky with drying blood. Look at me, my love. I'm here, you saved me. Open your eyes and look at me.

It happened during the fighting, they tell me, an hour or so before dawn. Eliza and Raven both saw it. Raven was a bird, soaring above the battle and the gunfire and the screaming, looking for the twins. Eliza was looking for a weapon. She'd dropped her knife in the dark somewhere ten minutes earlier, and there was nothing she could do.

It was my fault. I lay amid the wreckage of a collapsed tent, unconscious. Hero was ten yards away, healing a girl who had been shot and who knelt, clutching her stomach, beside the dead bodies of her parents. Hero kept glancing over her shoulder to check I was safe.

Then, suddenly, I wasn't.

A Guardsman spotted me from somewhere in the dark. They had electric torches, sweeping the beams over the blood and the wreckage to find new victims, and he saw me. An easy kill, not even awake. He lifted his gun.

Pause, suspended in the darkness. In my head, I can see the dead, unseeing look on his face.

Then he shot me in the stomach. The spatter of my blood is still on my feet.

She cried out and lunged towards me just as the Guardsman

aimed again for the last, killing shot. He was walking towards me as he did it, very calm. I was bleeding from the wound in my stomach, blood oozing thick and dark on to the grass, still not waking. The Guardsman pointed his gun at me, and Hero . . .

Eliza and Raven say that something passed from her hands, a shimmer of air like heat, and into me. A pulse of healing. I've never seen her do that before, she must have got stronger since she left the orphanage. She was powerful enough to heal me fully, to wake me, and she didn't even know it.

The wound in my stomach closed, the bleeding stopped. Eliza says that she saw my breathing hitch, the rise and fall of my chest speeding up, though I didn't wake.

The Guardsman was still striding towards me as Hero turned and slammed a knife into his stomach. They stood there staring at each other, their eyes gleaming in the torchlight as his blood poured over her hands. Then he fell on to the grass.

Raven landed a few feet away and became a wolf, growling at him. Hero, her face sheened with sweat and blood, shaking, picked up a gun in the grass, checked it for bullets, and then threw it aside.

Before she could turn towards me, the Guardsman at her feet raised his arm. He was still holding his gun, and he was pointing it into her face. She looked down at him. Neither Eliza nor Raven knows for how long. Around them everyone was screaming, dying. But neither of them moved.

After a long time, he pulled the trigger.

CHAPTER 15

Ellara

I was dead.

I was *dead*, and Hero brought me back.

I died when Hero pushed us from the tower, trying to save us from the Guard. I died when I hit the water, bones cracking open in the icy moonlight. I hadn't seen the moon in so long. I remember how beautiful that first breath of cold air was, how I revelled in it, even as I fell. And then everything was over in a crushing snap of force, a rush of the drowning sea into my lungs. Everything was gone. *I was gone.*

Hero dragged me back to life on the beach, set my pulse moving again, put breath in my lungs and healed me, gave me back my legs, even. But she couldn't wake me until desperation, on the battlefield, gave her the strength.

My dark, brave, clever sister.

She was the best part of me. In my cell in Elida, I'd imagine she was with me, laughing and joking, holding my hand. *We'll be here soon*, she'd say. *Just wait, just be patient.* Wherever she was, I knew she was coming. She couldn't just leave me there.

I'm here for you, I told her, when I imagined her there. *I did it for you, love.* I had never called her that when I was with her, never told her how much I adored her. She was the one who kept me sane, all those terrible days inside the black tower. She kept me together, when all the pieces of my head were straining apart. Every day, when the door of my cell opened, I half-expected to see the barrel of a gun instead of a face. A garrotting wire, a knife. I nearly went mad with the fear of it.

But I knew that outside the black tower, Hero, too, would know that I might die, and she would have accepted it, and planned for it, because that was what Hero did with everything. She would have taken the possibility of my death and made her peace with it, and knowing that helped me make my peace with it, too.

And Joshua was with her, over the black hills.

Joshua . . .

I know what you did. Eliza told me.

You left her. You left *me*.

You lost your mind. I stayed sane but *you* lost your mind. What the hell kind of excuse do you have for that? All that time waiting for you in my cell, and the way you looked at me when you saw me in the tower room, like I was the only thing in the world. I was so grateful for you.

But then you woke on that cliff top driven mad with hatred and fear and you turned against her. Hero.

You tried to *hurt her*.

I don't understand that. I can't. I think about the words, and beneath them in my head there's just blankness and silence. An impossibility.

When I knew you, you would never have done that, never in a thousand years. You were brave and loyal and kind. I loved you for it. Was that all a lie, some delusion you put up to impress me? Or did that courage vanish the moment a knife was held to your throat? What did you become, when I wasn't there to watch you?

I wanted you both to be safe, it was all I wanted. You ruined yourselves, trying to save me.

Please don't have changed. Let it be some illness, some

madness that seized you and then left. Tell me you're still you, underneath.

Just don't be dead. Whatever happens, don't be dead.

Eliza comes to me in the morning, in the tent where Hero lies sleeping. The cries of the wounded have quietened now, and the dawn mist over the hills is thick and grey. She gives me food. Salt fish and bread and pale red berries. I thank her, then sit holding the food for a moment.

'Did you sleep?'

'Yeah, for a week and a half.'

'That's not what I meant.'

'I know what you meant.'

After a moment I bite into the bread. It's going stale, but I don't say anything. Eliza watches me eat. Then she says, 'I was up all night with the doctors here. This whole place is a tinderbox.'

'I know.'

'Do you?'

'I can feel it.' Hatred and anger and fear and grief are smells on the air in this camp. It makes me tense. 'What's going to happen?'

Eliza hesitates. 'I don't know.'

'What do you *think*?'

There's a pause. I can feel her giving me a long measuring look, but I keep my eyes on Hero's face. Knowing that Eliza's watching me makes me shiver.

'I think,' she says slowly, 'Anthony is going to blame us for the Guard finding the camp.'

They told me about him last night, about Cairn and the resistance. Cairn is dead, but they can't tell anyone yet, and Raven is her heir, the little dark-haired girl with the bright, magnetic eyes.

'Really? How?'

'He's going to say . . . I think . . . that we led them here. Deliberately or accidentally, I don't know, but it'll be our fault. He was always suspicious of me, even when I lived here. I don't know what Cairn told him.' She rubs her face. 'And since we showed up the day it happened . . .'

I look at Eliza and try to keep my mind clean and clear. She looks very tired, and much older than she did even a day ago. The veins stand out clear in her clenched hands, and she's cut her hair shorter. Her dark eyes are sunken in her face, gleaming onyx. She's beautiful, I realise suddenly, a heart-deep and painful beauty. When she turns the shadows deepen under her eyes, like paint on ceramic. I just want to sit and stare at her for a while. It would be so easy just to do that, and not to think.

Instead I say, 'Does he really *believe* it? That we're working for the Guard?'

Eliza shakes her head.

'But . . .?'

'But he needs a scapegoat. He needs to persuade people there's still a danger, *within* the camp, so they'll rally round him. He needs a reason to make people distrust us.' She rubs her eyes. 'I mean, the camp only has our word for it that Raven really *is* Cairn's intended heir. If he can paint us as liars, he can say that we lied about her, he's their only choice to lead them now she's gone. She's a child, after all. And . . .'

She hesitates, uncomfortable, then looks up at me.

'What?'

'The Guard let you out of Elida.'

The shock is almost physical. 'They didn't *let me out*. Hero and—' I can't say his name, not yet. The thought of him brings all the hurt and confusion rising to my throat and stops me breathing. I shake my head, trying to clear it. 'I was rescued. I *died*.'

'I know that. They don't.'

'I—'

'I know, Kestrel.' Eliza looks up at me. 'But you're human, you were raised in an Amareth orphanage full of Guardsmen, you were in Elida and now you're free. It *looks*—'

'Eliza.' My voice is cold, hard. 'They tortured me.'

She looks at me for a long dark moment. I know she can hear the truth in my voice. I close my eyes to push the pictures in my mind away and when I open them my fists are clenched again in my lap.

'I know,' she says.

She gets to her feet and starts walking slowly up and down, staring at the canvas walls.

'What about you? Why do *you* look suspicious?'

'I'm a truth-teller. People don't like what I do.' She's stopped pacing and is staring at the grass, a grim smile on her face like an inside joke. 'And I'm an outsider. Everyone knows everybody else in this camp, and I lived away from it for six years. People are tense. Give it a few days and supplies will start running low. A few days more and people will start to work out why Cairn hasn't found us yet. I think Anthony's guessed already. It was suspicious enough, the way we arrived.' She raises her eyebrows, her eyes unfocused. 'He might say *we* killed her, even.'

She sucks in a breath and looks up at me, gives me a quick, forced smile. 'It's going to be difficult.'

'I know.'

'If you wanted to leave, now—'

'No.' My hand closes around Hero's cold wrist. 'I'm not leaving.'

She hesitates, watching me, then takes something from her belt. A knife, the blade clear as glass, long and thin and deathly sharp. It glints in the dawn light through the canvas. The wooden handle is blood-stained.

'This was his wife's.'

'Anthony's?'

'Yeah. Her name was Beth. Caleb took it from her body after she was killed.' Eliza looks at the knife with distaste, then hands it to me. 'It's made of diamond. That's Anthony's demesne, diamond. He made a knife like that for Cairn, and a couple of other people. We all have our own weapons. You should have this.'

I look up at her.

'If Anthony *does* try to blame the attack on us, to say we're working with the Guard . . .' She rubs her face again, hesitates. 'A lot of people died that night. You should keep this. All the time. Keep it strapped to you, on your left side. You'll need a belt.'

'I don't know how to use it.'

'We'll teach you.'

I nod. A pause.

'Eliza?'

'Yeah?'

I hesitate, measuring the words. 'He's just lost his wife. Anthony. And if you're right, if he already knows, or he thinks, Cairn's dead . . . his sister . . .'

She looks at me, a long moment. 'You don't think he's in any state to be making plans. To be plotting to grab power.'

'Yeah.'

'I disagree.' I look up at her, see her watching me, onyx eyes bright in the darkness of the tent. 'Pain sharpens the mind.'

There's shouting from outside. I wake lying beside Hero, my throat cracked and dry. I get up, slowly, and go to the tent entrance.

Sobbing. The sound of feet scuffing against dirt. Someone cries, *'No!'* For a moment I think, with a slow heavy panic, that the Guard have found us again, but then I remember that Eliza said they couldn't. I believe her. I open the tent flap.

Luca is standing outside, tear tracks etched into the grime of her face. It's dusk. She's holding something, something that's twisting and struggling against her grip. I look at it and it's a ferret and then a bird flapping wildly and then a lizard, but Luca is too strong, and keeps it trapped in her arms.

Caleb is standing at her shoulder. I can see his eyes shining with tears. The eagle tries to flap out of Luca's arms, twists free and gets two feet up, three, but Caleb raises his hands and the eagle stops in mid-air, struggling, like it's being held with invisible ropes. It gives a terrible screaming cry of frustration and then drops to the ground.

I step forward and around Eliza, who's standing in front of my tent with her hands over her face. When my eyes adjust to the darkness, the eagle's gone and there's a girl with long black straggly hair curled on the ground, sobbing.

'Raven,' says Luca softly. Her eyes are bright with tears in the half-light, and when she kneels and reaches towards Raven I see her hands are trembling. 'Raven, I—'

'*You said he'd come back!*'

The girl's scream is high-pitched, anguished. Below us, on the hill, I see people push aside tent flaps to look out at us, exhausted and alarmed. When they see Raven, they step out further, draw knives from their belts. They mutter to each other.

'*Mala kralovna*—'

'Is she all right?' calls a tall man with dark hair, holding a bandage to his cheek. 'The little one?'

Caleb can't bring himself to speak. He nods. Raven is still crying, crumpled on the ground. They go slowly back into their tents.

Next to me, Eliza mutters distractedly, 'Get her inside. They can't see her like this.'

But she doesn't move, just clutches the tent canvas so tightly her knuckles turn pale.

'You said he was . . . you *said* . . .'

'Raven,' says Luca again, very quietly. The tears are rolling down her face, silver and gleaming. 'Raven . . . I'm sorry, I should have—'

'We did think he would come back,' says Caleb, very quietly. 'We didn't lie.'

Raven looks at him, bleak and terrible. 'You did. You *all* did. You're evil. I hate you.'

'Raven—'

He takes a step towards her but she scrambles back, staring at him, her small chest rising and falling quickly. He stops dead. In the dimness I can't read his eyes. Beside me, Eliza has her face in her hands.

'Raven . . . Raven, we tried . . .'

Raven's scream is appalling. It cuts through the soft dawn mist and I flinch. 'You *let him die!* You didn't take him. You should have left *me*, it should have been me, I don't care . . . Mark . . .' Her voice collapses, blood-stained sobs, a terrible moan of grief. '*Mark* . . .'

Silence. Luca is on her knees, arms outstretched towards the little girl, tears running over her bitten lips. Eliza doesn't move. Caleb turns away suddenly from us, pressing the heels of his hands into his eyes. I can see the hunch of his back in the half-light, shaking. No one else is watching.

'Raven,' says Luca, quietly. Her arms are still open, trembling. 'Raven, come here . . . come on . . .'

'*You said he'd come back! You said he wasn't dead!*'

'I know,' says Luca. Her voice cracks and she wipes her eyes. 'I know.'

Raven curls up on the ground, pressing into herself like she's trying to make herself vanish, howls still tearing in her throat. Luca turns and then suddenly without moving she appears beside Raven, puts her arms around her, crying too, and stroking her black hair. I flinch before I remember what she is, that her appearing and disappearing is nothing to be scared of. Not a trick my head is playing on me, a play of shadows in the darkness of my cell, designed to drive me mad. *Calm down.*

There's movement out of the corner of my eye and when I turn Eliza's gone. I hesitate and then follow her back into Hero's tent.

My eyes take a second to adjust to the darkness. Eliza is sitting in the chair beside Hero's bed, staring at her. There are tears running down her face and her hands are blood-stained. The shadows under her eyes are deep bruise-blue. I don't know what to say.

'I'm sorry.'

Eliza wipes her eyes slowly, still looking at Hero. When she speaks, her voice is dead.

'No, you're not. You didn't know him.'

I take the seat on the other side of Hero's bed. I changed the bandages on her face a few hours ago, but I can see the greyish blood leaking through the cloth, and something else, something yellowish-white, something unthinkable. I look away.

'I'm sorry,' says Eliza at last.

'Don't be.'

'I didn't mean that.'

'I understand.'

'Do you?' Eliza looks at me over Hero's sleeping body. 'I have . . . I have premonitions. I see the future. Sometimes.' She wipes her eyes again, leaving streaks of dirt like war paint on her cheeks. It takes her time and effort to speak again. 'I saw him die when I was nine.'

I stare at her. She looks down at Hero, not meeting my eyes. Her voice is slow.

'It was a dream. I saw . . . it was dark. I saw the knife go into his . . . his throat.' She stops, eyes on the ground, breathes long and deep and slow. 'I didn't know who he was. Then, years later . . . after the Guard killed Luca's parents, she and Caleb and Raven came to the camp, and Cairn sent us away to live with them. To *protect* them, train them. It was partly Raven, of course . . . Cairn wanted her watched, thought she had potential . . . but it was Luca as well. Vanishers are rare and precious, she said . . .' Eliza's voice is bitter, trembling. 'I'd never met Mark before that. Never met any of them. Cairn ordered me into her tent and he was standing there. She said she had a mission for us. That we were going to be spending some time together. And I looked at him . . . and I remembered . . . it was *him*.' Her voice breaks. 'In the vision, he'd been a man, but then, he was only a boy. I kept watching him, waiting, as he got older, taller . . .'

She is staring at Hero's face. Her hands are closed fists, blue-veined, trembling in her lap.

'In the dream he died in a field, at night. I was the one who insisted we kept night watches, I was the one who made sure we never camped in open fields. Like it would make any difference. I knew that if I'd seen it, it would come true. His hair . . .' Tears are running down her cheeks again, over the sound of Raven's sobs outside. 'In the vision, in the dream, it was down to his ears . . . I kept telling him to cut it . . . but he said it looked better long. He was trying to impress Luca, I think. The idiot.'

She puts her face in her hands again. All I can see is the grime of her fingers, pale in the dusk light, the shorn fur of her hair. Her slumped shoulders in the rough-hewn wooden chair.

Where are you now, Joshua? Are you dead?

Are you dead, or are you still wandering alone in those woods, on that cliff top? Or have you stumbled into the arms of the Guard, into their knives and gun barrels and their smiling teeth? Are you in Elida, in my old cell, waiting for me to come for you, the way you came for me?

But I can't leave Hero. And even if I could . . .

I loved you, before all of this. I don't know my heart anymore, not after the black tower and dying and Hero's ruined face, not with all these memories clamouring in my head. But I know that for sure. In the orphanage, when you kissed me, the love burst in my chest so fast it crushed my heart against my ribs. I was sick and light-headed with it.

Falling in love with you was terrifying. I didn't want it but there it was, like a magnet in my mind, a disease. It made me *feel*, in a way I never had before, like someone had peeled the skin from my heart and the nerves lay raw and bleeding. All I wanted was to look at you, touch you, like that would put the problem of you away in my mind so I'd never have to think about you again. And now . . .

I don't understand you anymore. I don't understand anything. Was everything a lie? Is this some terrible sick joke?

You tried to kill Hero, Joshua.

I don't know what that makes you. I don't have the words for it, there are none in my head.

I know the things you said to her. *Lying bitch*, you called her. You said she'd always wanted me dead. You said she'd been trying to kill me, when she pushed me from the tower. Didn't you understand it was the only way *any* of us could live? Didn't you think?

She saved us. And you turned against her, because you needed someone to blame for my death. You chose *her*, because of what? Because you resented her for saving you? You didn't like being in her debt?

I'm trying to come up with reasons but there aren't any. Just a deep, sickening evil, lodged somewhere in your beautiful laughing eyes.

Hero could forgive you. If she was awake, she'd forgive you

in a moment, she's that good a person. Maybe if I hold on to that tightly enough, I'll be able to forgive you too.

But I can't now. I have nothing left to forgive with, no spare feeling. My love burned low in that terrible place, and now all I have is exhaustion, and the thought of your face makes me sick and scared.

You *left*.

Movement in the dark around me. Someone's hand on my shoulder, shaking me. 'Kestrel. Wake up.'

Guardsmen. I kick out in wild panic. My foot hits bone. A grunt of pain.

Someone else's voice. 'Oh, crap—'

'*Kestrel.*' A more familiar voice, bright, a pull to it like falling water. 'Kestrel, look at me.'

I blink, breathing fast. A dim tent. Memory drifts slowly back into the darkness of my mind. I'm not in my cell.

I scramble to sit up, and feel Hero's congealed warmth beside me. Two figures are standing over me, a boy and a girl. The boy is clutching his stomach, taking rasping breaths through his teeth. When I look at him, he straightens up again.

The boy-twin. Caleb. Yes, I remember.

'What the—'

The girl, Eliza, puts up a hand to silence him. 'Kestrel,' she says, still with that soft pull to her voice, 'you're okay. You're safe. You remember where you are?'

Everything is coming back slowly. I look at them both, and nod.

'It's almost dawn. You need to come with us.'

'Where?'

'To the lake. Luca went to the camp to . . . to find Mark.' A slight break in Eliza's voice. 'She's just come back. She sent Caleb to find us.'

I shake my head. My hand is still in Hero's cold slack grip. 'I need to stay.'

'Kestrel, I'm not leaving you here alone. It's too dangerous. You remember what we talked about?'

Eliza's eyes are flint-hard in the darkness. I stare back at her, belligerent. She sighs.

'Fifteen minutes. Nothing will happen to her, Kestrel, I promise you. Raven will be here to look after her. Anthony's men won't hurt them.'

Caleb, behind her, is still eyeing my feet warily.

Eliza says, more firmly, 'Kestrel, you need to come with us. Hero will be fine. Do you understand?'

That pull is back in her voice again. I nod.

'Good.' Eliza opens the tent flap. I get to my feet slowly.

'I'm sorry,' I tell Caleb. He shakes his head.

'It's fine.'

'I thought you were—'

But I can't say it.

He has that too-understanding look in his eyes again. He says, gently, 'Kestrel, it's fine.'

I nod and look away.

Outside the tent are four men, standing close together. Only two of them are staring directly at our tents; the other two are looking, with carefully blank expressions, at the hills beyond the camp. Before we get near them, they turn and vanish down the hill, into the mess of half-erected tents and rows of wounded.

'Anthony's men,' says Eliza, as if either of us needed telling. 'Gone to tell him we're leaving.'

Caleb opens and closes his fists, watching them darkly.

'I could stop them.'

'No.'

'Eliza—'

'No. I don't want Anthony to be able to say we started this.'

He stares at her.

'Started what?'

'I don't know,' Eliza says. She's still staring after the men. 'Raven's his biggest problem right now. He can't risk going after her, she's a kid, so he'll come for me first. He'll try to paint me as a traitor, and her as my trained monkey. It's what I would do, if I were him.'

Caleb lowers his voice, aghast. 'You mean . . . he'll try to kill you?'

'Not directly,' says Eliza. 'I don't think so. I think he's subtler than that.'

She shakes her head as if to clear it, and walks faster. 'So long as you're with me, I don't think he'll try anything violent. He knows what you are.'

'Eliza—' Pain flashes across Caleb's face, brief as lightning. 'Look, if . . . if Mark were still here . . . but you can't just rely on *me* to . . .'

Eliza turns around to look at him for the first time.

'I'm not,' she says gently. 'Trust me, Caleb, I'm . . . there are things Anthony doesn't know about. I'm not just relying on you.'

Caleb nods, his throat tight. He tries to hide it, but I can see he's relieved.

Luca is waiting for us at the edge of the trees, where the earth is softer and wetter, before the ground slopes towards the flat gold lake, blinding in the sunrise.

There is a body at her feet. Caleb stops dead at the sight of it.

'Is that—'

'It's not him,' says Eliza quietly. 'It's a woman, look.'

He nods, too quickly. His arms are tightly folded.

Luca strides towards Eliza when she sees her, not looking at the corpse. 'Where's Raven?'

'Looking after Hero,' says Eliza. 'I didn't think she should see this.'

Luca hesitates, then nods.

'What happened?'

'I just got back. There's no one there. The Guard left hours ago. Just . . . just the dead.' Luca, too, looks pale, as though she hasn't slept in days; there are tears dried into the grime of her face. 'I found him. I didn't want to bring him back, I . . . I didn't want Raven to see him like that . . . and I thought the Guard might come back, and find him—'

She stops, and lets out a shuddering outward breath.

'Luca,' says Eliza. Her eyes are dry, but her grip on Luca's arms is iron. 'What did you do?'

Luca swallows.

'I burned him,' she says, in a small voice. 'I thought . . . I thought he'd want that.'

Caleb makes a choked kind of noise in his throat.

Eliza nods slowly. 'He would,' she says. 'He would want that. You did well.'

'I thought he'd be safe,' Luca says. Her arms are wrapped around her waist, holding herself together. 'I thought . . . I thought since he was human . . . they wouldn't hurt him.'

'He loved us,' says Eliza, quietly. 'He loved us so much they killed him for it. We were what he was prepared to die for, Luca. If he had to . . .' Her voice shivers and almost breaks. 'If something had to happen, he would have wanted it to be like this.'

Luca nods, presses a hand over her eyes, and breathes slowly.

Eliza looks beyond her, to the body at her feet, her face quite blank. 'Who is that?'

'She's a Guardsman.' Luca turns around to look at the dead woman. 'I brought her back. I thought you should see her.'

I look at the body, at the face. Everything in me has gone quite still. The wind is colder on my skin. I see her face in my head. Blue eyes, laughing. The smile on her face. I am very still because I am going mad. I feel the scream as it leaves my throat but don't hear it. A shining animal cry, shock and fear balled up in it like fists.

I stumble back, away from her.

Her clothes are cracked and black with dried blood, and the skin of her clawed hands is white and I can see the jagged bone beneath, but even though her stillness is absolute I can see the smile on her face, ghostly, her lips pulled back over the pale pearl teeth—

'Kestrel!'

– and I can't stop looking at her eyes. I swear she can see me. They're blue and milky and staring sightlessly at the earth beneath her hands but I know she's looking at *me*, she's smiling at me, she came here for me, she found me again.

'*Kestrel!*'

Someone grabs my wrist, the one with my diamond-blade knife in it. I try to pull away, but the grip is too strong.

'Kestrel! Calm down!'

'*Let go of me!*' I'm struggling, shouting. My breath is white-hot in my throat. I have to get free, I have to—

'Kestrel! *Stop!*'

Eliza steps up to me out of nowhere, grabs me by the chin, holds me steady. There's a moment of shocked silence. A heavy calm spreads over me, thick and milky as sleep. I realise I've stopped struggling. My breathing is quick, hoarse. The screaming in my head is coming from a deeper, darker place now, faint and echoing. I can still feel those blue eyes on me from the earth.

'Let go of me.' My voice is low and strong, surprising me.

'Not until you tell me what's going on.'

'Eliza.' Luca is standing at her shoulder. 'Just . . . just look at her.'

After a long moment, Eliza lets go of me and turns to stare at the body. I stumble backwards. Something sweet and aching lights up under my fear and panic, a longing dark as moon-light. I do not want her to stop touching me. I hold the feeling in my mind for a moment, cradling it. It's familiar, a precious thing.

Then I turn back to the body beside the lake, my breath steeled in my chest.

She's dead.

It sinks in slowly in a way it didn't the first time. Her shirt is covered in dried blood from the wound in her stomach. I remember all the times I imagined making a wound like that in her, taking a knife and sinking it deep into her flesh. The look on her face.

Her mouth is covered in blood, too. That's why Luca looks so sickened. Her mouth is covered in blood, but that blood is silver.

The implications of that take a moment to hit me, and then nausea rises up through me. The thought is cloying in my head, filthy. I want to be sick. My hands are shaking. I try to fix my eyes on the grey hills over the horizon, looking at them and only at them, but my gaze keeps drifting back to that silver wound.

Eliza is kneeling beside the dead Guardsman, examining her with disgust. 'Kestrel.'

'Yeah.' My voice is still oddly low.

'Who was she?'

'She . . .' The name swims back up through my mind, unwilling. 'Ellara. Her name was Ellara.'

Eliza looks up at me. 'How do you—'

'She told me. She came to my cell, the third day I was there . . . She was wearing different clothes . . . I . . .' Her voice seeps through my head, a low frightened whisper. *Hello? Hello, are you there?* 'She said she was a prisoner.' *Help me. We have to get out of here.* 'She had keys . . . unlocked my cell door. She had food and water. I was so thirsty and scared. We went down the stairs . . . spiral stairs, I was dizzy.' *I'm so glad I found you. Come on, hurry.* Her blue eyes, piercing in the torchlight that gleamed in the black corridors. Her slow, sweet smile. 'And then she led me . . . into a room . . .'

Luca is very still, listening. Eliza doesn't take her eyes from my face, but I can't say any more. My head is full of it, the moment the lights switched on in that room, the dim argon bulbs, and the Guardsmen standing around me, and Ellara at their side as they drew their knives.

The scars on my arms throb dully, and I pull down my sleeves.

Kestrel, she said then, a hunger in her voice I'd never heard before. I hadn't told her my name.

Eliza doesn't say anything. She looks at me for a long time, then back down at Ellara's dead body. She touches the dried blood on Ellara's lips.

'Where did this come from?' she says quietly.

'There was a man beside her,' says Luca. 'A . . . one of us. There was a . . . cut in his neck. There were tooth marks.'

Eliza looks up sharply. 'She *bit* him?'

Luca nods slowly.

'Why,' says Eliza softly, looking back down at the body, 'would she do that?'

'Because they're mad,' says Caleb harshly from behind us. He hasn't come any closer to the body, but is staring at it from where he stands in open disgust. 'They're all insane, the lot of them.'

A pause.

'How much did it bleed?' Eliza asks Luca, at last.

'What?'

'The wound in the neck. How much did it bleed?'

Luca looks bewildered. 'I don't know. Not . . . not that much. There wasn't any on the grass.'

Eliza looks up at me. I stare back at her. I can't speak. Caleb looks between us.

'What does that have to do with—'

'If it didn't bleed,' says Eliza, 'it means his heart wasn't beating. It means he was already dead when she did it.'

'*So?*' says Caleb, tightly.

'So *why* did she do it?'

He grits his teeth. '*How the hell am I meant to know?*'

Eliza looks at him steadily. Caleb swears and starts pacing furiously up and down through the mud.

'If this man was dead,' says Eliza, quietly, to his back, 'then she knew that. He died before she did, he wasn't the one who stabbed her. She knew she couldn't hurt him. It wasn't revenge. So why would she do it?'

He doesn't say anything. My hands are trembling and I close my fists, trying to stop it.

'It was her last act,' says Eliza. 'The last thing she ever did. She was wounded and dying. The last thought that went through her head. What was yours when they shot you, Caleb?'

He turns to her, eyes burning. 'Why are you asking *me*? They shot you too.'

I close my eyes. I think of the water as I fell towards it in Joshua's arms. And before that, as the door of my cell opened, and the Guard came towards me with the knives in their hands. The hundred times I thought I'd be killed, that this was it, it was over. The final thought that kindled panic in my bone-dry mind.

Eliza says it as I think it, so quietly I barely hear her.

'*I don't want to die.*'

There's a silence. A bird caws in the distance. Caleb is staring at Eliza.

'You mean she thought . . . biting him would *save* her? How?'

Eliza looks at me, then kneels down again beside the body

and, with the faintest shudder of disgust, prises open Ellara's mouth. She glances inside it, then rolls Ellara's head over to the side for Caleb to look at it, like pushing a book across a table.

I walk slowly forward. Luca steels herself and peers into Ellara's mouth, then recoils.

The backs of her teeth are silver. The roof of her cracked dry mouth. The skin of her throat.

'His blood,' says Eliza softly, nausea crawling in her voice. 'She was trying to drink his blood.'

CHAPTER 16

The Voice

We stay there a long time, the body between us. The twins don't speak. I'm trying not to think of anything, of Ellara or her body or the blood. Eliza is pacing up and down beside the lakeshore, deep in thought. Eventually she turns to me.

'Are you all right?'

I swallow, find my voice again.

'Yeah.'

'I'm sorry. If I'd known you knew her—'

'It's okay. You couldn't know.'

She's only half paying attention to me, I can tell, the other half of her mind is buried deep in her eyes.

Caleb says, 'Eliza.'

Luca is pulling grass from its roots beside the shore to clean her sword, she looks up at the sound of his voice. 'Eliza,' he says again, more quietly.

Then he's running up the hill, so fast his form half-blurs in the fading light. Luca looks after him, uncomprehending, and then with a sudden terrible cry she's after him. I don't understand what's going on, I don't—

The smoke. Our tents are burning.

The whole world vanishes from under my feet in a sickening rush of terror. The only word in my mind is *Hero*, echoing in my head, dizzying . . . no, not Hero, please, I'll do anything—

When I come to, I'm running, dirt under my feet and smoke through the treeline, and my whole mind focused on that tent and Hero inside it. Then I remember Raven, who is not comatose, a child alone in the flames and the smoke—

As soon as the word *flame* brushes my mind I realise that the tents are burning white.

There's a crowd in front of them, watching us run up the hill. Two tiny figures, dirty and crumpled, lie on the ground. A grey-haired man is standing over them, holding a knife. A woman and a girl at his feet. The woman bleeding grey.

Hero.

Hero and Raven are lying at his feet. Not burning, not dead.

Relief washes over me, and I stumble. Caleb is screaming in fury and fear, running towards the grey-haired man and the silent horde behind him. They're all very still, watching him.

'Don't get any closer,' says the grey-haired man quietly. There's a knife in his hand, the little girl at his feet. 'I'm warning you.'

Caleb slows and finally stops, panting, staring down at Raven. Luca stops behind him, staring at Anthony, pure hatred in her face.

'I surrender,' says Eliza behind me. 'We surrender.' She's holding her hands above her head, eyes on the grey-haired man. Everything is so quiet.

The grey-haired man is watching her. His eyes are dead in his face.

'Where's my sister, Ehler?' he says quietly.

Behind him, the flames crackle softly.

'She's dead,' says Eliza. 'Cairn's dead, Anthony, she died days ago. I'm so sorry. Please don't hurt them.'

'*Days* ago?'

Anthony's voice has risen, a harsh fever of pain. He lowers it. The crowd behind him is silent. They already knew Cairn was dead, they must have done, it was so obvious. They are not shocked, and therefore they're here for something else. Something else. *Think*.

'Did you kill her?' he says, and again his voice is dark and cavernous with pain.

'No,' says Eliza at once. 'No, Anthony, I promise you. The Guard killed her. They found us on the cliff tops at Elida, after we rescued the Fitzgerald girls. They killed Cairn and they attacked us and we went to the camp. We came to you for help.' Her voice cracks. 'Please don't hurt them.'

Silence.

'I'm not lying,' says Eliza, and for the first time I hear a note of fear in her voice. 'I swear to you, Anthony. There was nothing we could do. Please don't hurt Raven. Put the knife down and we can talk, I can tell you things—'

'You can tell me,' he says softly. '*You* can tell me.'

Silence again. At his feet Raven stirs. Blood trickles through her black hair from a cut in her scalp, and behind me Luca growls with rage. My heart grows steel tendrils, digs into the bone of my ribs and keeps me standing. I can feel anger pulsing slow in my blood now, too.

'You brought the Fitzgerald girl here,' says Anthony quietly, looking at me. 'You took her from Elida and you brought her into this camp. I want the girl.'

I feel completely blank.

Eliza's voice is steady. 'Kestrel didn't betray you, Anthony.'

'Oh yes?' A fissure appears in Anthony's voice for the first time. 'You think it's a coincidence, then? She walks out of Elida, she comes here, and then a day later they follow her? If she *isn't* working for them' – he looks me straight in the face, I can see his disgust – 'then they followed her somehow.'

'Anthony—'

He raises his hand. I can feel the eyes of everyone behind him on me, the hatred pulsing towards me, and I have no voice at all. In my head, the door to my cell swings open, and the darkness around me is thick and wet. I can taste blood and fear in my throat. I step backwards.

Veins of diamond trickle over the skin of Anthony's hand, hardening to blades in the light. I can't look away from them, they're so beautiful.

'You killed my wife, girl,' he says, very quietly.

'Anthony,' says Eliza. 'Anthony, no—'

I open my mouth to speak but no words come. I can't think, I can't breathe; fear is the air in my lungs.

And then he lunges for me.

Everything is silent. All I can see is him.

He leaps over Hero's body and then he's between us. His hands are raised. I step back, but I have no grace and no speed and no courage, and his eyes are bright and the certainty in them is terrifying. I can't even raise my hands to fight him, I'm pathetic—

'*Stop.*'

And he does.

Silence. I can still hear Eliza's voice in my head, deeper than light, a throbbing reverberation, shuddering in my bones. It's beautiful, magical, it commands. I want to do what it says, more than I've ever wanted anything.

I've stopped dead, and so has Anthony in front of me, hand still upraised. No one moves.

Then, at long last, he lowers it and looks at her.

This close, I can see he's too thin, wasted and trembling. I can see the bones in his arms, the lines in his face. Grief has hollowed him out. He looks half-mad.

He looks down at Eliza past me, and slowly sanity returns to his eyes. I am numb, floating, my breath harsh in my chest.

But her voice—

'Anthony,' says Eliza quietly, and there's still that timbre in her voice I've never heard before, a bright deep power, compelling. It speaks of *truth*, and the need to obey. Every eye is on her. There's complete silence but for the crackling of our tents burning silver.

'Listen to me. Don't hurt them. I know why you want to, I understand. But it won't help. I promise. Anthony. Let me talk to you.'

Everyone is quiet, listening to her, half-dreamlike. My eyes are on Hero's chest, rising and falling so slowly in the pale light. The bright echoing sheen of Eliza's voice still greases my mind, trust like a drug. She starts talking in a low rapid voice, holding Anthony's eyes.

'Anthony. Step away from the girl.'

A moment of silence. Then Anthony steps away from me, his diamond-bladed hands still raised. He's staring at her, eyes wide. Eliza keeps talking, low and intent.

'Anthony, listen to me. You need to know. The Guard drink blood. We went back to the camp, we saw it ourselves. They drink the blood of gods and half-breeds.'

He just stares at her. She's still talking, quickfire and staccato, holding his eyes.

'Listen. When they drink a god's blood, they get our powers for a few minutes, maybe hours, I'm not sure. But it only works *so long as the god is alive.* Anthony, it makes sense, it's the *only* thing that makes sense. It's why Elida exists. Why else would the Guard want to keep gods alive? They hate us, they want us dead.'

Still he just stares.

'Anthony, you know what this means. Your sister—'

'Don't you dare talk about her,' says Anthony suddenly. His eyes are dead. 'Don't you dare.'

Silence. Below us, at the bottom of the hill where the other tents are clustered, people have seen the smoke and realised what's happening. Some of them are running towards us. Anthony's crowd spreads out at the sight of them, encircling us, closing us off from their sight. They will not allow us to be rescued.

'What did you just do to me?' asks Anthony, at last. 'With your voice. What did you do?'

'Nothing,' says Eliza.

A pause.

'Look at her,' says Anthony softly, to the crowd, without looking away from her. 'Even now she lies.'

Eliza doesn't look at them. Her burning gaze is on Anthony, her voice low and fast and thrumming.

'It's true, Anthony. We saw it. They'd drunk blood, the Guardsmen, while they were dying, to try to save themselves. Because they must have thought, the gods *around* them would be able to heal themselves, so by drinking their blood, they could heal their own wounds, you see? But if they drank the blood of a dead god—'

There's a collective shudder at her words, a murmur of disgust. Even Luca twitches, still staring at her sister unconscious on the ground.

'If the god was *dead*,' Eliza presses on, 'nothing happened. The Guardsmen died anyway. It makes sense, Anthony, don't you see? And it explains how they got into the camp, how no one saw them coming, how they were suddenly everywhere, before we could fight back. They *vanished* into the camp. We know they have a vanisher, they captured Joanna years ago, they could have drunk her blood easily. Don't you see?'

She stops talking, breathless. Anthony is staring at her. Around us, beyond the wall of his supporters, people are starting to gather, watching.

Someone shouts, '*Mala kralovna!*' One of Anthony's men shoves him to the floor and kicks him. He looks up, spitting blood. Anthony glances at him.

'You believe this?' he says to Eliza. Contemptuously, but there's something else there, beneath it. 'You honestly believe this rubbish?'

'Yes,' says Eliza.

Anthony looks at her. There's hatred in every line of his face. 'Then you're an idiot,' he says. 'If they'd been doing this all this time, then we'd all be dead by now.'

'They haven't,' I say.

It's coming together in my head at last, slower than it would have for Eliza or Hero, but I understand at last. Everyone turns to look at me, and the air seems to turn solid in my chest. I take a long look at Hero, collapsed on the ground. *Breathe. You're braver than this. Be worthy of her.*

When I speak, everything is quiet. I can feel Anthony's eyes on me.

'When I was in the black tower, the Guardsman used to come into my cell, and . . .' *Breathe. Look at Hero. Say it.* 'About a week before I was rescued, I started seeing . . . There were shimmers on their hands. In the darkness. Like they were trying to gather wind, or light, or something. I recognised it.' *Joshua had that shimmer around his hands before he made a light appear. But I still can't say his name.* 'Maybe they were trying to . . . I don't know.'

'To master new demesnes,' says Eliza, watching me. 'If they started drinking blood *then*—'

Anthony shakes his head, slowly. No one else moves.

'None of this,' he says quietly, 'makes sense, Ehler. This is desperate. If you're saying they've kept gods in Elida for twenty years because of *this*—'

'Maybe not because of this, then,' she says. 'Maybe just to experiment. To find out how to get demesnes of their own, to work out how to use gods to their advantage. Anthony, look at me.' He regards her coldly. 'I'm not saying they *always* knew. Maybe they worked it out a few years ago and kept the gods alive in Elida just in case—'

'In case of *what*?'

He spits it, but she stays calm.

'A crisis. And then there was one. A god and a half-breed

escaped from an orphanage and got halfway up the country.
They fought their way out of a village. Maybe then the Guard
decided to start using it, to capture them. And then, when
Kestrel and Hero escaped Elida, they used it to attack the
camp.'

'And how exactly,' says Anthony, his voice very quiet and
dangerous, 'according to you, did they *find* the camp?'

Eliza takes a deep breath.

'That,' she says, 'I don't know.'

A long silence.

'You see,' says Anthony, and now I see how his hands are
trembling, 'that's curious, to me. Because it seems that that
would be the only thing in this of any use.'

'*The only thing of any use?* Anthony, this is how we defeat
the Guard!' Eliza's face is flushed, her voice deep and fluid
and strong. Everyone is watching her now, even the twins.
'The Guard were created to protect humans from us, and now
they're trying to *become* us! As soon as they try to get our
powers, our demesnes, they're no different from us! Anthony,
if we spread the word about this . . . this is how the Guard
lose support. This is how they're *overthrown*. This is what
Cairn always wanted. It's a masterstroke for us, it's an advantage like we've never had, it's—'

'Don't you dare say her name,' Anthony says, his voice
suddenly vicious with hate. 'Don't you dare talk about her
to me.'

Silence. Eliza stares at him, breathing hard, his eyes
narrowed.

'It seems to me,' says Anthony, 'that the most likely expla-
nation for how we were found is still *this girl*.' He spits the
word at Eliza, and gestures to me with a jerk of his thumb.
'She walks out of Elida and into our welcoming arms,' the
contempt in his voice is unbearable, 'and then not *twelve
hours* later—'

'I didn't walk,' I say. 'I fell.'

Anthony turns slowly to look at me. His eyes are ice-grey, devoid of feeling. I hold his gaze.

'You what?' he says softly.

'I *fell*. I fell from the tower.'

'You fell from . . .' He seems completely nonplussed. It wipes even the hatred from his face for a moment. 'How?'

'My sister. She healed me. I was dead and she healed me.' I nod towards Hero without looking at her. 'And as for whether I'm working with the Guard – whether I'm *loyal* to them—' The words burn my throat. I want to close my eyes. I take a deep breath.

And then I pull up my sleeves and show him my arms.

He looks down at them, and then steps slowly back. I can hear mutters from the crowd. I don't look down at my forearms, my wrists, the scars there. I don't want to see them ever again. Quick as a dragonfly over water I feel the brush of Joshua's lips on my skin. He loved my arms.

'They cut me to see what colour my blood ran, and then they kept cutting to see if it would make me talk, and then it did. And then . . .' *Please don't hurt me.* I can hear the Guardsmen laughing inside my head. 'They just kept cutting.'

The tents are burned down almost to ash, silver-white embers and soot. Even the crowd behind Anthony's men are silent. I can feel the touch of their eyes on me, but mine are on Anthony. There's confusion in his face at last, his certainty cracking under the weight of shock. The silence is absolute.

'I didn't betray you,' I say to him. Then with effort, so much effort, I look up at Anthony's men, meet each of their eyes with Hero's courage, and they look back at me. I say it again, because it is true, and my certainty strengthens my voice. 'I didn't betray you. I didn't know where the camp was, I didn't even know it existed, and if I had I wouldn't have said anything. I would *never* help the Guard. I—'

'It's all right,' says Eliza quietly, from behind me. 'It's okay, Kestrel.'

I swallow, and the breath comes out of me in a shuddering gasp. I look down again, at Hero. I pull my sleeves down again.

The shock is still there on Anthony's face. He glances at his men, uneasy.

Over my head I hear Eliza say into the silence, 'Please listen to me, Anthony. This is our way in. This is it. We're never going to have a better chance to convince the people that the Guard are evil.'

Anthony says nothing. Eliza turns to face the men behind him.

'The girl you attacked tonight,' she says, 'is Cairn's chosen heir. Not Anthony, whatever he might tell you. Raven was the one. Cairn told me herself, years ago.'

Anthony makes a sudden, violent gesture. The voices of the crowd behind him rise; someone shouts '*Mala kralovna!*' again. The circle around us tightens, trapping us in.

Eliza raises her voice. 'Cairn raised her and trained her almost from birth. She's a shapeshifter. She's braver than anyone I've ever met – cleverer, too – she's *good*, and innocent, and honest and loyal, and she's worth a thousand of Anthony Abernathy.' She's talking directly to his supporters now, whilst he stares at her, livid with rage. He's lost control now, and he knows it. 'She is the purest soul ever to be born of our blood, and she is *chosen*.'

'*Chosen!*' The roar comes up from behind Anthony's supporters, from the crowd who gathered around us at the sight of Raven. '*Mala kralovna!*'

'She fought in that battle,' says Eliza. She is not shouting; they all fall silent to listen to her, rapt and breathless. 'She was ready to die for you. *All* of you. And this is how you repay her?' She gestures to Raven, lying tiny and helpless at the woman's feet, blood trickling down her forehead.

Even some of Anthony's supporters are looking uneasy now.

'She is a child,' says Anthony, his voice trembling, 'and you are lying scum.'

Eliza turns to look at him. There's a strange light in her eyes.

'That's what you think,' she says, so softly only he and I can hear over the cheering. 'Do you want to bet that's what *they* think?'

'*Mala kralovna! Mala kralovna!*'

His eyes are burning. He knows he's lost. I see it in the way he looks at the men surrounding him.

Then something seems to break in him at last. Grief and exhaustion rise in his face, and something else, too; a white-hot hatred, a concentrated fury. His teeth are bared, his fists clenched and trembling. It seems to take him all the effort in the world to speak.

'Go,' he says at last, softly. 'Take them and . . . and go. But I swear, Ehler, you will not forget this.'

At his words, the woman holding Raven steps back, and the crowd behind her erupts. People are pulled backwards, shoved, punched, to make a path for us to walk through the crowd. Luca vanishes and reappears in an instant beside Eliza with Raven in her arms, and then she's gone again, casting a look of murderous loathing behind her at Anthony before she disappears.

The crowd are separating, stumbling apart, and half of them are cheering Anthony and hissing at Eliza and me, like children in a playground. But the other half are screaming for Eliza, who raises her head and walks slowly down the hill with Caleb and me two steps behind her, towards the sunset and the deep gold lake.

Anthony watches her go, his eyes alight with a fervent, burning hatred, surrounded by his own chanting men. He looks suddenly very alone.

I can still feel the ghost of my terror in my chest, the way he stood over Hero. Grief doesn't do that to you. I wonder what really lives in him, what he wants, underneath his burning fury and his sunken eyes. I look at Eliza, tall and bright in victory, and the power thrumming in her, and for the first time I have hope that we're going to make it out of this alive.

CHAPTER 17

Midnight

Before I change her bandages, I take Hero down to the lake. Dark has fallen, but the night is clear-skied and moonlit, and Eliza and the others will be able to see us from where they've pitched their tent. But nobody will attack us. Eliza is almost sure we're safe now.

In the silvery light, I can see Hero's face. I take off her filthy, blood-stained clothes, careful not to pull scabs from the sticky skin. Then I pull her by the shoulders into the water with me.

She floats when I let her go, spread-eagled, her single eye closed. The night is cold, but I'm not scared for her, even unclothed in the water. Her skin is hot and feverish. In the silence I watch her.

Everything burns and blurs in my head. Anthony's bladed hand, Hero limp on the ground at his feet, Raven in Luca's arms, so tiny and helpless. The dried, cracked blood in Ellara's mouth. And the Guard, the Guard, the Guard. The door of my cell closes inside my head with a soft thud that echoes over the lake in the smooth black silence.

I lie back, pushing at the water with my fingers together like fins. I learned to swim in the river that circled the grounds of Fitzgerald House, a glittering ribbon in sunlight. I duck my head under the water until my mind is silent and warm again.

The sun set hours ago over the trees across the lake, which means that way is west. So south is *that* way. Back towards the main camp. Somewhere beyond it, hundreds of miles away, is Amareth, the glass city. Our dormitory window, the curtains closed. Our empty beds.

And north . . .

The black tower. Elida.

Joshua. I think of him again, irrepressibly, though I don't want to. *Please don't be dead.* I think it with force this time, the words clean and clear in my mind. I see him in my head, my dark-eyed laughing boy.

Don't be dead. Just be gone.

Because I can see the other boy in my head, the one he became. The one who screamed at Hero in the tower. *You're not my master!* A child's words, spoken in petulance and spite, but with the power of life and death behind it. The shock on her face, and the weariness. *You've never cared about me!*

I know how badly he must have hurt her, to make her say that to him. And more than that, the words Eliza told me he said. *Lying bitch!* I can hear that in my head, in his voice, and I want to kill him for hurting her like that. But when I close my eyes I can still feel the sunlight on my face as we lay together on the riverbank at the bottom of the hill in the orphanage, my head on his chest as he stroked my hair, and I remember how my heart glowed with love. I can't shake the image of his face, the heat in his eyes just before he bent to kiss me. I can't forget who he was, and I can't want him dead.

So I stare out over the lake and think: just be gone. Don't come back, just stay wherever you are, stay away from her. Let me remember you as the boy with the dancing eyes who died saving me, and then maybe in five years or ten I can forget the murderous creature you became. Look, she's dying now. Isn't that what you wanted? I wish we'd never met. I would give anything never to have loved you.

I close my eyes and sink beneath the smooth surface into

darkness. I feel the dried blood pull gently away from my skin.
I run a hand through my hair, untangling the matted filth.

I know what I have to do now.

I lie back in the water, tasting the knowledge in my head.
It feels warm and worn, like tiredness. Anthony, the Guard,
the blood, my arms, Hero, Raven, Mark in the grave, and
Ellara's whisper in my ear, *you're free* . . .

I close my eyes and pull myself out of the water, shivering
in the cold. Take slow breaths to calm myself. I know what
I have to do and I will do it.

I sit there on the muddy bank for a while, then I pull Hero
out on to the shore, drying her off with a blanket, with all
the tenderness and love I have left in me. I sit there beside
her for ten minutes, just feeling the darkness and the cold
wind on my wet skin. Then I pick up the knife.

Later, at midnight, Eliza and I are sitting alone in the new
tent, not talking, just slumped on the grass in the exhausted
silence. This one is borrowed, I don't know from whom. Luca,
Caleb and Raven, the cut to her head healed, are asleep in
the tent next to us. The twins have refused to leave Raven's
side since Anthony's attack. His men came into her tent and
kept hitting her until she passed out, even though she fought
and kept fighting. She kept apologising for that, even though
they tell her it's not her fault, it could *never* be her fault. She
won't accept it. *I told him*, she kept saying, over and over, as
the twins tried to calm her down. *I told him I'd never get
caught off-guard* . . .

After a while, Eliza says quietly, 'Didn't you wonder why
Cairn didn't choose one of us?'

Shadows move slowly on the canvas wall. There's a torch
left just outside the tent, on the grass. I can smell the smoke,
it makes me very tense for reasons I can't quite remember
now. I watch its flickering for a while, then say, 'Yeah.'

Silence. Eliza doesn't speak.

'I thought she should have chosen you. I couldn't understand why she'd give it to a kid, when you were right there.'

Another silence. I stare at the canvas wall.

'Back there, on the hill . . .'

She looks at me, dark eyes gleaming in the torchlight.

'You saved my life.'

Pause. She doesn't contradict me.

'You did something with your voice. You said *stop*, and then Anthony did. *I* did.' I look at her. 'It felt like . . . like I had to.'

'I know.' Eliza looks at her hands, white and spectral in the flickering light, as though she can see the silver blood beneath. 'I didn't realise I could do that.' She laughs suddenly, bitterly. 'No. No, I did.'

'You've done it before?'

'Once, maybe. When I was a kid, in the camp.' She coughs again, wincing. 'Cairn was there. She saw me do it. That was when she started watching me. And when my mother died . . . Cairn took me in.'

'Because she knew you were powerful.'

'Yes. I was ten. I had no one else.' She looks at me. 'You think she was callous? That she only took me because I was useful to her?'

I don't say anything.

There's a rough edge to Eliza's voice now.

'You didn't know her.'

'I know.' I hesitate. 'Could you do it now? Command someone?'

'I don't know. Up on the hill, I was . . . desperate. Scared.' She looks at me, thoughtfully. 'Hero brought you back from the almost-dead, when she was desperate and scared. It does strange things to you. Gives you power.'

I think of Hero, of kneeling beside her holding the knife

in the darkness an hour ago, of what I did, and feel sick.

No. Don't think of that.

Think of this: Eliza was afraid that I would die.

I sit and look at her, heartbeats slow in my ears.

'You're a telepath,' I say quietly. 'That's what you really are. Truth-telling is only part of it.'

I can see the panic in her eyes. 'No. *No.* That's not it. I can't . . . read minds, or . . . the thing on the hill, I've only ever done it twice, I didn't even . . .' She falters. 'Kestrel, I swear, I'm not, I would never—'

'Eliza. I don't care.'

She looks at me. I've never seen her this frightened before. 'The others would.'

'No. You're good, you're a good person. They'd trust you. *I* trust you.'

She doesn't say anything. Everything is unfolding inside my head, moving into place, sense forming from confusion.

'That's why Cairn didn't choose you as her heir,' I say. 'Why she had to pick Raven instead. She didn't want you given more power. She thought you already had too much of it.'

Eliza rubs her face, very slowly, still staring at the tent entrance. Then at last she says, 'Yes. She used to say too much power can drive a person mad. A weak person.' She turns to me at last. She looks pale and strained, and somehow much younger. 'But I thought I could withstand it. I thought she would trust me that much.'

I don't know what to say, how to take the pain from her beautiful face. There's a long silence.

'Raven will be better,' she says softly. 'Cairn was right about her heart, at least. She's incorruptible. Her sense of right and wrong. . . And she's brave, braver than I ever was. She deserves it.'

'We don't need bravery,' I say. 'Not right now. We need cleverness. Cunning. We need ruthlessness.'

'You think I'm ruthless?' She tries to smile.

'Ruthlessness and cruelty aren't the same thing.'

'They can be, if you give it long enough. The ruthless become cruel, in the end.'

'Did Cairn?'

Eliza flinches, and I wonder if I've stepped over the line, but she doesn't say anything for a long time.

'I did wonder sometimes,' she says softly, 'if the reason she tried so hard to convince me I wasn't suited to power . . .'

She licks her lips, swallows.

'She was afraid of you,' I say, quietly. 'She thought if you believed you deserved power, you'd take it from *her.*'

'I would never have done that,' says Eliza, her voice tight. '*Never.* Not from her.'

'But you *could* have done.' The dizzying, limitless expanse of her power lies before me in the dark of the tent. 'Just by talking to her. You could have—'

'Don't,' says Eliza, with sudden vehemence. Her voice sounds constricted, and for the first time I can hear a crack in it. 'Don't say that.'

Her face is in her hands. I wonder for an awful moment if she might be crying, but then she swallows and raises her head, and I see her eyes are dry.

'Raven is righteous and brave,' she says, at last. Her voice is lower and steadier. 'She does deserve it. If she were grown . . . if this was peacetime—'

'But it isn't,' I say softly. She turns to look at me. 'The Guard hate us, and we're weak, and if we don't fight we're going to die. We can't be led by a child. We need *you,* Eliza.'

She's looking at me oddly.

'We?' she whispers.

That fire is alight in my chest again, sweet and blade-sharp. A bravery I don't feel I own thrums softly in my skin. The world is canvas and grass and silence, and *her,* face hollow and gaunt in the pale light. I just want to look at her. The word in my throat is *beautiful*, she's beautiful, but it goes deeper than that, a knife in my chest, my lungs, breathless and acidic.

I reach up and touch the skin of her throat, gently. I don't know what I'm doing, but the clouds in my head have dispersed and my blood is singing. I'm just staring at her, and happiness has settled over my mind like a silken veil.

In the very first, long moment of touch, the world around me seems to sharpen, and there's electricity bright as flame in my fingertips. I could look at her forever. And then the moment breaks and time restarts and I'm just waiting with my heart clenched in my teeth for her to push me away or say something.

But she doesn't.

'Be careful, Kestrel,' she says quietly. There's a strange light in her eyes.

We sit there in the silence, my fingertips still on her throat. I'm about to let them fall and apologise when she lifts a hand and presses my fingers with sudden strength against her skin, a flash of heat in her eyes.

Then finally, with the last of my strange courage, I lean forward on to my knees and kiss her.

Her lips don't taste like the cinnamon of Joshua's, but of sweat and metal and salt. She's kissing me back very gently. All I can see is her, her wine-dark eyes, and the sound of her voice in the cavernous darkness when I woke up that first time.

At first I think she's pulling back, and I move back too, ready to say sorry and run away, but then she kisses me harder and I can taste the salt of her open mouth and her quickening heartbeat and one of her hands is in my hair and the other is on my stomach under my shirt and I can't breathe at all.

I kiss her neck, gently, feeling the muscles shift as she leans her head back and makes a soft noise in her throat that lights my blood on fire. Skin beneath my hands, my lips, and my mind white-hot with hunger. I can taste her warm silver voice. I want to kiss it from her throat.

Some time in the depths of the night, I hear movement outside.

I sit up slowly. My jacket is lying beside me on the ground and I take the diamond-blade knife, scrubbed clean in the lake water hours ago after what I did to Hero, and get to my feet. Eliza is asleep next to me, wrapped in a sheepskin rug, and the torch burns outside. In its faint, flickering light, she looks like a river nymph, the soft bruise-blue of her eyelids darkened in the dim tent. I look away. I will not wake her.

A silhouette is framed against the tent entrance.

My grip tightens on the knife. I stand there in the warm silence with my heartbeat in my throat, the canvas walls fluttering slightly in the night wind, my mind alight.

Someone is here to kill us in our sleep. I raise the knife in front of me, gripping it with both hands, pointing it at the tent entrance. Let them try. They're not going to hurt Eliza or Raven or the twins while I'm here.

The tent flap opens, and my pulse quickens in my chest. I grip the knife tighter and step forward. And then the woman steps into the tent and the pale torchlight falls on her face and I see her.

Hero.

I drop the knife and it hits the earth with a soft black *thud.*

She's standing right there in the tent entrance. Her face gleams softly with pale pink scar tissue, tracing the path of the bullet up through her cheek and over where her right eye used to be. She's wearing the same clothes she was in when she left the orphanage, torn and dark with dried blood, and she's shivering in the cold autumn night, dark hair still wet from the lake. She looks bewildered, hugging herself.

Then at last, her eye adjusts to the light and she sees me, standing there watching her in the dimness of the tent.

She stops dead.

Everything is still and silent. All the colour leaves her face. Her mouth opens slightly, soundless.

'Kestrel?' she whispers. '*Kestrel?*'

Hero looks at me and the light in her face is growing and then she makes a choking noise that I realise is laughter only when she starts running towards me and she does a kind of jump and we collide in mid-air, and then her arms are around me and she's laughing and crying and so am I and I'm hugging her as tight as I can.

'Kestrel, Kestrel, *Kestrel*—'

I laugh into her wet hair, because I can't help it, I'm going to collapse with the joy of it. I want to tell her that I love her and I was so scared for her and I'm so grateful to her, but I don't have the words or the breath. I'm putting all my strength into hugging her and hoping that says it all. It's been so long. Hero alive and laughing, I would give the world for this.

(Did I?)

'Kestrel, *Kestrel* . . .'

(but don't think of that, don't think of what you did by the lake)

'Kestrel, you're *alive*—'

(it doesn't matter what you did if Hero's okay, nothing matters so long as she's okay)

She releases me at last, pulls back to look into my face, watching me hungrily. 'Kestrel.'

Hero's just staring, open-mouthed, at my face, and she's so alight with joy, and all I can think is *finally, finally.*

'Oh, Kestrel . . . I don't . . . what happened? How did you wake up?'

I kiss her forehead, marvelling at the living warmth of her.

She's so thin I can feel the bones of her ribs pressing against her arms. 'You. You did it. You saved me. You woke me.'

'I . . . when? How?'

'Before.' I don't look away from her ruined face, I know it will hurt her if I do that. 'Eliza says you did something with your hands, you healed me, and then afterwards I woke up.'

I turn. Eliza is blinking, propping herself up on an elbow, watching the two of us blearily. Her eyes settle on Hero and after a moment the sleep clears from them and her mouth falls open.

'Hero?'

Hero looks at her and smiles. 'Eliza.'

Eliza gets slowly to her feet, a hand to her throat. She walks slowly towards Hero, who doesn't flinch. She touches Hero's scar very gently, as if checking it's real.

'You healed yourself.'

Hero nods, still watching her uneasily. I let go of her and step back, picking up the diamond-blade knife from the grass. 'I woke up. I was injured, but I could take away the pain. Everything was half-healed already. I think I did it in my sleep.'

'That's impossible. No one can heal when they're unconscious.'

Hero shakes her head slowly. Her eyes keep flickering back to me, the smile still there on her face. 'Eliza, what *happened*? Where are we?'

Eliza studies her for a moment, an oddly closed expression on her face. She glances at me and I see something flicker in her eyes. She suspects already, I can see it.

'Eliza. *Kestrel*.' Hero looks between us both. I stare back, unable to believe she's alive and standing there. Everything I did by the lake was worth it, for this. 'What *happened*? Is everyone okay?'

Eliza and I look at each other, over Hero's shoulder.

'The Guard found the camp,' says Eliza eventually. 'There was a battle—'

'I know, I remember—'

'Luca got everyone out, or most of us, anyway, and we came here.'

'Luca's okay?'

Eliza nods, her throat tight. I can see the muscles in her neck. 'And Caleb. And Raven. But, Hero . . .'

'Where's Mark?' says Hero. When Eliza doesn't answer, Hero looks at me. 'Kestrel, where did Mark—'

'He's dead, Hero,' I tell her softly, knowing Eliza can't say it. 'The Guard killed him.'

'The . . .'

Hero's voice dies in her throat. She stares wildly between me and Eliza and when Eliza doesn't deny it she sinks slowly down into the grass, her hands over her face.

I kneel down beside her and wrap my arms around her. 'I'm sorry.' Eliza has turned away, staring at the canvas tent walls.

'He was . . .' Hero presses her knuckles into her forehead, breathing in. 'He was . . . he was brave. He was kind. He saved my life, I mean – Eliza, I'm so sorry.'

Eliza's face is expressionless. She throws Hero some food from the pack. 'Take this,' she says. 'You should eat.' Her voice is thick, and when I look at her she turns away, a hand covering her face. It's a few moments before she comes back to sit next to us again beside the fire, and she doesn't speak for a long time.

Hero eats slowly, still staring at me as if she can't believe I'm real. She is thin and gaunt, and her hair is shorn, but her eyes – her *eye* – is still bright and alive. She's still my sister, still the girl who undid the bonds tying me to my chair in the black tower, talking slowly and softly to calm me down. And sitting there between Eliza and Hero, my heart sings with happiness, full and warm and pure, for the first time since I was taken from the orphanage.

She asks questions as she eats and I tell her everything we know. About the camp, about Anthony and what he did on the hillside, about the Guard drinking blood to get people's gifts, keeping them locked up in Elida to drain them. Hero absorbs this quite calmly, her eyes flickering between me and Eliza. After a while she holds out her hand silently and Eliza accepts it, and I watch the cuts and bruises fade from Eliza's arms like puddles drying in sunlight.

There's a silence. I lean my head against Hero's shoulder, like I used to when we were younger. She's so warm, so wonderfully alive.

'That makes sense,' Hero says at last, once we've told her everything. 'About the blood.'

'Does it?'

'The light on the Guardsmen's hands. The night we took you from the tower. Don't you remember?'

I remember. I can see it, in my head, the strange gold shimmering.

'It looked like—'

I can't say his name. Hero looks at me.

'Yes,' she says, 'I think it was his. He was shot in Seaborne and he left his blood over everything. It would have been easy for the Guard to get it. And it explains . . . on the cliff top, some of them who had been blinded were healed, and I didn't understand . . .' She trails off.

The wind outside is high and whistling and cold. Autumn is deepening rapidly to winter now. I was taken in summer; it seems years ago now.

'Joshua's alive,' says Hero quietly, at last. 'I know it.'

I look back at her. 'Hero, I know what he did.'

'What, run away?' Hero's voice is oddly rough and high, as if she's about to laugh. 'He did more than that, Kestrel.

You weren't there. At Seaborne. And after . . . he—' She stops, closes her eyes. Then at last she says, 'He did a lot. He was a coward, and he . . . but he's still ours, and he's *alive*, Kestrel, I know it.'

Silence. Eliza's eyes meet mine and then she looks away to the tent entrance. I don't say anything. She turns to Hero.

'If we find him,' says Eliza gently, 'if we get any indication of where he is—'

'We *know* where he is. If he's alive, he'll be in Elida.'

'You can't ask us to do that, Hero.'

'I'm not asking you to do anything.'

'Yes, you are.'

There's a long silence. Eliza gets up and walks once round the tent, staring at the floor. I don't meet Hero's eye.

Finally, Eliza says, 'Hero, I don't want to . . . I mean . . .' She looks down at her, standing with her clasped hands behind her back, and Hero looks back up at her steadily. 'Your eye.'

Hero doesn't say anything. Slowly, she touches her face, the mass of scar tissue where her right eye should be. Then, when Eliza looks like she's about to speak, Hero says hoarsely, 'Joshua had a vision about my getting shot in the face. Just like it happened. I should have realised . . . He didn't see the tents in the vision. Or he didn't tell me about them. That was why I didn't realise where I was.'

I take her hand and hold it.

When she has the strength to speak again she says, 'No, I don't think I can heal it. I can't grow it back. I'm not . . . that's not healing. I can't make something again, if it's lost.'

'It's okay,' I say quietly. 'It's all okay.'

Hero looks at me, breathing slowly and deeply, and Eliza is watching us with an odd look in her beautiful face, and all is silent.

From outside the tent comes a terrible scream.

A moment of quiet. The scream dies. We've all frozen.

Then all at once Eliza's running, so fast she blurs, out of the tent into the wide black night. I'm following her even though I'm still half a thought behind her, still on *maybe we imagined it*, and Hero is behind me, stumbling with fear crystallised in her dark eye. Something is terribly wrong, but the grass is cold under my bare feet and it's so dark I can't see anything.

When my eyes adjust to the torchlight, I see Luca crouching in the grass outside her tent. Her face is torn and bleeding, and she's sobbing in pain, her scream choking in her throat. Something gleams near her foot—

In her foot.

Someone has driven a metal stake through it and pinned it to a steel block and they're pulling it forward, dragging her, and she's crying with the agony of it.

My breath leaves me, and I can feel bright fear swimming in the darkness of my head.

Eliza shouts, '*STOP!*'

There's the ring in her voice, the timbre that makes you want and need to obey. I stop where I am in the grass, swaying, and so does the man dragging Luca.

My mind is suddenly cloudy, slow. I shake my head to clear it.

Eliza runs forward, and with an effort I follow her, Hero right behind me. There are more torches studded in the earth beside Caleb and Luca's tent, and in their light I can see what's going on.

A tall man is standing beside Luca. He's a holding a steel chain, trailing down to the block pulling Luca forward, and when I follow it I realise that the steel is part of his arm, the metal melting smoothly into the flesh of his wrist. He stands barefoot on the grass, so Luca can't vanish away.

Behind me Hero is bent double, heaving. I reach backwards and touch her shorn hair with shaking fingers and feel myself steadying. Breathe in, breathe out.

Distantly, I hear Eliza saying, 'Let her go or I'll kill you right now.'

Hero crawls forward, past me, and puts a hand on Luca's neck, and her screams stutter and fade as Hero takes her pain. Love swells in my shattered heart. The man's eyes are on Luca as the cuts on her face seal and fade.

He says, 'Go away and we'll leave the rest of you alone. We just want the vanisher.'

Eliza looks at him. I see a thousand thoughts, quick as birds, flicker across her face and vanish, and then she looks as dead as Anthony did, in the moment he let us go.

She says, 'Kill yourself.'

Something changes in the black air. A fluttering, winged something, a heat shimmer, seems to pass from Eliza into the man. His breath catches, and he steps back, and for a moment everything is silent and dead. Then the metal chain on his fingers snaps, with a sound like breaking ice. It hangs in the air as the steel melts from his fingers, drips into the grass, and then thins and hardens and sharpens into a long thin blade. His trembling hand moves slowly upwards. His eyes are on Eliza, terrified.

'No,' Hero says behind me suddenly, 'wait, no—'

Then everything happens at once.

Behind us from the darkness there's a terrible roar like a wounded wolf, and Caleb comes stumbling out of the tent, his head bloody, Raven tiny and filthy and unconscious in his arms.

At the same instant, the blade pierces the man's shirt.

Hero lunges forward, clumsy and slow with horror, but it's too late. The shirt is deepening black beneath his bulging-eyed touch, blood spreading through the fabric and dripping on to the grass, and I can just *smell* the fear on him.

There's silence. Then Caleb sees Luca's foot and screams.

The man is still standing. I can see him looking at Eliza,

terrified, as he pushes the blade slowly further into his chest, his fingers slick with his own blood, and she's looking back at him and there's no colour in her face at all.

The blade touches something within the man's chest. The light in his eyes goes suddenly out. He falls to his knees. *Thud.* Onto his face.

All is still.

Silence and darkness. The man is sprawled on the ground, a mess of collapsed flesh and silver blood. I can see his head where it lolls on his shoulder, his eyes still open. I turn away. My ankle gives way in the movement and I stumble. I look at my hands and see they're trembling.

Caleb is kneeling beside Luca. Hero is crouching with them, speaking softly and calmly even though her face is dead grey. I can barely hear what they're saying.

'– not going to lose her foot, Caleb, let me look at Raven—'

'They knocked us out.' His face is contorted and blood trickles slowly down his forehead. 'Me and her, *again,* they came when we were sleeping. I said they'd never hurt her again, I swore it. Luca, I'm sorry . . .'

Luca is looking at Hero. 'You're alive,' she whispers blankly.

Eliza is standing behind me, staring at the dead man. The light is suddenly back in her eyes, although her hands are trembling. I walk over to her and hold her hands to stop them shaking. I kiss her, very gently, because it's the only thing I can think of to do. 'Eliza,' someone says with my voice. 'Eliza, it's okay, it's all okay.'

But the man is dead on the grass, and his chest is soaked in blood, and she said *kill yourself*—

'I made him do it,' says Eliza, and swallows. Suddenly she sounds much younger, without that thrum of power in her voice. 'I . . . I made him do it.'

Behind us, I hear Caleb and Luca moving. Raven is awake and murmuring in Caleb's arms, bleary and confused. I walk between Raven and the man Eliza killed, shielding him from her view. My hands have stopped shaking and I feel a warm numbness alight in my chest, a sallow strength.

Eliza turns with a shuddering effort back to Luca, shivering beside Caleb in the dark. She walks back towards them.

I hear her say, 'You'll be okay?'

'She'll be fine,' says Hero, before Luca can answer. She's watching Eliza very intently, her hands covered in grey blood. Her eyes keep moving behind her, into the darkness where the man's body lies crumpled.

Eliza looks away from her, into Luca's face. 'What happened?'

Luca swallows. Her voice is shaky and hoarse from screaming. 'They came into the tent. Knocked out Caleb. Raven woke, tried to fight, but he knocked her out too. I thought for a moment . . .' Anguish drifts like smoke across Luca's eyes. 'I would have vanished, but I couldn't leave them, and he was between me and Caleb. Then he . . . speared me. Dragged me out of the tent.'

Eliza takes a deep breath. I grasp her hand, trying to help her calm down. I see Caleb glance towards us.

'It was a kidnap attempt,' says Eliza, flatly. She turns away from me and puts a hand over her face, her eyes, takes another deep breath, then says, 'Anthony wanted to take Luca to stop us being able to leave. He's planning . . . to kill us, all of us. Maybe tonight. We need to go.'

The silence is brittle as glass. Raven slides from around Hero's neck and shifts in the darkness into a girl again. She walks slowly towards Eliza, then stops.

'Eliza, we can't go. I have to stay here.' Her eyes are burning in the dark. 'I'm their *leader*.'

'Sweetheart,' says Eliza, 'no you're not.'

Silence. Just the crackling of the flames, and Luca's harsh breathing.

'No,' says Raven at last. 'No. I can't *leave*. They need me. They shouted for me, they followed me into the fight—'

'Some of them. Not enough. We didn't have time to get them all. If the whole camp had been on your side, Anthony would never have got close to you, yesterday or tonight. It didn't work. I'm sorry.'

'I can get more of them,' says Raven fiercely. 'I can stay. I can talk to them. Cairn wanted me to . . . I *have* to—'

'You can't,' says Eliza, softly. There's a tremor in her left hand, and she clenches it until it stops. 'Cairn would understand. I thought you could, but you can't, not now. It's too dangerous. If you go back up there, if you stay here and try to build a following, Anthony will crush you. We know that now. He'll kill you. And they' – she points up the hill, into the dark – 'those people, the ones who followed you, they won't like it, they'll grieve, they might even hate him for it, but they'll keep following him, because they're safer with him than alone.' Her voice breaks. 'Sweetheart, I'm sorry.'

'But Cairn . . .' whispers Raven. She looks tiny, bewildered, pitiful. 'Cairn wanted . . .'

'Cairn's dead,' says Eliza, 'and she loved you, Raven, she'd want you alive. We have to keep you safe. That's the most important thing.'

'No,' says Raven. Her face is set. 'No. This is what I'm *meant* to do. Cairn said. It's the . . . I have to *stay here*.' Her jaw is clenched tight, her arms crossed. There on the bloody grass, she looks like a child's idea of bravery, angry and stubborn.

'Raven,' says Eliza, and suddenly her voice is very different, colder, 'Mark died for you. You think I'm going to risk losing you now? Not for a moment. You're coming with us.'

Raven looks stricken, but Eliza turns away. I see her fists are still clenched at her side, her jaw set, but she speaks calmly.

'Luca, do you think you could get us out of here? I know you're weak—'

'I'm not,' says Luca. Her eyes are still on Raven, trembling in the dark. 'Where do you want to go?'

'I don't know,' says Eliza. She rubs her face, exhausted. 'Somewhere close.'

'Eliza,' says Hero quietly, from the fireside. 'If we leave, we can't come back, Anthony will seize everyone who supported her, or convert them . . . and if we try to walk back in—'

'He'll kill us if we stay, too.'

'That depends. How many people do you think he'll send?'

'Enough,' says Eliza. 'Enough that even if we survive, they'll find us tomorrow surrounded by bodies and covered in blood, and how do you think that will look for Raven?'

Hero inclines her head. Raven is staring between them, still hugging herself. Caleb walks over and wraps her in his arms. She clings to him. His eyes are on Eliza, over her head.

'I hope you know what you're doing,' he says, at last.

Eliza's eyes fix on him, and I half expect her to shout at him, or to snap at last and collapse weeping on the ground. But she just stands there alone in the firelight, her shoes covered in blood, her face grey and taut, beautiful.

'Yeah,' she says. 'So do I.'

CHAPTER 18

Just Say the Word

When dawn comes we're on another hilltop.

We set up our blood-spattered tents. Caleb tries to make Raven go to sleep, but she's having none of it, so he lights a fire instead for something to do. We haven't gone far. We can still see the camp over the crest of the hill. Eliza says that if something happens, she wants to be the first to know. No one says anything to that.

Raven is restless. She keeps turning into her white owl and flying around our hill, looking down on our tiny fire. She hasn't spoken to anyone since last night. Caleb's eyes follow her silently.

After we've eaten, he says, 'I thought the camp was invisible.'

'It used to be.'

'The people who made it invisible—'

'Dead in the attack,' says Eliza, staring at the camp.

Caleb nods slowly.

Eliza puts down her beef strips and looks up at him. 'Are you angry with me?'

He doesn't answer immediately. He chews his stale oats, swallows them, and then looks up at her.

'You didn't need to talk to her like that,' he says finally. 'Last night.'

I expect Eliza to be irritated, defiant, but instead she just looks weary. 'I know. I'm sorry.'

But this only seems to make Caleb angrier. 'She never wanted the bloody thing in the first place, and then you – I mean, *we* – we convinced her that it was Cairn's dying wish, or something, and she had to do it for the good of the camp or whatever, and you know how much it took out of her – she risked her *life* that night—'

'I know,' says Eliza. 'I do know.'

Caleb takes a deep breath and keeps his voice level with what looks like enormous restraint. 'So *why*, then?'

'Why what?'

'Why did you take her out of there?'

Eliza looks at him, bleakly. 'He tried to kill us, Caleb.'

'Don't give me that. You'd decided before then. I know you. If you'd thought there was a chance, you'd have fought harder. There was something else.'

Luca's eyes flicker between them. Eliza is looking at Caleb very shrewdly, and I can tell she's impressed, very slightly. Then she looks away.

'There was a council,' she says softly, staring down at the camp, over the hill.

'What?'

'There was a council. Of people who were meant to take over the leadership of the resistance if Cairn died before Raven came of age. She knew it might happen, she knew she wasn't invincible, she always said that. She told me on the cliff top, when we were waiting for the Fitzgeralds to get out of Elida. She'd planned it in secret, to make sure Anthony didn't get power by accident.' Eliza pushes her hair out of her eyes. 'When I left you by the fire that night, before the Guard attacked . . . I was trying to find them, to tell them Cairn was dead. They might even have believed me, about every-thing.'

She looks up at him. She seems suddenly much older.

'Raven wasn't meant to be a true leader for years, Caleb. Please believe me, that was never the plan. She was meant to be a figurehead, while they trained her for real command.'

Caleb looks aghast.

'A council? Who are they? *Where* are they?'

'They're dead,' says Eliza. 'Every last one of them.'

'When did they die?'

'Two nights ago,' says Luca, her eyes on Eliza. 'Fighting the Guard. Right?'

'No,' says Eliza. 'No, they died before the Guard came. Two of them got suddenly ill, another three drowned, one just disappeared. All very mysterious. All in the last couple of months.'

Absolute silence. The fire crackles softly at Eliza's feet.

'Anthony found out?' asks Hero, beside me. I jump. She hasn't spoken for hours.

Eliza nods. 'Once I knew that, I realised we'd underestimated him. That *Cairn* had underestimated him.' She looks exhausted, rubs her eyes. 'It didn't matter how much the people loved Raven. Everything I said last night . . . even if they *were* ready to follow her, obey her, it wouldn't matter. Anthony would never let her live. He'd die before he lost his chance at power. A man like that . . . and deranged by grief, into the bargain . . .'

She stares up at Raven's owl, circling slowly fifty feet above our heads, looking down at us with dark, soulful eyes.

'That's why I ended it,' says Eliza at last. 'That's why I knew we had to get her away from here. I wasn't going to outsmart him. If he'd been working for months, I didn't know what other plans he had. And I wasn't going to risk her. I'd *never* risk her.' She looks at them. 'Do you get that?'

Luca and Caleb exchange a look, and then Caleb nods. 'All right.'

'It's not *all right*,' says Eliza through gritted teeth, and gets to her feet. She walks once, twice around the fire. Hero and Caleb's eyes follow her. Luca is shivering and staring into the flames, one hand stroking her newly healed foot absently. Eliza stops suddenly and looks into Caleb's face. 'There are things I haven't told you.'

'Yeah,' he says, 'I know.'

'I'm a telepath.'

'Yeah.'

'I can make people do things. With my voice.'

'I got that.'

'It's my demesne. Truth-telling . . . that's just part of it.'

'I guessed.'

Eliza stares at him. 'You're very calm about this.'

'Did Cairn know about it?'

'Yes.'

He shrugs. 'That's good enough for me.'

'Caleb—'

'What do you want me to say, Eliza?' he says, suddenly fierce again. 'You want me to scream at you? Tell you I never want to see you again? I can do that, if you want.'

She stares back at him, aghast. 'No, I—'

'The way it looks to me,' he says, 'you're all we've got. Yeah, do I wish you'd told us, sure, but to be honest, Eliza, I've got other things to be angry about right now.'

A silence.

Eliza looks at Luca and takes another shuddering breath, steadying herself. 'The man . . . the one I killed . . .'

'I'd have killed him if you hadn't,' says Luca quietly, looking up at her. 'And he'd have killed you, if he'd had the chance. Don't beat yourself up about it.'

Eliza stares between them. She looks lost.

'I thought you'd hate me,' she says.

'Then you were an idiot,' says Luca, looking back into the fire.

'But I . . . the way he . . .' Eliza runs a hand through her hair and swallows. It's strange to see her looking for reassurance, after her murderous calm last night. 'The way he died . . . the way I killed him . . .'

'It was no better or worse than putting a knife through his chest,' says Caleb. 'He's just as dead.'

A silence. Eliza looks lost for words. I want to speak, but I have no voice left. I'm so tired.

'So Anthony wanted to kill *you*?' asks Luca at last, hoarsely. 'To kidnap me, and kill you?'

Eliza starts pacing again, scratching the back of her neck. 'Yes. I think so.'

'Why?'

'He's afraid of me as much as Raven. I'm a threat to him too, I proved that yesterday. I should have seen it coming, I knew I'd provoke him if I showed him what I . . . but I couldn't let him kill Kestrel . . .' Eliza looks at me, and when our eyes meet I feel a shimmer of heat between us, a bright joy in my heart, despite everything.

She was scared I'd die. That will never lose its bright miraculousness.

'So what do we do now?' There's a slight plaintiveness in Caleb's shadowed eyes. 'Eliza, couldn't we—'

'Leave?'

A silence.

'Yes,' he says. 'Yes, couldn't we leave? After everything . . .' He closes his eyes and swallows, speaks with difficulty. 'After *Mark* . . .'

Another silence, longer.

'We can't,' says Eliza softly. 'Caleb, I'm sorry, but if Anthony wanted us out of the way, it's because he's going to do something and he thought I would try to stop him. I can't leave. It's what he wants.'

'What he . . .' Caleb looks lost for words, aghast. 'Screw what he wants!'

At his sudden, violent shout, Raven soars down to the

ground at last and turns back into a girl, staring at him. He looks back at her, his eyes suddenly glistening, then puts his face in his hands. Luca puts her arm around his shoulders.

'I'm sorry,' says Eliza. 'We have to stay. I'm sorry.'

He doesn't look up.

We need water. Hero and I have taken the iodine and gone down to the lake. I had to fight with Eliza about it. I told her, as reassuringly as I could, 'We're on the other side of the lake from the camp. We'll be hidden in the trees, no one will see us.'

'It's too dangerous.'

'That's just the dehydration talking.'

'Don't joke about it.'

There was a pause. I wanted so much to make her smile, to take the weariness from her eyes. She pushed her hair out of her face.

I said – suddenly, calmly – 'I love you.'

She just stared at me.

I don't know why I said it. I don't even know if it's true. It occurs to me now that *she* must know, with her demesne.

I think about that for a while.

After a few minutes Hero says, with a good attempt at a casual tone, 'Tell me what's going on with you two.'

I look up. We're sitting in the shade of the trees beside the lake, letting the iodine sink in slow dark tendrils through our water. The camp is on the other side, distant, tents dotted against the grass, smoke rising in greasy columns.

'Nothing,' I say.

Hero laughs. 'You're a terrible liar, you know that?'

'I do know that. In my defence.'

She grins at me, and then it fades. 'Joshua . . .'

'Hero—'

'I just want to know how you feel about him.' She's suddenly grave. 'I need to know.'

'How do *you* feel about him?'

A long silence. The sun is rising, but the dawn is still thin, here in the shade of the trees. The lake glitters gold. I stare into it, wanting to blind myself with it, to drown in light. In my cell it was so dark. I would have killed for this.

'I don't know,' says Hero, at last. 'I can't hate him. I don't know why, I feel like I should, but I . . . I can't.' She turns to me. 'I keep remembering him when he was a kid. And the things I said to him, to try and control him—'

'No,' I say at once. 'Don't think like that. He tried to *kill* you. It doesn't matter what you said, you could never have deserved what he did.'

'I said I loved him,' says Hero softly. 'No matter what.'

'I said that, too.'

'And now?'

'I don't love him anymore.' I say it baldly, simply, and am relieved that nothing in me twinges or struggles against it. 'Anyone who says *no matter what* is kidding themselves. There are things you can do to stop someone loving you. And he did all of them.'

She looks out over the lake, the blinding sunset, the sweet autumn air. I close my eyes.

'The night before we rescued you,' says Hero after a while, 'I was on a cliff with Joshua, and we were talking.' She turns to look at me again. 'I asked him what he wanted, after we had you again. How he wanted to live. I knew we couldn't just run from the Guard forever. I thought, when Cairn had us, that we might live in the camp, but now . . .' In the silence I see Anthony's insane gleaming eyes, his snarling face. 'What do you want, after this?'

'I . . .' I don't know. When I close my eyes and ask myself all I see is Hero and Eliza, safe and whole and happy, alive. I cannot see myself. 'I'm not sure.'

'Joshua wanted to leave,' says Hero, watching me sideways.

'Get a boat and go somewhere else. South, across the other sea, to Karkaran. What do you think about that?'

It frightens me more than I can say. 'I don't know.'

She nods and looks away. Then she says, 'You and Eliza . . .' She trails off, and for a moment I think she's going to say something else, but then I realise it's a question.

I owe her the truth. I owe her so much. 'Yeah.'

She looks at me. 'I didn't know you even liked girls.'

'I . . .' *Girls.* The word seems strange, gaping and hollow, when chained to Eliza, her glittering eyes, the deep brightness of her mind, her fleeting, grim smile. *Girls* are the laughing, quick-eyed creatures we lived with in the orphanage. Eliza is different.

'Neither did I. But I . . . I hadn't liked any other boys before Joshua.' His name tastes strange in my throat. 'I didn't like anyone before him.'

The truth closes around me, its cold hand sliding under my shirt to ball a fist against my stomach. I need to tell her what I did. She deserves that. My heart is fluttering, humming-bird-quick, against my ribs. I lower my head, close my eyes, breathe. She's already watching me, I can tell.

Someone says, in a voice that sounds like mine, 'You didn't wake up on your own.'

'What?'

'I . . .'

Hero turns to me. The flask of water sits between us. I want to look away.

'You drank my blood,' she says softly.

'I . . .' The words are so stark. 'Yes. I . . .' And the memories are flooding back before I want them to, kneeling beside Hero in the moonlight, on the other side of this lake, the diamond-blade knife trembling in my hand. The cut on her wrist, the blood that welled there. Hero is half-god and half-human, so her blood tasted of rust and salt and iron, and then a silver note beneath it, sweet and singing. Honey and nectar, and the rush of power in my own veins, narcotic. It awoke a thirst in my stomach, my chest, that made me want to throw up into the dirt. I felt the heartbeats that surfaced inside my head like pebbles in water, and the power in my hands. Watching new skin form under my touch on her ruined face, half-healed. I never wanted it to end.

'I'm sorry,' I say, because it's all there is in the revulsion and the horror and the guilt. 'I'm sorry, I'm . . . I didn't want to do it. I'll never do it again. I swear it.'

A silence.

'I know why you did it,' she says. She doesn't look up at me. I'm on her right, so when I look at her I see the long scar, the mass of skin where her eye used to be. She's looking out over the lake. 'You saved my life.'

'I wasn't going to tell you. If you'd just woken up, half-healed, and thought you'd done it yourself . . . I thought lying would be easier. I'm sorry.'

She looks at me at last, face intent in the dappled sunlight. There's a moment of hesitation, and I see something dark cross her face. *I hate you*, she's going to say. *You're worse than Joshua. You traitor. I never want to see you again. Get out of my sight.*

But she says, quietly and with a bright intensity that breaks my heart, 'Kestrel, I love you. You couldn't do anything to make me not love you. Listen to me.' She touches my face. 'You saved my life. It's okay.'

I nod. Sway slightly in the grey dawn, relief like warm water in my veins. Cover her hand with mine in the grass. She lets me, and for a while we just sit there in silence. When I close my eyes I can still see the revulsion that flashed across her face. I feel the bulge in my pocket, the hard glass of the vial I keep there, hidden. I close my heart. That's a truth too far, I think.

*   *   *

We carry the water back up the hill and Hero says to me, 'We could leave if you wanted.'

I keep my eyes on the leaf-strewn ground, not wanting to look at her. 'You mean that?'

'If you wanted it. We don't have to stay here. It's not our fight.'

'It *is* our fight.'

I can hear a slight smile in her voice. 'I know.'

A pause.

'You'd have liked Mark,' says Hero quietly. 'I only knew him for a couple of days, but I still liked him.'

I push my hair from my eyes and try to look calm, but my heart is still thudding, my fingertips numb. If she'd said she wanted to go, I'd have done it. Of course I'd have done it. I couldn't say no, not to Hero, not ever. I'd do anything for her.

But Eliza . . .

'Hero,' I say at last, 'maybe we should—'

Then I stop dead.

My heart is thrumming in my throat. Fear jolts awake in my throat, a touched nerve. A voice has echoed me somewhere in the depths of the woods. Between the trees, distant.

Someone else said her name when I did.

The silence reverberates. Neither of us moves. Then Hero's hand goes to her belt, but there's nothing there. I draw my diamond-blade knife.

'Up the hill,' she murmurs, almost too faintly to hear. Her eyes are on the trees, searching.

'Who? Not the others—'

'*Hero?*'

Something trickles through my brain, down the base of my spine. A shiver made liquid. I know that voice.

'Oh,' whispers Hero, staring through the trees, her hand gripping mine so tightly it hurts. 'Kestrel—'

And his voice says suddenly, clear and close and desperate, 'Kestrel?'

I don't feel myself move. The world blurs, darkens with shock, and then suddenly I'm running towards it, towards the voice that sounds so like Joshua's, through the woods, panting and heedless. I can't breathe. I will not hope, I can't hope, I—

And the trees clear, and—

And there he is.

I stop dead. Gravity swoons around me, the trees rushing up. I fall to my knees and I'm level with his death-blue face. He stares at me. Face frozen, lips moving soundlessly, tracing my name.

'Joshua,' says Hero breathlessly, from above me. Her voice thrums with astonishment and wonder. '*Joshua.*'

He doesn't look up at her. His eyes are fixed on me. There are tears in them. He starts to struggle, and then I see he's bound with steel ropes to the tree. He's half-naked, covered in bruises. There are long, deep, half-healed cuts on his arms.

'You're hurt,' says Hero. 'Joshua, you're *hurt*.' She walks towards him quickly, hands outstretched.

His head jerks up to look at her at last. His gaunt face stretches in terror. '*YOU!*'

She stops dead, ten yards away from him, staring down at him.

'YOU!' he screams. '*YOU!*'

He thrashes against the ropes, trying to snap them, and the look on his face is wild with hatred. '*Kestrel!* Kestrel, run, get away from her! She hates you, she tried to kill you—'

'Joshua,' I say quietly, because all other words are dead and floating inside my head. 'What are you talking about?'

Movement in the trees, footsteps. I whirl, knife raised, but it's Caleb, Luca just behind him, and a wolf with Raven's dark eyes, growling. Caleb looks wild, frightened. 'What the hell is—'

He sees Joshua, tied to the tree and wild-eyed, and stops dead.

'Oh, crap,' he says, eventually.

More footsteps, and Eliza comes through the trees, panting. 'What's going on?'

'It's him,' says Caleb, eyes still on Joshua, who's fallen silent, panting. 'Eliza, he's here. How is he *here*?'

Eliza stares at Joshua for a long time, very still.

'He was left here,' she says, after a long time. 'The Guard left him here for us. They know where we are.'

Caleb whirls, aghast. 'They *know* . . . then we've got to get away from here! Eliza—'

'No,' she says shortly. Her eyes are still on Joshua. 'We can't.'

'Eliza,' says Luca quietly.

'No.' Eliza whirls, her hands over her face, and speaks through her fingers. 'We can't leave. If they found us, then they must have found the camp. We have to stay. If there's an attack, we have to help get them out.'

'You mean *I* have to help get them out,' says Luca quietly.

Eliza doesn't say anything. She lowers her hands and turns back around to stare again at Joshua.

'Kestrel,' whispers Joshua, eyes on me, full of tears and wonder. 'Kestrel, run . . .'

Silence.

'Look at the cuts on his arms,' says Eliza finally, as though he weren't there. 'They took his blood. That's why he's too weak to break those ropes, too weak to heal. But the blood's no use to them if he's dead, and it's a risk keeping him with them, so they left him here for us to look after.' She laughs, bitterly. 'It's a threat. A sick joke.'

There's an odd, familiar shimmer on his hands, mesmeric. His fists open and close convulsively. I can see Hero staring at them.

Eliza turns back to Hero. 'Can you heal him?'

It's a question, not a request. Hero looks at her blankly. She seems to pull the words from somewhere deep within her, underneath her thoughts, speech clumsy in her mouth.

'I . . . yes.'

'*Will* you do it?' Gently.

Hero's voice is dead. 'If he lets me.'

'She's not coming near me,' whispers Joshua. 'She's a traitor, a lying bitch, she tried to kill us. I *trusted* her—'

The shimmering on his clenched hands grows suddenly brighter and I shout too late, and the bolt of light, weak and flickering as candle flame, shoots from his hand towards Hero, who ducks.

My eyes are tight shut. Someone's screaming. There's the smell of smoke. Someone pulls the flask of water from my hands. 'Shut up,' says Eliza, her voice deep and thrumming with the command that cannot be disobeyed, and whoever is screaming stops, and then everything's quiet.

I open my eyes.

The bolt of light hit a tree, which has caught fire. Luca is pouring the flask of water on to its roots, trying to stop her own trembling, and with a hiss of steam the fire goes out. She looks up, fearful, and I know what she's thinking: if Anthony sees the smoke . . .

Hero is crouching, her hands over her head. The Raven-wolf is growling at Joshua, teeth bared. Caleb has his hands raised. Joshua is hovering in mid-air, suspended, thrashing, blood dripping from the cuts on his arms. He looks down at Hero and his face is so full of loathing and contempt that I want to throw up.

Caleb looks past me at Hero, breathing hard, still keeping Joshua hanging in mid-air. 'Say the word,' he says, 'and he'll fall.'

'He fell further than that and lived,' says Hero. I am

surprised for a moment at how calm her voice is. 'He fell from the top of the tower, the night we saved Kestrel.' She gets slowly to her feet. I go to her, wrap my arms around her, rest my head on her shoulder. I want her to know I'm here and that I love her and I don't believe him, not for a moment, but the words are shrunken and dry in my throat. She puts a hand on mine, grips it tightly.

Joshua is still spitting, struggling. 'No! Kestrel! Don't go near her. Get away from her! She's with the Guard, she wants you dead—'

Shock and horror are melting my thoughts into sludge.

'Just say the word,' says Caleb, again. 'I'll kill him for you, Hero.'

She's still staring up at Joshua, half-fascinated. I can feel the slow press of her heartbeat through her wrist. Then at last she shakes her head. 'He's not my brother,' she says quietly. 'He never was.' It takes me a moment to realise she's asking me a question.

I breathe in, breathe out, make myself say what has to be said.

'He was once,' I say, 'before it mattered. A real brother would have died before he turned on you.'

Hero nods again, more strongly. 'Yes. He wasn't real.'

Joshua stares down at me, his eyes suddenly blank with something terrible, with astonishment, with . . . betrayal?

And that's what makes me break, like the clean snap of bone. Fury, sudden and strong in my throat, my hands. How dare he be angry with me, when he says such terrible things to Hero. The arrogance, the breathtaking callousness. The cowardice.

'Say one more word against her,' says Eliza to Joshua, 'and I'll make you walk into the lake. I can do it. Believe me.'

He looks at me, pleading, and I don't say anything.

Eliza turns away, nothing but disgust in her face. 'Caleb,' she says. 'Deal with him.'

'No,' Joshua says suddenly, feverish, looking down at me. 'Kestrel, please, help me, I'll do anything . . . please don't hurt me, I'll . . .'

I don't say anything.

We look at each other, me staring into his golden eyes, his mouth half-open, breathless and terrified. And I feel nothing. There's a hole in my chest where he was, where he should be.

Then Caleb flicks his wrist and Joshua slams backwards into the trunk of the tree. There's a sickening *crunch* and his head flops on to his shoulder, unconscious. I don't even wince.

Caleb lowers him slowly to the ground, still bound by his steel ropes. I walk to stand over him. He looks so familiar, but inside his face there's no one I recognise. Hero is at my side, I'm holding her hand. I tell myself over and over, for what feels like hours, in the silence: forget who he was. He's no one now. A coward in a beautiful skin. Didn't you know that, before?

When we get to the top of the hill, Caleb carrying Joshua in a fireman's lift, the camp is still there.

Caleb sets Joshua down and brushes off his hands. He turns to Eliza, businesslike. 'What do you think's happening?'

'The Guard . . .' She's lost for words, staring out at the camp. 'I don't know. Maybe they're waiting.'

'They didn't wait before.'

'Yeah. Yeah.' She turns back to him, distracted. 'Maybe they've learned from their mistakes. They lost a lot of people in the last attack. Maybe they want to be cleverer this time.'

We sit in silence, watching the camp. Hero is behind me, silent. Our backs are to Joshua.

'We should warn them,' says Raven quietly. I didn't realise she'd transformed back into a girl.

'Sure,' says Eliza. 'Do you want to go talk to Anthony about it, or shall I?'

'I can—'

'*No, Raven*. It's too dangerous for any of us. Better to wait up here.'

I see the twins exchange glances.

'Or maybe,' says Eliza at last, 'maybe the Guard don't know the resistance only has one vanisher.' Her eyes are suddenly alight. 'Yes. So they think that if they attack, the resistance will just vanish away again, so there's no point!'

'So what are they going to do?' says Caleb.

'I don't know.'

'What do you think?'

Eliza strikes the ground with her fist with such sudden fury that we all flinch. 'I don't *know*, Caleb.'

Another silence, minutes long this time.

'If anyone has a premonition,' says Eliza after a while, 'and I don't care what it's about, *tell* me, okay?'

Everyone murmurs agreement. Hero glances at me and smiles wanly. I grin encouragingly back at her.

'If I have a premonition,' she murmurs, 'I'll *definitely* tell them.'

'Yeah. Me too.'

'If I think it's gonna rain—'

'Be sure to let her know.'

'Absolutely.'

Hero smiles again and leans against my shoulder. I stroke her hair. I want to say, *I'm sorry he's back*. But that sounds heartless even to me. Six weeks ago, before I was taken by the Guard, the news of his death would have been the end of me. But now he's just a gap inside me, a torn-out emptiness where feeling should be.

'I'm so sorry,' Hero says, hoarsely.

I wrap my arm around her shoulder, rub her back gently, like I used to do when she was younger. 'He's not your fault, Hero.'

'He was with me for five weeks, when you were gone. I wasn't careful enough. The Guard had him, they tortured him.'

I try to keep my voice calm and soothing. 'He believed this stuff before they took him. You know that.'

'Yeah, but . . .' I can't see her face, only the muscles in her neck, tense. 'What if it's not his fault?'

'What do you mean? How can what he thinks not be his fault?' I stroke her head, trying to keep myself cold and unforgiving. 'I was in there for much longer than he was, and I promise you, there's nothing they could have said to me to make me hate you.'

Another pause.

'He didn't used to be like this,' she says.

And I say what I know to be true, the realisation that came to me in the darkness of my cell. I've never said it aloud before. It sounds harsh, and very cold.

'He was. When you think about it. He never believed anything was his fault. He'd blame anyone but himself. You just got in the way of that, this time.'

She's quiet for a while. She pushes her hair out of her eyes.

'I keep thinking about the time I was sick,' she says. 'Remember? He wouldn't let you go near me in case you got it. He stayed with me for days.'

I do remember. I was in the next, empty bedroom, kept away by the nurses for my own safety, sick to my stomach with worry. I thought, *what if she dies?* The words hung in my head, terrifying. I'd only known her three years but I was fifteen and she was the world to me. The only person who'd ever told me she loved me.

Joshua always bathed carefully before he came to tell me how she was doing, scouring the illness from his skin. I remember him like that, younger, his hair wet, full of fierce love, golden eyes blazing. Coming into the sterile, silent bedroom to tell me she was still delirious, and a day later that she had woken, the day after that she had asked for water, that her eyes were no longer bloodshot.

I remember the moment he came rushing in to tell me, breathless, 'The fever's broken, she's gonna make it, she's gonna be okay.' I couldn't breathe. It was like everything had broken and I could barely stay standing. I was burning with relief, I wanted to see her, but he said it was still too dangerous, and that was when I noticed the drop of water still on his upper lip, trembling as he spoke. I raised my hand to brush it away, without thinking.

And the moment I touched him, the air changed and we were standing there in silence and our shared joy, looking at each other, closer than we'd been since the night when we were twelve and he had the dream, when I held him down to stop him screaming.

He looked at me. Then he lifted my hand and folded it gently in his, looking carefully at my face, trying to read me. Then he stepped closer and he was kissing me, the first boy I'd ever kissed, warm and soft and sudden. And that was it: I was his, for the next two years.

I am still sitting here, my hand in Hero's hair. She's waiting for me to answer. I say, 'This doesn't mean that wasn't real. Everything he did, in the orphanage . . . he loved you. He was your brother. That still happened. Nothing can take that away from you.'

My voice is strong and certain, and it sounds for a moment like I believe it.

The whole day passes watching and waiting, with Caleb and Raven walking down to the lake every few hours to get water. Once, Raven bounds back from the lakeside as a river dog, holding a huge flapping silver fish in her fanged mouth, looking very pleased with herself. Caleb ruffles her hair. She is still very quiet, watching Eliza all the time. We roast the fish over our tiny fire, over the crest of the hill so it won't be seen, and eat in silence.

At dusk, Hero finally curls up and goes to sleep while I stroke her head. Caleb and Raven drift off as darkness falls, but Luca stays up, striding restlessly around the fire, one hand on the hilt of her longsword.

'How long has it been since she slept?' I ask Eliza quietly, when she comes to sit beside me.

'I don't know, a day? She doesn't sleep a lot.'

'Doesn't she get tired?'

'Not according to her.' Eliza smiles slightly, wry and weary. I want suddenly to kiss her again.

'You should get some sleep,' I tell her.

'I will if you do.'

We sit like that for a while. Her hand is flat on the grass, and I run my thumb over her knuckles, trying to relax her. Her hands are so cold.

'What do you think's going to happen now?'

'I don't know.' Her eyes are so beautiful, lit by the firelight in the darkness. 'If the Guard don't attack soon, I'm going to get worried.'

'Why?'

'Because it'll mean they have a bigger plan. And I don't know what that would be.' Eliza presses her hand against her face. 'The more I think about it, the less their attacking the camp – the old camp, I mean – makes sense. There were thousands of people there, and most of them had demesnes, divine speed and strength, even premonitions. The Guard must have known they couldn't kill all of us.'

'The Guard had all of that too. They were drinking blood. And they had guns.'

'Yes, but . . . still. They were so outnumbered. And they knew we had vanishers, they knew we had the means to escape . . .' She bites her lip, and I fight the urge to kiss it. 'If they attack again, they must know we'll get away again. They must be planning something else. But I can't think what it would . . . I can't *think* . . .'

She looks so strained and exhausted, I don't want to worry her any more, but I have to ask. 'If the original attack wasn't meant to end us, then—'

'I don't know what it was meant to do.' Eliza runs a hand over her face. 'Provoke us, maybe. But I can't think what . . .' Pause. She shakes her head to clear it. 'What do you want to do about him?'

A weight settles slowly into my stomach. I don't have to ask who she means. 'I don't know. What do you think we should do?'

Eliza shakes her head slowly, looking into my face. I know what we're both thinking, and despite everything the idea pulses panic into my blood.

'Don't kill him,' I say, quietly. I don't know why I care anymore, but I do. 'Please.'

'I'm not going to kill him. But he'll be difficult to restrain. We'll have to keep him unconscious. And then . . .' Eliza sighs. 'Kestrel, in any court . . . he'd be convicted for three attempted murders. At least. He'd go to prison for a long time.'

'There aren't any courts out here.'

'There are,' says Eliza softly. 'In the camp, there are. And ways of restraining gods.'

A pendulum of silence hangs between us.

'Anthony won't be there forever,' she says. 'Not if . . . well. Sooner or later he'll try to kill the wrong person. And then we'll go back.'

You're the wrong person, I want to say. *Attacking you should have been his last mistake.*

'And Joshua will be tried. Locked up.'

Eliza searches my face, her gentle eyes tender. 'I think so, yes. How do you feel about that?'

The thought quickens my breath. I can hear the door of my cell slam shut, the sound echoing over the hilltop. Never, never again, I'd die before I let that happen to me. Was Joshua locked inside the black tower, too? Is that why he went mad? Is it really his fault, everything he thinks? But if it *isn't* his fault, how could I live with myself for letting him be imprisoned again? After Eliza—

'You could change his mind,' I whisper to her. I see her eyes go cold. 'You could talk to him. Make him stop believing . . . all this. About Hero. You could *make* him stop believing it. I know it.' I've heard it, the rippling power beneath her voice when she gives a command. Making people tell the truth, making them stop talking, that's only a fraction of what she could do. She could go inside someone's mind, strip it down and rebuild it, just by talking. I know it. I *know* it.

There's a long, long silence.

'I don't know,' says Eliza softly. 'Maybe I could. If you asked me.'

Another long quiet, solid and impenetrable. I can't break her piercing gaze.

'Please,' she says, 'don't ask me, Kestrel.'

I know why, of course. I try to imagine what it must have been like to grow up with such untouchable power. To know that she could have bent the whole camp to her will, whenever she wanted. And she never did it, never *dreamed* of doing it, because she knew it was wrong, and now here I am with my pleading eyes, asking her to take a hammer to the iron walls she's built inside her head, to look at another person and see them as clay, to be reshaped, remade . . . The evil of it, the breathtaking wrongness of it.

I'm filled with shame. I take her hand gently away from her face, enclose it in mine. She looks at me, her face unreadable, the silence between us solid. I touch the smooth skin of her face and kiss her, long and deep in the soft cowl of darkness. Let me stay here, smear this moment over the rest of my life, smother me in it. I will live in the taste of her, the warmth of her, and never move again.

But eventually she breaks the kiss and puts her hands on mine. 'When you said,' she says softly, and swallows, I see it in the smooth expanse of her throat, the shifting skin. 'When you said you loved me . . .'

It's not a question. I run my hands through her hair, cradle her face, the only real thing in the salt moonlight silence. 'I meant it.'

Her eyes are liquid and she kisses me again. I smooth all thought from my mind, flat and dark as the still, black lake water below us. I am so happy, suddenly, and when we break apart I laugh softly, before she kisses me again to silence me. I can taste her smile, though. And the words beat then in my head at last, sure as the blood in my palms: *I love you, I love you, I love you.*

It's quiet. Eliza is asleep beside me. Even Luca is still at last, breathing slowly by the embers of the dying fire. The camp, below us in the valley, is dark, lit only by pale starlight.

I feel empty, the way I felt at night inside my cell. The darkness is so complete, I think I can reach out and brush the walls with my fingertips. Feel the glossy stone, the drying blood. If I don't keep my eyes open, I'll wake from this dream and be back in my cell, insane at last.

I get to my feet and walk slowly, stepping over the girl-wolf curled beside the fire, careful to preserve the silence. The grass is damp against my skin. I turn against the pale-blue horizon, where in an hour or so the sun will brim slowly over the hills. I sink to my knees beside him.

He looks younger asleep. He's so thin already, and the scars on his arms are not yet healed. His skin is blue-grey beneath its soft brown. I'm watching his eyes. In the darkness, when they open, they're black, not gold.

He looks up at me, his eyes wide. His lips part, an *o* of perfect joyful surprise.

'Don't look at me like that,' I say, very quietly. I don't want to whisper; whispering is conspiratorial. I don't want him to feel like it's him and me against the world. I don't want him to think I'm on his side.

'You're alive,' he says, simply. He doesn't whisper either. I glance up, but the others are still asleep. His eyes rove over my face, hungry, adoring.

'I need to talk to you,' I say. I look down into the valley. I can't bear to look at him.

'Yes,' he says.

'Yes?'

'Yes.' His gaze is intent. He's biting his lip. 'How are we going to get away?'

His tries to get up, but he's still weak and I push him down hard.

'We're not leaving.'

'Of course we're leaving. We have to get away from them, and if we leave when they're asleep—'

'We're not,' I say, looking at him very hard, 'leaving. Do you understand me?'

He doesn't. I can see it in his fevered eyes. 'Kestrel, if we stay here, they'll make us fight for them. They'll make us one of them.'

'I *am* one of them.'

He stares at me.

'I don't understand,' he says.

'Don't you? They saved our lives, Joshua. How much simpler does it get?'

'Only for their own sake,' he says.

I spread my arms. 'Look at me. Do I look like a fighter to

you? A valuable soldier? Would *you* have risked your life for me, if you were Cairn?'

'I'd do anything for you,' he says quietly.

I look away. 'Yeah.'

Silence. He starts struggling against the bonds tying his wrists again, but he's too weak.

'Kestrel,' he says, 'help me with these—'

'Why should I help you?'

I didn't mean to get angry with him, I was going to be all calm and dispassionate, but suddenly I'm so full of rage I can barely breathe with it. All I can think of is Hero's face, her broken heart, the light around his hands as he summoned it to kill her. 'Why the hell should I ever help you with *anything?*'

I look down at him. He's stopped struggling and is just looking at me blankly.

'Kestrel,' he says softly, and he smiles a little. 'Kestrel, you don't understand. What I went through to get you out—'

'What *you*—' I might actually die from the indignation and the fury, I think numbly, might pass out and die from it right here on this hill. 'You coward. I know what happened. I know about Seaborne. I know what you did. *Hero* rescued me, and you did everything you could to screw it up.' It's unfair, I know, but I want to hurt him for his arrogance and his cruelty and it's worth it for the look on his face.

'What has she told you?' he whispers.

I run my hands through my hair, trying to keep myself calm enough to stay quiet. I don't know why I'm even talking to him. 'The *truth*. You tried to kill her—'

'*She* tried to kill *us!*'

Luca stirs beside the fire and Joshua lowers his voice to a hiss, his eyes wide, insane.

'Kestrel, she pushed us from the tower—'

'I know.'

'She was trying to kill us. We could have died.'

'We *could* have died,' I say, trying to keep my voice low and steady, 'but if we'd stayed in that tower we *would* have died. Hero did what she had to do. I admire her for it, I'm grateful for it. You'd have stayed there and got us all killed—'

'I'd have fought our way out. If she'd really wanted us to live, she would have let me fight.'

My hands are so tight in my hair they're going to pull it out by the roots. 'Joshua, there were *dozens* of them. You'd never have made it three feet. I couldn't even walk.' The rage is back, bubbling in my brain. 'Just because she didn't do what you wanted, doesn't mean she was secretly trying to kill you, you selfish idiot. She needed you, I was dead, and you turned on her.'

But he's shaking his head slowly, staring up at me, almost pitying.

'She's working with them, Kestrel,' he says. 'She was *always* working with them. It was all worked out between them, before we even got there. I suspected it before, but . . . they told me. They told me everything.' His face crumples suddenly, a deep well of pain. 'They told me and *laughed* . . .'

'Who told you?'

He raises his face to me, open, his eyes full of agony. 'The Guard,' he whispers.

'Oh, come on, Joshua.' Everything is falling away; I am numb, exhausted. 'What the hell are you talking about?'

'They told me,' he says. 'When they captured me . . . I was in the forest, and they said, *look, that's him* . . . and one of them said, *just where she said.*'

'That was Cairn, you idiot. *Cairn* gave you away. They tortured her before they killed her, Eliza told me.'

He's still shaking his head. 'They said it was her. They told me – *your sister's a clever girl*, they said. They said she'd told them she always hated us, she couldn't wait to see us dead.'

'The Guard *lie*, Joshua!'

It takes all my effort to keep my voice low enough not to wake Luca on the other side of the dying fire. I'm so furious I can barely breathe. My heart thrums with rage against the vial in my pocket, and beneath my anger there's a strain of guilt, because how can *I* talk about betraying Hero, when I—

I shake away the thought. My own guilt is nothing, *nothing* to the white-hot fury burning in me. Joshua is still looking up at me with his stupid, desperate eyes.

'The Guard lie, you idiot! They try to drive you mad, they try to crush your hope, they want you broken and dead inside before they kill you, that's what makes them *happy*! Do you have any idea the crap they told me when I was in there?' The darkness has solidified into the stone walls of my cell, crushing my breath from my lungs. 'They told me you were dead, or that you'd started killing people, that you'd abandoned Hero, that the two of you were heading south, back towards the city. They told me you'd been captured and you were in the cell above me, that it was *you* I could hear screaming—'

The memory is suddenly, crushingly bright: the profound silence on this hilltop is just a ringing in my ears, and beneath that are the echoing shrieks of agony and a darkness that will never ever let me go, I'm still in my cell, this is all a dream . . .

My fist is clenched so tightly it hurts. I open my hand with a painful effort. My palm is slick with blood. I try to breathe in the cold night air. No salt, see? You're hundreds of miles from the ocean.

'I never believed them,' I say at last, my voice soft and shaking. 'I always hoped. Because *the Guard lie*, Joshua.'

He's standing above me, the Guardsman, right there, a knife in his hand, smiling with white teeth, his hungry eyes on my face. I can't look up.

'You're disgusting, Joshua,' I tell him. 'You're *disgusting*. You believed them over her? You're a traitorous, two-faced—'

Joshua's staring at me, open-mouthed. I can't bear to look at him anymore.

I get up and walk away, as quickly as I can without waking anyone, and lie face-down in the grass beside Eliza, shaking. I can feel a slick, bloody hand on my shoulder. A Guardsman's whisper in my ear. *You taste of salt. Delicious* . . . The caress of a blade before the cut. The *thud* of a cell door closing, echoing over the hills towards me, over a thousand miles.

CHAPTER 19

The Vow

I'm standing on the island. The sunset is golden on the polished obsidian in front of me. I shouldn't look at it, I know that. If I just don't look at it I'll be free.

But still I turn, helpless. I raise my head and stare up at it, hating myself, dread in my stomach. Please, no . . .

Gleaming and black, a knife against the sky, and the air suddenly thick as ice around me. I know that black stone, it lined the walls of my cell, and then suddenly the beach is gone and I'm *in* my cell, and I hear the echo of a door closing and the blood comes to my mouth as the breath leaves me. Darkness all around me, and the Guardsman standing over me with his blade, smiling. Beneath the knife Hero's shade would vanish, I wasn't strong enough to keep her there, I couldn't, I—

'Kestrel.'

But I'm not in my cell, and Hero is here, and I—

'*Kestrel!*'

Hands close around my wrists and I jerk backwards, stifling a scream that will choke me if I let it, and my hand meets grass and suddenly I'm awake I'm on the hilltop with them all staring at me. Words die in my mouth. 'Please don't hurt me,' I was saying, 'please don't hurt me,' and bile rises to my throat, the savage blade of self-hatred sharp in my chest. I press it down and gather my breath.

Hero is kneeling beside me, anxious, her single eye golden in the dawn. Eliza's on my other side, one hand still on my shoulder where she was shaking me. My breaths are still too quick.

'Kestrel,' says Hero, half-whispering, 'Kestrel, it's okay. It's okay, it was a dream, just a dream. We're here. You're safe.'

She's here. I'm safe. Just a dream. Breathe in. Breathe out. Steady hands and still muscles, my body is my own to control. Fear is a part of me, a poison of my own making. It cannot hurt me unless I allow it.

Voices around me. Raven. 'Is she okay?'

Caleb, bleary. 'Yeah, sweetheart. She had a nightmare. She's all right.'

Luca says suddenly, 'Eliza.'

Eliza draws her legs underneath her, watching my face intently. 'What was it?'

'I was . . . the tower. The black tower. I was in my cell again.'

Behind her, I can see Joshua. He's still asleep, feverish and shivering. He's still so weak, blood loss and sickness and fury sapping his strength. What will he do when he regains it?

Eliza is still looking at me and I remember in a sudden rush what we talked about last night, and what we didn't say, and—

She knows.

I saw the flash of suspicion in her eyes when Hero returned. She knows what I did, what I had to do to save Hero. Our eyes meet and the knowledge lies between us for a moment, suspended in her gaze. My mouth opens. If she asks me, and I lie—

And if she sees the vial in my pocket—

'*Eliza,*' says Luca again, fear sudden beneath the steel of her voice, and Eliza looks away.

Silence. Caleb and Raven have stopped talking. Eliza gets to her feet, turning from me at last, and over her shoulder I see Luca point silently at the camp. I pull myself up to my elbow and turn.

The valley is empty.

The lake is silver and mirror-smooth in the dawn. The camp is gone. The tents in their swirling formations, the little silver campfires, all disappeared into nothing.

My brain goes silent, uncomprehending.

'They're invisible again,' says Caleb after a moment. 'They got someone else—'

'They can't have done,' says Luca. 'Declan and Anna are dead. I saw them die.'

'But they said there were six of them, maybe with the other four—'

'Shut up,' says Eliza. There's no pearlescent shimmer to her voice, but the twins fall silent at once. I get up, swaying slightly, and Hero grasps my arm to hold me steady. I pull away from her, pull down the sleeves of my shirt. I don't want her to see my arms.

'Raven,' says Eliza at last, 'I need you to do something for me.'

'Anything you want,' says Raven at once. Her voice is slightly hoarse from lack of use, but her eyes are alight. There's no fear in her voice at all, nothing but trust. My hand finds Hero's in the dawn's sunlit warmth.

'I need you to fly over the camp. Be something really small, a sparrow, something that won't be noticed. Look around, come back and tell us what you see.'

'No,' says Caleb. 'Eliza, you said the Guard are watching the camp—'

She shakes her head. 'This whole valley is full of sparrows. They can't see us from here, they won't think twice about one more bird.'

He's suddenly angry. 'Oh, and you're sure about that, are you? Like you were when we left her in the tent?'

'Look, Caleb, if I could do it myself, I would, but I can't, and I need to know what's going on, all right?' Her voice is rising, I can hear the strain in it. 'Every time I haven't, people have died, or people have been hurt, or—'

'It's okay,' I say. 'Eliza, it's okay.' I can't bear the pain in her voice.

'No, I . . .' Eliza steps back from me, her hands over her face, and I flinch. 'I *need to know what's going on!*'

Silence.

'It'll be fine,' says Raven to Caleb, softly. 'I'll be five minutes. It'll all be okay.'

'Sure,' he says, at last, but his eyes are still on Eliza.

We watch Raven until she's too small to see, an inkdrop of wings in a pure white sky.

Then Caleb says, almost casually, 'Out of interest, when would you have *made* me say yes?'

The silence suddenly thickens. All the colour has left Eliza's face. Even Luca looks shocked. I could hit Caleb.

'Never,' she says. 'Never, Caleb.'

He looks calmly back at her. 'I need to know,' he says at last. 'I need to know what you'll do.'

'To *you?*' Her eyes are suddenly dead. 'Nothing, Caleb. As long as I live, I swear.'

Raven comes back after three minutes instead of five, materialising from a sparrow six feet above the ground and hitting the grass with a sudden, alarming thud. She raises her head, panting, and looks around at us.

'They're gone,' she says. 'I went right to the middle of the valley. Past where the boundary would be. There's no one.'

'Are the fires still there?' says Eliza.

'They put them out.'

'Can you see the marks of where the tents were? Footsteps?'

'Yeah.'

Caleb starts to speak, but Eliza holds up a hand to stop him. 'Did the footsteps lead away from the camp? Through the hills, into the lake, anything?'

Raven shakes her head slowly.

Eliza closes her eyes and takes a deep breath, in and out. 'They vanished away.'

'They can't have done,' says Luca at once. 'There's no one else who can do it. That's why Anthony wanted to take me, you said—'

'They have no other vanishers,' says Eliza softly, staring down at the camp. 'They do have a vanisher's blood.'

Silence.

'No,' says Luca. 'No, no.'

'They put a spike through your foot. We left it there on the grass. If he got there before it dried, he could have used it. He'd only need a drop.' Eliza strikes the side of her leg with sudden, alarming violence. 'I should have *thought* of it!'

She turns on the spot, spinning in a slow circle, like a dancer, hands over her face.

'When I told him about the Guard drinking blood . . . Anthony . . .' Eliza raises her head to look into Luca's horrified face. 'He must have thought it was something he could *use*. He tried to take you because he wanted your blood . . . and he tried to kill *me* because he thought I would stop him if he left me alive . . . and of course, that's why he had Caleb and Raven knocked out instead of killed, he wants your demesnes, too, he thought he could use you . . . and . . .'

Caleb has turned away. Luca is retching into the grass. Silence, but for Raven padding over on wolf's paws to nudge at her head, comforting. Then Luca says hoarsely, wiping her mouth, 'He drank my *blood?*'

'Yes,' says Eliza softly. 'He drank your blood and took the resistance, he went . . . where did he go?' She spins again, looking mad, stops facing me, staring without seeing. 'The Guard knew he would go somewhere, they wanted him to go there. That's why they waited to attack. They attacked the camp to *provoke* him into doing something. That's what they

want.' She turns to Hero, desperate. '*Help* me, I can't think
. . . what did they do, what else did they do?'

'They killed his wife,' says Hero quietly.

'Yes.' Eliza seizes on it, feverishly. 'They killed his wife.
What does that mean? Why did they make sure to kill her?'

'To anger him,' says Hero. 'To make sure he'd want revenge.'

'What does revenge look like? Where would he go to take
revenge on the Guard?' Eliza's eyes are wide, unseeing. 'Not
Elida. It's too well-guarded, especially after Kestrel broke out.
Where would Anthony go, if he wanted to crush the Guard?
Where?'

They stare at each other, and the gaze is living, seething,
thoughts flickering silently between them like ripples in water.

'Amareth,' says Eliza, finally.

Caleb looks up at her sharply. 'What?'

'It's the only other place he'd go,' she says quietly, still
staring at Hero. 'He just wants to end it. The war, the . . .
the Guard, everything. He's going to march on Amareth and
try to . . .' She spins again, hands over her eyes. 'The idiot.
He's going to try to destroy the Guard by sheer force of
numbers. In *Amareth*.'

'Wait,' says Hero, 'no, wait, hang on—'

Eliza stops and looks at her, breathing hard.

'You told me,' says Hero, looking at her intently, 'that the
camp was a place for rescued gods. Children, the old, the sick
and injured. People who needed refuge. It's not an army. If
they had enough fighters to defeat the Guard, it wouldn't
have been such a bloodbath the other night.'

'Yes, but—'

'Anthony knows that,' says Hero patiently, 'right? He knows
he's got maybe a few hundred fighters, and the rest are useless.
And you're saying he's going to attack Amareth anyway? He'll
be slaughtered. They'll *all* be slaughtered.'

A short pause.

'Maybe he doesn't care,' says Eliza at last. 'They killed his wife—'

'And getting the resistance wiped out isn't going to bring her back. He knows that. Eliza.' Hero's voice is low and kind. 'This doesn't make *sense*. Anthony plotted for months to get power, he killed the council; he's not the kind of guy who's going to blow up his whole life just for *revenge*. You know that. He's cleverer than that.'

Eliza stares at her. I know she knows Hero's right.

'So what's the bigger plan?'

'Maybe there isn't one,' says Eliza, softly. 'Maybe he's doing exactly what we think he's doing. Maybe it's just not revenge making him do it. There's something else. Something making him so stupid and desperate he'd do this.'

'Like what?'

They look at each other.

'I don't know,' says Eliza. 'I need to go to Amareth. I need to see if we're right. I need to know what's happening.'

She breaks Hero's gaze at last, turns back to Caleb. 'We need to go now. We don't have a lot of time, we—'

'Go *now*?'

'Yes. Now.'

'Eliza . . .' He looks lost for words. 'We're not ready, there are *six* of us, we don't have a plan—'

'It doesn't matter. There's no time to plan.'

'We can find time.'

'Really? Where?'

'Eliza.' He moves forward, catches her shoulders, trying to keep her still, to look into her eyes. 'Eliza, listen to me. No one here is in any condition to go to Amareth. We've barely slept, we haven't eaten, you're exhausted, you're not thinking straight—'

She wrenches away from him. 'And while we rest? What happens then?'

'Nothing happens. Eliza, Anthony wouldn't rush to rescue *you*. Why are you saving him from himself?'

'*Him?*' Her voice is high-pitched, the residue of the madness staining it again. 'You think I give a damn what happens to him?' She gestures down at the empty camp, the silent lake. 'You see any injured people here? Any children, any pregnant women? Anthony took all of them with him, Caleb. *All* of them.'

'But he won't have sent them to fight.'

'That doesn't matter.'

'Why not?'

Eliza makes a strange high-pitched growling noise in her throat, a shriek of frustration, as if at his stupidity. 'Because there isn't going to be a fight! It's going to be a *slaughter*! Caleb, where do you think the Guard are right now?'

Silence. Everyone's staring at her, her grey colourless face.

'They went to Amareth! This is what they *wanted* him to do! They're ready for him, they're lying in wait for him, and when he does they'll fall upon him and they'll kill every man, woman and child he has with him. Everyone we know will die. *Everyone.* And we're the only ones who can stop it and we'll just be sitting here on this bloody hill, *resting* and *recovering* and—'

'All right, all right,' he says. 'I understand.'

'Do you, Caleb? Because if we stay here, Mark will have died for nothing! Do you understand *that*?'

He looks as though she really has hit him. 'I understand,' he says at last, his voice shot through with fury. He turns away.

'I'm missing something,' says Eliza. She looks up at Hero, eyes burning into her. 'Something important. Tell me what it is.'

Hero glances at me before she looks back at Eliza. 'I don't know.'

'Tell me everything we don't know.'

Eliza's hand finds mine and squeezes it. I squeeze back, helpless, unsure how to ease this panicked, feverish madness.

'We don't know how the Guard found the old camp,' says Hero. 'Or this one. Or us. We don't know why they left us alive.'

'We do,' says Eliza. 'They wanted us to keep Joshua alive. To heal him. So they could use his blood.'

Hero glances at me. Something passes across my mind, numb.

We should kill him. So they can't use his blood to slaughter the resistance.

I stare at that thought for a long, long time.

'Yes,' says Eliza. Her eyes burn into Hero's. 'More.'

'We don't know . . .' Hero looks up at me again, as if hoping I can explain what Eliza means, what she's thinking. I almost laugh. 'I mean . . . you say Anthony's gone to Amareth, but we don't know where in Amareth. It's a big city.'

'He'll go wherever the Guard have gone. He wants to attack them.'

'Then we don't know where the Guard will go. Eliza—'

'Keep talking.' Eliza's voice is whispery, feverish. She tightens her grip on my hand. 'That's it. That's what I'm missing. Where would the Guard go, in Amareth?'

'I don't know, Eliza, I don't know the city that well.'

'Neither do half the Guard. *Keep talking.*'

Hero hesitates. 'They'd go somewhere easily defensible. They know the resistance want to come at them. They'd go somewhere . . . somewhere that puts the resistance at a disadvantage attacking them.'

'What kind of disadvantage?'

'I don't know, Eliza!' Hero's voice is rising, angry. 'Do I look like a Guardsman to you?'

There's a silence. Eliza is still staring feverishly at Hero, who swears and lowers her head, her eyes closed. I can hear her breathing slowly, as if gathering her strength.

'Visibility,' she says at last, without looking up. 'They wouldn't stay in the city itself. They wouldn't want the resistance to be able to hide in back streets, to sneak up on them from alleys. They'd make sure the resistance had to be out in the open when they attacked.'

'Which means?'

Another pause. Hero raises her head very slowly. 'Eliza,' she says quietly, 'if you're saying what I think you're—'

'I don't know what I'm saying.'

'Yes you do.'

Eliza just looks at her.

Hero swears and turns on the spot. 'I'd get to high ground,' she says, rubbing her forehead and looking away from us. 'Just outside the city so there were no streets, somewhere on top of a hill, easy to defend, on one side of a river, to stop the resistance escaping too easily.'

My head is buzzing, her words crushing the base of my skull. My hands are numb, and I know only by looking that I've let go of Eliza. 'No,' I hear myself say. 'No, no.'

'What?' says Caleb impatiently. 'What are you talking about, where?'

Hero has turned round and is looking back at Eliza. Fury is there in the set of her jaw. I should be angry, too, but my anger died in the black tower, and I have only fear left now.

'The orphanage,' says Hero. 'She's talking about Fitzgerald House.'

CHAPTER 20

Amareth

'It's beautiful,' Raven says, when she sees the city. Caleb pulls her back, behind him. His knives are drifting around him again, like raindrops suspended in honey.

Eliza's breath has gone out of her. I heard it, the rush of air. I twine my hand in hers, not knowing what to say to her.

I've never been inside the city itself, unless the Guard's van passed through it on the road north to Elida on the day I was taken, while I sat chained at gunpoint in the back. I know the landmarks well enough, though, because we could see the skyline from our dormitory window. The spiralling crystal towers of the Palace of Peace, the fifty-foot steamed-glass greenhouses of the Institute of Discovery. There are a thousand different kinds of plants in there, the nurses told us, sprung from the seeds of a hundred lands, brought to Amareth by sailors from merchant ships and the galleys of explorers. And there beyond the city itself, where the mud-brown river opens into the sea, is the port. Ships teem in the mouth of the river. I watch them for a little while, fascinated by their slow dance, the gliding of oars through the water.

Fitzgerald House stands alone and watchful on its hill below us. It's barely sunset this far east. We're standing on a hilltop a couple of miles outside the city, looking down at the orphanage, the glittering river that borders it, and the thick woods that surround it. There is no wind.

Anthony's army is gathered beneath us in a ragged forma-
tion, milling nervously about on the grass. They have surrounded
the hill.

'They're inside the orphanage,' says Eliza after a moment.
'Oh, crap. The Guard are *inside*.' She runs a hand over her
face, not looking away from the brick house on the hill, the
glowing windows.

'But the kids—'

'The kids are still inside. It's a threat.'

The horror of it has its own silence, thick as cold water.
Joshua is crumpled on the ground behind us, still unconscious,
huge in his stillness. He draws the eye. Look, I want to say
to him, you're here, you're back, you never really escaped.
The idea brings a terrible laugh to my lips.

'The Guard would never kill human kids,' says Hero. 'They
went to every length to avoid it when we were there. There'd
be huge protests. It'd be too dangerous.'

'Not this way,' says Eliza. 'No one will find out. They'll
only kill the kids if Anthony attacks the orphanage, and if
he does that, they'll say *he* killed them.' Something carefully
blank passes across her face, and her shoulders move in a way
that isn't exactly a shrug. 'It's quite clever, when you think
about it.'

Anthony's battered army crawl like insects at the bottom
of the hill. They're no match for Guardsmen, they have no
discipline, you can see it even from here. All the Guard will
have to do when they attack is lean out of the windows of
the orphanage and open fire, and they'll be mown down by
the hundreds, clambering uphill over corpses. *If* they attack.
I think with a lurch of the tiny faces of the children in Corridor
One, not yet old enough to go outside, the laughter and sobbing
that used to echo up the stone stairs to our dormitory as we
lay awake. They're too young even to understand this fight,
to know what the orphanage was for when it was first created.

Anthony can't, he *can't* attack.

'Where are the resistance's kids?'

Eliza points. 'Right there. He's put them at the back.' Tiny figures in rags are clustered together near the woods. Their silence is unnerving. None are even crying.

'Maybe he thinks he's protecting them,' says Hero quietly.

'He's not. They'll be the last to die, but they'll still die.'

'I should go down and talk to them,' says Raven, from behind us.

'No, Raven.'

'Not Anthony. The children. I could get them away.'

'*No*, Raven. They'll have orders to kill us as soon as we get close. None of us can risk it.'

There are furious tears in Raven's eyes. 'Why won't you ever let me do things?' she says to them. 'Cairn thought I was ready. You told her, you told me I was ready, on the cliff top—'

Eliza laughs. 'To be presented to the camp, sweetheart. Not to *lead*.'

Raven stares at her, stricken. She stands there for a moment and then turns and walks back down the hill towards her brother. Eventually Luca follows her, throwing Eliza a guarded look.

Eliza stares after them, and puts her face in her hands. For the first time, I can see the world slipping away from her, out of her control.

And now, we wait.

Sunlight on the grass, brimming over the horizon like treacle in glass. Joshua is still unconscious. Hero is sitting alone on the edge of the hillside, staring down at the orphanage. I recognise her calm, blank expression: she's searching for heartbeats in the orphanage. But they're half a mile away, well out of her range. I resist the temptation to go to her. I know she wants to be alone.

'You haven't been talking much.'

I turn. Eliza is next to me, shredding grass absently and staring down at the orphanage, her eyes flat and gold in the dying sun. She sits very slightly closer to me than she would have done before the night in the tent, close enough that I can smell her sweat, that I could lean over and kiss her without shifting on the grass. Sometimes I forget that night happened, it felt so dreamlike. But then she looks up at me, and I'm close enough that I can see the silken strands of grey in her black eyes, and the warm glow of the memory catches and lights within me again.

She's waiting for me to answer, I realise.

'I watch. I listen. You two are clever enough for all of us.'

Eliza studies me.

'You knew that. You knew how clever she was. That's why she had to be the one to escape the orphanage.'

I nod.

Eliza cups my face in her warm callused hands. 'You're the bravest woman I've ever met.'

I smile. 'You're a good liar, considering.'

'I'm not lying.' She kisses me, hesitates. Then she says, 'I love you. Did you know that? I wasn't sure.'

I touch her face. 'I do now.'

She smiles and kisses me again, and for a moment we just sit there, our hands entwined, as close as we can be to each other. I'm lost again in the cut-glass beauty of her, the miracle of my sitting here with her, alive. She is why I didn't die in the black tower, I realise now; so I could wake up, in the dimness of her tent after the battle, and see her grave, dark eyes.

'We're all going to be okay,' she says. 'I won't let any of you die. I promise. I'll make sure of it. It's why I was born, to keep you safe. I know that now.'

I don't trust myself to say anything else. I try to lean my head against her shoulder, but she holds me sitting up. I look back at her. Something in her eyes has changed.

She says, softly, without moving her gaze from mine, 'You drank her blood.'

Fear surges through me, violent and jarring as lightning, and then it's gone. It's not a question. She already knows, she knew long ago. I can't lie to her.

'Yes.'

'You knew it would save her.'

'I didn't know. I . . . I hoped.'

Eliza stares at me. I can feel the intensity with which she is reading my face, white-hot, like touch.

'It didn't disgust you?'

'Of course it . . . of *course* it did. But I had to do it.' There's a note of pleading in my voice now, of panic; I need her to understand. 'She'd have died.'

I can't read her eyes. There's a deep, bright silence. I expect her to say, *You appal me. Get away from here.* Pushing against my chest, across the grass. And then I will be alone again, as completely and overwhelmingly as I was in my cell.

But instead she touches my chin, gently, and kisses me.

'That was incredibly brave,' she whispers.

I look down at her. I don't understand.

'You're not . . .'

'Disgusted?'

I nod.

'A little,' she says eventually. 'But so were you, weren't you? And you did it anyway. Because it would save her.' She kisses my forehead again. 'You're so brave, Kestrel.'

I wonder whether she can feel the vial in my pocket, the one I kept. I wonder if she'd hate me, if she knew. I couldn't bear that.

'Listen to me,' she says at last.

I look up at her. She swallows.

'Cairn used to . . . she used to test me.'

'What do you mean?'

It's a moment before she answers. The expression on her face makes me think of the look in Hero's eyes before she pushed us from the tower.

'To see what I could do. If I could. . . control her. But I never could, not really. That's why she took me in. She knew I was never a real threat to her.'

I don't understand what she's saying. I sit up straighter. She swallows again, her hand on the back of her neck, as if to steady herself.

'She was too powerful. I couldn't overwhelm her. I could make her sit or stand. Speak and shut up. Little things. But if she really wanted something – I could never stop her.' She rubs the back of her neck slowly, her eyes unfocused. 'Slow her, maybe. But not hold her. Some gods . . . they're too strong. Stronger than me.'

'Eliza, what are you?'

'Kestrel,' she says softly. 'Do you get what I'm saying? The next time Anthony comes for you – if he wants to kill you, if he really wants it – I might not be able to stop him.'

Silence. The lights are coming on in the orphanage windows, warm and golden in the thickening dark.

'You did before. He was going to . . .' I can't think. 'He was going to kill me, and you said *stop*—'

She shakes her head. 'He was weak. He was exhausted, he was grieving. I can't count on that again. And even if I could . . .' Fierce anguish in her eyes. 'I'm not losing you. I can't take any more risks.'

I want to touch her, to calm her, but something is alight in her that I can't put out. I don't dare move.

'What would happen to the others? If you died and I – I was – I mean – if I couldn't think, if I couldn't protect them anymore?'

'Eliza. I'm not going to die.'

'I won't risk that. I can't.' Something in her voice has broken, and whatever is beneath it is bloody, anguished. 'I *can't*. Do you understand? Kestrel, I'm sorry, I'm – I'm so sorry – I just – I just need to be *sure*—'

I don't understand what's happening, all I want is to reassure her, to quiet the panic in her trembling hands.

'*Eliza*. Look at me.'

She takes deep breaths to steady herself, closes her eyes. I watch, very still, waiting. Part of me wants to run to the twins, to call for help. I've never seen her like this before.

Then she says, more quietly, 'Kestrel, do you trust me?'

I don't even have to think. 'Absolutely.'

She breathes out, and opens her eyes.

'Okay,' she says, softly, and I see something in her eyes has changed, become harder and colder. She looks up at me.

Panic lights within me at last, far too late.

'Eliza—'

But when she speaks, her voice is shimmering with bright power, the kind that swims inside the darkness of my mind and can't be disobeyed.

'Get up, Kestrel,' she says.

She sounds so sad.

I'm stronger than I think – I hold out one second, two, against the tide-pull of her voice, and then I watch as my legs unfold and carry me, staggering, to my feet. My mind has gone out, suddenly, like a light. It's just the two of us, in the darkness. All I can see is her eyes.

CHAPTER 21

The Orphanage

AWOOOOOOOOOOOOOOOOOOOOOOOOOOOOOOO.

I wake in near-darkness, deafened, and for the first time in my life I can't remember where I am.

My brain is fuzzy and warm. My head is in someone's lap. I struggle, disoriented, and grab an arm. Familiar skin. *Joshua*, is my first, insane thought, and then everything comes back to me and I remember. Soft voice, dark eyes. *Eliza*.

The noise comes again.

AWOOOOOOOOOOOOOOOOOOOOOOOOOOOOOOO. Like the cry of some terrible wounded beast, long and deep and *everywhere*, loud enough to push you to the ground. Coming from the bottom of the hill.

We're on a hilltop. Yes. I remember.

I try to get to my feet and for a moment I don't know where the ground is. There's a thin layer of grease over everything in my mind, smothering my thoughts. I don't know what's happening. I don't remember the sun dipping beyond the hills. I don't remember falling asleep. Something happened and I—

I was talking to her, and she said, *what if you died?*, and I said, *Eliza, I'm not going to*, and something . . . something happened *after* that, but I can't . . .

There's an aching wound where memory should be and when I try to push against it and remember, it says to me gently, *no, forget that, don't go there, think of something else.*

And I can't *think.*

AWOOOOOOOOOOOOOOOOOOOOOOOOOOOOOOO.

Caleb stumbles in front of us, his hands over his ears. 'What the—'

'It's a war horn,' says Hero, from our right, as the echo finally fades. She's scrambled to her feet from where she was sitting, listening for heartbeats, staring over the hill. 'The *idiot*. He's attacking the orphanage.'

From the distance, beyond the treeline, starting slow and then rising, comes the battle cry, the screams and roars of Anthony's army as they run up the hill.

Luca has pulled Raven to her feet and is saying something to her, slow and comforting. Raven looks terrified, but is trying to crush it beneath a stubborn determined courage. She reminds me so much of Hero.

Think, why am I thinking of that now, I have to concentrate, I have to—

But something is screaming inside my head, loud enough to block out anything else. *The children*. The Guard have the children. They'll kill them now that Anthony's attacking. They're going to kill all of them.

Oh no, no, please no—

The world comes back slowly. I'm breathing too fast. Someone has taken my wrists in their hands, trying to calm me, but I pull away from them, stumbling backwards. The children. My head is full of the Guard, the *thud* of my cell door closing, the cold dark and the gleam of the Guardsman's teeth as he raised the knife to his lips. *You taste of salt . . .*

Someone is calling to me.

'Kestrel!'

'Luca,' I say back, feverish. 'Luca.'

'Kestrel, what are you—'

'Luca—'

The world returns. Eliza is standing in front of me, her eyes burning into mine. There's something a little like panic in her when she looks at me, a tightly controlled fear.

'Kestrel. Come on. Stay with me.'

Words come to me, stumbling and feverish. 'Luca – she can get inside.' She can stop this, I know it. She can vanish inside the orphanage, surely, she can kill the Guard before they kill the children, she can—

'Kestrel, no.' Eliza grips my wrists more tightly. Her eyes are shining, as close to tears as I've ever known her. 'Luca *can't* get inside the orphanage. Kestrel, can you hear me? She can't go in there, she hasn't ever *seen* it, that's how her gift works or Anthony would have vanished inside there himself by now. No, *Kestrel!*'

Her words don't make any sense, my head is still ringing, I've pulled away from her and I'm running down the hill towards Luca and Raven. Terror is a hammer in my head, crushing my brain, but I'm still on my feet.

They're running towards us. By the time I reach them they're nearly at the crest, staring down at the army and the orphanage and the screaming and the rattling of gunfire and—

No, I can't look at that. Nothing else matters apart from the children, don't think about anything else. Eliza is running after me, calling me back, but there's no power in her voice and so I can keep running.

I seize Luca's shoulder when I reach her. She wrenches away instinctively, pushing Raven behind her, but her face changes when she sees me.

'What?'

'You have to vanish there. Inside the orphanage, Luca. We have to get to the children.'

'Kestrel, no, I—'

'You can *get* to them, Luca.'

She pulls away from me, anguish twisting in her eyes. 'I *can't*, you idiot. Don't you understand? I need to *see* it, in my head.' She takes another step back, furious again. 'Don't you think I'd be in there now if I could?'

'Kestrel.' Eliza is at my side, her arms around my waist, pulling me away. 'Kestrel, you have to calm down.'

'Luca,' I tell her. 'The children.' I must sound mad, I realise, and the thought is so terrifying I laugh aloud, high-pitched as a bird. 'We have to get to the *children*—'

'Kestrel,' whispers Eliza in my ear. She wraps her arms around me, half-trap and half-embrace, kisses my neck. I can feel her tears on my cheeks. 'Kestrel, calm down.'

I feel dizzy, sick. I can hear Hero's voice in the distance, calling my name, or is it just in my head? *Breathe in.* Beyond us over the hill is screaming and gunfire, war cries and the thundering of running feet. I have to stop it.

I need to see it in my head, Luca said.

I need to see it in my head.

I can see it in my head, vivid as a dream. Our dormitory, stone-walled, the curtains fluttering in the breeze, the shimmering river and the glass city out of the window. Our beds unmade. The last time I was there, I kissed Joshua – for luck, I said, though I knew it was goodbye. I can see it when I close my eyes. If I could give Luca my mind . . . if I could *make* her see it . . .

I pull free of Eliza, grab Luca again. She nearly hits me this time, I can see it in her face.

'Let *go* of me!'

'Look at me.'

There are tears in her eyes too, shining. 'What do you *want*?'

'Listen to me. Our dormitory is in the east wing of the orphanage. The window faces the city. There are three beds in it—'

'It doesn't *matter*, I can't—'

'*Listen to me!*' I shout it at her with such ferocity that she stares, shocked and angry. I lower my voice.

'There's a desk underneath the window, a bookshelf on the back wall, a door, there's . . . I mean, there's a—'

I'm not doing it right, this isn't right at all. I close my eyes, *seeing* it, my hands still tight on her wrists. I need to *make* her see it.

And suddenly my hands move, cleverer than my brain. I am further along the road to terrible things than I knew, and my hand is on my knife, and the knife is out of my belt, even as I realise what I'm doing, even as Luca starts flinching away, and *no*, whispers something inside me, *no, what are you doing—*

Wham.

Pain like fire, broken ribs. A rush of air. The ground is gone from underneath my feet, a swooning absence. I kick and splutter for air, breathless and agonised. The knife is still clutched in my hand.

Caleb is standing below me, hands upraised, holding me suspended and flailing in the air. His face is contorted with rage.

'What the *hell* are you doing?'

'Let her down, Caleb!'

'What the . . . Eliza—'

'*Let her down.*'

Her voice is full of power. The invisible ropes binding me loosen, and the grassy hilltop slams into me. The impact rips seams of fire through my ribs, and I scream. The knife is gone from my hand.

'Eliza—'

Caleb is staring at her. There's no shock on his face, nothing. Eliza has stopped, her hands half-raised to her face. She looks suddenly exhausted again.

'Caleb. I'm sorry. I didn't mean—'

He turns and walks away from her, down the hill.

Pain is still crackling through my chest. Luca watches her brother go, a torn, dead look in her face. She doesn't call after him.

Below us, there are screams, gunfire. Eliza puts her face in her hands.

'What the *hell* were you doing?' says Luca to me, taking her eyes off her twin at last. Her voice is shivering with suppressed fury. It almost surprises me that I'm not scared of her.

'I can see it,' I say, breathless with pain, 'I can *see* our room in the orphanage. Inside my head. And you can't.'

'What the hell does that mean, you lunatic?'

'Your blood, Luca,' says Eliza. She's watching me with a curiously blank expression. 'She needs to drink your blood.'

The look of pure revulsion that passes across Luca's face makes me wince, and that sends another shot of pain across my chest, forces a sob from me.

Behind her, I see Hero running towards me, over the crest of the hill.

Luca stares at me for a long time. It occurs to me that we have never really spoken. I wonder if she hates me. It was my being in Elida that brought them to the cliff top in the first place; it's my fault that Cairn is dead, that *Mark* is dead, Mark who grew out his hair to impress her . . .

Her hand moves to her wrist, without her taking her eyes from me. Slowly, as the screaming and the rattle of gunfire echoes up from below us, she pushes up her sleeve.

'You only had to ask,' she says.

I open my eyes with my mouth full of blood. The hilltop is gone, and I am inside the room in my head.

There's wood beneath my feet, instead of grass. I stumble and crack my head against stone, crumple to the floor, clutching my scalp, burning ribs.

But the smell, I know the smell. Linen and wood.

I roll over and look up. A stone ceiling, grey slate. The sound of the battle has shifted. It's much closer, to my left, muffled through stone walls.

Our dormitory. We're in our dormitory. We're *in* Fitzgerald House.

I start laughing, hoarsely. Something thuds to the ground in front of me. Some*one*. Luca, disoriented and stumbling. She's not as used to this place as I am. I bet she tripped over the chest at the end of Joshua's bed.

She insisted on coming with me. She was holding on to my arm as I lifted my cupped hands to her mouth; as the blood touched my lips, sweet-salt, and the power rippled through me, shimmering . . .

The blood.

The way Eliza and Luca looked at me, their disgust and their horror. My mouth still tastes of it. My veins are buzzing with it, and my head is full of Hero's face—

I throw up on the floor.

'Shut *up!* If they hear us—'

Luca hits me on the side of the head and I start coughing. Her hand is slick with blood. She hisses in pain and grasps her bleeding wrist with her other hand, and I see the wound heal beneath her grip. *See, no harm done*, I think, and that insane laugh bubbles up to my lips again.

'We should go back,' says Luca, very softly, watching the door. 'I should get Eliza. I should have brought her, I didn't *think*—'

'The more of us there are, the more easily we'll be heard. If they find us they'll kill us.'

Luca glances at me, sour. 'I don't have to bring *you* back with me.'

I am dizzy with flushed new courage and self-revulsion. 'Oh yeah? How do you get to the entrance hall from this room?'

She glares at me.

'You need someone who knows this building.' When I try to push myself to my feet, the floor presses the vial in my pocket into my chest. I can feel the hard glass edge of it.

I can't check now. Luca's still scowling at me. I look back at her, trying to seem dispassionate, and at last she looks away.

'Where do you think they'll be?' she says at last.

I try not to let her dislike get to me. I close my eyes. If I had Hero's powers, I could feel their heartbeats, but—

I don't need her powers, I have my ears. Silence on this corridor, over the rattle of gunfire and the screaming outside. Silence in the corridor below. No one's here. *Or they're all here*, says a voice in my head, quietly malicious, *and they're all dead*. But they can't be dead, if they're dead I'll go mad.

'They must have gathered them together.' I'm lying, I realise, at the foot of my old bed. The room seems much smaller than it was when we left, but I can see all the old marks on the ceiling, dents like constellations in the grey stone. I used to lie awake staring at them, worrying and planning. 'All the children in the orphanage, they must have taken them somewhere. Kept them together. It would make sense. It'd be easier to watch them.'

Luca looks down at me. 'Where?'

No classroom is big enough. 'The dining hall.'

'Where is it?'

'Right in the middle of the building. The ceiling is glass, it acts like a skylight.'

'How do we get there?'

I close my eyes, seeing it. 'Down to the ground floor. Through the nursery, the language classrooms, right across the courtyard, then . . .' It seems so long ago I knew this place, memories glimpsed through deep water. 'It'll be guarded. Heavily. All the Guardsmen will be in that room.'

Luca touches the knife on her waist. A little jerk of her head.

'They'll have guns.'

'Then what do *you* want to do?'

I think she's only being half-sarcastic. I can hear the trep-idation in her voice, low and fiercely veiled. If I close my eyes again I will have to listen to the screaming and the rattle of gunfire outside. The Guardsmen are firing from the upper windows now.

That's the reason people are dying right now. The Guardsmen are firing on the resistance, killing them. My resolve hardens, a fist closing in my chest.

'I'll go to the dining hall. You take out the shooters. They'll be the next floor up, looking out of the windows. If you vanish from person to person you could take a dozen out before they even know something's wrong.'

'They'll be harder to kill if they've drunk blood.'

'They won't have done. It would be a waste of blood. They don't need demesnes. They have guns, and they're firing down. They'll think they're safe so long as they stay in the building.' My head is oddly clear; the way forward is glimmering through darkness. 'If you're in danger, if they realise something's wrong, go down to the resistance and bring as many people as you can to help. There'll be no point in stealth if they know you're here anyway.'

'And you? What will you do?'

'I'm going to the dining hall. I told you.'

'And doing what?'

I don't know what to tell her. I just want to hurt Guardsmen, to take some small revenge on them for what they did to me. I hear again the sound of a cell door closing from somewhere deep in me. Like shrapnel lodged beneath my heart, embedded in the half-healed flesh. It will always be with me.

'I'll fight,' I say. 'I have a plan.'

When she's gone, I walk through the halls like a ghost.

Once you get far enough away from the windows the cries

of the battle outside fade and everything is stone walls and torchlight and silence. It's very strange with everyone gone, as if someone has stripped the soul from this place. If I meet a Guardsman, or even a nurse, I'll be in danger, but I have my diamond-blade knife in my hand. I have strength and purpose, my head is buzzing and full of light, and the people I love are far away from here. No one's life is in my hands but my own.

The classrooms are empty. I wonder where the nurses are and hope they're safe. They tried to protect us from the Guard as much as they could.

I walk slowly across the courtyard, trying to block out the screaming and gunfire outside as much as I can. No one here. I am invisible. It's exhilarating.

The gunfire should stop soon. That's Luca's job, to stop the gunfire.

And mine . . .

My heart flutters. The strange grease in my mind is still there, slowing my thoughts. I try to concentrate. I need a plan. I don't have a plan. If I try to do this without a plan, I'll die, and my death won't make anything better. I need to think of something. I—

Come on, breathe in, breathe out. You're not stupid, if you were stupid you'd be dead by now.

Think.

You can't go to the antechamber. If you go to the antechamber now, you'll get killed.

But what if—

And suddenly, from far away, rippling through the silent corridors, comes a voice. I throw myself against a wall.

'– all of them?'

'And guards. Guards to hold them. As armed as we can manage. They're strong enough to tear through the walls.'

I press myself hard against a wall, heart hammering. It

takes a moment to slow my breathing beneath a panicked rasp. I know the voice. *You taste of salt.* . . The blood-drinker. In the tower, he said to Hero, *Jessica Markham*, and smiled.

He told me his name, one day when he was cutting me. Roman.

I want to be sick, I want to run. I make myself keep my eyes open.

He and the other Guardsman are walking behind me, the other side of the courtyard, near the entrance to the dining hall. I am hidden, they are not looking for me, they will not see me. I cannot breathe from terror. I can feel his fingers on my skin.

They speak in soft, intent voices.

'It might be best,' says the other one, after a slight pause, 'not to discriminate. The threat was clear. If we don't go through with it—'

Roman, soft-voiced and very calm. It physically hurts, to hear him speak again; the scars on my arms throb. 'The threat didn't work, in case you haven't noticed.'

'Because they didn't think we'd do it.'

'Because they didn't care. These people don't care about human children. This is *Anthony Abernathy* we're talking about. He only cares about his own kind. We need to show him we mean what we . . .'

They walk into the hall and their voices fade until I can't hear them anymore. I lean my head against the wall, steadying myself.

They're strong enough to tear through the walls.

His own kind.

Think. What does it mean?

Eliza would know, or Hero, they're cleverer than me.

His own kind . . . human children . . .

They're the Guard, they don't want to kill human children. They only want to—

The antechamber.

I turn around and start heading in the other direction.

It takes me perhaps three minutes to reach the dining hall, and another two to find a window. I can see a slice of the room through the smudged glass. I duck to make sure they can't see me.

They've cleared all the tables away and have the children sitting in neat rows on the floor, confused and frightened. Some of the Guard are leading the children into the hall, their wrists bleeding red, some weeping, some pale and stoic. Others are leading the kids out, towards the antechamber.

In the sunset through the glass ceiling the Guardsmen's teeth shine silver when they speak. *Blood drinkers.*

Hands bleeding red.

Human. Human children. Bleeding from the wrists. They passed their blood tests.

And two and two come together in my head with a sound like a cell door slamming.

The Guard are blood testing all the children in the orphanage. All those old enough for their blood to show, old enough to have been born in the few years it took for the gods to be eradicated, fifteen and older. They're trying to find the gods and half-breeds, purge them all for good.

He only cares about his own kind.

They think that by threatening Anthony with killing children of the blood, they can stop him attacking the orphanage.

The antechamber. They're putting all the god-kids they find in there, under armed guard.

But there can't be more than three or four of them left in the orphanage; the Guard are too good. Of the kids old enough to have been born before the gods were wiped out, most of them would have been rooted out years ago. Of the thousand children here, maybe only three or four gods will have been clever and lucky enough to have survived the Guard's relentless purge. But that's enough. And if they're being watched by Guardsmen who have drunk blood . . .

I press my hands to my face. How am I meant to fight them if they've got guns *and* demesnes? I'm human. I just have a knife.

My hand tightens on it.

Beside me, a door opens, and I press myself against the wall again.

The slam makes me twitch. My heart is furious in my chest, my mind suddenly blank. I press myself against a wall.

'Keep your hands where I can see them,' says a voice from around the corner, suddenly close. I flinch from the wash of terror that floods my brain. I'm so tired.

No. Do what has to be done.

My hands are at my pocket before I realise why. The vial, the secret. But when I reach inside it there are two vials there.

I pull them out and look at them.

Why are there two? I don't remember the second one, I don't know where it came from. When I press against the memory the voice in my head says *look away*, a threatening blankness.

I'm so tired, and anyway it doesn't matter. I know which one is right. It feels warm and known in my hand, and the viscous liquid in it is soft grey, not deep silver.

I put the unfamiliar vial back in my pocket and look at the one I know. Dirty stoppered glass, filled with something congealed and grey, gleaming in the torchlight. My brain opens and tells me what it is. Blood, Hero's blood. I took it from her after I drank it to heal her.

Never again, I told myself, would I put her life at risk. I would always have a contingency plan. Hero's blood, her healing powers, kept on me always. Just in case Hero herself was unconscious, or exhausted, or gone, and there was no darkened lakeside to take her blood.

And now . . .

A few minutes' worth of blood, of healing. To use on myself instead of her.

Slowly, watching the movements of my own hands, I pull the stopper from the glass and pour the blood into my mouth.

It comes unwillingly. Salt and then sweet, the deep thrum of power in my veins, like adrenaline. I close my eyes and lean back, the bone of my head against the wall. My hands are shaking.

'Your hands,' says the voice again. 'I want to see them.'

'They're right here, moron.'

A boy's voice, sullen and defiant. Footsteps, clumsy. I keep my eyes closed, feeling the taste of Hero's blood in my throat, revulsion beneath my terror. Slowly, the pulse of heartbeats comes into focus around me, pulling at the thread of my thoughts.

Heartbeats beyond count in the hall to my right, the children and the Guardsmen. A pulsing mass faintly outside the building. Above my head, the heartbeats of the sharpshooters, far apart. I hear them speed and falter and hope desperately that one is Luca's.

'Where are we going?' The boy again, his voice vaguely familiar.

'Upstairs.'

'If you're going to kill us, do it here.'

Another of the gods starts to cry. One of the Guardsmen swears viciously.

'We're not going to kill you.'

'Put down your guns, then.'

A thud and a grunt of pain. One of the Guardsmen has kicked the boy. I close my eyes more tightly and feel their heartbeats, try to count them, six seven eight nine, but how many are children and how many Guardsmen? They'll be strong, crushingly strong with the blood they've drunk, and

I won't be, Hero has no particular strength. So I need surprise, surprise is all I have.

That and the knife in my hand.

'I don't *want* to go!' A girl, sobbing. 'I don't *want* to—'

The Guardsman's voice, low and dangerous. 'I said, keep your *hands*—'

My heart is in my mouth, they're so close, and I'm not breathing in case they hear me. Everything in my mind is numb, but at last I have the courage to do what needs to be done. I know where to hit. Even with a god's healing powers, no one can survive a blow to the heart or the head.

Breathe.

One of the Guardsmen backs around the corner. The knife shifts in my hand, viciously quick, and moves up with all my strength into the neck, underneath the base of the skull and into the brain above.

I wrench it out before anyone can cry out or breathe, and as the first Guardsman is falling I go for the next one.

He fires, but his gun still halfway in moving from the wailing girl to me and the bullet hits the floor. I'm not going to reach him in time, I know, I'm three yards away and it might as well be three miles because there are two other Guardsmen and their guns are moving too, over the teenagers chained together in a circle and crying.

I take aim – *the heart and the head* – and throw it with everything I have at his eye.

I don't miss. I see it go in, the dark splatter, the sickening grating of metal through bone. He hits the ground with a *thud* I feel in my ribs. Then, at last, the first bullet hits me.

There's no pain yet; I can feel the cut sealing over. I duck, trying to push the gods behind me, but they're all screaming except the defiant boy and a hard-eyed teenage girl, who are shouting and trying to pull the others with them by the chains on their wrists that link them together.

A stab of pain in my arm and my leg, but I focus and heal them, an intoxicating rush of blood into melding flesh and sinew, and then something metal is in my hand.

A gun. The gun of the Guardsman I killed. *Concentrate.*

I stand up, aim over the heads of the teenagers, and fire twice at the Guardsmen. I feel a stabbing pain in my shoulder. One of the Guardsmen is hit in the throat and goes down in an explosion of blood, but that's not the head, it might not kill him. Damn. *Breathe.*

My blood is thundering in my brain. I duck behind the corner again, pulling the kids with me, still holding the gun. They must have heard something in the dining hall or the antechamber by now, there will be more Guardsmen coming soon, and when they do I'll die, but this isn't so bad, is it? As deaths go. I am lightheaded with fear but I am not in pain. Let it come soon, let it be quick, before I lose my nerve.

Behind me, a noise like splintering metal.

Someone shouts, 'Go! *Run!*'

Someone else grabs my arm. I turn, ready to kill, but it's the defiant boy, the one who the Guardsmen kicked. His wrists are stained silver with his own blood, and the remnants of those chains hang ruined from the cuffs. He pulled himself free, with divine strength. He's dark-skinned like Eliza, dark-eyed. I *know* those eyes. Hero used to whisper to me about them, shamefaced and lovestruck.

Idris.

'You're alive,' he says to me, blankly.

'Yeah. Go. *Run.* If you die, Hero's gonna be cut up.'

'Hero's with you?'

'Yeah. She's out there, on the hill. Go to her.'

A slight hesitation. Then his eyes harden.

'No,' he says. 'I'm staying. I'm fighting them.' He reminds me a little of Hero, with that same grim determination. He must have been waiting for this moment his whole life, the day he could finally hurt the Guardsmen who have made his life hell, and I can't bring myself to stop him.

Footsteps thundering down the corridor. Above my head I can feel heartbeats winking out like stars. Please let it be Luca killing sharpshooters. Please, *please* let it not be more gods.

'Why are they not attacking us?' Idris whispers. He's knelt down beside me, closer to the corner and the blood-stained corridor. Protecting me, I realise. He must be able to see my shaking hands. I grip the gun tighter, trying to steady them.

'I don't know, maybe they're wait—'

A hail of gunfire, sudden as thunder. The Guardsman has appeared around the corner. I scramble to my feet. One bullet hits my stomach and there's a blaze of agony, but even as it heals I'm firing back. I can't see because there's blood running into my eyes. My scalp is bleeding. *The heart and the head*, if it gets my brain I'll die. But I can't feel any pain at all.

Everything is a blur. Idris leaps at the Guardsman with a wild howl of fury and they collide. He knocks the gun out of the Guardsman's hand and they're both on the ground, flailing and wrestling with each other. The Guardsman's teeth are stained silver, he has divine strength as well as Idris, because he's drunk blood. Why was I so slow to realise that?

He aims a blast of ice from his hand at Idris's face, but Idris is dizzyingly quick, his teeth bared with rage. His fist turns to stone as he raises it and he smashes it into the Guardsman's face with such force I hear the crack of bone, and what the hell am I doing just standing here?

Another Guardsman, there was another Guardsman.

When I move round the corner he's lying on the ground, twitching, trying to heal the wound in his throat. His hands and the floor around him and his uniform are dark red and growing darker. The blood he drank must be wearing off.

He tries to lift his gun to point it at me when he sees me, and with my last bullet I shoot him in the head.

There are no heartbeats above me anymore.

I turn to look at the Guardsman fighting Idris, both covered in blood and still grappling wildly, and the gun swings from my slack grip. A wave of exhaustion sweeps over me and I nearly fall.

'*Stop.*'

The gun slips from my hands and clatters on to the floor. My legs nearly give out. I want to turn, to look at her, but my muscles will not move. *Stop*, said the voice, low and slow and deep, and with a thrum in it that commands, sinks into my chest and stays there. She said *stop*, so I cannot move.

Everything has gone quiet. Idris and the Guardsman are no longer fighting.

'Kestrel,' says Eliza behind me. Her voice trembles slightly with relief. 'Oh, thank . . . turn around. Are you okay?'

My feet move without my telling them to, shifting on the cold stone, pulling me along. At the other end of the corridor are Luca and Eliza, swaying and covered in blood.

Eliza goes very pale when she sees me, the bloodstains in my clothes from the bullet wounds. 'Kestrel—'

'I'm okay,' I say. 'I'm not hurt.' The words come easily, the magnetic pull of her voice drawing the truth from me. *Go on*, I think. *Ask me how. Ask me how I didn't get killed.* I can feel the empty vial in my pocket, burning into my chest. And the second, full, inexplicable one, heavy and unfamiliar and cold.

Am I going mad? Is that what this is?

Eliza is walking towards me. Luca puts out a hand to steady herself against the wall. She looks exhausted.

'I brought her here from the hilltop,' she says when I look at her. 'The sharpshooters are dead.'

And she's right, the silence outside is pure and unbroken. The fighting's over. I want to laugh with relief, but I can't.

When Eliza gets to me she touches over my shirt, looks

at the blood that comes away there, sticky on her palms. 'Kestrel . . .'

'It's not mine,' I say, 'it's the Guardsmen's.'

Too late I remember how stupid it is to try to lie to her. She looks up at me. I can see her reading my face, that white-hot gaze. I can't look away. And suddenly I'm so tired. *Ask me*, I want to say, *just ask me. I took my own sister's blood when she was sleeping, to save myself.* And then she can tell me she hates me and I can stop being so afraid of the moment she finally realises what I am.

But she doesn't, she just stares at me. She takes my hand. Her other hand is still on my cheek. She looks exhausted, and so relieved.

'Eliza,' says Luca suddenly.

Running footsteps from around the corner. Guardsmen, coming towards us from the dining hall. They will have guns. My heart beats faster again and I tighten my grip on the gun. It sounds like hundreds of them.

'Eliza,' says Luca, her knife in her hand. 'Eliza, are you sure—?'

'I can handle them,' says Eliza softly. Her hand is in mine. She stares ahead, at the corridor beyond us. 'Don't worry, Luca. It's okay.'

Luca turns back to look at her just as the first Guardsmen appear around the corner, out of breath, guns raised.

Eliza says, 'Don't move.'

They stop at once. A sudden silence spreads back down the corridor. Some of the Guardsmen have stopped mid-step and teeter, unstable. Their expressions are frozen too, their eyes. It's a bizarre sight.

Luca tries to say something. The sound is muffled, unintelligible. I can see the tension in her arms.

'Oh, I'm so sorry – of course – you can move, the two of you.' Eliza sounds anguished. 'I'm sorry, I can't – put your hands over your ears, block me out—'

Luca coughs. I feel freedom return to my arms and legs, and nearly collapse again.

'How long do you think you can hold them?' asks Luca, when her coughing stops.

'Long enough,' says Eliza, after a moment. 'You're safe.'

She bends down beside Idris and the blood-stained Guardsman, who are suspended mid-wrestle, arms and legs frozen in the air. Idris's fist is clenched and made of stone, three inches above the Guardsman's face. His eyes are full of terror as she crouches beside him. The broken chains are still dangling from his wrists.

'What's your name?'

'Idris,' he whispers.

'He's of the blood, Eliza,' I tell her. 'He was Hero's . . . I mean, he fought . . .' The words are numb and clumsy in my mouth. Eliza glances back at me.

'All right,' she says. 'You can move now, Idris.'

Idris collapses, gasping. He crawls off the Guardsman and curls up on the floor, his fist turning back into flesh again, staring around at the corridor. Then he catches sight of the dead Guardsman next to him and edges away, slowly, pressing his back against the wall, not taking his eyes off it.

'What are you going to do with them?' says Luca, eyeing the Guardsmen uneasily. 'I mean . . .' She swallows. 'If you told them not to breathe, would they . . .?'

Eliza pushes her hair out of her eyes. 'Do you want me to do that?'

Luca doesn't answer. Eliza nudges the Guardsman on the floor with her foot. 'Get up.'

He does, clumsily, his hands slick with blood, staring at her. There's shock and hatred in his eyes, but no fear yet.

'Where are the rest of the Guardsmen?'

It takes me a moment to realise that Eliza is talking to me. She doesn't look away from the one in front of her.

'In the dining hall, or the antechamber.' My voice is raw, it hurts to speak. 'They were blood testing the children. They thought if they killed gods or half-breeds in front of Anthony, or threatened to kill them . . .'

'That it would stop him attacking? They haven't met Anthony.' Eliza's voice has the sharpness of cracked ice. 'Go back to the dining hall. You.' She points to three of the Guardsmen. 'Get your colleagues from the antechamber. Use force if you need to. If any of the children have been harmed, kill all the Guardsmen in that room. Then follow us.'

We walk slowly, the Guardsmen marching in time, down the bloody corridor towards the entrance to the dining hall. Halfway there, Eliza looks at me. Before she can speak, I squeeze her hand.

The Guardsmen look up when we get to the hall, startled, but before they can move Eliza says, 'Put your guns to your heads. Turn off the safety.'

They do it in a single smooth movement, barrels against their temples, faces flat and expressionless. The children stare round at us, murmuring to each other. A girl of about six edges towards the door on her knees, clutching a baby.

'Go,' says Eliza to the children. 'Run. Over the hilltop to the north. You'll find protection there.'

There's no thrum in her voice, no command: she lets them do it of their own free will. They go slowly, uncertainly, older children grabbing younger ones, hesitant footsteps speeding up to a run. I can't feel their heartbeats anymore. Hero's blood is wearing off inside me. I feel light-headed.

When they're gone and their footsteps have faded to echoing silence in the glass hall, Eliza says, 'I could make them pull the trigger.' She doesn't look at either of us. 'Would you do it?'

Luca glances back at her. 'I . . . maybe. Yes.'

'*You* don't have to. You don't have to live with it.'

'I know.'

'Kestrel?' Eliza turns to me, and though her tone is still casual I can see the fear in her face 'What would you do?'

I look around as the other Guardsmen, the ones from the antechamber, file into the hall. Two are wounded, clutching bloody arms and limping, and the Guardsmen Eliza sent to fetch them are pointing guns at their heads.

'What the—?'

'Guns to your heads,' Eliza says to them, the power in her voice again. It goes through my lungs like water, trembling in my bones. They obey at once.

Then the whole Guard are standing in front of us, pistols pressed against their temples.

It is intoxicating. All those weeks in the black tower, alone and terrified, and now . . .

I can see Roman's face, just another nameless blood-stained Guardsman amongst the hundreds here. I can hear the door closing in my head, but it's further away now, throbbing gently across a black lake. The diamond-blade knife is cold in my hand.

'I never wanted this,' Eliza whispers again. She licks her lips, takes a step back. 'I never wanted this.'

'No one wanted any of this,' I say, but that's a lie; of course I always wanted them here, powerless, at my mercy. I remember eating breakfast here on our last day, knowing what I would have to do to save Joshua and Hero. The terror in me and the sadness and the grief, because I knew I would have to lie to them and leave them. And all because of these people. All because of the Guard.

Please don't hurt me, I said, in the cell, in my nightmare. *Please don't hurt me anymore.*

'Would we be safer?' she says, softly. 'Really? If they were all dead? How many lives would it save?'

I look around at them, then down at my bloody hands. I have killed four people today. I want to cry, to throw up, to scream.

'What else will we do with them, if not kill them?' asks Luca.

'Imprison them,' says Eliza.

'In the black tower.' I raise my head slightly. 'That would be good.'

Luca glances at me. 'They'd escape and kill us all again.' Her voice is flat. 'We'll never be safe while they're alive.'

I don't dare to speak. Roman's hand trembles on his gun. I can feel his eyes on me.

'Kestrel,' says Eliza at last, 'it should be you. You're the only one with the right.' She turns to me. 'They tortured you. This is your decision. Tell me what you want.'

I just stare at her.

I want to say, *kill them all*. But then I will walk out on to the hill, to Hero, and she'll ask me what happened, and I'll say, *they're all dead*, my voice light like it was nothing to me, which will be true, and she'll look at me like she doesn't know who I am.

Hero, in my place, would not carry out mass murder, not even on the most deserving people in the world. Hero is a better person than I am.

'Let them live,' I say, after a moment.

I see Roman's pupils dilate. Luca glances at me, her eyes unreadable.

Eliza stares at me for a long time. I look back at her, impassive. I have to do what Hero would do, even if it breaks me.

'All right,' she says at last, breathing out. 'All right.'

She walks forward and turns around so that she can see all of the Guard, guns pressed against their heads. There's a long silence, long enough that for an instant I think with a thrill that she'll ignore me, that when she speaks she'll say *fire*.

'In a minute,' she says at last, 'you'll put down your guns. You'll take off your uniforms. I want you to run. Far from Amareth, far from the places you were born. Somewhere you're alone and unknown.'

The one in front of her is trembling. His eyes are screwed up against the press of tears, his hand shaking as he presses his gun to his own head.

'Then,' says Eliza, 'you'll forget yourself. Everything you were, everything you've done. You'll forget that you hate people of the blood. You'll forget your names. You'll start new lives. Harmless lives.' Eliza glances at Luca, hesitates, then says, 'But if you ever hurt anyone of the blood ever again, if this hatred ever takes root again in your heart, you'll open your wrists. Do you hear me?'

They nod, compulsively, a mesmerising rippling movement.

Eliza looks around, swallows. 'Do it, then.'

When the room is empty but for the pile of guns and uniforms on the floor, Eliza says, 'That was mercy. Wasn't it mercy?' Her voice is oddly flat.

Luca isn't looking at me. I feel sick inside.

Do what has to be done, I think, but instead I say to Eliza, very calmly, 'Yes, it was.'

CHAPTER 22

Premonitions

We walk out on to the hill, gold bleeding from the horizon, my hand in hers. The air is brittle and cold, and I breathe it in with my eyes closed and Eliza's warm hand in mine, and in that one moment I feel truly calm.

Then I open my eyes.

The hillside beneath us is covered in bodies. Dozens, some still living and bleeding silver from the arms.

Arms, I have time to think. The Guard wouldn't have aimed for their arms. The Guard would have aimed to kill.

Eliza knows it too. She looks like someone's shot her again, and for a moment I have to hold her as she sways.

'What happened?'

Luca is running down the hill, past the groaning injured – not dead, I see as I look at them, just too weak to heal – screaming for her brother and sister. *Hero*, I think with a jolt.

It takes us ten minutes to find them, beyond the crest of the hill. Caleb is covered in blood. He cries out when he sees Luca, a half-sob of relief, and they collide with such a ferocity of love I don't think they'll ever break apart again. Raven hugs them both, human for once, and sombre.

'She had to kill someone,' Caleb tells us later, quietly, his hands still shaking in his lap. 'Raven, I mean. A couple of them came running down the hill, right at us, and they had guns, and . . . I was trying to keep them away from her, but they had demesnes too, and one of them was right on top of her. She had to bite his throat before he got to his gun. I couldn't hold them all.' His voice is full of grief. 'I didn't want her to have to . . . we always promised her . . .'

Luca puts her arm around his shoulder, rubs his back. Raven's eyes are empty, unblinking. She stares down at the hill of corpses.

'What happened?' asks Eliza, urgently. 'Who cut these people? Was it the Guard? Did they do it as they ran?'

'No,' says Caleb, hollowly. 'The Guard went straight past us into the woods. It took us a moment to even realise who they were. They didn't touch us. They didn't even look at us. It was Anthony. He attacked them.'

Only then do I fully realise Anthony's army is gone.

There are children gathered beside the twins, around their fire, shivering. *Protection*, Eliza told them they'd find here. I remember it and want to be sick.

I find Hero sitting in the shadow of some oak trees, a few yards away from Joshua, who is still bound and unconscious on the ground. She is with Idris, leaning against his shoulder. He's staring at his hands, and does not look up at me.

Hero scrambles to her feet when she sees me and runs towards me, her eyes wide. '*Kestrel!* You're . . . where the *hell* did you—?'

'I had to do it.' The words are clumsy in my mouth again. 'I had to . . . I couldn't let you—'

'You should have taken me with you.'

'I couldn't risk you. I had to go—'

'It's not your decision to make, Kestrel!' She looks like she wants to hit me. 'Don't *do* that, don't try to be heroic. I nearly lost my mind. If you get hurt—'

'I'm sorry.'

'Kestrel, look at me.' She takes my hands, looks up into my face. 'You have to stop trying to protect me. I want to fight with you. I'm not a child.'

I think of the taste of her blood in my mouth and close

my eyes. I should be protecting her from *me*. I swore I'd never take her blood again.

Behind us, Eliza is giving orders, tearing up shirts for bandages, sending children down our hilltop to tie the wounds of the injured below. If they can't heal, they'll bleed to death. Hero runs towards her, wanting to help, but Eliza sees the blue-black shadows under her eyes, the trembling exhaustion. She looks half-dead, she's been awake for almost two days, and even now I watch her anxiously, worried that at any moment she'll stumble and fall to her knees and pass out and not wake up again. Eliza orders her sternly to stay behind, and Hero grits her teeth but obeys.

I want to be by Eliza's side, helping her, giving her strength, but I can't leave Hero. I sit with her underneath the oak trees, beside Idris.

'Caleb said Anthony attacked those people.'

'We didn't realise. It was chaos, we thought the Guard were still firing, we didn't know what was going on. If we'd known it was Anthony we would have stopped him.'

I don't understand, I'm too tired for understanding. 'Why?'

Hero runs her hand through her hair. 'After the sharp-shooters stopped firing . . . he must have realised the Guard were defeated inside the building, so he turned for the city. His army, the resistance, they were walking in a crowd, carrying their dead and wounded . . . and someone saw Anthony, they said later . . .'

'What?'

'He attacked the ones at the back,' she says at last. 'Anyone slow, alone, behind the others. He took them aside and cut them and . . .' She swallows. 'He drank their blood and left them in the grass.'

Horror washes over me like dizziness. 'How many?'

'I don't know.' Her hands are in her hair, eyes fixed on the grass. 'A dozen. Maybe more by now. The army itself – the resistance – they may not realise what he's doing. They might not miss anyone for hours. They're exhausted. And they trust him completely.'

'Why?' It doesn't make sense, nothing makes sense. 'Why would he need all those demesnes? If the Guard aren't in the city anymore and no one else in Amareth has guns, and they're all human—'

'I don't know,' says Hero. She looks back at Idris. 'I really don't know anymore.'

After that, I go to Eliza.

'We can leave him,' I tell her, because someone has to. 'Anthony. We don't have to do this anymore. We can just go. We can run, and deal with him later.'

'We don't have to deal with him at all,' she says quietly.

When I stare at her, she smiles wearily.

'I'm just tired, Kestrel. I know what we have to do.'

I take her hand.

The children are the problem. They want to come with us, the ones who aren't injured, the ones with demesnes but who aren't old enough for their blood to have turned silver. The hard-eyed teenage girl who fought with me against the Guard leads them in their protest. Eliza tried to reason with them, to stop them joining the fight, but they were adamant. There are more of them than I thought, five or six at least.

I look at them and think: some must be human, surely? Some must be brave enough to know what's right. Even that young. At thirteen, I would have been one of them. I knew Hero and Joshua by then, I loved them. But at eleven? I don't know. Would I have come to know what was right, if I hadn't stood to lose anyone to the Guard? Would I have believed gods dangerous and hateful, if I hadn't been put in that dormitory with Joshua and Hero, and fallen in love?

The thought makes me shiver, a bone-deep tremor, a strange kind of fear, like reaching for your soul and not finding it. I put my hands to my temples, steadying myself. Don't think like that.

The girl says to Eliza, 'You can't stop us.'

Eliza looks her up and down, her hands in her pockets. 'You don't really believe that.'

'There are more of us than there are of you.'

'Kid, you're not part of this. Stay out of the city and keep yourselves safe. Anthony is *my* fault.'

'We're on your side!' She steps forward, and suddenly Luca appears from the air at Eliza's shoulder. Some of the children scream, but the girl stands her ground. 'You don't know anything about what's going to happen! None of us do! We're not children, we can fight, you *need* us—'

'I know,' says a voice softly behind her.

Eliza turns. Raven is standing at the very top of the hill, her arms folded. At the sight of her, a murmur passes through the gathered resistance fighters behind her. One man gets to his knees, a hand pressed over his heart, head bowed. A woman with half-healed arms cries, '*Mala kralovna!* He said you were dead!'

'I'm not dead,' says Raven. 'I'm right here.'

The smiles on their gaunt faces are pure light. They watch her, rapt. Eliza's eyes move between the kneeling man and Raven's face.

'I know what's going to happen,' Raven says. 'I had a premonition. Someone here is going to die tonight.'

Eliza turns to Raven. 'Who?'

'I don't know.'

'Where? *Here?*'

'I don't know that either.'

Everyone is watching her now, but it doesn't seem to scare her. She walks towards Eliza and looks her straight in the eye, holding her small frame straight and steady, and for a moment, even though Eliza is at least a foot taller than her, Raven seems level with her.

'We shouldn't fight,' she says to Eliza. 'We should all be together. If bad things are going to happen we shouldn't be apart.'

The children are nodding. Eliza stares down at Raven, her face unreadable. The fighters on the other side of the hill are watching her, hypnotised. I'm willing Eliza to realise what's happening here, to get that it's bigger than her, to understand the power burning in the eyes of this child. But of course she's so much cleverer than me, six steps ahead.

She drops to her knees at Raven's feet and puts her hand over her heart. '*Mala kralovna,*' she says. And there's almost nothing in her voice. Nothing you would hear if you weren't listening for it, if you didn't know her. Just the thinnest, electric thread of power, lit up in the base of her throat, so that when I listen, I hear my own voice, compelled, rising to the chorus, feel my knees give out beneath me, and I hit the ground.

'*Mala kralovna!*' I cry, with the rest of them.

With my head lowered I have just a glimpse of Raven's face, astonished, at the top of the hill, as we shout her praise. '*Mala kralovna!*'

One last thing, before we go into the city.

The sun has fully set now, and his skin shimmers faintly in the soft blue twilight. There's a cut on his shoulder, I notice, raw and half-healed. The Guard don't cut there, they don't usually cut there anyway. At least, they didn't cut *me* there. No, don't think like that.

Eliza, standing beside me, says quietly, 'We could leave him here.'

'No,' says Hero at once.

'Hero, the first chance he gets he's going to attack you again. You know that, right?'

'I do know that, yes,' says Hero. There's a slight edge to her voice, and after a moment Eliza looks away. 'But with his blood, Anthony could kill us all if he wanted to. The Guard had it in the tower and they nearly finished us.'

Eliza is staring down at Joshua with that odd, closed look on her face again. Then she nods, slowly.

'We'll have to hold him,' I say, because no one else looks about to say anything.

'We can use the ropes,' says Eliza. 'He was bound when we found him.'

'He could melt them,' says Hero quietly. 'If he really wanted to.'

Eliza stares over his body, into away from the city.

'Eliza?'

She comes back to herself suddenly, looking first at me and then at Hero. 'Yes,' she says. 'Yes.'

Hero glances at me. 'If he—'

'If he tries to escape,' says Eliza curtly, 'I'll take care of him.' She strides away down the hill.

Hero and I look at each other for a long time.

Tell her, says the voice in the back of my head, urgently. *Tell her what you did. She'll forgive you. She'd have given you her blood willingly, if you asked. Tell her now.*

But I don't say anything. Even after everything, I'm still a coward.

Hero says, quietly, 'Is she okay?'

'I don't know.'

'You love her.' She says it flatly, baldly.

'Yes.'

Hero gives me a searching look.

'What?'

She hesitates. 'You've known her, what, a week? Less?'

'She saved our lives, Hero.'

'And I'm grateful for that.' She gives me another flickering glance. 'But you're . . . more than grateful. And I just . . . I worry about you. Sometimes.'

A silence. Her words trickle through my head like rain down a window.

'You're saying. . . you think she tricked me? Controlled me? Into . . .' I don't know what to call it. 'Into *this*?'

'No. No. Of course I don't.' Hero looks fixedly down at Joshua, even as I stare at her. 'But . . . I'm just saying, she could have done. And I don't think any of us would know. She's more powerful than any of us know. I don't think *she* knows how powerful she is.'

I just look at her, aghast. I don't have the words for it – how obscene the suggestion is, how unspeakable. At last she turns to me, biting her lip.

'What were the two of you arguing about? Before you fell asleep?'

'What do you mean?'

Hero waves a hand impatiently. 'Tonight. You were arguing, it sounded like she was shouting, and then you got up and the two of you went over the hill and came back and you just lay down and went to sleep.'

'What are you talking about?'

There's a longer silence, and when she speaks again her voice is much lower, aghast. 'Are you saying you don't *remember*?'

'I—' *Don't think about that*, says another voice in my head, the one that lives next to the memory. I push against it but it won't give. 'No.'

'Kestrel,' says Hero, 'you know I love you, right?'

'Of course.'

She glances down the hill, towards where Eliza vanished into the dark. 'You need to be careful,' she says. 'We all do.'

Anger rises in me, sudden and white-hot. 'You're saying not to trust her?'

'Of course not,' says Hero. 'I'm saying to be careful. People with power, real power, they can suppress it as long as they want, but once they start using it, they don't stop.' She looks down at Joshua. 'It becomes natural to them. Addictive. They can never really . . . put it away again. You know?'

Silence.

'It's just because we let the Guardsmen go,' I tell her. I want to reassure her, I can't bear the idea of her being scared of *Eliza*, of all people, after everything else Hero's been through. 'She's just anxious. She wanted to kill them all. We should have, it would have been safer. But I said let them go.'

'What? Why?' Hero's looking at me again, her gaze sudden and sharp.

I thought it was what you would do. 'It was the right thing, I thought. She wiped their memories and sent them away, and I—'

I falter at the look on her face.

'Kestrel,' she says quietly, 'you're the bravest person I've ever met.'

I think of Eliza, in the sunset. *So incredibly brave . . .*

I think again of the taste of Hero's blood and feel sickened with myself.

I say, 'I did it for you.'

Hero steps closer, kisses my forehead. 'I know.'

We both look down at Joshua. I can feel the wind on my face, the gentle edge of winter.

'Who's going to wake him up?' I say, at last.

Hero takes my hand and tugs me gently away.

'It's okay,' she says. 'Someone else can do it. He's not our responsibility anymore.'

CHAPTER 23

Rebellion

This time we are armed, prepared.

We have the guns the Guard left behind, wooden handles clutched in our sweaty grips. The injured who have recovered enough to walk are behind us, seething with fury. I can feel it from here. They trusted Anthony, and he betrayed them.

Raven walks at our head as we make our way down the hill, her head raised. Eliza and I are on either side of her.

The streets are clear and quiet in the moonlight. I see faces pale in torchlit windows, doors barred against us. The humans trying to hide from us don't understand there are two sides in this. To them, Anthony and Eliza are as good as kin. That brings wild laughter into my throat again, but then I taste Hero's blood still in my mouth, the rank stench of guilt and furtive wrongdoing, and I choke it down.

It doesn't matter, we might be dead in an hour.

That makes me want to laugh too, laugh until I collapse on the grey cobblestones.

The darkness thickens as we walk through silent streets, past drawn curtains and ghostly houses, until alleyways deepen into warm black abysses, the gleam of stray cats' eyes.

'Eliza,' says Raven suddenly. 'Eliza, look.'

There are people standing beside her, like an honour guard, walking with the twins, protecting her. One of them rushes forwards.

'*Mala kralovna?*'

Eliza holds up a hand and the woman stops at once. Before

I can speak, I hear what Raven heard: a groan of pain from the darkness beside us. The drip of blood on stone.

'Light,' says Eliza quietly, and I think for a brief, insane moment of Joshua. 'We need light.'

Someone lights a torch. The firelight seeps into the alleyway, illuminating the cobblestones with a cold pallor, and we see the injured man, the cuts to his arms deep through the fabric of his shirt, bleeding silver on to the ground.

Then the light moves further and the moans of pain separate and multiply, rise to a terrible deafening chorus.

Raven gasps, and Eliza pulls her gently back.

Fifty at least, stretching back as far as the flickering light extends, and who knows how many more sheathed in darkness beyond. Anthony has sat them, almost gently, against the red-brick wall like limp rag dolls. Men and women and children with pale, bloodless faces and long cuts down their arms. They blink at the light, like newborn creatures.

'Are they dead?' whispers Raven beside us.

'Of course they aren't,' says Eliza, after a moment. She doesn't look away from them. 'Their blood is no use to him if they die. Bandages, who has bandages?'

We took bandages from the nurses' stores at the orphanage. The injured who followed us here, and have regained their strength enough to heal themselves, peel the binds from their own arms; we tear up shirts. When the wounds are all bound we break open the door of a deserted house beside the alleyway and lay them down inside. Hero is by my side, helping me silently, wrapping her hands around deep wounds and closing her eyes so that the cuts seal over, her hands grey with blood.

'How did he manage to overpower them all?' she asks, when the worst of their injuries are healed, and she stands beside us. She looks exhausted; I can see the skull beneath her skin. 'If they're of the blood—'

'The more blood he drinks the stronger he gets.' Eliza rubs her face. 'And they were weak anyway. Tired and scared. Unprepared to fight. Most of our real fighters died when the Guard found us. The camp was a refuge, not an army.' She stares down at them, scratching the back of her neck. 'Cairn always said she wanted to make us stronger . . . but that was in twenty years, we thought we had *time* . . .'

She trails off, then turns away, coming back to herself. 'We'll need food for them. And water. They're so weak, we need – Hero, what else do we nee—'

BANG.

Screams and cries behind us. I turn, staring wildly into the darkness.

Then I see it. A man is standing above us at an open window on the other side of the street, staring down at the crowd, a gun in his hand. There's a blast from behind us from one of Raven's protectors, a rush of scalding air and a crack like a gunshot, and the man at the window goes down in an explosion of blood. I can see a woman in the darkened room behind him, screaming his name, her back against the wall, terrified.

People are shouting questions. Eliza beside me. 'Was anyone hurt? Was anyone hit? Tell me—'

'Kestrel,' says Hero beside me, softly. 'I think—'

I turn.

She has one hand to her shoulder, and when she takes it away it's soaked in grey blood. She stumbles and starts to fall, but it's Luca who catches her, who brings her inside and lies her down on the carpeted floor. The shock is white-hot in my mouth, the blaze of her eyes on mine. Suddenly I can't breathe again.

I kneel on the carpet and watch her grey blood soak into it, unseeing, my mind quite blank. All I can think is, *no, please.* The world blurs around me, and suddenly I am in the camp again on that first night, newly woken, with Eliza gripping my wrists. *What's your name?* And I remember the way the world looked without Hero in it, the scoured bleak emptiness. Her lips are blue-tinged again. Sweetheart, *please . . .*

Eliza is crouching beside me. 'Hero? Can you heal? Can you heal it?'

Hero gives a shudder, and then falls still.

I cry out, half sob and half scream. Eliza grabs my shoulder, her other hand on Hero's wrist for her pulse.

'She's not dead. Kestrel – *listen* to me, she's just passed out. We need more bandages.'

I stare down at Hero, at the spreading blood through her shirt. 'She can't heal if she's not awake.'

'I know. We'll have to leave her here.'

'No! *No!*' I want to shake Eliza, to hit her for suggesting it. 'I can't leave her, I won't *leave* her.'

'Then you can stay here too.' Eliza's face is hard.

'No! Give her a few minutes, she'll wake up.'

'Kestrel. Look at me.' I do. Onyx eyes gleaming in flickering light. 'We can't wait for her. Look how strong Anthony is, look what he's already done. We need to find him *now*.'

'But—' Panic is pulsing in my veins. Hero's blood has long since worn off in me, or I could have used it to heal her. Damn it, *damn* my stupid selfish cowardly— 'I can't leave her. Eliza. Not again.'

'She's hurt, Kestrel. I won't take her into more danger.'

The blood is spreading through Hero's clothes, down to her stomach now, thick and dark. I crawl over to her and kiss her forehead.

'Hero, wake up.' I can feel her breath on my hands. 'Please.'

Someone returns with bandages and I bind Hero's shoulder myself. She's so pale, her blood pooling on the tiled floor. But she won't die. If she stays here she can recover. If I drag her to fight Anthony, and she gets killed . . .

Her blood in my mouth. I promised her I'd never take her blood again, I *swore* to her, I broke her trust.

I broke one vow to her, I can break another.

I can leave her. And she'll be safer by far with Anthony defeated, even if I die.

I kiss her forehead again, the mass of scarred flesh where her eye used to be. 'Please,' I say aloud, 'wake up,' but even as I say it my resolve is hardening. I see her as she was, standing in the tower room of Elida as I struggled, bound to a chair, my angel come to save me. I won't let her get hurt ever again.

I kiss her forehead one last time and tell her that I love her. I think something moves in her face, but then the light shifts again and she lies still on the blood-stained carpet.

I get to my feet. Behind Eliza, I see Caleb talking quietly to one of the women who followed us here from the hilltop, with newly scarred arms. She nods.

Eliza holds out a hand to me and I take it. 'We need to leave,' she says.

I turn to the scarred woman. 'Please look after her.'

The woman nods. Eliza takes my hand and we walk from the room. I don't look back. If I look back I know I'll break at the sight of her, unconscious and bleeding on the floor of a strange house.

In the hallway, Raven looks sombre. 'Is she going to be okay?'

'Yes,' I tell her, my voice very steady. My head is full of shimmering light, but I am calm. 'She's going to be fine.'

Caleb is here again, avoiding Eliza's eyes. I saw him come running at the sound of the shot, his face suddenly grey with fear. He hasn't left Raven's side. He searches his pockets as we walk through the doorway and into the cool blackening night.

The woman in the house opposite has stopped screaming,

and there are no more faces in the windows. Everything is silent, dark. The humans are hiding from us again.

'This isn't what Cairn wanted,' says Eliza quietly. 'All this bloodshed . . . Anthony doesn't know how much damage he's doing. He could turn them against us forever if he—'

Raven's watching Caleb.

'What's wrong?'

'I . . .' He looks up from checking his pockets. 'Damn it. I think I left my knives in that house. In the bag.'

'I think I saw them,' says Luca immediately, with half a glance at him. 'You left them on the carpet, should I—'

'I'll get them,' says Raven quickly. 'Wait, I'll be right back.'

I only have a glimpse of the look on Caleb's face before she turns and runs back into the house. As soon as she is over the doorstep, Caleb raises his hands.

The door slams shut behind her. Above us, the windows swing closed. Through the plate-glass of the door window I see Raven turning, blank incomprehension on her tiny face.

Luca steps forward, lifts a plank of wood from the alleyway with unnatural strength, and fits it across the door, barring it.

From inside, Raven starts screaming and pounding on the wood.

'Can she break through it?' says Luca quietly, stepping away from the door. She presses one hand to her mouth, as if trying to stop herself calling back to Raven, trapped in the darkened house. Her eyes are full of tears.

'I don't think so,' says Caleb. 'She hasn't got the strength.'

He walks forward to lay his hand on the door, presses his cheek against the wood. He closes his eyes.

'Sweetheart,' he calls over the sound of Raven's screaming. 'Raven, calm down. It's okay.'

'Let me *out!* I'm coming with you! I want to fight, let me *out*—'

'I can't, sweetheart.' Caleb's voice breaks. 'You've done enough, you've fought enough. It's over now. You'll be safe in there.'

'I can't leave you! I can't stay here!' Panic splits open Raven's voice. 'I can't, I'm meant to fight, Cairn wanted me to fight—'

'Cairn is dead, sweetheart. It's just us now.'

'*No!* I have to lead them—'

'No, you don't.' Caleb reaches behind him, still with his forehead pressed against the door, and Luca takes his hand. 'We have to keep you safe. That's our job. You'll be safe in here.'

Raven's voice rises to a scream again. 'Let me *out!* I hate you!'

'No, you don't,' says Caleb, and there are tears running down his face now, silver in the light. 'No, you don't, Raven.'

'I *do!* I do, Caleb, let me *out!*'

He hesitates, then walks away. Luca stays with her hand against the door, still rattling as Raven pounds on it. 'We love you,' she says. 'We'll be back when it's over.'

'*I hate you!* Please, Luca, let me *out!*'

'*Mala kralovna!*'

Raven's protectors are muttering amongst themselves, alarmed. One of them runs forward. He squares up as Caleb turns, brushing tears out of his eyes.

'Let her out,' says the man. 'She has to be with us.'

'No,' says Caleb.

The man clenches his fists. 'Listen, she's our—'

'I don't give a damn who she is to you. She's our sister. She'll be safe in there. I'm not bringing her one step closer to Anthony.'

The man steps forward, his fists raised. 'Look, kid—'

Caleb raises his hands, his eyes cold, and the man slams into the ground. The man howls and clutches his broken leg. It's strange to see human flesh snap like that, so quickly and with such force, like someone dropped a hammer from a hundred feet up.

'I'm not going to warn you again,' says Caleb to the man, his voice dead.

'Let her out,' says Eliza quietly.

She hasn't spoken until now, just watched, her eyes unreadable, standing beside me.

Silence.

Luca looks between Eliza and her brother, and stays where she is. That's her mistake. I know that already.

Caleb steps forward. His eyes are burning, like Eliza's did on the hilltop. Eliza puts her hands in her pockets, looking at him. For a moment they stare at each other.

'Eliza,' he says finally, in a very deliberate voice, 'don't do this, please. I don't want to fight you. I'm just trying to keep her safe.'

'Let her out,' repeats Eliza. Her expression is impassive.

Another silence.

'If you think I won't hurt you,' he says, 'you're wrong.'

Eliza raises her eyebrows slightly but says nothing. This only seems to make Caleb angrier. He steps forward, over the still-sobbing man with the broken leg, towards Eliza, through the deep bright silence.

'Every time you take us into a fight,' he says, '*she* gets hurt.'

'That,' says Eliza calmly, 'is not true.'

Caleb's fists twitch. I see Luca's eyes move between him and Eliza. I don't know what to do.

'You keep risking her,' he says, and I can *see* the anger rising in him, the colour in his face. 'You put her in danger, over and over again. And every time you tell us she's going to be fine and she isn't. Anthony attacked her *twice*, she nearly died fighting those Guardsmen. She's ten years old, she's been through enough, she—'

'Caleb,' says Eliza, very quietly, 'we need her with us. I've been trying to keep you safe.'

'Oh, yeah? And how's that been working? How *safe* is Mark right now?'

I hear Luca's quick, sharp intake of breath. Eliza goes suddenly still.

'You're not Cairn,' says Caleb. 'I'm not just going to blindly obey you. Not if it means putting Raven in danger. Not again.' The tears are back in his eyes and he wipes them away furiously. 'We have to *protect* her, Eliza, why don't you get that? You used to love her.'

Thick, ice-black silence. I don't dare move.

'Get her out,' says Eliza again, and this time there's a silken power in her voice.

Caleb's eyes widen. At last, I can see fear in him. His hands go to his ears, too slowly.

Eliza says again, quietly, the power irresistible and overwhelming now, '*Get her out*, Caleb.'

Luca steps forward. 'Eliza, no, what are you—'

'Be quiet, Luca,' says Eliza, her eyes still on Caleb. 'Caleb, do it.'

Luca coughs, her hands going to her throat. Caleb raises his hands, muscles taut with the strain of resisting it, face contorted in rage. He doesn't take his eyes off Eliza, as if the force of his hate could burn through her, cut her down.

She looks back at him steadily.

'Do it,' she says.

He stares at her. Slowly, the plank of wood rises through the air, hovering above the doorknob, until at last, with a crash, Raven falls through the open door, panting.

The resistance fall to their knees, crying her name in relief. Raven scrambles to her feet and looks around, at Caleb in his contorted fury, Luca's wide-eyed breathless shock, Eliza with her hands in her pockets. She looks at Eliza, confused.

'What's happ—'

'Come on,' says Eliza. Her eyes are still on Caleb. She turns away from him. 'We have to keep walking.'

There's no thrumming command in her voice, but Raven turns anyway, uncertain, glancing back at her brother and sister, and begins to walk ahead of the mob, who follow her with cries of '*mala kralovna!*' There is no power more acute, I realise, than the trust of a child, and Raven trusts Eliza absolutely. Eliza knows that.

Something cold and metallic, a slow sinking weight, trickles into my stomach and stays there.

The crowd walk away and then it's just us, Eliza and me and the twins. Two men have stayed behind and stand on either side of Eliza, their eyes slightly blank. Did she order them to do that? I don't remember.

Eliza turns to Caleb and folds her arms. Her eyes have gone cold.

'You ungrateful bastard,' she says.

He struggles against his own locked muscles, teeth gritted so hard I think they'll snap. Luca looks terrified, clutching at her throat. Eliza inclines her head slightly.

'Go on,' she says. 'You can move.'

Caleb collapses at her feet and then almost as quickly staggers up again, throwing himself at Eliza. The rage on his face is transcendent, insane.

'No,' says Eliza softly, 'no, I don't think so.'

He goes suddenly still and teeters on one foot, terrifying in his absurdity, and then falls again. Luca makes a horrible strained noise in her throat. Her face is turning blue.

'Eliza,' I say, and my voice sounds so weak. She does not look at me. 'Eliza, *stop.*'

Eliza takes a step back, but the curtain that has fallen over her eyes does not lift. Her eyes are still on Caleb, and I know that look, I wore it when I stood over Joshua in the darkness after he told me Hero was a traitor. But I was hurt and confused, and there's none of that in Eliza now, just rage.

'I never wanted this,' she says to Caleb, paralysed and struggling on the ground, her voice soft. 'Don't you get that? I never *wanted* any of this, but there was no one else to do it. If you'd wanted to make the decisions –' She pushes her hair out of her eyes, staring down at him. '– I'd have stepped aside the moment you asked. But none of you did. None of you had the courage to do what has to be done. Rather sleep at night, wouldn't you? So you made *me* do this. Cowards.'

'Eliza,' I say, but she ignores me, staring down at Caleb. Luca's face is turning purple.

'You think it's just your sister who's in danger? There's a whole *city* full of kids who'll be hurt if we don't get Anthony under control. There are things more important than our lives. Why am I the only one who gets that?'

'*Eliza!*'

She turns to me at last, her eyes still flat black and dead. Caleb is struggling on the floor.

'Don't make me do this, Kestrel,' she says quietly.

I stand my ground, my hands shaking. It takes all my strength. 'Do what?'

Luca drops to her knees, her hands over her throat, eyes widening, her face turning reddish-black. With an enormous effort, fighting his paralysed muscles, Caleb pulls himself into a sitting position and reaches for her.

I step between him and Eliza.

'Stop,' I say, and my voice is trembling. 'Eliza, *stop* this.'

She looks me up and down, her hands in her pockets.

'When you said you loved me,' she says, 'you lied. You know that, right?'

'What?'

Something changes in her eyes. She steps back, puts her hands over her face.

'All right, you can move,' she says through her fingers. 'Breathe, Luca.'

Movement behind me, rasping. I turn. Luca is on all fours, gasping and retching. Caleb crawls over to her, puts his arms around her. When he looks up at Eliza, there's nothing but hate in his face.

'Get the hell away from us,' he says, panting. 'You're a monster.'

Eliza gives a very thin, sad smile, and in it I can see her heart breaking.

'You made me do this,' she says, 'so you wouldn't have to do anything that was hard. All you had to think about was Raven. You took the easy stuff and left me all of this.'

Silence.

'But I need you on my side,' she says, almost to herself. I can see her eyes unfocused, lost in thought. 'If you think I'm the enemy, if you don't trust me, everything will fall apart. There'll be chaos. Anthony will slaughter you.'

We just stare at her, alone in the shadows. She pushes her hair out of her eyes, holding it at the back of her neck, staring into space.

'I swore I'd never do this again,' she says. 'I swore it to *you*, Caleb, didn't I?'

She closes her eyes. She laughs, a bitter half-laugh with a crack through its centre. Then she licks her lips.

'Screw you,' she says. 'You made me do this.'

Caleb's eyes widen. He tries to scramble to his feet, but again he's too late. Eliza opens her eyes and says, in a deep rippling voice that gets inside my brain and stays there, '*Forget.*'

Cobblestones and cold moonlight. I wake slowly. The world above me sways gently in the wind. I'm lying on the ground. Everything hurts.

Someone's cool hand on my forehead. Eliza. 'Kestrel,' she

says, far away, and then, 'Kestrel,' her voice louder and brighter in my ear.

I struggle to sit up.

Luca is sitting across from me. Her face is very red, but she's taking slow deep breaths. Caleb's arms are around her. We're alone in a darkened street. The window above us is shattered, bloodied curtains billowing in the soft breeze.

'What happened?'

I don't know who says it, it might be me. There's a bruise on Eliza's forehead. When I try to touch the memory it pushes me back gently, saying, *no, look somewhere else.*

I don't know what's happening. There are chunks of my mind missing, torn out and bleeding. Am I going mad?

'We passed out,' Eliza says, evenly. I can see the marks of knuckles on her forehead. Who hit her? 'It was a gas attack. A trick of the Guard's.'

'Where are the others?' Luca's voice is hoarse. She coughs. 'Where's Raven?'

Eliza gets to her feet. 'I don't know. They'll come back for us.'

Caleb is standing, swaying slightly. 'Where is she? Where did she—'

'The Place of Peace,' I say. Something swims up through the cold water of my brain to float on the surface. 'That's where they were going.'

Caleb sets off at a run and Luca stumbles after him.

'Are you all right?' I ask Eliza.

'Yes,' she says, and kisses my head. 'Yes, I am.'

Only when we are three streets away do I remember that I left Hero behind, in the house with the broken door. She was shot, Eliza says. The gas has left a strange fog in my brain.

'Is Hero going to be all right?' I ask Eliza.

She pushes her hair out of her eyes.

'Don't worry,' she says. 'Everything's going to be okay.'

CHAPTER 24

The Child

The square at the centre of Amareth, its pulsing bloody heart, is called the Place of Peace. It's full of bodies. There are cuts on their necks and arms. They lie groaning on the ground. Losing so much blood has weakened them, so they can't heal, so they lose more blood. A slow cycle, a spiral towards exhaustion and death. I feel dizzy for a moment. I want to sleep.

'Bandages,' says Eliza curtly when she sees them.

The twins have run into the crowd to find Raven, so it's me who has to say, 'We won't have enough.'

Her head twitches slightly, irritated. 'Tear up shirts, then.'

Two are dead, half-breeds who could not heal and who bled out on to the granite paving stones, alone in the darkness. The living ones, twenty at least, lie moaning or quiet on the ground. We walk through them, surveying the carnage, watching Eliza's people tie bandages and pour water down dry throats. Raven walks amongst them, and they clutch at her hand, wanting her blessing, calling her *mala kralovna*.

The Palace looms in the gleaming dark at the end of the square, marble and spiralling glass. The centre of Amareth, its government and history. We could see its towers from our window in the orphanage.

'He's in there?' I ask, quietly.

'Where else?'

'But it's so . . .' I can't find the word.

'Obvious?' Eliza gives a weary smile.

'He wants you to go in there,' I say, slowly. 'He *wants* you to attack him.'

'I imagine he does.'

'And you're just going to—'

'I'm not *just* going to do anything. Kestrel.' Eliza touches my face, turns it towards her. I realise with a slight shock that I am taller than her. 'I'm going to do what I have to do.'

'I'm coming with you. It's my decision.'

She looks at me for a minute that might be a year, the silence slow and black as river water. The twins have come up behind her silently, arms crossed, like bodyguards.

'Okay,' she says at last. 'But not without him.'

She nods over my shoulder to the body curled behind me in the darkness, the one we carried with us from the hill. He's still unconscious, but I can see the glint of the steel ropes binding him.

'No,' says Caleb at once. 'No. Absolutely not.'

'He's stronger than any of us,' says Eliza. Her voice is hoarse, but calm. 'If Anthony attacks—'

'It's not Anthony we'll have to worry about, if *he's* with us.'

'I don't think so,' says Eliza. 'It's Hero he wants dead. And we have something he wants.'

'What?'

Eliza's eyes flicker towards me. I look back at her. A slight shock ripples through me, more like a shiver, at the stillness in her, the impassivity.

'If you need me to do it,' I tell her, 'I'll do it.'

A slight pause.

'Thank you, Kestrel,' says Eliza, softly. Her eyes don't leave mine.

Waking Joshua isn't hard; he was always a light sleeper. I think again of the hilltop, the night I woke him, thinking I could talk him out of his insanity.

I kneel down beside him and touch his shoulder. 'Joshua,' I murmur. 'Joshua, wake up.'

He blinks for a moment in the darkness. I see everything return to him, the way his eyes widen before they focus. He tries to roll over, struggles against the ropes. The cuts on his arms are healed to thick purplish scars now. He looks so achingly familiar, the light in his eyes. The pale, mangled ghost of the boy I loved.

'Kestrel?' he whispers.

'Yeah, Joshua. It's me.' It breaks my heart, the hope in his eyes. He thinks I've come to save him.

'Where are we?'

'In the Place of Peace.'

'In *Amareth*?'

'Yes. Listen, Joshua.' He tries to sit up, staring at me. 'We need to go into the Palace. We need to stop Anthony. Will you come with us?'

Lay it all out, everything open; I don't want to delude him. This is what his choice is now, and he can make it freely.

'You're . . .' He struggles with it, confused. 'You're going in there? With who?'

Eliza steps out of the darkness, her hands in her pockets. She doesn't say anything, just looks down at him. He goes very still.

'You're with *her*?'

He says it blankly and I know he doesn't mean what comes to my mind – he can't know about that, he can't possibly know – but I can still feel Eliza's eyes on the back of my neck, and fight to keep it from showing in my face. I know he can still read me.

'Yes.'

His eyes widen. 'Kestrel, you have to get away from them, they're dangerous—'

'*Listen to me*, Joshua.' I try to make my gaze as white-hot and piercing as Eliza's. 'I'm with them now. Come with us or don't.'

He stares at me.

'You're going in there?' he whispers. 'To fight someone?'

'Yes.'

'Then I'm going with you.'

I twist to look up at Eliza. Behind her, I can see the twins' uneasy faces.

'I'm going to untie you, Joshua,' says Eliza, 'but if you try to run, or hurt anyone we don't tell you to, I will make you hang yourself with them. Do you understand?'

He glares at her. 'Fine,' he says at last, flat and petulant.

Caleb steps forward and unties the ropes with sharp, forceful movements, as if he's trying to touch Joshua as little as possible. He steps away very quickly.

Joshua brushes himself off and gets to his feet. He glances at me, and I step away towards Eliza. I turn away at his stricken look. Even after everything, I don't like seeing him hurt.

Eliza inclines her head towards the Palace of Peace, not taking her eyes off Joshua. 'Come on,' she says. 'Let's go. Before Raven sees us. I don't want her following.'

We do it now, while everyone is busy tending to the wounded, Raven kneeling beside a bleeding boy, surrounded by her pack of watchful, reverent protectors. She does not look up. Nobody notices us climbing the blood-slicked stairs in the black of night, cold wind on our faces, walking into the darkness.

We studied the Palace of Peace once in the orphanage, when I was a child. It was destroyed twenty years ago in the rebellion that slaughtered the gods, and then rebuilt again – the spiral towers taller still, the webs of gold thread on the walls more intricately woven, its glass towers brighter in autumn sunlight. The walls are marble, but in the dark everything is colourless and grey.

'Lock the doors,' says Eliza. 'If they realise we're gone, they'll try to follow us.'

Caleb does it. The doors are stone too, and their thud echoes through the dark entrance hall like the toll of a bell. For a moment I feel the walls of my cell solidifying around me again. My nails dig into my palms. *I'm not mad, I'm* free. The Guard are gone and cannot hurt me. But Anthony, *Anthony* can hurt me . . .

Breathe, I tell myself, but I can feel the panic beneath the thought, a rising songbird note. The darkness is sudden and absolute.

It'll never be over, says Roman softly in my head, and I feel the caress of his knife over my face. *You'll never be free. No one ever leaves here, not really . . .*

'Eliza,' I whisper, because I'm shaking, and she says, 'I'm here.'

Hands groping in the dark. I feel the brush of her fingers against mine. The known, warm shape of her under my hands, smooth thin arms and hard lips. She is here, so I'm safe, I'm not in my cell. I kiss her, clumsily, the warmth of her mouth beneath mine. She is the last good thing in the world, and if she's here *I am not in my cell.*

'Kestrel?' she murmurs. 'What's wrong?'

I don't have the words for it. 'I'm sorry.'

'Don't apologise. Don't ever apologise to me.' She touches my cheek in the darkness, her voice a low warm whisper. 'It's okay. You're okay, you know that?'

'I know that.'

Her hand tightens in mine. 'Stay close.'

'I will.'

Our footsteps echo as we walk into the darkness. I can hear my heart pounding in my head, aching, but Eliza's hand is in mine so I am safe. My diamond-blade knife is in my hand. And then Luca cries out from the darkness to our left, sudden and sharp.

'What? Luca?'

'Luca, are you okay?'

I hear Caleb shifting, trying blindly to find her. He stumbles, I hear the thud. 'What's wrong?'

'My hand,' says Luca. Her voice is tight with pain. 'I . . . I touched the wall, and something . . .'

'Joshua,' says Eliza sharply. 'We need light.'

For a moment I don't think he'll do it. Then I see faint golden light blooming in the palms of his cupped hands, his sullen face lit by it. I look away.

Luca is standing beside the wall. It's like molten gold in Joshua's light. The stone is coated in rough mountain ranges of razor-sharp glass. Luca's cut heals as she makes a fist, grey blood dripping from the inside.

'What the hell is that?'

'Diamond,' says Eliza quietly. 'It's his demesne.'

Her eyes widen suddenly, and she takes half a step forward.

'Luca, is your blood on it?'

'Why? It doesn't—'

'Of course it matters. *Listen* to me. Is your blood on it?' She turns in the dark. 'Joshua, we need more li—'

Something moves at the end of the hallway.

'Eliza,' I say, but too late. There's a soft thrum like a loosed arrow, a rush of air, and then with a *crunch* Joshua is blasted off his feet. His light goes out, and far behind us I hear him slam on to the stone floor, and then everything is quiet.

I feel the twins turning around towards the end of the hall, hear their gasps.

Then no one moves.

Silence, thick black darkness. My heart is inside my head,

beneath my skull, beating too fast for thought. If we don't speak Anthony can't tell where we are.

I let go of Eliza. My knife is in my hand. I raise it in front of me, holding it out, like a sacrifice. I'm not a fighter. If he comes for me I'll die.

'Anthony,' says Eliza loudly, and the thrum is in her voice now, the deep compulsion of power. 'Anthony, st—'

A deafening rumble like the crush of an avalanche, the whole hall reverberating with it so that Eliza's voice is drowned. The sound is beyond loud, deeper than the bones of my chest, and I fight the urge to cover my ears.

Where is Anthony? If I knew I could throw the knife. Caleb could throw him . . . *dammit*—

What else can he do, what other demesnes does he have?

And then, suddenly, a hand around my throat.

I try to scream but he lifts me off my feet and slams me against the wall. I feel blood trickling into my eyes, and the crunch of bone breaking, but the fear drowns the pain. I can smell his sweat, his panting breath; his closeness is obscene.

You're the only one he can kill, says the voice, *he wants their blood, he needs them alive, but you're human, he has no use for you.* Mad laughter in my throat again, choking me. His voice in my ear, a terrible snarl, I can taste the scent of sweet blood in his throat. *Eliza*, is all I can think.

'Where's the girl?'

He's not Eliza, he can't make me answer. I struggle to draw breath through the tightness of his hands around my throat and realise with dull surprise that I can't. I'll lose feeling soon, touch and sight and sound. There are worse ways to die, but if Eliza—

'*Where's the girl? Tell me!*'

He grinds his knee against my broken left hand, and I scream in the blazing agony that shoots up my arm. My right hand is fumbling at my waist, his body against mine.

'*The girl – she killed them—*'

My right hand twists, the edge of the knife finding his stomach at last, and I push it in as deep as I can. I feel his jagged gasp of breath, but his wound heals as soon as I make it, the knife forced out of his flesh, muscles pressing against my hand. *The heart and the head.* I can't hurt him like this. He tightens his grip, and deeper darkness blossoms at the corner of my eyes, my lungs collapsing. *The heart and the head—*

Then he jerks and releases me, a splatter of blood on my face. Beautiful air in my lungs, my throat bruised and agony, my left hand a broken mess, but I can breathe. I can *breathe*.

Light, sudden and flickering. A ball of fire in Anthony's hand as the gunshot wound in his back heals. The gun we took from the Guardsmen is in Caleb's hand. I can see Luca sprawled unconscious on the ground, Joshua behind her, stirring on the blood-stained marble floor, his wounds healing, his eyes are open, but where's Eliza?

Caleb fires three more times at Anthony, but Anthony moves so quickly I swear it's like he vanishes away and he sends the ball of fire at Caleb's face. It flowers in the black air and then dies against the cut-diamond wall when Caleb ducks.

'*Where's the girl?*'

The gun is floating in mid-air in front of Caleb's face, pointed straight at Anthony's forehead. Caleb's fists are closed, the muscles in his face standing out at the temples.

Silence, at last. Anthony has stopped, narrowed eyes on the gun inches from his face. *The heart and the head.* If Caleb fires, Anthony will die, but Caleb doesn't. *Fire*, please fire.

'What?' he says. 'What did you say?'

'Your little girl. She's the reason they died.' Anthony licks his lips, eyes still on the gun. His eyes have lost all life, they pool the light in them, reflect it, flat and white and dead.

'Raven?' says Caleb, at last. 'What are you talking about?'

'I found a Guardsman. Cut him till he talked.' Anthony half-smiles, licking his lips again, staring at the gun, diamond rivulets trickling down his fingers to harden into blades. I'm trying to pull myself towards Joshua, grasping for my knife along the marble floor with my good hand, but every time I move a sheet of agony flares up my arm. *Where's Eliza?* 'The Guard were in the mountains, looking for us, the night of the attack. Seventy miles from the camp. They didn't know where we were. We could have been a hundred miles in any direction. They never would have found us. But they had telescopes. And one saw a bird . . . an owl, a white owl, flying over the woods . . . but they knew there were no owls like that this far south. No woods for it to live in.' Anthony's eyes are fixed on Caleb, his voice curdled with hate and pain. 'It seemed strange, to them. So they went closer.'

All the colour has drained from Caleb's face.

'*That* was how they found the camp. The night Beth died. The little shapeshifter girl gave us away.' His voice is low, rough with menace.

'No,' whispers Caleb. I've stopped crawling. My head is full of her. I see her the night Anthony drove us from the camp, that first bleak dawn. Eliza and Caleb arguing. Raven flying around us, a white owl in the pale sky, watching. Being watched. Oh, no.

And then Joshua appeared in the woods, and—

'*Where is she?*' Anthony whispers.

Caleb hesitates, staring at Anthony. *Pull the trigger*, I want to shout at him, but I have no voice and I know he won't. Eliza told me, Caleb doesn't have the strength or the ruthlessness to do what has to be done, he's not a killer, he has no true steel.

'Far from here,' says Caleb at last. 'Safe from you.'

'Shame,' says Anthony, and before I can cry out the crusted diamond on the wall behind Caleb sprouts thin ropes and twist around him, pulling him closer. He screams as the edges cut into his skin, a sob of agony, blood welling in webbed lines to soak his shirt, dripping from his fingers.

Anthony snatches the gun from the air in front of him as it falls, and when Caleb tries to blast him backwards Anthony closes his fist. The ropes of diamond tighten and cut deeper, and the pitch of Caleb's screams rises, blood running into his eyes. The more he struggles, the more he bleeds, until at last he goes limp, his breath coming in agonised rasps. The blood drips on to Luca, unconscious at his feet.

Anthony points his gun backwards at me just as my good hand closes around my knife.

I stop dead. Anthony raises his other hand so that the light from his ball of flame spreads further down the corridor, and I see another huddled, unconscious figure, sprawled on the marble floor a few yards away.

Oh, no, please let her not be – don't let Eliza be dead.

Anthony twitches. Something moves from his hand to rush over her, like a pulse of air. She stirs at its touch, raises her head to blink at the dim light.

From behind me Eliza says, 'Wait.'

I twist around and see her struggling to her feet. She's bleeding from the temple, staring past Anthony.

Towards the unknown figure at the end of the hall.

I am bleary, my mind pain-dulled. Luca and Joshua are unconscious behind me, and Eliza is here, so who is—

'No,' Eliza whispers. Her eyes are wide.

The girl tries to pull herself up on one elbow, but the movement hurts and she winces and cries out and clutches her shoulder. And all the air leaves me, sudden as flame catching to wood.

Oh no, no, please no. *Sweetheart, I'm sorry—*

'You thought,' says Anthony to Eliza in a low rasp, 'that I wasn't having you watched? You thought that I wouldn't leave

some of my people behind, to see what you did? You thought
I was an *idiot?*'

Behind him, on the ground, Hero's eyes flicker open,
adjusting to the light. Her gaze moves over all of us, Caleb's
blood dripping on to the floor, my crushed hand. She breathes
deeply, her eyes wide and steady, and doesn't move.

'The scarred woman,' says Eliza evenly, at last. 'The one I
left her with. She gave you her blood willingly. She stayed
behind on your orders.'

'She was loyal. She knew why I needed it.'

'And why did you need it?'

Anthony raises a bloodied arm to point straight into Eliza's
face. Diamond is crusted into talons on the tips of his fingers.
He looks insane.

'You,' he says. 'You were working with the Guardsmen, I
know it. You betrayed us to them, you helped them kill Cairn.
You know what they know. You can help me.'

I expect her to be shocked. I expect her to say, *no, of
course I wasn't*, that Anthony is insane, that she loved Cairn
and would never have betrayed her. I expect her to tell him
what I told Joshua – that this is what the Guard do, what
they love. They want to turn us against each other, so we'll
destroy each other for them. I expect her to shout at him.
But of course, Eliza is much cleverer than I am. Her eyes
move from Caleb to Hero to Anthony to me. She doesn't
answer for a moment.

Then she says, 'Help you? How?'

Anthony's face contorts.

'The *child*,' he hisses. 'You know where they took her. Tell
me or I'll kill her.' He jabs a finger behind him at Hero, who
has one blood-soaked hand pressed to her shoulder. She
flinches. Eliza's eyes flicker towards her.

'Raven's not here, Anthony,' she says, 'and she's surrounded
by people ready to die for her. You'll never touch her.'

'Not *her!*' He almost howls it; he looks quite mad, with his blood-stained teeth and his sunken eyes. 'The *child!*'

Eliza just stares at him.

He reaches into his pocket and throws a scrap of parchment at her. It flutters against the air, crumpled, and drifts to the marble floor at her feet. 'This. Your *friends* in the Guard left this for me.'

Slowly, not taking her eyes off Anthony, Eliza bends down, one hand still pressed to her bleeding temple, and picks it up. She stares at him for a long time before she reads it. Then she looks back up at him again. The only sound is Caleb's panting, agonised breathing.

'*We have the girl,*' says Eliza, softly.

Anthony nods. He's shifting his weight from foot to foot, his eyes darting, between us, too quick. 'They left it in the tent. The night they killed Beth. I knew they must have her here. In Amareth.'

Another long silence. Eliza stares at him. Her face is completely expressionless.

'You had,' she says at last, very slowly, 'a daughter.'

Anthony nods, rapid and manic.

'Outside of the camp.'

'Cairn knew,' he whispers. 'She said it was the reason – the reason I could never follow her. As leader. She thought the Guard might find out. I argued with her. I thought they were *safe*, Adara and the baby, I took every precaution, I—'

Eliza is still looking at him. Her face is quite empty.

'You had a child,' she says, 'with a human woman.'

Anthony rubs his face. I see, suddenly, the terror that has worn itself into him, his sunken eyes, gaunt yellowish face. The white in his hair. He starts talking, jerkily, compulsively.

'It was Cairn's fault. I always told her that. She thought, we'd been in hiding for ten years, we needed to make more *progress*, people were getting restless – so she sent some of us to Amareth. To hide. Find out what was going on. How to defeat the Guard. And Adara – the woman who gave us shelter—' He rubs his face again, too fast, and I can hear the rasp of palm on stubble, see the way the skin reddens. 'Two years later she got a letter to me, in the camp. She said there was a child, that she was mine, that she wasn't human, she could make plants grow just by touching them. That ivy grew around her cot. Neassa.' Anthony smiles thinly, quick and blank and mirthless. 'I went to visit her in Amareth. As often as I could. I couldn't take her to the camp, she looked too much like me, it would have been obvious she was mine. If Beth had ever seen her it would've destroyed her. I promised Adara no one would know, ever.'

'But the Guard found out,' says Eliza. Her voice is still slow and soft and empty. There's a look of transcendence about her, everything coming together at last. '*That* was their bigger plan. That's why they killed Cairn. Because they knew you would replace her. They wanted you to be leader. They knew they had something they could use to control you. And the night they attacked . . . they left you the note . . .'

'They thought they could turn me. They thought they could use her against me. Make me act against my own people. *Never.*' He spits on the floor. 'I went straight to Amareth. To find Neassa, to get her out of their hands—'

'But they knew you'd do that,' says Eliza. Her voice is quiet, her face still quite blank. 'That was part of their plan. They knew the resistance was weak. We'd lost all our trained fighters in the first attack. They *wanted* you to attack Amareth. They were waiting for you at Fitzgerald House.'

I don't think he even hears her.

'I thought they'd have her there. At the orphanage. And then they stopped firing, and the Guardsmen were gone, and

I didn't know where. I needed all the power I could get. I thought they might have taken her here . . . and I knew you would follow me.'

'You drank blood to rescue Neassa,' says Eliza. 'To defeat the Guard, and rescue her.'

'Yes,' whispers Anthony. 'But she's not here.' He jabs a finger into her face again. This time Eliza does flinch. 'But *you* know where she is. You were working with the Guard, to kill Cairn. Tell me where she is, or the healer dies.'

Eliza says nothing, still staring at him in shock. This is what lay behind Anthony's crazed blood-thirst, his will for destruction. Just this. A little captured girl.

Anthony points back at Hero. She's taken the hand away from her shoulder, which has stopped bleeding. His voice rises, a high insane rage. 'You think I won't kill her, Ehler?'

Eliza's eyes flicker to me. I try to burn into her eyes with mine, hoping desperately that somehow she can read my mind. I don't care what happens now, I try to tell her. I just want Hero alive.

'I believe it,' she says.

But too late, I realise Anthony has noticed the look between us. I try to stare at the floor, make my face neutral, despite the white-hot pain in my hand. Try to pretend she's nothing to me.

He looks between the two of us, his eyes widening.

'Oh,' he whispers. 'Oh, I see.' He moves the hand with the diamond-blade claws slowly through the air, to point at me instead of Hero. 'It's not the healer you love, is it? It's *this* one. The human girl.'

Eliza stares at him, her face quite blank. Joshua, behind her, has come round. He pushes himself slowly into a sitting position, his eyes moving between Anthony and me. I can see his hand shimmering, but he doesn't do anything. Anthony's hand is pointing straight into my face.

'Tell me where she is,' says Anthony, his voice shaking, 'or I'll kill the human girl.'

I close my eyes, breathe in and out. I can feel Hero watching me. I need to be brave for her. My hand pulses, a slow throb of agony, steadying me.

Eliza says, evenly, 'Don't do this, Anthony.'

But there's no thrum of power in her voice, no magic. She doesn't want to risk aggravating him; he'll hear the power before she can give a full command, and shoot me. I want to scream at her, and at Joshua, too, with the light in his hands that could kill Anthony in an instant. Not even Anthony, with all his blood-drenched power, could move faster than light. They could both kill him right now. *Do what has to be done!*

'I never worked with the Guard,' says Eliza to Anthony, quietly. 'I need you to know that.'

The diamond-blade claws on the hand pointing into my face grow longer, sharper. I don't look away. I will not die a coward.

But then, into the silence, Eliza speaks.

'Kestrel,' she says to me. Her voice is soft, and she doesn't look round. 'I need you to remember, now.'

There's a white-hot thread of power into her voice. It reaches into my mind, and unlocks a door that was shut and barred. The flesh of my memory, the part of it that was torn away, is suddenly healed and whole.

I fight the urge to look at the memory. I need to stay here, with Hero and Eliza. But Eliza turns back slightly to look at me. Her voice low and urgent, her eyes burning. The voice I cannot disobey.

'Kestrel,' she says, and I'm falling, 'I need you to *remember—*'

And I'm on the hilltop, a thousand years ago. Eliza has tears in her eyes. She says, *When Anthony comes for you, I might not be able to protect you. Some gods are too strong. Do you understand that?* Her voice rising, panicked. *I need to keep you safe. I'm sorry.*

And then the power in her words, silvery and bright, her face so sad. The resolve of years snapping, irretrievably, like Hero said it would.

You won't remember this, she says. *Stand up.*

The memory that was taken from me dribbles slowly back to me, slow and cold and metallic, like mercury.

I cannot think; Eliza has my mind. *Come with me*, she says, and I do, over the hillside to where Joshua lies unconscious, bound with ropes.

Eliza takes out a knife and a vial. She makes a deep cut on his shoulder, where the skin is thin and tender, and holds the vial to it as the silver blood wells and beads and dribbles from the room. She is taking slow, deep breaths. She stoppers the vial and hands it to me. Her eyes are dry again, and her face set. I put it into my pocket, next to the one Eliza doesn't know about, the one full of Hero's greyish blood.

If Anthony realises I can't control him, she says, *he'll stop being afraid of me. He'll realise I can't stop him killing whoever he wants. So I can't risk trying and failing. Do you get that? It's too dangerous.*

I just stare at her, my mind warm and numb and empty.

If he comes for you, she says, *you have to drink this and kill him.* Her voice full of power, jewelled and glittering. Her eyes alight. *Kill him, Kestrel. Do you understand me?*

My mind goes numb.

I understand her.

The world comes back, tearing through layers of memory. I am on my feet, blood dripping from my mangled hand. A vial in my other hand. I look down at it.

It's unstoppered, empty. I can taste sweet blood in my mouth.

Everything around me is clear and cold. I can see Eliza,

watching me intently, and Hero, confused and afraid, her mouth moving very slowly, trying to say, *Kestrel*, but I don't hear her. Everything is quiet.

My mind is greasy and numb.

There's a jolt like a second heartbeat, the power seeping through my veins, sweet and sickening. This is what I was meant to do, what has to be done. A pulse of searing heat in my hand as it heals, broken bones fusing and skin sealing over.

I look at Anthony. His hand has moved as I got to my feet, the diamond-blade claws still pointed straight into my eyes. He's looking at me in confusion. He doesn't understand yet.

Eliza's eyes are moving from my face to my hands, and in the thrill of the power in my veins I realise how hot my skin is. Light lives in me, white-hot and blazing. The light concentrates, grows in my hands, the heat of it rippling over my face.

Anthony's mouth is opening, the diamond rivulets on his hands stretching in trickles towards me, to pierce my skin and tear out my heart. Everything moves slowly, so slowly.

Don't be afraid, I want to tell him.

The light leaves my hands.

I watch it move through the air, its glorious dragonfly speed, white and blinding. Everything is lit by it, the darkness outside it absolute. Nothing exists in the world in that moment but me and it and Anthony. I can see his face, every bone in it, in the hard light as it flies towards him.

Then it goes out, sudden and sharp, and darkness falls. Everything is quiet.

'Kestrel!'

'Eliza—'

'Kestrel, where are you, what—'

My hands are glowing again. I pool it in my palm and the

hallway slowly reappears, golden and glistening. My teeth are silver-stained, and I can feel Caleb staring at me from his diamond ropes, covered in blood.

'Anthony,' says Eliza's voice in front of me, urgent, 'where's Anthony?'

I look down, stretching out my arms so the pool of light in my palms covers him. He's on the ground too. His face is burned black. *The heart and the head.* I can see the skull beneath the peeling grey skin.

I turn away and vomit on to the floor. Eliza holds me tight.

'You did so well, love,' she murmurs to me. 'So incredibly well.'

It's a while before I can breathe again.

I say, in a rasping acid-scoured voice, 'You didn't need to make me kill him.'

'I did, sweetheart,' she whispers. 'I did. Or we'd never have been safe. I'm sorry. This is what had to be done.'

She kisses my head. I just gaze at Anthony, dead on the marble floor.

Joshua is still on the ground by the wall, panting. His hands are over his face. He doesn't look at me.

Anthony was still carrying one of his diamond-blade knives. We use it to saw through Caleb's thin ropes to release him. His cuts are many and painful, but not deep. I tear off strips of my shirt to make bandages, but he won't look me in the face, either.

Eliza wants to go outside, to tell her people that it's over. We walk out of the hall, past Joshua and the twins, and out on to the glass steps. I stay in the shadows, feeling Joshua's blood still thrumming in my veins.

The tiny lights he conjured have vanished, but the injured and their helpers in the square have lit small fires. There are many more of them than there were when we went into the

Palace of Peace. They have gathered in the greying dark: hundreds more, maybe thousands, packed into the stone square, nervous and silent.

Humans have come out from their houses, some of them holding guns, but no shots are fired. They're still too confused. They've noticed the Guard are gone, but they know this doesn't look like an attack. I'm not sure they know who we are. That's good, that's very good.

There are children asleep in corners, the wounded propped up on beds that have been dragged into the square from houses. And I think, numbly: they cannot ever know what happened tonight, what is behind me in the entrance hall of the Palace of Peace. If they ever know that this began in blood, it will break this fragile peace, these fragile people.

Eliza must know that, too.

I stop just outside the door, in the shadows. Eliza walks halfway down the steps and then comes to a halt, staring at all of them. I can see the tears in her eyes, glistening in the firelight, tears of pride, I think, or maybe just exhaustion.

Raven sees her first. She is easy to find: in the very centre of the square, surrounded by people, all bowed heads and hands laid on hearts, all wanting to talk to her, to see her, to lay eyes on the wondrous child who saved them from the Guard. They kneel when they see her and stretch out their hands like a blessing.

When she sees Eliza, her face lights up. They follow her gaze and stand.

The noise of the crowd quietens and a deep silence spreads out from the stairs of the Palace, rapt and waiting. But she doesn't say anything. She just stands there on the steps, alone in the moonlight and the silence, looking out over the gathered crowd with fervent hunger, taking them all in, the injured gods and half-breeds, and the frightened humans with their upturned faces.

Slowly, something builds in their midst as they watch her, a deep rumbling, the thunder of low voices. I wait, hand on the knife at my belt.

Then at last it breaks like a wave, and they're shouting, screaming her name, crying out their gratitude, jumping up and down and hugging each other in their joy. They clamber up the steps towards her and she disappears under a wave of them, half-laughing and half-crying, all trying to touch her, hug her, shake her hand, tell her they love her.

The wave of people draws back like a breath, and through it I see Raven with Eliza's arms wrapped around her, raising her fist into the cold night air like a prize fighter, and they all kneel, every single one of them, and cry with a single screaming roar of a voice, 'Mala kralovna!'

She turns to me and smiles, and says, 'Go back inside, Kestrel.'

And I do, because it's all okay now.

We have to move the body, Eliza says when she returns, and clear up the blood. There can't be any remnants of this by the time the others get here.

I am standing beside the wall. My hands are still shimmering. Hero has healed Caleb's cuts and is sitting beside me. No one looks at Anthony's body.

'This place is made of stone,' I say, at last. 'Where will we bury him?'

'We don't need to bury him. We can burn him.'

'What about the kid?'

To my surprise, it's Joshua who says it. Everyone turns towards him. He's on his feet at last, still shaking slightly. The scars on his arms are almost fully healed now. He's still refusing to look at me or Hero.

'What about it?'

'The Guard said they had his kid. What if she's here?'

Eliza looks at him for a long time. 'She's not here, Joshua.'

'How do you know that?'

Hero and I glance at each other.

'She's dead,' says Eliza shortly. 'As soon as Anthony started heading to Amareth, the Guard would have killed her. They'd got what they wanted out of her. They wouldn't have risked letting her be rescued.'

Joshua stares at her. 'Do you know that, or are you guessing?'

'I'm . . .' Eliza closes her eyes, takes a breath to calm herself. 'I'm as sure as I can be,' she says eventually.

'What if she's not, what if she's in a basement somewhere? We should check—'

'No.' Eliza covers her face with her hands, as if she could blind herself to him. 'We can't . . . we can't deal with that right now. We have to take care of this first.'

Joshua's face darkens. 'Don't tell me what I *have* to do, bitch.'

I'm about to say something, to hit him maybe, but before I can, Eliza says through her fingers, 'Shut up, Joshua.'

There's a silvery, garrotting-wire thread of power in her voice, just enough to compel, and the silence that follows it is absolute, deep and dark and oily.

And then Joshua says, 'No.'

Eliza's head snaps up. Everyone stares at them. Joshua's eyes have widened.

'I said,' says Eliza after a moment, her voice soft and dangerous and with a liquid sheet of power I can feel in my ribs, deep and electric enough to stop my heart, '*shut up.*'

A pause.

'No,' says Joshua again, quietly.

Absolute, heart-frozen silence. Nobody moves.

Some gods are too strong, Eliza says in my head. *I could never control Cairn.*

I think of all the times she threatened him – *I'll make you hang yourself* – and he looked at me and saw in my eyes that I wouldn't defend him from her, and that was enough, and she never *had* to—

Eliza's face is completely blank, and I can almost feel how fast she's thinking. I can see the world falling away from her, through her slack hands.

Joshua raises his hands, the light shimmering on them. He doesn't take his eyes off Eliza. 'You can't control me,' he says quietly. And then he smiles, a wide sharp-toothed grin.

She says nothing. The light in the room from the cracked-open door is oozing towards him, coalescing in soft gold sinews on his hands.

Everything happens slowly; everything blurs, and I'm not quite sure of all of it. I know that Hero beside me goes still, and I know I'm a second late in understanding the vicious joyful madness in Joshua's eyes. I know his gaze moves towards her – honey-slow, it seems to me in the darkness – and the light on his hands grows brighter, but I'm not sure, yet, what he's going to do next.

What I know is that the light on his hands brightens, and his eyes move to Hero, and in that moment Eliza says, her voice glowing with electric-bright power, 'Kestrel, kill him.'

The blood is still thrumming in my arms. My mind goes quiet.

I raise my glowing hands.

Joshua sees it. He jerks backwards – his movements are slow, so slow to me – and raises his hands in front of his face, the light still glowing in them, his eyes widening. It's instinctive, he's not afraid yet. He doesn't even have time to reach fear.

I release the light.

It flies towards him. Everything slows, and I see everyone's faces lit by it, and the silence pure, the last true silence in the world.

My light collides with his. There's a deafening *boom* and then an explosion, sun-bright, electric and agonising, white-hot enough to obliterate him.

I can still see his face, frozen in shock and not-yet-fear, as the explosion swallows him whole. I will see it, I think, for the rest of my life.

Then the blast hits me, and the world ends.

CHAPTER 25

Mercy

I wake at last. I am lying on stone. Someone is stroking my face. Everything hurts, my skin is tight and white-hot. I wonder if I'm dead.

'Kestrel,' says a voice, softly. 'Kestrel, look at me.'

I try to move my hands. I know I'm bleeding. I try to open my eyes, but I can't.

'You're going to be fine,' says Eliza's voice, from above me in the darkness. Her hands are cool on my burned face. Her breathing is ragged. 'This is never going to have happened for you, sweetheart. You're going to be okay.'

Hero. Is Hero alive? My throat is red-hot, rasping. My heart seems to be beating very slowly, the blood in it thick and cold.

She kisses my forehead and lays her head against mine for a few seconds. I can feel the tears on her cheeks.

'I'm so sorry,' she says at last. 'For everything I did. Cairn was right. I was never *good* enough.' She gives a terrible choked laugh. 'Oh, what am I going to do without you, Kestrel?'

I hear her wipe tears away again. She takes long deep breaths to steady herself.

'I didn't want to do this,' she says. 'Any of it. Kestrel, please, just . . . I don't want to do this.'

And fear moves slowly into my heart, icy and black, beneath the love and the grief.

'Eliza,' I try to say, but the word won't come. The fire burned away my voice.

'Sweetheart,' she says, 'Kestrel, I love you. I meant it. I love you.' I try to breathe through my burn-scoured throat, try to speak.

'The twins are dead,' she says at last. Her voice is full of pain. 'They were standing too close to him. It's . . . I . . . '

Then she's quiet.

'All right,' she says softly, as if to herself, as if I'm already not there. 'All right. I can do this alone.'

I can feel the heat, still, the crackling of the flames. Outside, the chanting of voices. *Mala kralovna*, they're shouting.

'Don't be scared, sweetheart,' she says. 'This is mercy. I'm saving you. You see?'

I can feel her, even through the excruciating pain of her voice, trying to smile.

Panic rises in me, slow, because deep down I know there's no real point fighting. I try to raise a hand, to touch her face, tell her *no, stop*—

But it's too late, she's already talking, and the power is velvet steel in her throat and the rhythm of her voice is warm and sweet and soft, and I fall into it, scrabbling at the edges of my mind to hold on as she drags me down to the black water.

Epilogue

Before I take the boat in I hang around the coast, just floating, watching the water darken, the sunset burning on the soft green hills. It's beautiful here. Winter came and went, and there was a revolution in the city, but it doesn't touch us here. Spring brought blue-veined ocean fish, eels, sharks whose teeth and meat we could sell at market. It's a good spring this year. We don't want for anything.

My sister is waiting for me back at the house when I come in. She's wearing a dark blue dress.

'I bought basil at the market,' she says. My sister is a healer, one day she'll be a doctor, but she's a terrible cook. I say, 'I'll make the tomato stew,' and she smiles and says, 'Thank you.'

The revolution happened suddenly, news of it spilling down to us like water from a bucket. There are no Guardsmen anymore, so my sister is safe, and there are two queens in Amareth now, one a soft-voiced young woman and the other only a child. I don't know their names and I don't care. It doesn't matter here, nothing matters here. It's very peaceful.

My sister only has one eye, and a scar on her shoulder she doesn't remember getting. It looks like she was shot. She could heal it, but she wants to know where it came from. I have no scars, because my sister heals them all. My sister is called Josephine.

'Don't you sometimes feel,' she said one night as we sat

drinking sweet red wine in our tiny house, talking and laughing, 'like your name is wrong?'

And I said, 'No.' I know what the right answers are to these questions. 'No, I don't.'

My sister and I grew up here on our own. She wasn't always my sister, we had different parents, our blood is different. My parents are shadows in my mind, but my sister is real. One day she will be a doctor, but I don't care what I am after this.

My sister comes into the kitchen while I'm cooking. I ask her, 'Are you going to see him tonight?' Arlen, I mean, the boy with the dancing eyes who she met at the school for healing, who's clever and funny and calls her beautiful.

She pushes her hair behind her ears. It's longer now, down to her ears. 'Maybe,' she says.

I don't remember why she cut her hair. I don't remember her cutting her hair.

I grin. 'Don't be coy. You want to see him.'

'I might,' she says. 'But that's not why I'm going.'

I turn suddenly, heart racing. I get scared sometimes for no reason when she leaves me. I'm just being stupid. 'Why are you going?'

My sister lays her hand on my shoulder. She's always been braver than me. 'There's been an accident. A boy fell into the water. He's broken pretty much everything. They need me. I'm sorry—'

'Don't apologise,' I say. 'Go.'

'Okay. I love you.'

The words are important, we say them every time we part and sometimes when we're only going to different rooms.

'I love you, too,' I say.

When she's gone I keep the stew hanging over a low wood fire and go out on to the beach. I light a cigarette and sit on the sand and tilt my head back to the moonlight and let the wind wash over my face.

Am I doing okay? I say to Elizabeth.

You're doing great, love, she says.

Elizabeth isn't real, she's just a voice in my head. I've known her since I was a kid. Imaginary people are something you're meant to lose as you grow up, but I talk to her more and more these days. Sometimes, like tonight, I can feel her next to me, sitting on the sand, her hair floating in the wind.

How are you doing? I say to her.

I'm fine. I miss you.

I'm right here.

I miss you, she says again, more softly. *You should be here with me.*

I turn my head to look at her, as if I could see her sitting there, like I could read her face. Stupid.

Where are you? I say.

She doesn't answer. Then she says, *Are you happy?*

Of course I'm happy.

Then it's all okay.

Good.

We sit there in silence, in the wind, until I can feel that she's faded and gone. The ocean glitters in the starlight and the spring breeze is cool on my face, like a touch I can't remember. I sit there for a while, listening to the ocean, until the cigarette burns down to the acrid stub and I crush it in the sand and get up and walk back towards the house.

ACKNOWLEDGEMENTS

This was a difficult book to write. It has been a yearslong process, with a lot of false starts, wiped drafts and rethinks. And here we are at the end of it, with *The Orphanage of Gods*. I am so proud, and so grateful that I was able to write it – but that's been possible only because of the endless patience, generosity and support of the people I work with and the people I love.

At Hodder, thank you to my editors, Thorne Ryan and Kate Howard, for your brilliant insight, your guidance and your tireless enthusiasm for this book. Thanks also to Kay Gale, who copyedited it, for your quick-witted thoroughness. And thanks especially to my agent, Meg Davis, for your depthless kindness and unfailing support. This book owes you its existence, and I my sanity.

To everyone who helped and supported me, in moments of euphoria and of exhaustion: to Cat, as always; to Hanna and Carlotta, the reasons I made it through school, I am so grateful for you; and for the later drafts, thank you to Ane, Felicity, Emma, Chris, Jorik, Sophie, Charlie, and Hannah. You have all my love, and I can never thank you enough.

To my parents, always and for everything.

And to Catherine, cleverest, wisest and best of sisters. I love you so much, and I am so proud to be a part of your life. Thank you for everything.